American Nightingale

Debra Scacciaferro

To my parents, Frank and Connie Scacciaferro, and my Aunt Angie and Uncle Larry Scacciaferro, who first took us children to visit North-South Lake campgrounds, the site of the real Catskill Mountain House.

The once-famous hotel burned down in 1963 after being abandoned for years. The site is now part of a state park with a spectacular view of the Hudson River Valley, where I live. Many names and dates from its history were carved into the large rock ledge that fronted the hotel, including the ornate script of "Smith's Cornet Band, 1866," which inspired me to write this book.

More thanks to author and historian Roland Van Zandt, whose definitive and vivid history book The Catskill Mountain House, described so many of the details and colorful history of this wonderful part of New York's history. And thanks to the citizens of New York State, who still maintain the site, as well as the Kaaterskill Falls described in this book, as a state park for the enjoyment of all who love nature.

One

May 1865
Manhattan

"Hurry, Amanda. We don't want to miss Papa's streetcar!" Bella Smith gripped her four-year-old daughter's hand and stepped into the crush of people on the narrow street. They dodged two boys who streaked out of the alleyway. Elbowed their way through a throng of shoppers and vendors.

"On-i-yons! Onions!" one vendor called.

"Hot soup! One penny!" cried another.

Bella allowed only one quick stop at Amanda's favorite bakery. They looked longingly at the rows of pink-frosted cakes and whipped cream confections, inhaling the intoxicating aroma of sugar and fresh baked bread.

At the junction of Park Row, Bella stood on tip-toe to peer down the avenue between stalled carriages and pawing horses. The buildings were still draped in black bunting from President Lincoln's recent funeral. Bella could just make out the green-trimmed, horse-drawn streetcar far ahead. It advanced quickly along its iron tracks, bringing her husband Daniel home from his job as senior clerk of Vanaford's Fine Books Emporium.

Since his return from the war six months ago, Bella and Amanda had made a ritual of meeting his trolley at noon on his half day off. Then they would all stroll down the avenues together, window shopping mostly. Daniel would treat them for the midday meal to one of the many delicacies that could be bought on the street: Perhaps a bowl of the delicious oyster chowder from a stooped, elderly man and his fat wife; or a paper cone of hot roasted chestnuts from the red-headed boy who tended the copper roaster. Whatever they chose, Daniel always insisted on buying a confection for Amanda from Kleekfield's bakery.

"It's coming, Amanda! Papa's trolley will be stopping soon. Let's hurry to meet him!" Bella tugged at her daughter's hand and quickened her pace to match the hum of activity on the great avenue. Her spirits were buoyant as the spring breeze. "It will be so much fun to surprise your father with this telegram from your Uncle Zachary."

How Daniel's blue eyes would sparkle when he caught sight of them! Bella pictured his delighted grin on hearing the news that his brother was alive and well. Daniel had prayed for that news ever since he began sending out letters in hopes of locating his older brother.

Anticipation burst through Bella. "When Johnny comes marching home again, hurrah! Hurrah!" she sang. "We'll give him a hearty welcome then, hurrah, hurrah."

"Is Papa's brother nice?"

"I've never met him, but I'm sure he's particularly nice." Bella frowned, wondering if a man everyone referred to as "the black sheep of the family" could be nice. It didn't matter. Daniel worshipped him. "At any rate, we shall soon meet him and find out for ourselves..."

The metallic grind of brakes and a loud crash cut off her words. A huge delivery wagon had sideswiped the green streetcar. Horses bucked, stumbled and screamed in fright as their drivers swerved to avoid the wreck, crashing into others in the chaos.

"Daniel." Bella whispered his name like a prayer.

A second wagon plowed into the streetcar, pinning half a dozen men who rode on the top, or clung to the outside platform. Screams of agony and sharp moans rose in a persistent staccato above the crowd's sustained murmur of horror. Slowly, the streetcar caved in. It rocked on its tracks. Then it turned over. The crowd roared. Bodies tumbled into the gutter.

"Daniel!" Bella screamed his name now. Scooping Amanda into her arms, she began to move, swept up in the tide of pedestrians who stampeded to the wreck. "Oh, God, please, not my Daniel!"

Tears stung her eyes. Her heart drummed out a message of fear. Vaguely, she was conscious of Amanda's sobbing, of the child's legs tightly wrapped round her waist. "Shush now," she whispered, automatically patting her daughter on the back. Yet, all her attention was focused on the chaos of the street. She stumbled, regained her footing. Jostled by the crowd, she fought to get closer.

"Daniel!"

The crowd pressed in from all sides. Bella clutched Amanda tighter, confused, and fearful of being crushed or pushed to the ground. Then the crowd shifted as the special squad of traffic police ran into the morass. They directed pedestrians around the fire brigade, who were struggling to pull out survivors from the overturned car.

"If you've a strong arm, lend a hand!" shouted one officer.

"Let the doctor through!" shouted another.

Bella plunged forward, her arms trembling from the exertion of carrying her daughter. "My husband. He was on that omnibus!"

The policeman nodded and pushed her through.

Bella's vision was blurred by tears. She wiped her eyes on her sleeve. Shifting Amanda to her left hip, she scanned the bloodied and bruised faces in tangled heaps, searching for a pair of familiar blue eyes. As she picked her way past sprawled, twisted bodies, a woman next to her wailed and collapsed to the ground.

"Don't look!" Bella instinctively turned Amanda's face into

the crook of her neck to avert her gaze from the horror. The four-year-old clung tightly to her.

Then she saw Daniel. His left hand was flung out above his head. His face twisted in agony. His lower torso disappeared beneath the overturned streetcar.

Bella's mind shut out the babble of chaos that swirled around them. Dazed, she bent to put Amanda down.

"Daniel?" Her voice was so choked she could barely whisper his name. She sank next to him on the hard bricks, gazing helplessly into his unfocused blue eyes.

They flickered in recognition. His lips curved slightly.

"Bella." He spoke her name so softly, Bella wasn't sure he had actually said it. Her spirits soared with a glimmer of hope. He was alive!

She leaned closer to smooth back the familiar stray blonde curl, her thoughts flowing back into serenity. "Daniel, I'm here. Don't worry. I'll make you more comfortable." She reached behind his head, intending to use her soft drawstring reticule as his pillow. Her hand felt something sticky. Blood. She stared at it in shock.

Daniel moaned and then his body seemed to relax with a long, deep sigh.

"I'll take care of you, my love." Bella lay her hand in his open palm, expecting his fingers to curl around hers. But his fingers did not bend. Confused, she squeezed his hand, but it remained unresponsive. Tears welled up in her eyes. She bent over him and kissed his still warm lips and knew that he was dead.

Bella felt an insistent tug on her sleeve. Bewildered, she turned to see her daughter.

"Is Papa all right?" Amanda's face was pale. Her china-blue eyes were wide with fear.

For a moment, Bella could not answer. Her mind refused to think. Her throat was so constricted, she could barely breathe, let alone talk. Tears ran down her cheeks. She took Amanda's hand, wondering why she could not feel its weight against her palm. All she could was shake her head in mute sorrow.

Without a word, Amanda knelt down next to Bella and put her arms around her mother's neck. Softly, the child patted her mother's shoulder in an attempt to comfort her. Bella clasped her daughter tightly to her chest, still unable to make a sound. Then she collapsed against her husband's lifeless body.

Two

Bella sat beside the open coffin that held her husband's body and stared into space.

She felt her breath come and go in counterpoint to the persistent tick-tock of the old grandfather clock. The ticking annoyed Bella. For her, time had stopped yesterday afternoon when Daniel died. Everything from that moment on seemed like a dream.

Her upstairs neighbor, Mrs. Porter, had sent her sons to fetch the doctor and purchase a simple coffin. She had helped Bella prepare Daniel's body for burial. She had lent Bella her old black dress to wear, for Bella had no money to buy fabric to make her own widow's weeds. The dear neighbor had even trimmed Bella's old bonnet with black lace and ribbons.

A few neighbors, friends and colleagues, and Pastor Millmann had come to pay their respects to Daniel after yesterday's accident. Now they were gone. The house was empty. Amanda was taking a nap. There was nothing left to be done until tomorrow's burial. The late afternoon sun cast its dusky shadow across the darkening room. Yet Bella ignored its call to light the lamps.

Her thoughts retreated to the past; namely, to the first moment she spied Daniel in Vanaford's Fine Book Emporium. Watching him through the window, she noticed how he dusted each volume as lovingly as a piece of fine porcelain. Intrigued, she had entered the shop and inquired about the latest volume of poetry by Alfred Lord Tennyson. His blue eyes lit up, and as they chatted about England's poet laureate, they fell in love.

Bella trembled as her gaze fell on her husband's body, now so stiff, so silent in the simple pine box. He was handsome, dressed in his dark blue Union uniform. Had she forgotten anything? She rose to double-check.

Anxiously, her fingers smoothed his collar, brushed back a stray tuft of hair, adjusted the brass buttons for the tenth time to ensure their perfect alignment. Smoothing the blanket she had used to cover his shattered legs, Bella stared into Daniel's face, searching for some small sign of life.

There was always the fear that he was simply unconscious. She had read about people being buried alive and stared at him all the more closely, hoping to catch him blink or wink at her, as if all this was some outrageous joke by God to test her love and vigilance.

A shudder of loneliness swept through her body. Cradling Daniel's cold hand, she bent her head and wept. He was no more alive than the table he lay on.

A sharp rap at the door hammered through her numbed senses. Bella commanded herself to rise, blinking through her tears. She opened the door. "Mrs. Oster!"

Her landlady stared back at her through squinting beetle-black eyes, her bony fingers toying with the fringe on her shawl. "Mrs. Smith. I have heard about your husband's death. My sympathies."

"Thank you." Bella was touched by the normally aloof woman's gesture. She opened the door wider. "Please come in."

"No, no," the woman hastily replied. "I won't disturb you. I had come to collect the rent." Her voice was reproachful. "You owed me for two weeks. It's past due."

Bella stared at her for a moment. She took in her cold demeanor, ramrod posture, disdainful glance. For the first time since the policemen had brought Daniel's body home, Bella felt emotion burn through the numbness. Anger boiled up inside her.

"If you recall, Madam, my husband had promised to pay in full on Wednesday."

"But now your husband is dead. And I doubted that you would keep his promise."

"Doubted?" Bella softened her voice but did not bother to conceal her contempt. "When have I not kept my word?"

"I simply thought a reminder was necessary."

"And haven't you chosen your moment to remind me so well? Yet, you have that knack, haven't you, of finding the most vulnerable time to attack."

Mrs. Oster's face contorted into open-mouthed outrage. "How dare you suggest...?"

"How dare you come in here," Bella raged, her voice rising, "when my poor husband is laid out cold and stiff, to hover like some black crow picking at the remains!"

"Crow! Humph!" Mrs. Oster snapped her mouth into a tight line. "You go too far, Mrs. Smith. I have a business to run." She took in a deep, noisy breath, her fingers twisting more furiously at the fringe. "If you cannot pay by Wednesday, I shall let the rooms to someone else. As a widow myself," she said pointedly, "I have learned to look out for my own interests." She spun on her heel and left.

Bella slammed the door and then collapsed against it. "That hateful woman. She couldn't wait just one day. Oh, Daniel, why did you leave me like this?"

The full weight of her situation hit home. There was enough money to pay the rent this time. But what then? She shuddered, thinking of the hat factory, where her aching fingers earned her only fifty cents a day after twelve hours of work. No, she mustn't think of that.

"Mama? Mama?" At the sound of Amanda's voice from the bedroom, Bella calmed herself with a deep breath and forced a smile. "Coming, my darling!"

They met halfway. Amanda flew into her mother's arms. Bella hugged her fiercely, then carried her to the big wing chair that had been Daniel's favorite. She sank into it, cradling Amanda on her lap.

"Shall I sing you a song, my love?" She smoothed her daughter's golden hair. "When Johnny comes marching home again, hurrah, hurrah." She sang the words softly, in slow cadence, as they had sung so many nights when Daniel was off at war. "We'll give him a rousing welcome then, hurrah, hurrah..." Her voice broke and she leaned over to kiss Amanda's brow.

"Mama, where will we live?"

"Don't pay any attention to that old Mrs. Oster face," Bella murmured. "We'll find a nicer place to live. In a pretty little cottage." Bella lapsed into their familiar game of what would happen when Papa came home from the war. "With lots of pretty toys for you."

"And pink sugar cakes?"

"By the dozens. And a big garden with sweet peas, and roses, and purple lilacs."

"But who will buy us the cottage if Papa isn't here to take care of us? Mama, what does 'in a bad way' mean? I heard Mrs. Porter tell Jimmy we would be in a bad way from now on."

Bella felt hot tears slip down her cheeks again. "It means we shall be very sad without Papa. And things will be hard again, like when he was away at war. But someday, I promise, I will buy you a pretty little cottage, just like we dreamed of. But first, I must go to see Mr. Vanaford and see about collecting Papa's pay." She gazed down at her daughter and kissed her on the forehead. "Will you stay with Mrs. Porter for a few hours again while I do?"

≈

No money, no home. No money, no home.

The sound of the carriage wheels squeaked out the accusation over and over during Bella's ride home from Vanaford's Fine Book Emporium.

She had spent a quiet hour with Daniel's employer in the back of the bookstore. Mr. Vanaford had been more than kind, offering her tea and cake. He praised Daniel's diligence, his attention to detail, his patience with the customers, and his love of books and poetry.

Bella had been touched by the stories and grateful for the man's generosity. He had handed her an envelope containing a full month's wages, even though Daniel had not finished out the month. He had insisted on hailing a carriage and paying the driver to bring her home. The wages would be just enough to pay the back rent and buy a little food. But after that? Her numbed brain refused to think beyond the moment.

By the time the carriage dropped her off, Bella was exhausted. She dragged herself up three steep flights to her landing, trembling from the exertion. Aside from the few bites of cake she had chewed out of courtesy, she hadn't eaten all day.

She breathed a sigh of relief as she reached the dark landing, then stumbled over someone lying in the dark by her door.

"What? Where?" a man sputtered. "They're charging, boys!" He shook his head. Jumping up from the floor, he raised his arms as if to attack.

"Oh, God in Heaven!" Bella shrank back, clutching her velvet reticule to her breast. She raised her other hand to ward off a blow. "I beg of you. Don't hurt me. Please. I have no money. I have a child to care for. Don't hurt me!"

"What? Ah...oh. Huh? Sorry." The man slowly lowered his arms and stepped out from the shadows into the sputtering light of an overhead gas lamp. He peered at her and rubbed his eyes. "I won't hurt you. No, no. I'm sorry I frightened you. I was just dreaming." He peered at her again. "Do you by any chance know the Smiths? I was told their rooms were on the third floor."

Bella stared, not daring to breathe, not registering the words he spoke. For the face she saw staring at her, illuminated in the flickering light, was Daniel's.

"Are you a ghost?" she whispered.

"A ghost?" For some reason, the question seemed to strike the man as funny. He let out a short burst of laughter. "Not unless someone stabbed me while I nodded off."

Bella shrank back in wonder. Surely, that musical laugh was Daniel's. And just as surely, it could not be Daniel. "Who are you?"

The man clicked his heels together and bowed low, sweeping his arm in a broad gesture. "Zach Smith of Smith's Cornet Band. Daniel Smith's half-brother. I'm waiting for him to come home." He smiled and waited expectantly. Then he asked more gently, "Have I got the right door?"

Bella stared at him, struggling to take in what he had said.

Her mind cast back to yesterday's events before the crash. Before they had gone to meet Daniel's trolley. It seemed a lifetime ago. Then she remembered. "Telegram." Her throat was so dry, she could barely get the words out. "Your telegram came yesterday."

He looked puzzled. "Then, are you Daniel's wife?"

"Yes." Her head spun. Her legs felt wobbly. "I'm Mrs. Smith."

"Well, I apologize. I was dreaming of the war and I..." He broke off and peered again at Bella. "Are you ill?"

Dots swam before Bella's eyes. The room spun, and she staggered back against the wall, her black skirts billowing out around her.

Three

Zachary Smith caught the woman as she collapsed. Gently, he eased her to the floor. "Poor thing. Wake up, Mrs. Smith." He patted her cheeks, then unlaced the ribbons under her chin to loosen her bonnet. "Can you hear me?"

Her head lolled back in response. Her oval face was as still as a marble statue, framed by wisps of dark hair that fluttered when he pulled off her bonnet. His half-brother had certainly married a beauty, thought Zach as he knelt by her. He lowered his head and was relieved to hear her soft breathing. Her eyelashes fluttered.

"Well, well. Coming around." Zach watched as she tried to focus her gaze on him. He smiled to reassure her. She looked so tired. "Did you have anything to eat today?" he said in a gentle voice.

"I...no."

"Are you ill?"

Bella brushed her hand across her brow. "What happened?" Her face was troubled.

"You fainted." He was squatting in front of her, noting how her eyes struggled to focus on his face in the dim light. The poor woman must be pretty ill, Zach thought. Or possibly with child. "Do you have a key? I'll open the door for you."

She stared at him, then fumbled for her black silk bag. "There's a key in my reticule." She fished it out of the black drawstring pouch and tried to rise.

Zach took her by the arm and helped her up. "Lean on me."

Her hand shook noticeably as she tried to fit the key to the keyhole.

"Here. Let me." Zach's hand closed over her gloved one and he helped her turn the key until it clicked. She looked up at him, still saying nothing. Her stare unnerved him. He released her.

"Where is Daniel? Should I fetch him?"

Daniel's wife didn't answer. She swung open the door and took a step, then hesitated on the threshold.

"Will he be home soon?"

"He's home now." Her voice was faint, barely a whisper in the quiet gloom of the room. "I'll just light the lamp."

Zach stared into the dark room. Home now? He had knocked on the door for a quarter of an hour, at least. No one had answered. Puzzled, he wondered if his half-brother was hiding from creditors.

Drawing out a match from the metal box on the wall by the door, Bella turned to light the kerosene lamp next to a large wing chair.

In its glow, Zach saw that Bella had dropped her reticule on the floor. He bent down and held the purse out to her. Slowly, she took it, her fingers grazing his hand. She jumped back from the contact.

Her reaction startled Zach. She was frightened of him. What the hell had Daniel done? Poisoned her against him before they even met? Anger rose inside him, mixed with bewilderment. Daniel's letter had been so friendly, so eager.

"Well, where is that brother of mine?" He tried to keep his voice light. "Does he work nights? Or has he just changed his mind about wanting to see me?"

She looked past him, her features suddenly contorted with grief. "He did so want to see you."

A shiver crawled up Zach's spine. Turning, he saw the large, sturdy table. He recognized its clawed feet and beveled edges; it was his father's refectory table, the one he had used for communion in his small church. Only now, a pine box was laid out on top of it.

Slowly, Zach approached the table and stared at the face inside the coffin.

"My God."

He caught his breath. The face he saw there was older than Zach remembered, but there was no mistaking Daniel's features. He felt a strange sense of doom creep down his spine. Except for the blond hair and the hated blue Union uniform, Zach felt as if he was looking at his own reflection.

For a while, he listened distractedly as Bella told him about the accident that took Daniel's life.

His mind reeled from the sight of his brother dressed as the enemy. True, he'd known from Daniel's letter that his brother had fought on the Union side. What else would he expect? Their father, the Reverend Jeremiah Zenobia Smith, had been an ardent abolitionist.

Zach had joined the Rebel cause as much to defy his father as to support his beloved Southern uncles and defend his mother's homeland. Now the horrible irony of it hit home; if he had met Daniel on the battlefield, he'd have been sworn to kill him. Instead he came here hoping for reconciliation yet been denied the chance by a freak accident.

"It was horrible," Bella said. "It all happened so fast."

Zach pulled his thoughts back to the present. "You saw the accident?"

Bella nodded and sank into the chair next to the pine box, laying a hand gently on the wood. "The worst of it was, my daughter Amanda was there, too. I would have done anything, anything to spare her that."

"Your daughter." Zach gazed around the room. He saw no sign of a child. "Where is your daughter? She wasn't with you when you came in."

"Oh, my goodness! She's upstairs with Mrs. Porter. I...I had to go out."

Bella squeezed her eyes shut. Zach saw a great weariness pass through her, the same way overwhelmed survivors on the battle-field simply gave up the fight. Filled with sympathy, he went to her side. Kneeling to take her hand, he noted the irony of giving aid and comfort to the enemy's wife.

Stop thinking like a soldier, he told himself.

"You'll be all right." He tried to think of something encour-aging to say. "You just need time to recover."

"Recover?" She gazed up at him, her face etched with sorrow. "How can I ever recover?"

Not knowing how to reply to that, Zach simply squeezed her hand and rubbed her fingertips. They were cold. Her grip, however, was surprisingly strong.

"But I'm forgetting you!" she cried, clutching his hand. "You've come to collect your father's things. It's been just a year since his death. And now, poor Daniel, dead, too."

Bella started to rise, but Zach laid his hand on her shoulder. "Don't get up. You need to rest. And I need a whiskey, if you have any."

"Whiskey?" She stared at him. "There may be some blackberry wine. In that cupboard."

Zach rose, embarrassed at his need of a drink, for the first time thinking of it as a weakness. Hell, if the shock of seeing Daniel in that coffin wasn't enough excuse for a drink, what was?

"I'll go and find it," he said.

Zach hadn't realized how badly he had wanted to forge some kind of friendship with his half-brother. His most vivid memories of Daniel were of a blond, bright-eyed toddler who begged for piggy-back rides, a song, or a lullaby on the cornet. And of the awkward and awestruck lad, twelve years old to Zach's nineteen, who eagerly devoured his stories of travel and romantic exploits on Zach's last visit back home. That was eleven years ago, long before the war, long before they lost touch.

When he'd arrived back in New York only a week ago and found Daniel's letter about their father's death, Zach fantasized about their meeting. He imagined how Daniel and his wife and child would take him in like the prodigal son, feasting and laughing with him, welcoming him with open arms. Zach had planned to take them out on the town, shower them with presents, take them to hear his band rehearse.

So much for fantasies.

Rummaging through the white pine cupboard, painted with delicate sprays of roses, he extracted a decanter of wine and two glasses.

"Have you written his mother? Is she still living in Hartford?" His hand shook as he poured the sherry and thought of the unfriendly woman who had replaced his own mother less than six months after her death.

"No, poor dear," sighed Bella. "She passed on in the influenza epidemic of 1863. Daniel and his father were so distraught... Your father survived her only by little more than a year." Bella's voice trailed off.

Zach set the full glasses on the table next to her chair, trying to steady his hands. "Drink this. It'll do you good."

She took a small sip, then looked back up. She seemed to scrutinize Zach, her head shaking back and forth in awe.

"It is uncanny. You do look so much like him. Like Daniel, I mean." She gestured to the table. "I dressed him in his uniform. He was very proud to serve the country. He wrote me every day." She clasped her hands together. "I prayed so hard for him to come home. And he did. He did. And now this!"

A fresh flood of tears obliterated her words.

Awkwardly, Zach patted her heaving shoulders. He gulped down his wine and frowned. He needed stronger stimulant than this. Her grief, on top of the shock of Daniel's death, had begun to penetrate the fortress of bravado and charm he kept as his outward armor. He belted down a second glass, hoping for the familiar fire to warm his veins. He was disappointed.

"You'll stay, of course, for the funeral?" Bella's voice was shy. "We, Daniel and I, we planned to give you Amanda's bed if you came. There, by the alcove. It's not a real room, but there's a curtain for privacy."

Zach hesitated. He felt uncomfortable about staying here while Daniel's body lay next to the alcove. He'd been near enough dead bodies these last years to last several lifetimes.

"You'll want to see Amanda, won't you?" Bella twisted her hands in her lap and slowly stood up. "I'll just go and get her now."

He thought of the boys in his band, of their laughter and whiskey and the girls they might romance tonight. He pulled out his pocket watch. It was after nine. He had already missed the last omnibus.

Bella's eyes filled with tears, her expression pleading with him.

"Of course I want to see Amanda," Zach told her. He flashed his most engaging smile and tried to sound enthusiastic. "Let's go get her right now."

～

"You're not my Papa!" On her first glimpse of Zach, Amanda frowned suspiciously. "Who are you?"

"Sshhh, darling," Bella soothed her. "It's Uncle Zachary, Papa's brother. You remember. Papa told us all about him. That he was coming to visit?"

Amanda stared at Zach, her bottom lip pulled into a pout. She popped her thumb into her mouth and began sucking it very hard. The gesture and her features—golden blonde curls, china blue eyes, even the arch of her mouth and eyebrows—reminded him of Daniel as a child. But her slender neck, oval face and high cheek-bones were unmistakably her mother's.

Zach held out his hand. "Miss Amanda Smith, I am very pleased to meet you."

After a hesitant glance at her mother, who nodded in eager encouragement, Amanda gravely took his hand with her free one, keeping the thumb in her mouth. Zach was charmed.

"Do you know how much you look like your Papa when he

was your age?"

She eyed him narrowly.

"Yes, you do. Just like him."

"Do I really?" She glanced over at her mother.

"If your uncle says so, it must be true. He watched Papa grow up."

The child approached Zach, stopped short and stared up at him, her expression changing from skepticism to trust. He lifted her up. She threw her thin arms around his neck and clung to him, bringing an unexpected lump to Zach's throat.

"Please make Papa wake up," she whispered.

"I wish I could, honey." He hugged the child to him and felt her soft sobs against his chest. He patted her back and smoothed her golden curls. He was totally unprepared for the strong protective instinct that swept through him.

With his mother's people in Georgia wiped out in the war, this child was his only link to the past. The only family, perhaps, he would ever have.

He drew back from her, intending to say something funny to lighten the situation. But the words died on his lips. Amanda's bright baby face, full of sorrow and glistening tears, smashed through all his emotional barriers.

"Don't worry, Little Missy." He clutched her tightly. "I'll take care of you."

Four

The following morning's funeral service was a blur to Bella. She hardly heard the words.

"Ashes to ashes, dust to dust," the reverend intoned.

She stared at the coffin, now waiting to be lowered into the pit that would be his grave; an ugly, gaping scar in this otherwise green plot. She held back a moan. This was not the way she wanted to remember Daniel, alone and cold and covered by dirt.

Zach took out his gleaming cornet, pressed it to his lips, and blew a haunting rendition of taps.

The melancholy tune tugged at the shards of Bella's broken heart and lifted her grief up and into the air, leaving a fresh note of beauty in its place. It awakened sweet memories of nights spent reading poems by candlelight with Daniel. It conjured up a kaleidoscope of emotions: of Daniel's gentle lovemaking; the warmth in his letters from the front; his tender hands against her expanding stomach when she was expecting Amanda; his awe at being presented with their tiny daughter on the night she was born.

Yes, she thought, that was how she wanted to remember her dear husband. She opened her eyes to watch her brother-in-law, amazed at the healing power of his music. She hoped to catch his eye, so she could acknowledge her gratitude with a smile.

But as the last lingering note drifted into the air, Zach abruptly turned away. Bella saw him flick his hand against his eyes, then bow his head. He did not turn around again until the coffin had been lowered into the grave.

~

For two days after the funeral, Bella had felt as if the world had caved in.

She drifted in and out of the present, where memories of long ago became more vivid than what was actually happening around her. Mostly, she slept a kind of twilight sleep; not restful and deep but hovering on the edge of jumbled dreams and hallucinations.

Zach had been kind enough to offer to stay for two more days, until he was due at a job. He took charge of Amanda, ordered food from the grocery and butcher, sent out the laundry, and even insisted on paying the undertaker for his services. It was, he told her several times, the least he could do for Daniel.

Bella had been gratified to see how exceedingly patient he was with Amanda. She watched them now, as Amanda giggled over some new game he was teaching her.

"Now you put your penny here," Zach instructed Amanda. "And then you take this penny and use it to flip the other one into the cup. See?" He leaned over the white linen tablecloth and flipped the copper coin neatly into Amanda's tin cup.

Amanda giggled. "Oh, Uncle Zach. It's in my milk!"

"Sorry about that," Zach said, picking up a spoon. "Here. Fish it out. Go on!"

Bella smiled at the pretty scene they made. She felt as if she were in a dream, watching Amanda and Daniel at play. But it wasn't Daniel.

She shook her head to dispel the strange feeling. The base of her skull ached. She stared at the table, cluttered with dishes of half-eaten food. Zach had ordered entirely too many expensive delicacies: hot oyster soup, tinned salmon, green peas, and pink sugar cakes for Amanda.

None of it stimulated Bella's appetite. She hungered for conversation about Daniel, about the brothers' childhood. She wanted to paint over her grief with a vivid picture of their boyhood. But memories were not something her brother-in-law seemed interested in pursuing. In fact, her questions only seemed to irritate him.

"Oh, Uncle Zach, I did it!" Amanda clapped her hands as her copper penny plunked into the tin cup. "Another penny, please! Please!"

Lightheaded, Bella rose to join them. She needed to connect with someone; to throw off this sadness or be crushed under its weight. She automatically picked up an empty plate and a bowl of peas, intending to take them into the pantry.

In a trick of her confused mind, the action brought back snatches of a conversation she had with Daniel only days before. His voice as clear and strong as if he were standing beside her, reminding Bella to give his brother the few things their father had left.

With a cry, she dropped the bowl. It shattered. Peas bounced across the floor. "Forgive me!"

Amanda gasped, looking up from the game.

"What's wrong!" Zach ran to Bella's side and took the remaining plate from her outstretched hand. He placed it on the table. "Are you all right?"

"I'm sorry. It slipped." Bella's hands shook as she tried to get down on her knees to clean up the mess. "It's just that Daniel was saying, I mean..."

She stopped, confused, as she saw Zach looking at her with an expression of alarm.

"You're upset. Maybe you should lie down." Gently, he took her arm to help her rise. She hesitated, but his grasp firmly lifted her to a standing position. "Be careful where you step." He smiled, his eyes crinkling at the corners just like Daniel's used to do, as he guided her around broken crockery and scattered peas.

"Listen, please!" Bella tried to explain. "Daniel left some things for you. From your father. I should have remembered earlier! I suddenly realized."

"Don't bother with that." He pushed out a chair for her. "Come and sit down."

She sat down as he asked. "You don't seem to understand. Your father's things. That he left you. Don't you want them?"

"Not just now." Zach's voice was sharp.

"But you must! Otherwise, I might forget. And Daniel would never forgive me. He'd..." She broke off, realizing that she still thought Daniel might walk through that door any moment. Yet the urge to finish this last task for her husband was too strong. "You must," she repeated. "He would never forgive me."

Zach sighed. "All right. All right."

"I'll just be a minute!" she said softly.

Bella hurried to her bedroom, driven by a feeling of urgency. She threw open the trunk where Daniel had always kept his most important papers. She filled her arms with three bulky bundles tied in brown paper and twine.

As she rose, her eye fell on the chest of drawers. Her father-in-law's gold pocket watch, which he had left to Daniel, lay there. She hesitated a moment, then hooked her forefinger under the chain.

Zach wiped up the mess, while Amanda picked up peas from all over the rug.

"Don't touch the broken pieces," he told the child in a gentle voice, trying to hide his rising irritation as he used his handkerchief to pick up bits of broken crockery. "I don't want you to cut yourself."

Zach really didn't want to deal with his father's belongings right now. All he wanted to do was push away the grief that surged inside him, threatening to burst through his defenses. Playing with Amanda had helped him do that. Everything had been quite peaceful. But even in death, his father had managed to shatter Zach's fragile peace of mind.

"Thank you, Amanda," he said as they got to their feet.

Amanda held out her collected peas and poured them into Zach's handkerchief. Then she smiled at him; one of those shy, sweet smiles that caught him by surprise again and filled him with tender feelings.

Zach reached into his pocket and brought out two pennies. "This is for you. I expect you to be tiddlywinks champ next time I visit."

Amanda's smile was broad. Her eyes shone with excitement as she took the pennies from his open palm. "Now run along and practice."

When Bella returned, she laid an armful of bundles in front of him. Shyly, she held out a gold pocket watch, dangling from a long chain.

"Your father left it to Daniel. But I think you should have it now."

Zach fought down an urge to swat the watch from her hand. To sweep everything off the table. There was nothing he wanted from that hateful old man. Not a damned thing. Reluctantly, he pulled out his fancy pearl-handled pocketknife and slit open the first bundle. It contained sermons written in his father's fastidious hand. The dedication read: "To my sons, may they publish these to honor my name."

"Publish indeed," he muttered, flipping through the pages filled with the all-too-familiar bombastic rhetoric. "No one would publish this tripe."

Bella gasped at the vehemence of his words.

"I'm sorry." Zach tried to soften his words, but he was caught in the old grip of unfinished family business. "Never mind."

He opened the next bundle, rifling quickly through a copy of the will and other legal papers that held no interest for him. Six letters written in his mother's florid handwriting caught his attention. Those he gently removed and laid to one side.

He sliced through the rough twine of the last bundle. The brown paper fell away. Zach stared at the top page. In a familiar script, embellished with many curlicues and flourishes, were words he thought he would never see again:

A Composition
Symphony of Life
by Zachariah M. Smith.

Trembling with rage and wonder, he ran a tentative finger over the page, unable to believe that something he had mourned over for so long still existed.

His puritanical father had not destroyed his unfinished symphony after all.

"What is it?" Bella stood up, clearly intrigued by Zach's reaction to the contents of the last bundle.

Zach felt embarrassed. So he did what he always did when deeply self-conscious; he struck out at the person nearest. He glared at Bella. "It's nothing!" He slapped the brown paper back down on the contents. His hands trembled. His mouth was dry as sawdust. "Fetch me some string!"

Startled, Bella slipped off toward the pantry.

Left alone to stare at his past, Zach clearly recalled his father's face; eyes blazing, towering over him clutching the sheets of music, roaring at his fifteen-year-old eldest son like a madman.

"The devil's work! You do the devil's work! And on the Lord's Day!"

Zach remembered grabbing at the remaining pages, but his father had wrenched them away. They had never really understood each other, but Zach had at least respected his father up until that moment.

Over the years, Zach fanned the sparks of his resentment over the incident into an inferno of hatred against his father. The loss of his creation, his musical composition, had colored everything else in his life and spurred him to run away to his mother's family in Georgia.

As a youngster, he had spent many long and happy visits at his uncle's plantation. He'd played Beethoven, Mozart, Handel and Bach at Saturday evening family concerts. He'd drunk in the mesmerizing rhythms and dance tunes sung on summer evenings down at the slave quarters.

It was where he had started to compose his symphony, only to have it snatched away from him on his return to his father's home in Malone.

And now, here it was, real and tangible.

Snatches of the melodies that made up the themes of his interrupted symphony drifted in and out of his mind. Perhaps he had embellished the fragments over the years, giving them a power and beauty they did not really possess. He had once tried to recreate the composition, but soon gave up. He had turned away from classical composition altogether, taking up more popular forms of music. It had been easier to let the ghost of his old ambitions fester along with all the other resentments of the past.

Now the very notes on the yellowed pages seemed to shimmer before his eyes, as if mocking him. He'd spent his life blaming his father for destroying his work. What if the symphony turned out to have no merit, after all?

"I've found some twine." Bella's voice from the kitchen penetrated his thoughts. She approached him warily, holding it out at arm's length.

"Just a lot of old memories," he said gruffly. "Unpleasant memories."

"I'm sorry."

"No need to be." Warily, he rewrapped the bundles. "How much did Daniel tell you about me?"

"Not very much." Her voice sounded soft and far-away. "He said you were a splendid musician. That your music was like poetry."

Zach grunted and pulled the twine into a knot. "What else?"

"That you ran away from home because your father was too

strict. That you were always in trouble." She hesitated. "He felt that somehow, he had gotten you into trouble."

Zach said nothing.

"He said you were the black sheep of the family. He thought that was very romantic," she added hastily.

"Did he? Well, it wasn't romantic to me. I can tell you that!"

"I'm sorry," she said quickly. "He told me about your visit when he was twelve. When they were living in Tarrytown. Remember? You brought him back picture post cards from Paris and Vienna."

Zach allowed himself to smile at the memory of that visit. "Yes, I remember. I think I came back mostly to impress them, their small minds in their small towns. Now, Paris." He blew a low whistle. "There's a city! The food, the music, the women..." He broke off and glanced at Bella. "Sorry."

She looked down at the floor but said nothing.

Somehow, her wistful attempts to get him to remember happier times made Zach feel even more like a fool. And he hated feeling foolish. It was the only feeling that made him panic; made him feel as if he were losing control. He longed to be back at the hotel with the band, back on familiar ground where he could finally slip back into his old life and the comfort of old, easy routines.

"What about you?" Zach suddenly asked. "Who's going to look after you, now that Daniel's gone?"

Bella frowned. She started to say something, then only ended up shaking her head.

Zach sighed. "I suppose a clerk in a bookstore wouldn't have made much money."

"That's true," she whispered. She cleared her throat and spoke a bit louder. "Daniel didn't have enough to put anything aside. During the war, he sent home what he could. I made a few dollars a week in the hat factory. We always managed to pay the rent." A faint smile hovered on Bella's lips. "Daniel used to say we could live on love and hope."

"Love and hope, huh? Sure, sure. Lots of people living on that, now." Zach shook his head at the naive sentiment, sounding like something from his father's sermons. He gazed at Amanda curled up asleep in the wing chair, her chin resting on her doll.

"So what will you do with your portion of love and hope now?" he said softly, almost to himself. Then he looked at her. Taking in her forlorn expression, he asked more kindly, "No family?"

"No. My parents are both dead."

"No relatives?"

"None that I know of." Her lower lip quivered as she tried to smile.

"Any friends to take you in?"

Bella's lips tightened. "Our closest friends are the Crains. They have nothing to spare and two aged parents to care for."

Zach snorted with frustration. His brother was a fool to think he could live on love. Dreamers always made him uncomfortable. Invariably, they left their problems for others to solve.

"I suppose you haven't the skills to even earn a living?" The question came out more roughly than Zach had intended.

Bella winced at his tone. "Not a decent one." She drew in a long, quavering breath and abruptly turned her back on him. "How foolish of me to be born a woman. I've regretted it. More than once."

He noticed how tightly her shoulders tensed, how rigid her back was. When she threw back her head and made a choking sound, he felt a rush of sympathy.

It occurred to him that he'd been taking his own bitterness out on her. What he should have done was offer some comfort. Why did any brush with his past always bring out the worst in him? Ashamed, he felt compelled to offer her at least a glimmer of hope.

"Listen, I'll leave you something..." He fumbled in his coat pocket for coins. "I'm a little short right now, but here's...five, six, seven, eight dollars." He neatly stacked the silver dollars on the table.

Bella stared at the money, then pushed the stack back toward him. "You don't have to give us charity."

Zach frowned. She was making this very hard on him. "It's not charity. It's family." He pushed the money back in her direction and the coins toppled over, sliding every which way. "Tomorrow, when I get to my next job, I'll send you some money. Enough to tide you over for a few months, until you can get back on your feet."

Bella whirled around, anxiety flooding her features. "Where are you going?"

"I can't stay," he explained. "I'm off to a job at the Catskill Mountain House tomorrow. My band is engaged there for the summer season."

A dreamy look came over Bella. She repeated the name with a reverence normally reserved for something beloved.

"You know it?"

"Yes." She blushed and smiled. "Who hasn't heard of the Mountain House."

Zach had a sudden thought. "You never know. They may need a maid or governess or something. I'll see what I can do."

"Oh, could you? Would you!" She gazed at him with renewed hope.

"If something comes up, I'll put your name in and send for you right away. I promise. I know the hotel manager." He stretched his arms wide and yawned. "I'll be leaving first thing in the morning. Five at the latest. Got to get down to the pier by six-thirty sharp!" He looked back at Amanda, curled up in the chair. The child's expression was so peaceful, it made Zach smile. "Look at her. She's fast asleep. Would you like me to carry her to bed?"

"Thank you."

Zach bent over the child and gently lifted her. The warmth of her small body and the clean-scrubbed scent of her skin soothed him as she snuggled deeper into his arms. "Listen, if you wouldn't mind, I'd like to keep in touch. Send Amanda something now and then. You, too."

Bella nodded. "It's kind of you." She followed Zach into her bedroom and pulled down the covers. "Do you really think they'll need a maid at the Mountain House?"

"It's a big place." He laid Amanda on the bed, then turned to go.

Bella stood in his path. There was an urgency in her voice as she asked, "If they did need someone, wouldn't they fill the position right away?"

"Maybe." He pushed past her, slightly uncomfortable with her questions.

"Don't you think it might be better if we went with you?" She tagged after him. "If they saw I was willing to do anything, anything, then I might have a better chance."

"I don't know." Zach headed for the table. This woman was asking far too much of him. He wasn't ready to take on the responsibility of his brother's family. Or anyone's family, for that matter. It just wasn't in his plans.

"Because it could take days to receive your letter," she persisted, hovering over him as he scooped the bundles into his arm. "Unless you telegraph us. But that's costly."

Her sad violet eyes pleaded with him, swallowing him whole with her hunger for an answer. Her vulnerability stirred something deep inside him, but it also made him want to run from the whole situation. He'd had all the heartache he could stand during the war.

"It would make so much more sense if Amanda and I came with you tomorrow."

Zach took a step back. The familiar cynicism rose up inside him. "Now listen to me. That's crazy! I just made a suggestion, that's all."

He tried to give her a stern look, but her eyes seemed to plead with him.

"This is my first time back at the Mountain House since before the war. I don't know if there is a job, any job. Much less whether I can get it for you."

"But you said..."

"I said *if* there was a job, I'd send for you. If. If." Reaching into his pocket, he jerked out his money clip and peeled off a ten dollar note. "That's a ten note and with the silver dollars, that should be more than enough to get you there and something to eat on the steamer, if I send for you." He held out the bill and shook them. "Take it."

"But..." Bella stared at him, her eyes still pleading.

Zach grabbed her hand and stuffed the bill into it.

She continued to stare at him, silently, with the money balled up in her hand.

"Just take it!" Zach turned his back on her, bracing himself with both hands on the table. "Now go to bed. I could use some privacy around here."

He held his breath, waiting until he heard the bedroom door shut between them to exhale. In the morning, he would be gone, safe from the past. Safe from this unwelcome request to look after his half-brother's family.

Five

Bella lay rigid and wide awake as the clock struck three.

It was pitch dark in that dismal predawn hour. Her daughter's soft, rhythmic breathing lent some small comfort. But she craved Daniel's familiar warmth and the feel of him curled spoon-fashion against her in their sleep.

She tried to ease her grief by concentrating on more mundane matters. Tomorrow was Wednesday. The back rent was due. The last of Daniel's pay had covered the funeral expenses. The remainder, plus Zach's money, would just stretch to cover the rent, steamer and coach fare to the Mountain House.

The Mountain House. The words filled the air with their coolness. Her memories of the place were happy ones, of soft breezes and shaded grounds, and hours spent in play with her mother and father, when Bella's family had lacked for nothing. Amanda deserved to spend her summer there. To escape the simmering heat of the city, its noise and disease, the crush of people, the bad smells.

You must go, she imagined Daniel whispering to her. She smiled and stretched her rigid muscles. Yes, he was right. She must go.

She turned over the possibilities in her mind. If she waited,

Daniel's brother might forget about his promise. Or they might hire someone else on the spot.

Better go tomorrow, she thought. If they wouldn't hire her, Daniel's brother wouldn't simply throw them out on the street. He felt something for Amanda. She could tell. Or there might be old friends, families she had known in happier times, who might be willing to let her be a governess to their children.

Restlessly, Bella rose from her bed and lit a candle. In the flickering light and the silence, the room reminded her of a tomb. Once, it held the promise of Daniel's return from the war. Now the memories tore at her soul, offering no solace for her grief.

Holding the candle aloft, she padded barefoot on the cold floor toward the trunk that contained Daniel's papers. Softly, she lifted the lid. Her hands shook as she removed a packet of Daniel's war letters tied with a blue ribbon. She hugged them to her breast and began to cry.

When the wave of misery had passed, Bella laid his letters carefully on the floor next to her. Methodically, she removed books and papers to make room for clothes and necessities, leaving only those of Daniel's possessions that were dearest to her.

She rose, knees aching, and opened the heavy doors of the pine wardrobe. Hesitating over Daniel's few clothes, she stroked them longingly. She buried her head in his comfortable brown waistcoat and a fresh wave of grief took over as she cried again.

Finally, she began the task of packing. She laid her husband's white silk cravat and the embroidered vest, her wedding presents to him, into the trunk. She added three of their favorite volumes of poetry, and the framed daguerreotype taken on their wedding day —she was seated on a chair in the photographer's studio, clutching a small bouquet of violets, smiling at the camera, while Daniel stood behind her, his right hand resting on her shoulder, gazing down at her with a tender expression. Whenever Bella looked at the photograph, she could remember every detail of that happy afternoon and its promise of a life together, now lost to her forever.

Gently, Bella closed the lid of the trunk. In the half-light of dawn she washed and dressed, then woke Amanda.

"Sshhh, my darling. Time to get up. We must be ready to leave with Uncle Zach."

Amanda rolled over and rubbed at her eyes. "Where are we going?" She opened her mouth in a wide yawn.

"To a wonderful place with an eagle's eye view of the world." Bella stroked her daughter's hair. "I used to go there as a little girl. Uncle Zach will find me a job there and there will be lots of children to play with. Oh, you'll like it."

After helping her sleepy daughter to dress, Bella tiptoed to the door and listened. Not a sound. It was now or never. She turned the knob and slowly opened the creaking door.

"Sshhh!" she told Amanda. "Help me tuck this blanket under the trunk here. Good." Bella began to inch the trunk across the floor, walking backwards, crouched and straining against its weight. It caught on the cracked door sill. When she tugged it free, it banged against the jamb.

"Sshhh!" Amanda said.

Bella nodded. "I know," she whispered in return. "We don't want to wake Uncle Zach."

~

"Just what in damnation do you think you're doing?"

Bella dropped the trunk with a thud. "Oh!" She turned to face a pair of angry eyes. Then she gasped.

Zach was naked from the waist up, emerging from the kitchen with a towel. His face was wet, a line of lather still defining where he had carefully shaved around his mustache.

Without his clothes, he looked very different from Daniel. Bella's eyes took in his hard, sharply-defined muscles, dark curly chest hair that glistened with water droplets, his broad shoulders and trim waist. She couldn't help but stare. Then she quickly averted her eyes and pushed Amanda behind her to block her view.

"I...I...I thought you were still asleep," she stammered.

He stared back with an expression of disbelief that made her cringe. "So you thought *that* would be a good time to go banging a trunk around! When I was still asleep?"

Amanda peeked out from behind Bella's skirts and giggled. "Mama, Uncle Zach's got no shirt on," she whispered.

"Please cover yourself," she reproved him gently. "For Amanda's sake."

Zach scowled. "Sorry." He strode to the curtained alcove that held Amanda's bed and reached for his shirt. Keeping his back to them, he pulled it on over his head. "What's the trunk for?"

"I packed our things."

Zach pivoted back, his fingers still fumbling with the buttons. "What do you mean?"

Bella hesitated, then shrugged. "We're coming with you."

"You're what?"

"Amanda and I. We're all packed. Except for Amanda's dolls and a few household—"

"Packed?" He glared at the trunk.

"Yes." Bella's voice was calm, but her body was braced for his rebuke. "I thought I'd have a better chance—"

"Are you demented?" he shouted.

"Sshhh!" Bella hissed, as Amanda scooted behind her at his shout. She clung to Bella's skirts with surprising strength. "You're frightening my daughter."

"And you're frightening me!" Zach finished tucking in his shirt, then jerked his suspenders over his shoulders. "Lady, what are you up to?"

"I simply thought I'd have a better chance at the job if I went now," Bella began again. "You could introduce me to the person who does the hiring."

"I don't know who's in charge of the servant staff these days!"

"But you said..." She covered her mouth with both hands. Her body went slack. All the certainties she had planned for vanished with his words.

"I know what I said." Zach pointed a finger at Bella. "I know the hotel manager. But he doesn't hire the maids himself. Someone below him does. You, on the other hand, apparently heard me say what you wanted to hear. I never said I could get you a job. I said there might be a job up there. Then again, there might not. What then?"

"I'll find something else," Bella said quickly. "There are other boarding houses. Factories."

"Well, I'm not taking you." Zach began to throw towels and shaving gear into his satchel. "That's final. I'll mention you to Gabriel Kramer and send for you if there's a firm chance of a job."

"But we can't stay here!" cried Bella. "There is not even enough work here for all the men back from the war!" A note of hysteria crept into her voice. "I am coming. I have the money you gave me."

"Fine, fine, do what you want." Zach buttoned his vest in short, jerky movements. "Just don't expect me to look out for you every step of the way. Daniel and I were never close. So I'm not looking to take on his entire family."

His harsh words appalled Bella. But she refused to give up. She must not think of anything except getting what she needed to survive. "We're coming, nevertheless."

A sharp rap on the door made them both freeze.

"Mrs. Smith? It's Mrs. Oster. I hear you. Open the door this minute."

"It's the landlady." Bella moved to open the door. "At this hour?"

"I thought I heard a man's voice in here." Peering round the door, Mrs. Oster spied Zach.

"That's my husband's brother. I told you that he was staying here with us."

Mrs. Oster's beady eyes fixed themselves skeptically on Zach. "Are you? His brother?"

"Half-brother." He folded his arms across his chest. "What business of it is yours?"

"There's a matter of twelve dollars on the rent owing. And I see that Mrs. Smith is fixing to sneak off without paying." She nodded toward the trunk.

"I was doing no such thing! Here!" Bella dropped Amanda's hand and strode to the mantelpiece to snatch an envelope. "Here's your twelve dollars, with a note that I am leaving. You can rent your precious rooms to someone else!" With a hand trembling as much from anger as nerves, she flung the envelope, relieved to vent some of her anger and misery at the old skinflint.

Mrs. Oster stooped down to retrieve it, slit it open with a flick of a practiced fingernail, then silently counted the dollars. "Well. It's all here."

"And why wouldn't it be?" In three strides, Zach was at the landlady's side, fixing her with an angry stare. "You owe Mrs. Smith an apology."

"Oh, I think not," she answered imperiously. "If I hadn't come to collect it, I doubt it would still be there waiting for me. Humph!" With that, the widow turned and sailed out of the door.

Zach slammed the door after her. "Good riddance!"

Now that her anger was spent, Bella could hardly bear to look at Zach. She opened her mouth to apologize. "I'm sorry... about..."

"Well, ain't this just dandy!" Zach stomped back to collect his things. "Yes, dandy. A few weeks ago I'm feeling fancy free. Happy to be back to my band. The stink of war behind me." He flung rumpled clothing into the satchel. "A couple of new suits. New shirts. Felt like a new man! Now I'm nursemaid to a bunch of relatives I don't even know and yelling at people I don't want to know."

Stung by his outburst, Bella's humility vanished in a wave of indignation.

"Please don't worry about us!" She used a curt and formal tone of voice. "I wouldn't dream of being a burden on you. We'll do nicely on our own, thank you kindly." She strode to him, folding her arms across her chest and fixed him with a stare.

"All I want from you is an introduction to the hotel manager and a recommendation. And then you're," she shook her hand at him, "you're fancy free again! Get your dolls, Amanda. We'll find a real gentleman to help us carry down the trunk."

Regally, she swished her skirts and marched past Zach to the pantry, where she began to gather some more belongings.

Zach threw up his hands in a sign of resignation. "Don't get on your high horse," he groused. "I'll take the damned trunk down for you."

"I'll thank you not to swear around my daughter," Bella said firmly, as if she were talking to the rowdy boys across the street. She quickly put her belongings in a carpet satchel. "Just because you are a black sheep of the family doesn't give you license to be rude."

"I'll try and remember my manners, ma'am," Zach growled back. He grabbed his cornet case and tugged on the trunk. "Don't just stand there, get my things if you're coming! If we miss that boat, you're going to hear a lot more swearing, Mrs. Smith." He dragged the trunk out the door and banged it hard behind him all the way down the stairs.

Elated by her victory, Bella quickly tucked the cornet case under her arm, and bent down to pick up the two heavy satchels. She staggered to the door.

"Come along Amanda!" she cried. Amanda scooted past her. As Bella reached the threshold, a wave of sorrow mixed with fear swept through her.

She turned to look around the familiar room one last time. Her tears began to flow. "Goodbye, my love," she whispered. "Goodbye, Daniel."

Squaring her shoulders, with tears still blurring her vision, Bella marched through the open door without bothering to close it behind her.

Six

The Thomas Powell steamboat waited on the dock, its red, white and blue flags and banners rippling in the breeze.

This and its sister ship, the Mary Powell, were most fashionable of the side-wheeler steamboats, plowing the waters of the Hudson between New York and Albany every day.

The crowd inched their way to the ramp of the steamship. Zach hadn't spoken more than two words to Bella on the way to the docks. After the porters took their baggage and they finally reached the deck, Zach handed Bella his cornet case so he could hoist Amanda up on his shoulders to see over the crowd.

"Ahoy there, Zach!" A tall, thin man waved his hat energetically from the deck. He tapped the shoulder of the lady next to him, who immediately turned to smile and wave at Zach, too.

The gaily dressed woman in a canary yellow gown and bonnet caught Bella's immediate attention. Zach grinned as soon as he saw them hurrying over.

"John! Good to see you." Zach shook hands with the gentleman, then bent to kiss the lady. "Nancy, my love. Missed you both. Everyone get aboard all right?"

"Without a hitch," John answered. "The boys are relatively sober and in high spirits. They said to join them in the bar. Your first drink is on them." He nudged Zach with his elbow. "They'll rib you no end for returning with two such beautiful peaches after all!"

"God save us!" Zach said. "By the way, this is my niece, Amanda Smith." He craned his head to look up at Amanda still riding on his shoulders. "Say hello to John Halley, Amanda. He's the band's fiddler.

John reached a hand up. Amanda shook it tentatively. "Pleased to meet you, Miss Smith. And what instrument do you play?"

For a moment Amanda was silent, then she answered gravely, "I play my dolly."

The three adults burst out laughing. Bella stood just outside the circle of mirth, feeling small and insignificant.

"Well, that will add a novelty to the band," John said. Then he turned to Bella. "And who is this beautiful lady?"

"Mrs. Daniel Smith, my half-brother's widow." As John's eyebrow's rose in shock, Zach quietly explained the details of his brother's death.

Bella felt the double sting of Zach's introduction. The term "half-brother" sounded like a deliberate insult to her ears, while the word "widow" opened a fresh wound.

John's face showed great compassion as he took her hand with gentle grace. "I'm so sorry to hear of the death of your husband. Zach had such hopes of seeing him again."

Bella looked into his brown eyes and immediately felt comforted. "Why, thank you for your concern, Mr. Halley."

The woman in the yellow bonnet stepped in, extending her hand as well. "I'm John's wife, Nancy. My deepest condolences for your loss. Oh, you must be tired. Come with me. There's a place where we can sit and take refreshment. It'll be lovely to have some feminine companionship."

A long, piercing whistle signaled the departure of the steamship. Zach swung Amanda down from his shoulders and grabbed his cornet case back from Bella. Nancy ushered Bella and Amanda through the dispersing crowds.

Quickly, Zach filled John in on the last few days.

"So now, I put my foot in my mouth and said I'd try and see if there were any jobs at the Mountain House. And she thinks that means she can tag along and I'll take care of her. John, I don't know what the hell to do." He leaned over the railing and watched the shore as the boat pulled away from the docks.

"Shouldn't be too hard to find her a job," John said. "They have a big staff at the hotel."

"That's not the point. Now I'm responsible for their welfare. Just what I need, with everything else." Zach scowled, jamming his free hand into his pocket, thumping his hat against his leg. "An instant family, with none of the benefits."

The violinist grinned and slapped him on the back. "This will put a crimp in your love life, old boy! The ladies will be calling you Papa Zach."

"Not if I have anything to say about it." Clapping his hat on his head, Zach straightened up. "Where's the bar, old man? Let's start this journey off properly!"

※

Bella toyed with a salmon paste sandwich and listened to Mrs. Halley prattle on.

The woman was obviously starved for companionship. What a life, Bella thought, traipsing with a bunch of musicians all over creation! Not the life for her. She wanted a home of her own, with a garden of roses where she and her family would sit of an evening.

Bella had hesitated when Mrs. Halley suggested taking tea in the salon, too embarrassed to admit she couldn't afford such luxuries. The woman had generously insisted on treating them to sandwiches, tea, and ice cream for Amanda in the ornate parlor filled with miniature gilt tables.

"How kind of you, Mrs. Halley," Bella said.

"Nonsense. And call me Nancy. May I call you by your Christian name? It makes me feel as though we were old friends. And that's ever so much nicer, don't you think?"

Bella blushed. This woman was so informal. "Of course. You

may call me Bella."

"Short for Arabella?"

"No, just Bella."

"What an unusual name. Not Belle, as in the South?"

"No. It's Italian. It means Beautiful..." Bella stopped.

"How lovely!" Nancy said.

Bella had almost said, "Beautiful Wind," which is what Daniel had called her the first time he heard her full name. Bella Gale, his Beautiful Wind. Just the thought of Daniel filled Bella's eyes with tears. She hastily took out a handkerchief.

"How long have you known Mr. Smith?" Bella asked, eager to change the subject.

"Oh, ages and ages," Nancy said with a laugh. "The boys were playing at the Rogers Hotel in St. Louis, where I'm from. It was back in Fifty-three. I was all of sixteen, working in my daddy's telegraph office." She tapped out a message rapidly on the table. "Well, Zach came in. The band leader had left them stranded with pennies to their names! Zach asked me to wire a man he knew for some money. I was closing up, but I did it as a favor. John had such a kind face." She took a bite of cucumber sandwich and wiped her fingers daintily on the white linen napkin. "Aren't these divine?"

"Delicious," Bella agreed. "Then what happened?"

"Imagine my surprise in the morning when I found the boys still there! They had waited outside the telegraph office all night, poor dears. They had nowhere else to go. I took them home with me for a bite of breakfast. Mama said they could sleep in the barn and help out with chores for their keep. That man never did send them any money. I found out later it was Zach's father. Isn't that terrible?"

Bella was shocked at the disclosure. Her father-in-law had always been so kind to her and Daniel. She couldn't imagine him committing such a betrayal. She felt a pang of empathy for her brother-in-law.

"Zach's uncle down in Georgia finally sent him some money. Then Zach found work at another hotel. He and John put together a new band and Zach became the band's leader. John and I grew friendly, and, well, I married him. Been a gypsy ever since."

"It must be a hard life."

"Oh, not at all." Nancy licked her fingers. "The boys are like family. It's like having seven brothers. There's always some fun going on. And I love to travel. Why, we've been all over the country, even Europe. Well, that was before the war. Now that it's over, perhaps we'll visit Paris again."

"Wouldn't you rather settle down in a home and raise a family?"

"Oh, well." Nancy's smile dissolved into an expression of vague sorrow. "Well, the good Lord has never seen fit to give me children." She quickly recovered her cheerful demeanor. "Besides, John loves being with the band. It's like meat and drink to him. I couldn't take that away. He wouldn't be happy."

"Yes, I understand." Bella was touched by Nancy's obvious devotion to her husband. Her heart ached for Daniel.

"May I ask you a rather personal question?" Nancy stared at Bella, as if appraising her. "Bella is such an unusual name, and ..." she hesitated. "Aren't you Bella Gale, the daughter of the Silk King?"

Stunned, Bella caught her breath. How did this woman know?

"It's just that, when you said your name, I remembered why you looked so familiar," Nancy Halley said. "I do keep up on all the gossip columns and the stock market news. A friend pointed you out at the time of your engagement party at the Regency Hotel, and I never forget a beautiful face. I remembered it doubly, because the next week I read about your father and the embezzlement at his company, and the stock that crashed. I only owned a few shares at the time, thank goodness, but I knew a lot of people who lost everything in that scandal. Terrible business..."

Bella began to tremble, unable to catch her breath. She felt cornered by the old memories of that terrible night.

"Then, of course, what was it?" Nancy chattered on, oblivious to Bella's discomfort. "A month later, I saw in the papers that the Silk King died and that you broke off your engagement to one of the richest young financiers on Wall Street."

Bella looked back at Nancy coldly. Amanda was quietly feeding cake and tea to her dolly. "It was a terrible time. One I prefer not to talk about."

Nancy looked up at Bella's face, which had gone quite pale. "Oh, how awful of me. Please." Nancy put a hand on Bella's arm. Her expression was as contrite as Amanda's when she was caught being naughty. "I meant no harm. I always wondered if your father had been innocent of the embezzlement. John's always telling me to think twice before I prattle on."

Bella looked away, fighting back tears and a surge of anger.

"Oh, dear, oh dear," Nancy said. "Now you'll think I'm awful, and not want to have anything to do with me. I'm sorry, really I am. Please say you'll forgive me."

Nancy continued apologizing with such dramatic fervor that Bella turned back to her and forced a weak smile.

"Please," Bella said quietly. "I forgive you. You couldn't know how awful it is for me to think about all that again. My father did not embezzle the money. He was so distraught after my mother died, that he just left his business in the hands of his partner's sons, and well..."

Bella stopped for a moment to calm her feelings of anger and sorrow. "Anyway, I suppose I'll be recognized by other people at the Mountain House, and have to endure their questions, their stares. Poor Bella Gale. Her father ruined and her fiancé left her all in the same month. She married a poor clerk and now she's a widow, scrubbing floors at the Mountain House."

She tried to say this with a light heart, but the last words caught in her throat. She couldn't stop herself from crying.

Amanda looked up from her ice cream and put down her spoon. She snuggled closer to her mother and put her arms around Bella's neck, one tiny hand patting her mother's shoulder.

Nancy was contrite. "Oh, my dear. You poor thing."

"It doesn't matter," Bella said, taking the embroidered handkerchief that Nancy offered. "Thank you." She dabbed at her eyes, then kissed Amanda on the tip of her nose. "There, there, sweetie. Finish your ice cream, now, before it melts."

Amanda wore a skeptical expression, but Bella gave her another kiss. "Honestly. Mama's fine now."

Bella took a sip of tea to calm herself. "I only hope my brother-in-law can find me something, any kind of job at the Mountain House."

"But you can't take a maid's job! Such terrible work! Zach can't let you do that. If you need some money, I'd be happy to…"

"I'll do what I have to." Bella laid her hand over Nancy's. "All I beg is, please, don't go around telling people about me. Or talking to my brother-in-law about this. Not until I've found a position. He already feels, well, angry at me for coming." Her eyes filled with tears again. "But I had nowhere else to turn."

"Oh, my dear! I'll keep your secret to the death!" Nancy plucked an imaginary key from the air and locked her mouth with it. Her obvious sincerity made Bella feel that, unexpectedly, she had found a strong ally.

~

As they left the tea salon, Nancy heard the music first.

"It's John and Zach and some of the boys," she said. "Oh, let's hurry!"

"How can you tell?"

"I'd know the sound of John's fiddle anywhere!" Nancy laughed and caught Bella and Amanda by the hand. The three hurried to join the swirling couples who were enjoying an impromptu concert by four of the musicians.

Amanda's eyes grew wide at the sight. "Mama, there's Uncle Zach!"

There he stood, head thrown back, eyes shut tight, his whole body poised triumphantly on the edge of a high note that held the crowd's attention.

In that moment, Bella understood that Zach possessed a

charisma she had seen only once before; in his father, the Reverend Jeremiah Smith, whom she had once watched deliver a stirring sermon to a packed church. The difference, however, was in the message. Zach embodied an exuberance and joy, whereas his father had held his audience spellbound out of terror for their immortal souls.

Bella smiled. She much preferred Zach's message. Her own feet began to tap in time to the lilting tune. To her amazement, Nancy whisked Amanda off in a waltz. Bella laughed at the spontaneity of it. As they whirled, Amanda kept turning her head to follow Zach's every movement.

The song ended to loud applause. John Halley inclined his head graciously, almost modestly. The French horn player and the hefty man who played the bassoon grinned and waved. Zach lifted his cornet high in the air, then scraped the ground with a deep, solemn, theatrical bow that Bella found quite charming.

"Thank you, thank you! Glad you enjoyed it, folks. I'm Zach Smith. This is John Halley and a few of the boys from Smith's Cornet Band. We're engaged for the season at the famed Catskill Mountain House. We'll be playing there for your musical enjoyment." He bowed again. "Now, John, let's do the doggy!"

John swung into the ditty that had become so popular this year. Zach began to sing in an exaggerated German accent. "Oh vere, oh vere has mine little dog gone? Oh vere, oh vere can he be?" He barked like a dog.

Bella laughed and pushed through the crowd after Nancy, who had whirled Amanda right to the front.

"Mit his fine fur coat and his little brown eyes, of vere, oh vere can he be? Arff! Arff!"

The crowd was now laughing and clapping to the beat, as Zach continued to sing and clown his way through the comical song, punctuating the end of each verse with a fanfare or a drop-tone riff.

Bella reached Amanda and tapped her on the shoulders. "Mama, isn't he funny?" Amanda exclaimed with a soft giggle. Bella nodded. Zach was a wonderful performer, with a honeyed baritone voice. He moved with vigor and athletic grace, changing expressions with all the delight of a young child suddenly finding himself the center of attention. Bella applauded enthusiastically with the crowd.

"Thank you again, friends." Zach bowed low, then winked at the crowd. Catching sight of Amanda, he seemed to pull back in surprise. Then his expression softened. "Ah, there is a very special little lady here. My niece, Amanda Smith. This next song is for her."

Amanda's cheeks flushed with color at the mention of her name.

Zach raised his cornet to his lips, bent at the knees, and then swooped into a bright rising note that hovered in the air. The note fell away and then rose again, creating a gentle rocking lilt of a tune that was clearly a lullaby, although Bella could not place the song. The other musicians joined in, their hypnotic music holding the crowd. People began to sway, drifting away on their private dreams, as the steamboat churned gently through the sun-dappled river, past the green-capped highlands toward the hazy, purple mountain peaks beyond.

Bella moved closer to Nancy and tucked one arm around her new friend's waist, stroking Amanda's blonde curls with her free hand. As it had at the funeral, Zach's music reached deep into her broken heart, coaxing forth loving memories of her beloved Daniel. Lost in those memories, Bella was startled only by the silence the followed when the last note died away. The crowd was too swept away to respond, or perhaps they hoped to hear one more sweet refrain.

Amanda cried out, "Oh, that was lovely, Uncle Zach! Play it again!" The spell was broken. People laughed and drifted away, satiated with the music and scenery.

But Zach seemed lost in thought, staring intently at Amanda. In a moment, he was at Nancy's side, lifting Amanda into his arms. "Do you know," he told her, "that your father used to say the very same thing when I played that song for him?"

"But he didn't call you Uncle Zach, did he?"

Amanda's forthright question made Zach chuckle. "No, he didn't. He did love this song. I'm glad you like it, too."

Bella was touched. "It's a beautiful song. I've never heard it before. And I thought I knew all the new songs."

He looked at her, his dark eyes intense and unnerving. "You wouldn't have heard this one. It's called 'Daniel's Song.' I wrote it for him when he was a baby."

"It's a wonderful lullaby," Bella insisted, touched by the image of a young Zach humming the song to her husband as a child.

"It was part of a larger piece." Zach hesitated, his speech guarded. "Part of an unfinished symphony."

"A symphony! How grand!" Bella conjured a picture of Zach in evening dress, conducting an orchestra at Niblo's Garden or the New York Music Society. She was intrigued by the image of Daniel's brother being a classical composer. "When did you write it?"

"A long time ago. It...it was lost for a while." Zach put Amanda down.

Oh, but you should finish it and publish it. I'm sure that..." Bella began. But Zach narrowed his eyes, warning her against further questions. "I only meant..."

With a last sideways glare, Zach turned on his heel. "I'm going to get a drink. Coming, John?" He packed up his cornet, snapped the lock shut, and strode off in the direction of the bar.

"What did I say now?" Bella knelt to hug Amanda, feeling miserable. Once again, her enigmatic brother-in-law was angry at her, but this time the reason was as mysterious as the wind.

Seven

The stagecoach rattled and swayed as it climbed to the famed Catskill Mountain House, jarring the occupants with every turn of the wheel along the rutted road.

Bella was glad she had not had much of an appetite when the boat arrived in time for lunch, for the jostling trip had upset her stomach as well as given her a headache.

Bella's arm tightened around her daughter's shoulder and smoothed her golden hair.

"It's all right," she murmured. "Nothing will happen."

Amanda's body tensed against Bella's grip. Perhaps she is fearful, Bella thought. Fearful that the carriage might overturn like the streetcar that killed her father.

On the other side of Amanda, Nancy huddled next to her husband, uncharacteristically quiet on the bone-shaking trip.

The five young musicians opposite Bella, however, seemed to be in high spirits. They fidgeted and poked each other. They snickered over Lord knows what dirty notions, she thought. They were as rude now as when they had first been introduced to her on the steamship, making snide remarks about her being the "peach" Zach had gone to see after all.

Zach had silenced them with his curt introductions of his widowed sister-in-law—with heavy emphasis on the sister-in-law.

And the boys had become subdued and properly courteous, offering muttered sympathies to her and to Zach. But once in the carriage, Zach had tipped his hat over his eyes and fallen asleep. And soon, the bored young men had reverted to their whispered, vulgar jokes and teasing comments.

Bella leaned forward to peer out the window. Huge trees along the road framed a dazzling view of distant mountain peaks and blue sky. Gazing down, she saw the abrupt edge of the road, a precipice that plunged headlong down among scattered rocks into a deep ravine. She shut her eyes and fell back against her seat. As a child, cosseted between her adoring parents, the trip had always been an adventure. But now, after Daniel's accident, the view of that steep gorge conjured up dreadful scenarios in her mind.

The steep gorge seemed to bring out the braggadocio in the musicians, as well.

"Whoa! What a drop, eh Peter?" The mischievous blond musician opposite her flashed a sly grin and poked his partner. "I hear there are carriages that have gone over whole, still lying on the bottom of the ravine."

"I don't believe you, Billy," said Peter. He jabbed the musician with his elbow, provoking a good-natured groan.

"Oh, believe it," Billy replied, tracing a cross on his heart with his finger. "They say the souls of many a poor pilgrim lookin' to spend a few months at the Mountain House are now wandering' 'round the ravine at nights. Imagine it, Whoooohoohooo!"

The two men snickered.

"Yes," a third musician, Paul, added. "The ghosts flit about the mountain house to scare off the guests who sleep in the rooms they had booked." He poked Big Harry in the stomach, and the rotund bassoonist let out a belch. The others howled with laughter, while John shook his head with an indulgent smile.

Bella narrowed her eyes at them and frowned.

"Mama, are there really ghosts down there?" Amanda asked.

"No darling," Bella replied, hugging her daughter tighter. "They are only trying to be funny."

Zach pushed his hat back. "All right, boys," he said. "Enough. You're frightening the little one."

"Don't you believe in ghosts?" Paul leaned across toward Amanda.

Bella pulled Amanda closer. She had a mind to scold the young man, but before she spoke, Zach reached across and cuffed him lightly on the shoulder.

"I said enough! Behave yourself!" Zach leaned forward to reassure Amanda. "You're not to worry." He looked deep into her eyes, and then smiled. "These coaches have never had an accident. Never. Mr. Beach, who owns this Mountain House, owns the stagecoaches, too. And he makes sure his guests arrive safely. And that's a fact, Little Missy."

Amanda nodded, but her eyes were still wide with fear.

"Come here on my lap." Zach reached out for her. "Sit up here with me."

Reluctantly, Bella let her go. The child quickly scrambled into his lap and buried her head against her uncle's chest, just as she used to do with Daniel.

"Enough ghost stories. Let's sing a song." Zach began to tap his foot, bouncing Amanda on his knee. "Shall we sing 'A Froggy Went a Courtin'? A one, two, on the downbeat... "He launched into the song. The other lads in the band joined in, their voices vibrating with each jolt and jerk of the carriage.

"'A froggy went a courting' and he did ride, uh huh. Uh huh..."

Soon Amanda chimed in, clapping her hands to the beat. Bella tried to catch the spirit of the lively song, but nodded off instead, her dreams a jumble of images and snatches of sounds.

Her eyes flew open as the carriage lurched to a stop, the wheels grating against the huge, pointed brake that kept the carriage from rolling back down the steep incline. With a heavy head and bleary eyes, she gazed out the window onto a spectacular sight. Perched on a shelf of rock above was the Mountain House, its thirteen Grecian columns glistening white in the sun.

It looked so near, but Bella knew from past experience that the distance was an illusion. They were stopped at the bend, yet the road climbed on for another mile and a half, twisting and turning and steeply pitched.

"Everyone out!" the driver cried. "Stretch those legs."

It was customary to encourage the travelers to walk the last and steepest three-quarters of a mile to relieve the strain on the horses. As a young girl, Bella had always welcomed the opportunity to walk. But now she had misgivings, exhausted by the last few sleepless nights.

The musicians jumped down from the carriage. John helped Nancy down.

Zach waited, holding Amanda on his knee. "Let me take Amanda for you," he told Bella. "When she tires of walking, the boys can take turns letting her ride on their shoulders."

Bella smiled at him. "Thank you."

"Need a hand, ma'am?" One of the lads on her side of the carriage held out an arm. Bella grasped it and held her skirts back, careful not to catch her hem on the corner of the door or the jutting step. Gingerly, she stepped out. A pair of hands grasped her waist and swung her to the ground.

She gasped and looked up into the face of the bright-eyed Billy, the drummer. "Thank you, sir."

"My pleasure, ma'am," he answered with a grin. His hands tightened around her waist.

"Thank you," Bella said. "I can manage from here."

He only grinned back. Alarmed by his insolent attitude, she squirmed, wondering whether he would let go at all.

"Billy-boy! Wake up!" Zach's voice held a warning note. "Let Mrs. Smith go and take Amanda for a ride, how about it?"

"Sure, Zach! Sorry, Zach!" Billy immediately released his hold on Bella's waist. "Sorry, ma'am," he stammered. "I just... ah. You're so pretty, I was just kind of admirin' you. Didn't mean to be disrespectful or nothing. No, ma'am."

Bella's mouth dropped open. She didn't know whether to slap his face for his insolence, or to laugh at his awkward apology.

Before she had a chance to do either, Billy swung Amanda up on his shoulders and galloped off up the path.

"Be careful!" she called after them. "Hold on tight, Amanda!"

The other musicians loped after Billy. The one they called Big Harry huffed and puffed his way behind them. John and Nancy fell in behind the boys. Zach turned to join them.

Bella sighed. They had forgotten she was even there. She was truly on her own. Which was fine with her. Life had been cruel in its lessons. She had learned to take care of herself after her father's death and again during Daniel's enlistment. Now she would have to learn to provide for Amanda. Sweeping her skirts high to avoid the dust of the road, she plodded along, pacing herself to the long incline and kicking loose stones with a vengeance.

Her mind cast back to happier times of childhood. Her gaze swept over the budding wildflowers, and she breathed in the sweet mountain air. She noticed the little pools of water, where birds dipped their beaks to drink before flitting off again. It was all just as she remembered it. Wild and beautiful, with the scent of pine on the breeze. Daniel would have loved it here. She wished they had been able to come here when he was alive.

Yet, walking up the steep mountain exhausted Bella. Her underclothes clung damply against her skin. The stays in her corset gripped her like an iron band. She glanced up, dismayed that the others were so far ahead of her. Hurrying to catch up, she stumbled on the side of a deep rut. Her pulse raced, her heartbeats thudding in her ears. Spying a little outcropping of rock near a shady glen, she veered off toward the spot where a trickle of water ran down the cliff nearby. She stumbled to the rock and collapsed, thinking she would just rest a minute. Closing her eyes, she lifted her face to the late-afternoon sun. A slight breeze tickled her cheeks.

She had no idea how long she had sat there. A crunching sound penetrated her stupor.

"Decided not to take a job at the Mountain House after all?"

Bella jerked her head up. Zach stood over her, shaking his head in amusement.

"I'm fine," Bella quickly answered, smoothing out her skirts. "Just catching my breath."

"It is a long walk." He held out his arm. "May I escort you up the hill, Mrs. Smith?"

Bella hesitated and then smiled. She rose, unsteady, and gripped his arm.

"Think of it as a stroll in an Alpine garden," Zach continued. "Nothing more."

Zach's surefooted steps steadied her own. His body sent other signals to hers—a pleasant warmth and solidness that emanated from his rolling gait. His mouth moved sensuously, with a lazy flash of smile that punctuated his stories.

He told her about Paris, but his words soon blurred. She concentrated on his face, still amazed by the similarity to Daniel, but now more cognizant of the differences. His curls, for one, seemed longer and wilder than Daniel's. His dark eyes were flecked with amber sparks. The tilt of his head and swing of his gestures exuded an edge of excitement so different from Daniel's gentle, steady demeanor.

She wondered what he had really done to earn his reputation as "the black sheep." At times, it seemed as if he could have done something dangerous—perhaps even scandalous.

"In Paris, there's a place called Montmartre," said Zach. "They have these cabarets with singers, comics, a magician, and always these lovely dancing girls. They were quite the flirts..." He glanced at her. "Sorry. I forgot I'm in the presence of a lady."

Something in the way he said it sounded sarcastic, rather than truly sorry. "Never mind," Bella said. "I confess I wasn't fully listening. And here I was, thinking how gallant you are to help me up the road. Just like Daniel."

His wry smile faded. "I'm not at all like Daniel." Bella felt his arm tense. "We had nothing in common except a father. That's all." His tone was light, but somehow the words sounded cold.

Bella released his arm and looked him right in the eyes. "I

don't know what came between you and Daniel. Nor do I care. But it's all in your head. Daniel never spoke ill of you to me."

Turning on her heels, she trudged up the hill as fast as she could in her long skirts. She was determined to get as far away from this odious man as fast as she could.

~

Zach hardly saw the angry woman who stomped away from him. He was lost in a flood of memories from the Sunday morning when his eight-year-old brother Daniel had burst in on him.

Zach was laboring over the notations for the horn section, straining to hear it in his head. He dared not play the notes on his cornet; playing music, unless it was Christian hymns, was forbidden on the Sabbath in his father's house. Daniel ran in, chattering excitedly about something, shattering Zach's fragile concentration.

"Go away!" he shouted at his little brother. "I'm busy."

"But Papa told me to come get you..."

"Go away!" In frustration, Zach struck his little brother. "Go bother someone else."

The next thing Zach knew, his father was grabbing him by his collar and hoisting him up out of his seat. His stool tumbled to the floor. His pen blotted and scraped across the notes of his symphony as he was dragged away. His father raged at him, snatched up the pages of music, and accused him of doing Satan's work...

Wearily, Zach's mind shut out the rest of the memory, unwilling to relive the terrible fight with his father over his symphony.

Had it been Daniel's fault? Of course not, he reasoned. Did it even matter any longer? Bella said Daniel never spoke ill of him. Probably his step-brother had forgotten the entire incident. But Zach couldn't. The wounds were still as fresh to him as if it had happened only yesterday. Why would his mind never let that humiliation fade?

Glancing up, he watched Bella in the distance. She struggled up the road, her head drooping, her bonnet askew. Suddenly, he felt ashamed. She's got no family. No husband. No money. And a child to care for—a child who was his only living relative.

"Damn! What's wrong with me!" he chastised himself.

Too much death, he realized. What he needed was life again. The band. The music. Who knows, maybe even a pair of lost relatives.

"Bella! Wait!"

Bella continued walking.

Zach trotted, then ran. For some unfathomable reason, he felt compelled to put things right. He raced up beside her, his mind searching for the right words to say. He was not used to apologizing.

She quickened her pace.

He matched her stride. Just say it straight out, he told himself. "I apologize."

She stared straight ahead, puffing hard with exertion.

"Don't run away, damn it." Zach grabbed her arm, and she turned to glare at him. "I'm trying to apologize for what I said before. It's all old family stuff. Nothing to do with you."

"That's hardly an apology!" She flicked off his hand and turned her back on him, breathing hard.

"What kind do you want?"

"Well, well! I don't know! Perhaps if you got down on your knees and said something nice about my husband, that might do." She folded her arms, glaring at him.

"Well, I'm not getting down on my knees for anybody. Sorry, ma'am." Zach was silent for a moment. "Daniel was a sweet and clever boy. A good boy. My father doted on him. He liked poetry, books, music, and peppermint sticks. I'm sure he was a good and loving husband and father."

"He was."

"To be honest, I didn't know him that well. I left home when I was fifteen."

"Sometimes you make it sound as if Daniel was the reason you left." Bella's voice was angry.

Zach said nothing. He kicked a stone, which skittered to the side of the path. "No, Daniel had nothing to do with my leaving. He was just...a pawn in the eternal war between me and my father."

Bella's eyes softened. "Nancy told a story about your father not wiring you money. When you were stranded."

"She did, huh?" Zach kicked at another stone, watching it skitter to the left this time.

"It is hard to believe he would do that to his own son," Bella admitted. "He was always so nice to Daniel and me. I guess I have a hard time thinking of him as..."

"A monster?" Zach interjected.

"Surely not a monster."

"Only to me."

"He must have hurt you very much for you to think that," Bella said. "I'm sorry."

"It was a long time ago." Zach sighed. "And I don't want to talk about my father. Listen, we keep getting off on the wrong foot, you and I."

Bella frowned. "You're not the easiest man to deal with. One minute you're charming, the next you're ready to bite off someone's head."

"You're not exactly easy to deal with yourself," Zach said. "You have this little habit of forcing me to deal with things I'd rather not." He formally offered her his arm. "Shall we declare a truce? Otherwise, we shall never get to the Mountain House."

She stared at him for a long moment, thinking it over. "Truce." Primly, she took his arm, and they continued up the road in mutual, but wary silence.

Eight

The Catskill Mountain House once more came into view, teasing them with a glimpse whenever the road curved into the next rise. They approached the back end of the giant hotel. The jumble of buildings that protruded from the main house held an array of storehouses, workshops, and servants' quarters. Amanda ran to greet them.

"Mama! Mama! You must come and see!" She laughed and tugged on Bella's hand, dancing in delight.

Bella chuckled. "Yes, yes. I'll come."

"Uncle Zach, you come too!" Amanda reached out took Zach by the hand and led both adults toward the hotel. "Come and see! Over here!" She broke away from them and began to run.

Zach knew the spectacular view that awaited their eyes just beyond the hotel. It was always fun watching a newcomer's first reaction to the sight. Running after her, he scooped up Amanda and felt her body quiver with excitement. He carried her across the grassy lawn and onto the bare, smooth, sandstone ledge that jutted out into space.

"Mama! Mama! I'm higher than the whole world!" Amanda cried.

Zach gazed out on the familiar view. He hadn't seen it in nearly five years. The panorama was just as awe-inducing as he remembered. From the stone ledge, which dropped away from the edge in a sheer cliff, the green valley stretched out below them for miles in all directions. Through it ran a twisting ribbon of river, which glinted like silver in the sun. On the horizon, the valley melted into a shimmer of gentle mountain peaks.

This was the view that drew the wealthy to the Catskill Mountain House. Artists and writers and poets came here to romanticize the wilderness, inspired by the carpet of pristine beauty spread out quite literally at their feet.

Before the war, this view had inspired Zach to write a symphony about the place. The idea seemed childish and absurd to him now, after so much carnage. Picturesque countryside had been ruined for him, forever linked in his mind with the mangled bodies of dead soldiers, the smoke and mud of Antietam and Gettysburg, and of his uncle's plantation burning in the aftermath of the Union's rampage in Georgia.

Bella touched his arm lightly. "Should we see about getting settled?"

He set Amanda back down on the ground. "Good idea. But there's no need for you both to come inside just yet. Stay here and enjoy the view. I'll go in."

As he turned to leave, a well-dressed woman approached them, waving a handkerchief to catch their attention.

"Is it really Bella Gale! It is you, isn't it? I thought so. How nice!" The woman headed straight for Bella and took her hands. "I haven't seen you in ages."

Zach watched as Bella stared at the woman. Then her eyes opened wide. "Oh, my goodness!" she exclaimed, as her face brightened with recognition. "Why, it's Mrs. Grayson. Oh, my goodness, I almost didn't recognize you. How lovely to see you again."

"And this is your husband and daughter?" The gray-haired matron turned to Zach and Amanda. "Delightful. So nice to meet you. I was always so fond of Bella as a young child. She and my daughter Hermione played together, right here. But that was before all those unfortunate occurrences. Oh, dear." She turned back to Bella. "Well, well. So wonderful to meet again, back at the Mountain House. You and your husband must—"

"I'm not her husband," Zach said curtly. "She's my step-brother's widow."

Both women's expressions immediately changed at his words.

Mrs. Grayson looked horrified. "Widowed? Oh, my Lord. Oh, my Lord! In the war?"

Bella glowered at Zach, then looked back at Mrs. Grayson. A red blush of either anger or embarrassment—he wasn't sure which —swept over her cheeks as she stammered out an explanation. The older woman fluttered her hands and kept murmuring condolences.

"Oh, poor Bella. You have had such terrible misfortunes. I'm so sorry..." Mrs. Grayson's voice trailed off and she awkwardly patted Bella's hand before making her excuses and hurrying away.

"Was that your maiden name? Gale?" asked Zach.

Bella didn't answer.

"How did you know that woman?" he persisted.

Bella's voice trembled. "She was a family acquaintance." Then she turned on him with an angry hiss. "How could you be so...so rude!"

"I was just correcting her assumption. Which I noticed you didn't bother to do."

"You didn't give me a chance." Bella looked around, calling out to Amanda, who was showing her doll to another youngster. "That's too far away, Amanda. Come back here!"

"And while we're on the subject," Zach continued, "you said you had no family. You said you had no money, no friends to take you in, and now this woman..."

"I haven't seen Mrs. Grayson ever since..."

"Ever since when?"

"Ever since we stopped coming here when I was fourteen."

"Your family came here every summer? As a guest?" Zach asked, with renewed interest. He folded his arms, now highly suspicious of his sister-in-law's intentions. "That takes a great deal of money. Your father was wealthy?"

Bella said nothing. She began walking toward Amanda.

"So he was wealthy." Zach followed her. "And?"

"And what?"

"So where's your money? How come you don't have a penny to your name?"

Her mouth opened in mute protest, then closed firmly.

"Ah, I'll bet I know," Zach continued in a wheedling voice. "You hated your family and ran away to marry my penniless brother, right? And your father cut you off!"

"Your assumptions are highly insulting, sir!"

"So, tell me the real story," Zach said, glad to finally have the upper hand with his sister-in-law.

"You don't want a real story," she accused him. "You want a Cinderella story, don't you? With a happy ending so you don't have to worry about a widow and her daughter anymore. Well, there is no happy ending. My family was well off once. And I loved them very much. And everything is gone now."

Bella moved off again in the direction of Amanda.

Zach ran after her. "Bella, wait!"

She stopped abruptly. When Zach reached her, he saw that her features were etched with sorrow. "What really happened?" he asked gently. "I do want to hear the real story."

Bella moved away from Zach and gazed around her for a long moment. "Not here. Not now. It's too painful."

"Sit down." He took her arm, intending to lead her to a bench in front of the mountain house.

She began to cry. Then she sagged, and he scooped her up and carried her to the bench. It took her a few minutes to calm herself. Zach gave her his handkerchief, and she dried her eyes and blew her nose.

"My mother used to come here and paint every summer," Bella finally said. Her voice was quiet. "This was her favorite place on earth. Even when she was dying, slowly wasting away to nothing, my father arranged to bring her here. I was fourteen on her last visit. He would carry her out to lie on a camp bed beneath that tree over there, so she could look at the view."

Zach slid his hand into hers and squeezed it. "I'm so sorry."

Bella sadly shook her head. "We couldn't bear to come here after she died. My father lost interest in everything. His silk business, his bank, his shops. By the time I was sixteen, he had left it all in the hands of his partner's two sons. They ruined the business. Wrecked his reputation. And they blamed it all on him. If I had been a son, not a daughter, I could have run it for him. I could have..."

She stopped and choked back a sob.

"What happened then?" Zach's voice was gentle.

"My father had a stroke. He died a few months later. They sold off everything, our house, even my piano, to pay the company debts. I was engaged to be married. But my fiancé's family was very clear. They had no wish to be connected to any financial scandal. So I agreed to break it off for a small sum of money."

Lifting her head, she glared at Zach. "A very, very small sum of money."

"I'm sorry," he murmured.

Bella turned her back on him to stare out at the view.

"Then I met your brother," she continued, her tired voice barely audible. "He was the most decent, sweetest man in the whole world. He cared for me. He married me. And we had Amanda. And we were *happy*! When he went to war, I worked in a factory for fifty cents a day while Mrs. Porter watched my daughter. You think that was easy?"

She lifted her face to him. Zach could see sparks of anger in her violet eyes.

"No," he whispered. "No, I'm sure it wasn't."

He reached for Bella's hand, wondering how to tell her that he understood what it was to lose a parent you loved above all else.

She flinched from his grasp. "You think you know everything!" she accused him. "Well, you know nothing about Daniel or about me!"

"No, I don't," Zach agreed. "I'm sorry." He wanted to make her feel better, but he knew he'd made a hash of it, for sure.

Bella did not acknowledge him but fixed her gaze on the view.

Zach sighed and stood up. "Rest here a while. I'll see to the rooms and luggage. We'll all get some supper. Then I'll find Kramer and we'll find you a job."

～

As he walked toward the hotel, Zach cursed himself for his prickly temper, for his cynicism.

Why was he so quick to think the worst of people? To think that Bella was taking advantage of him? If the poor thing had had any money, she certainly wouldn't be traipsing up to the Mountain House with a perfect stranger to take a job scrubbing floors.

He continued to berate himself silently as he walked through the hotel's front door. A familiar voice caught his attention.

"Zach Smith, as I live and breathe! Welcome back!" Gabriel Kramer, the hotel manager, strode down the last few steps of the center staircase and hurried toward Zach. He extended his hand. "Good to see you, you old dog!"

Zach smiled and heartily shook Kramer's hand. "Not such an old dog as yourself, eh?" It was an old joke between them, since Kramer was a good ten years older than Zach. But the two men had always liked and respected each other. For a moment, Zach felt lighthearted, as if time had shifted back. As if he had never been away. "It's good to be back. The place hasn't changed much."

"Oh, there's a been a few changes." Kramer's grasp was firm and warm. "I've missed you, you old scallywag." He slapped Zach on the back. "You don't look much different. Maybe a little scrawnier." His expression changed to one of concern.

"You do," Zach joked. "A few gray hairs there, old man."

"Come on, I'll get you settled and buy you a drink in the salon."

"I'd like that, but...I've got some people I have to attend to first."

Kramer's eyes widened. "I take that back. You have changed. First time I knew you to pass up a free drink."

Zach chuckled. "I'll take you up on the drink another time.

Right now, I have a problem. A slight problem." And he began to tell his old friend about his brother, his sister-in-law, and his niece. "It's a bit of a mess. She insisted on coming. I told her I didn't know what could be done."

Kramer looked thoughtful. "I might have something open. Martin Ruckler, the new staff manager, said something this morning about a maid who hadn't shown up. He might be shorthanded."

"Did Mr. Pruitt retire?" Zach asked.

Kramer sighed. "Poor old man, he passed away. Had a stroke. I tell you, they don't make them like him anymore. A real gentleman and a superb butler. Ran the kitchens and the maids as if this place were Buckingham Palace."

"I'm sorry."

"Yes, sir, lots of changes from the war." Kramer's expression was mournful. "It's damned hard to find anybody with experience now. Ruckler's been with us for a number of years, overseeing the bakery and laundries. He's a bit rough, compared to Pruitt. But we figured we'd try him out with the staff. Honestly, so many men went off to war, well..."

The two men nodded in silence for a moment. Then Zach changed the subject. "Are there any empty rooms? For my sister-in-law?"

"Only the deluxe ones, and they're very expensive. We can find her something suitable in the servants' wing, especially if she's going to be working here." Kramer walked over to the desk clerk to check on the situation. Then he motioned Zach over. "This is Mr. Farris. He'll take good care of you, Zach. And I'll get back to you this evening about your sister-in-law."

"Thanks, Gabriel. I'm in your debt."

Kramer grinned. "You always are, you old dog. You always are."

Nine

"**D**one this kind of work before?"

Bella stood stiffly at attention in the butler's pantry as the head of the servant staff, Martin Ruckler, looked her over.

Zach had arranged for her to be interviewed right after the last dinner seating. There had been no time to change clothes or even find her trunk. She'd scrubbed the dust from her and Amanda's face at Zach's washstand and straightened their hair before joining the musicians for dinner. Now, all she wanted to do was climb into bed, but she willed herself to act brightly in order to make a good impression.

Out of the corner of her eye, she could see her daughter waiting outside the door, seated on a low stool facing the enormous kitchen. A rhythmic thumping of knives came from Bella's left, where the kitchen help chopped vegetables and pounded meats. The click and clatter of china came from her right, where two young men on ladders were stacking plates on shelves that reached to very top of the lofty ceilings.

"We have no use for incompetence." Mr. Ruckler's voice was haughty and disdainful. He was a burly man, tall and imposing, but somehow ill-fitted to the elegant black butler's waistcoat and jacket he wore. His features were rough: a shock of brown hair tufted up from behind his ears; an unruly beard was streaked with gray; a pair of shaggy eyebrows gave him a hooded look; and a crooked nose looked as if it had been broken more than once. He rubbed his beefy hands together and tightened his lips into an unpleasant smile.

"I am very capable, sir." Bella lifted her chin high. "I'll work hard."

"You're expected to work hard." He continued to circle around her, his voice rising above the chopping and clatter of plates. "But you haven't answered my question."

Bella swallowed and crossed her fingers behind her. She'd never needed to lie before. "Yes, sir, I've done this kind of work before."

"Where?"

"At a small hotel in New York. It closed last year."

"The name, the reference?"

Bella thought quickly and made up a name out of two of Daniel's old friends. "The Blake West. Mr. Tom Spard."

"Never heard of it."

"Unfortunately, sir, no one ever heard of it. It was not well frequented. Mostly boarders. Not fashionable. Which is why it closed."

Mr. Ruckler stopped circling and fixed his watery brown eyes on hers. "Ordinarily, I wouldn't take a chance on you, with no references. But one of my girls never arrived. So you've got a week's trial." He stepped closer to her. Bella willed herself not to step back. "If you please me, you can stay."

Bella didn't care for his tone. She struggled to keep her voice neutral. "Thank you, sir."

"Right. Follow me. I'll show you to your room. Bring the child along." He stomped off without a backwards glance.

Bella grabbed Amanda's hand and traipsed after the man, out the kitchen complex, into another building and down a long corridor of rooms. Finally, he stopped and unlocked a door. "In here. C'mon, c'mon."

A smell of musty air and lye soap pervaded the tiny room. It held a bed barely wide enough for her and Amanda to share, and a miniature chest of drawers. At least there was a large wash basin and pitcher, and a mirror. A row of wooden pegs stood at one end of the room, and a chamber pot peeked out from under the iron bedstead. There was one small window so highly placed that Bella would need to stand on a chair to see out of it.

"I don't like it that you have a child with you." Mr. Ruckler jabbed a stubby finger in Amanda's direction. The child clung tighter to Bella's hand. "If she interferes with your duties or gets in trouble, you must leave. Understood?"

Bella patted Amanda's trembling hand and gritted her teeth. "My daughter is well-behaved. You shall have no reason to complain."

"See to it, then." The manager glanced around, then his eyes swept back to Bella's face. "Get settled. Report down to the kitchen in the morning. Five a.m. sharp!"

Bella locked the door after him, then fell onto the bed. It sagged to one side, and with it sagged her hopes. She regretted her haste in coming here. This wretched room made Bella's stomach churn. This was certainly a side of the Mountain House she had never seen before. Silently, she chastised Daniel for leaving her in this fix. This wasn't the way it was supposed to be.

"Mama, I don't like this place." Amanda stared at Bella from the corner of the room.

"Come here, my darling." Bella held out her arms, expecting Amanda to fly into them as usual.

But the child stood still. "Do we have to stay here?"

"Now, don't pay any attention to that awful man." Bella patted the bed next to her. "Come over here."

Amanda hung back, her mouth curled in a quivering pout. "I want to go home."

"I want to go home, too." She walked softly to Amanda's side, knelt, and kissed her daughter's brow. "But we can't, my darling. This is our home now."

Amanda squirmed. "I want to go home. I don't like it here."

Bella hugged her daughter, emotionally teetering between grief and panic. "You must promise to be good, my darling."

Amanda began to cry. Wriggling out of Bella's grasp, she flung herself into the opposite corner. "I want my papa!"

"I wish I could help you understand," Bella began. She knelt at Amanda's side, but the child faced the wall and would not be comforted. "Oh, darling, your dear sweet Papa has passed over. He's with God, up in heaven. And he's looking after us from up in heaven. Understand?"

Amanda raised both her fists, striking the wall with puny blows. "No! I want my papa! I want my papa!"

"Amanda, please!" Bella felt helpless. Amanda never acted like this. Not that she blamed the child. The stress and strain of the last few days had taxed both of them beyond their natural tolerances.

Banging from the neighboring wall broke into her thoughts. "Quiet in there!" came a shout from the next room.

Bella remembered Ruckler's threat. Amanda mustn't make trouble. "Sshhh, Amanda. Please. Stop that."

Amanda continued to wail even louder.

Desperate to stop her before someone complained, Bella shook her daughter by the shoulders. "Amanda! Behave yourself!"

Amanda stopped. Her face clearly expressed shock at her mother's actions. "I don't like you," she declared. "I don't like you and I don't like Uncle Zach. I don't like anyone!"

Bella stared at her daughter. What was happening to her? Bella breathed in short, frantic heaves. Her eyes fell on the small clock on the dresser. It was nearly ten o'clock. The child was just exhausted.

"We'll both feel better after a good night's sleep, Amanda." She picked up her squirming, wailing daughter and carried her over to the bed. She rocked her and softly hummed a lullaby, hoping it would calm them both down. Soon, Amanda's body relaxed.

"All right, sweetheart," she told Amanda when she finished the song. "Let's get out of those clothes and into a nightgown now."

But Amanda was already fast asleep.

≈

A loud knock roused Bella the next morning. She rolled over and nearly fell off the narrow bed. Totally disoriented, she was unable to see much in the darkened room.

The knocking grew louder.

"Mrs. Smith! Four-thirty! Be down in the kitchen at five sharp!"

"Yes!" Bella called, her voice hoarse with sleepiness. Her feet hit the cold floor. "I'm up!"

In answer, the sound of footsteps moved off, and the same knocking began further down the hall. The morning had begun. Bella lit the bedside candle quickly. She would have to hustle if she were going to report for duty on time.

She turned back to look at Amanda, still lying in bed. Her curls were tousled. Her dress was rumpled and stained with the remains of yesterday's chocolate éclair dessert. A half hour! She would let her daughter sleep until the last minute.

Bella flew to the dresser. She undid her braids and brushed them out. Hastily, she rearranged her hair into plaits, which she wound around her head.

"Where are my hairpins?" she fumed, frantically searching for where she had left the elusive pins. "Aha!" Quickly, she wound and pinned her braids in place, and pinned the white maid's cap on top. She wriggled into the gray and white uniform, using her button hook to close up the rows of tiny, bone buttons on the front bodice. Then she pulled the crisp white apron over her head, tying it the best she could behind her back.

Ten minutes to spare, she thought. Suddenly, she realized she hadn't given a thought to what Amanda would do while she was gone.

Last night at supper, Nancy Halley had casually offered to watch Amanda if Bella got the job. Bella wasn't sure if the offer was genuine, or if Mrs. Halley were even capable of taking care of Amanda. Perhaps she was only being kind. But in any case, Bella hadn't seen her since and doubted she would be up at this hour.

If only Bella had asked what arrangements other staff members made for their children. When she was little, her own governess had come to the Mountain House with them. There must be some kind of governess here for the children of the staff, surely in such a remote place as this. She would just have to ask Mr. Ruckler.

"Amanda darling!" Bella gently shook her daughter. "Amanda, sweetheart. Mama has to go to work. Wake up, darling."

Amanda woke, then whimpered as she sat up. "Mama!" she cried, wrapping her arms around her mother's neck.

"Sweetheart, we have to dress in two minutes." Bella gently pushed her daughter back, and quickly unbuttoning her pinafore and dress. Amanda squirmed as she pulled the clothing over her head, and quickly slipped on a new dress and pinafore. "Come with me. Quickly, now." She scooped up Amanda, swished a wet cloth over her face, and tweaked her nose to make her laugh. Amanda giggled and Bella breathed a little easier. She locked the door, picked up her daughter, and raced down the hall to the kitchen.

One of the maids stood at the back kitchen door, filling two buckets with water from the well. She opened her mouth in amazement as Bella rushed toward her, staring at Amanda as if she were some wild species of animal. She flung open the door, then jerked her thumb toward the far side of the large room. "Staff breakfast is over that-a way."

Bella didn't have time to wonder why the woman had reacted so strangely. She hurried inside and over to the table. Most of the kitchen and house staff were already seated, wolfing down huge stacks of buckwheat pancakes, fried potatoes, and hot black coffee. She lowered Amanda into one of the empty chairs, then sat down next to her.

A young boy in a white uniform slapped two plates of pancakes in front of them.

The old man in a black frock coat smiled at Bella from the opposite side of the table. He pushed over a pitcher of molasses. "For the hotcakes," he said in a friendly voice. "I'm Charlie Douglas, head waiter. Happy to meet you."

"Thank you, Mr. Douglas. I'm Mrs. Smith, and this is my daughter, Amanda." Bella took the pitcher and poured syrup over

Amanda's stack of cakes. Then she reached for the plate of potatoes.

"I'm Anna," said a red-haired woman, who reached over the table with a huge white porcelain pitcher. She poured a stream of milk into both their glasses. "Did Mr. Ruckler say you could bring your daughter to breakfast? It's not customary."

"I'm sorry. I didn't know," Bella apologized. "Where do the staff children eat?

"You can bring them a basket of food on your break times and such. Cook will do that for you," Anna said, indicating a large man in white chef's clothing down by the stoves. "Mr. Michaels. He's a terror though. Be nice to him."

Bella caught Anna's arm as she started to move off. "Is there a governess or someone to look after the staff children?"

Anna looked amused. "A governess? Not that I know of, but then I don't have children. Most of us don't. Ask Carrie over there. She's the mousey one at the end of the table." Anna rapped on the table. "Carrie? This new girl wants to know what you do with your brat while you're working. She seems to think you've got a governess."

Several snickers and giggles greeted Anna's remark. Bella felt embarrassed. She took a bite of pancake. She was starving. Mr. Douglas stood up. Carrie quickly slipped into his chair across from Bella.

"Hullo," she said. "Me name's Carrie Quinn, and that's me tall, strong husband Michelmas, over there." A young man with ruddy cheeks and dancing green eyes waved cheerfully from the far end of the table as he shoveled another forkful of pancake into his mouth. "This is our second season here," Carrie said. "Our son, Rory, is just two."

"What do you do with him when you're working?"

"Lock 'em in the room and check on 'em as often as we can."

Bella was horrified. "You just leave him? In the room?"

"Sure," said Carrie. "Where else would I be leavin' him, now? Can't afford no nanny. But he's all right, most of the time. He can't go nowhere. I leave him a few toys and come back to nurse him. And when he's really cranky, I just give him a bit of medicine that a doctor give me, and he goes right off to sleep."

Bella couldn't think of what to say. Carrie's shy expression didn't seem to be apologetic or even suggest such a situation was unnatural. In fact, she seemed to be proud of her resourcefulness when she mentioned the medicine.

"I can show you the medicine, if you need to get some," Carrie added.

Bella swallowed hard. The delicious buckwheat pancakes suddenly felt like sawdust in her mouth. "Thank you, Mrs. Quinn. I appreciate the information."

"We're in room twenty-three, if you're of a mind to visit."

Bella forced herself to smile. "Well, what a coincidence. Two doors down from my room."

Suddenly, the atmosphere in the room changed. People began pushing back their chairs, taking a last bite or gulp, and bolting up from the table.

"All right, people," bellowed the voice of Mr. Ruckler, who lumbered heavily in from the dining room. Everyone stood at attention. Everyone, that is, except for Amanda, who was calmly eating her pancakes.

Mr. Ruckler stopped in mid step. He pointed at Amanda. "Who is that?" he bellowed.

Bella hastily stood up. "My daughter, Mr. Ruckler. I'm Mrs. Smith, remember? I brought her to breakfast. I'm sorry if I wasn't supposed to."

For a moment, Mr. Ruckler simply stared at Amanda, who continued eating, completely oblivious to the commotion she had set off. "Mama?" she asked. "May I have some more 'lasses?"

Bella hurriedly reached for the pitcher, while Mr. Ruckler's features settled into a deep frown. "Children are not permitted in the kitchens. The cook will fix a tray for her from now on."

"Yes, sir." Bella put the pitcher down.

"Don't let it happen again."

"No, sir."

He stared at her for another long second, then took out a large, black book from under his arm and opened it flat on the table. "Now, here's the day's agenda." He began to tick off how many rooms were booked, how many new rooms needed to be readied for arriving guests, how many breakfasts, lunches and dinners would be served, and how many requests for picnic baskets. Special events were planned, including a formal afternoon tea, a croquette party, and an after-dinner concert.

As people received their assignments, they dispersed quickly to their duties. The kitchen bustled with activity.

"Mrs. Smith!" Mr. Ruckler bellowed. He crooked his finger at her. "Come over here. You will be working with Katie, here, learning to do up the rooms. You'll help with the breakfast trays first, go with Katie to do the rooms, then return to help with the picnic baskets. You'll help set the tables for the first and second dinner seatings. Katie will supervise your work, show you the ropes, and generally train you."

Bella nodded. She smiled at the young blonde woman who stood very close to Mr. Ruckler. She returned Bella's smile with a haughty nod of her head.

"You've got fifteen minutes to get that child out of here and start on those breakfast trays." Mr. Ruckler leaned forward. "Fifteen minutes. Understood?"

Bella swallowed. "Understood, sir." As Mr. Ruckler turned back to confer with Katie, she dashed over to Amanda and whisked off the napkin from around her neck.

"Mama! I'm not finished."

"I'll bring you something else in a bit, darling." Bella pulled back Amanda's chair and lifted her out. "But believe me, you are finished."

Once out the kitchen door, Bella had an idea. She turned in the direction of the hotel's small back porch and through the smaller set of double doors that led to the back of the grand staircase. Bella slipped up the stairs carrying Amanda. She huffed and puffed up one, then two, and finally the third flight of stairs that led to the Halley's room. Perhaps Nancy Halley would agree to take Amanda for at least a few hours. Please, God, Bella breathed. Please let her be up.

But when she knocked on the door of the room she had remembered from last night, there was no answer. Desperate, she walked on to the last room, which was Zach's. She knocked softly on the door, then a bit louder. "Zach! Zach, it's me, Bella."

There was no answer. Bella's shoulders sagged, and she knelt down to release Amanda. Dear God, what would she do?

Slowly, this time holding Amanda's hand, Bella descended the staircase. She stopped at the front desk. The dark-haired man looked up. "Yes?" Then he looked at her strangely. "What's the problem?" he said in a colder voice.

"I was looking for Mrs. John Halley," Bella said. Suddenly, she was conscious of the clerk's gaze, and realized that she was wearing a maid's uniform. "I wondered if you knew if she had gone out."

"I believe Mrs. Halley came down early this morning. I cannot say where she went. Shouldn't you be at work?"

"Yes, but first I need to leave Mrs. Halley a note. May I borrow some paper and ink?"

The desk clerk looked at her and shook his head. "Can you write?"

"Yes, I can certainly write," Bella snapped back.

He nodded toward the salon. "Paper and ink at the desk. In there. You can leave the note with me. When she returns, I'll deliver it."

Bella hastily wrote a note for both Zach and Nancy, leaving both with the desk.

Then she rushed back to her own room.

"Amanda," she said with a heavy heart, "I'm going to have to leave you alone for a little while. I'll come back soon, and soon Uncle Zach or Mrs. Halley will be able to take you with them. But for now..."

Amanda's face began to puff up with anger and tears. "I don't want to stay here. I hate it here! I want more pancakes!"

"Please, please be good now. For my sake." Bella could feel the hot tears springing to her own eyes. "I'll come back in a little while. Please, darling. Please..."

But Amanda would not stop crying. "I hate you! I hate you!"

Bella glanced at the clock in desperation. She was out of time. "I'll come back for you soon. I promise." The words were more for herself than for Amanda, who seemed not to hear her. Closing the door behind her, then locking it was the hardest thing Bella ever had to do, as Amanda's cries of "I hate you" rang in her ears.

She hated herself for bringing them here. Hated Daniel for leaving her with no other means to care for her daughter. Hated Mr. Ruckler for being so awful. And for the first time in her life, she hated the Mountain House.

~

A few hours later, Bella had something else to hate. Her new supervisor Miss Lindstrom.

"No, not that way! Here, do it again!" Katie Lindstrom reached across Bella and ripped off the sheets she had just tucked under the mattress. "Again." She flipped her long blonde braids behind her shoulders, then folded her arms and pursed her lips together in a smug expression.

Bella held her tongue and said a little prayer for patience. Once again, she spread the sheets on the bed, making sure to keep the overhang on each side even and smooth.

This was the kind of room she remembered from her stays at the Mountain House: Rich carpeting and fine polished furniture, hand-embroidered linen sheets edged with lace, and heavy silk draperies with multi-colored tassels. Only now, Bella would be keeping them clean for other people, some of whom probably remembered her and, no doubt, would gossip about her until something juicer came along.

"That's better. Square corners. Evenly spaced."

The woman, whom everyone called Katie, and whom Mr. Ruckler seemed to lavish open affection upon, was obviously glad to have a new charge to bully.

Bella tucked the last bit of sheet into place, then rose off her knees. "That's done."

Katie threw two heavy feather pillows at her. "Now these and sharply! We've wasted too much time already. And one more room still to be done." She turned and flashed her feather duster across the tops of the dresser, headboard, and chairs.

When Bella finished plumped the pillows, she surveyed the room. The furniture glowed from the beeswax she had applied. The windows sparkled, although Bella's fingertips were puckered from washing them with vinegar.

Katie clapped her hands. "One more room to go. Let's try and do it right this time, darlin'." She sailed out the door, leaving Bella to push the heavy cart laden with cleaning supplies and fresh linens.

"Witch!" As soon as she said the word, Bella felt frightened by how bitter she felt. Burying her feelings, she hurried after the woman.

The morning went by in a blur. At ten o'clock, Bella returned to the little room, which was dim despite the sunshine outside. She carried a basket of bread, an apple, a piece of pie, and a small bottle of milk for Amanda. Bella felt ashamed for not remembering to light a lamp for Amanda before she left for her shift. She reached up and pushed the long iron rod attached to the small transom window to let in some fresh air and a sliver of light.

"Amanda?" she whispered, lifting the candle high. "Are you asleep?"

Golden curls splayed across the pillow, obscuring her daughter's face. Steady breathing confirmed the child was deeply asleep. Bella laid the basket on the floor.

"Poor child. I won't wake you." She sat on the edge of the bed and stroked her daughter's hair. "Poor child. No one to look after you. At least in the city, Mrs. Porter looked after you while I worked. Maybe I should have stayed there."

She kissed Amanda's forehead. With a heavy heart, she rose and crept out the door, softly locking her daughter in for what she feared would be most of the day.

Ten

"All right, everybody awake now?"

In the deserted ballroom, Zach looked around at the sleepy-eyed musicians gathered for the mid-morning rehearsal. "Let's take it again from the top." He tapped his foot heavily on the floor. The sound echoed off the walls and twelve-foot ceilings. "And a one, two, three and..."

The band swung into a rousing polka. They played more than half-way through the piece before Zach stopped them. "No, no. Bah, rump TILLY ump. Not bah, rump tilly UMP. Hit that little trill. Got it?"

"Got it."

"Yes, indeed."

Eager to continue, the band members nodded and mumbled in agreement.

"Listen, do you really want me to come in on the third beat?" asked Clyde, the drummer. "I think it's better on the fourth."

Zach shook his head. "The third, I said. But attack it. Attack it." He demonstrated on the cornet. "Okay, everybody. Take it from the chorus."

The band worked through the rest of that song, then practiced four more before Zach was satisfied. He peered out one of the tall windows that overlooked the courtyard. The sun shone invitingly. "Nearly lunch time, friends. We'll take a break. Be back at three."

He watched the men run off, pleased at the rehearsal. John had done a good job of keeping the band together while he was away. Except for a few flubs, the young musicians sounded pretty good. Not as good as his old band, of course. Then again, nothing was the same as before the war.

But a little fine tuning this afternoon and by tonight, Zach felt they'd sound grand. Next week, he intended to begin rehearsing some Rossini and Mozart, as soon as he finished arranging the scores to fit his band's instruments.

"Too bad that last singer I hired last month didn't work out," said John Halley, breaking into Zach's thoughts. "Her voice would have sounded just right on that last number."

Zach nodded. "Not worth it unless we can find one who shows up on time, and cares more about the songs than her hat. I wish Nancy could carry a tune."

John laughed. "So do I. I'm off to take her to lunch. Will you join us?"

"Thanks, my friend, but no. Think I'll look in on my sister-in-law. See how Amanda's getting on."

John gave him a funny look. "See you at three."

Zach wiped his cornet with a soft cloth, then secured it carefully in its case. He felt good today. He was back to work, had a good rehearsal, and was settled for the season. In his expansive mood, he decided to surprise Amanda and Bella by taking them to lunch. He wondered if she had gotten the job after all.

Whistling all the way to the servants' quarters, Zach stopped outside the kitchen door and looked in. He didn't see Bella, and finally enquired which room Mrs. Smith was staying in. Still whistling, he walked through the kitchen, stealing two carnations from a silver bud vase on a tray. Once outside, he found the old wing with no difficulty and rapped smartly on the last door. There was no answer.

"Bella! It's Zach!" Putting his ear to the door, he thought he heard a faint rustling sound. "Amanda? It's Uncle Zach!" He smiled as he said the word, enjoying the sound of the title. "It's Uncle Zach come to take you for lunch and ice cream!"

The rustling sound grew louder. "Uncle Zach? Mama's locked me in."

"She what?" The idea of the pretty child locked up on such a grand day rankled him. "Is there a key?"

"No. She says I must stay in while she works."

"For how long?"

"Until she comes back." The child gave a muffled whimper.

That did it. "I'll break you out!" Zach called through the door. "Can't have you cooped up in a stuffy room like a chicken in a coop on a day like this!"

Zach fished around in his pocket for his own key. Experimentally, he fitted it into the keyhole and fiddled with the lock, wriggling the doorknob to jimmy it open. From past experience, he knew that with a bit of patience, any key could open most of the flimsy doors in the servant's wing. In fact, someone had once broken into his own room before he rigged up a better system. A soft click signaled success. Gently, he opened the door.

Amanda sat on the bare floor, stockings down around her ankles, no shoes, dressed in a rumpled shift and pinafore. She looked up at him with a dull expression. Her doll lay face down by her side. "Mama said I must stay here."

A swift glance around the dreary, stuffy room made Zach's stomach tighten. Something smelt bad. One high tiny window let in little fresh air and less light. No wonder the child appeared listless.

"Well, she didn't mean you couldn't come with me. After all, I'm your uncle. Right?" He held out a hand. "Up now. There's ice cream waiting."

Amanda's face brightened. "Vanilla?"

"I think we can arrange that!"

She scrambled to her feet. "Can I bring my dolly?"

"Sure." Zach scooped Amanda into his arms. "Hey, now. Can't have you looking like the rag-and-bone-man's daughter."

He tickled her under the chin, but the child's expression remained grave. "Where are your clothes?"

Amanda shrugged and stuck her thumb in her mouth. "I don't know."

Zach strode to the dresser. A basket held the remains of an apple and crumbs of bread, along with a bottle of milk. He picked up the bottle and sniffed, then wrinkled his nose. Sour. With one hand, he yanked open the top drawer. Empty. So were the other two.

The rosy image he had held of Bella faded. What kind of mother would leave her child like this?

"Let's try the trunk," he told Amanda, careful to keep the anger from his voice. He lifted the lid. "Ah, here we go."

Sorting through the carefully packed contents, he unearthed a tinted daguerreotype of Bella and Daniel, him gazing down at his seated bride with obvious affection. For a moment, Zach stared at it intently, trying to imagine his brother's feelings on that day. Hastily, he replaced the photograph and continued searching until he found Amanda's underclothes, stockings, a fresh dress, and neatly folded pinafore.

He tipped some water into the pitcher and lathered a cloth with soap. "Time for a wash first."

Amanda drew near and tipped her face up, squeezing her eyes closed. Awkwardly, Zach ran the cloth over her face and hands, then held her over the bowl while she splashed water to rinse. He splashed her, made her laugh, then threw the towel over her head. "Where did Amanda go? Amanda?"

"I'm here, Uncle Zach!" Underneath the towel, the child giggled and squirmed.

He whipped the towel away. "Aha! There she is!"

Enjoying himself, Zach made a game of removing her soiled clothes and dressing her again.

"There now." He surveyed her and frowned. "Your braids are a tangle. Where's the brush? Now, you'll have to be patient with me. I'm not too good at this, so tell me if I hurt you."

Gingerly, he brushed out the knots, but gave up on the

redoing the braids. "Well, you're respectable at any rate. Respectable enough to be seen with the leader of the best band in the land. Eh, Little Missy?"

She smiled up at him, nodding eagerly.

"Don't forget your doll." As he turned to leave, Zach glanced around once more, making a mental note to find them a better room. He'd say something to Bella, too, about the condition she had left Amanda in. A fine mother indeed.

~

Bella hurried down the narrow hall.

It was after one already, and that miserable Mr. Ruckler had refused to allow her to take lunch to Amanda. The poor child would be starving. Fingers of guilt stabbed Bella's insides, competing with the aches and pains of a busy morning of bending, toting, folding linens, and scrubbing. At least the cook had been generous, tucking an extra piece of apple pie into her basket of food for Amanda.

Bella pulled out her key. "Amanda! I'm here, my love." She fitted the key in the lock. The door swung open by itself. Her throat tightened. "Amanda?"

The room was empty. A pile of clothing was heaped in the corner by the trunk. In a daze, Bella walked to the washstand and lifted the rag. It was damp. She turned, her eyes taking in the rumpled bedsheets. She began to tremble with anxiety. "Amanda?"

Dropping the basket on the dresser top, she ran to the bed, pulling off the covers as though she might find Amanda playing a game of hide and seek.

"Amanda!" She raced to the trunk, heaved the cover open, and dug through the contents. "Amanda!" She dropped to the floor and crawled to the bed to look underneath. "Amanda! Come out now. Amanda!"

Tears were streaming down her cheeks, blurring her vision, choking her cries. She couldn't think. Where could the child be?

Panic took over her better senses. What if someone had kidnapped her daughter? Dear Lord, what if she was hurt? What if she had fallen off the ledge?

Blindly, Bella ran down the hall and out of the building. Spotting a group of rough-looking children by the smokehouse, she rushed over, but Amanda was not among them. She began to stalk through the throngs of people on the spacious lawns of the hotel, catching her breath each time she saw a golden-haired tot. No Amanda.

Then she saw her. She recognized Zach first, lining up a shot on the croquet field. Amanda was beside him, clapping her hands.

Relieved to see Amanda safe and unharmed, Bella breathed in deeply. "Oh, thank you, God, for keeping her safe. Oh, thank you, thank you for not letting her get hurt!" she whispered as she ran to her daughter. Bella shivered, as the fearful scenarios she imagined during her frantic search came back to her.

"If she had just stayed put, as I told her," she fumed. "But no, he steals her away without a word."

"Mama!" Amanda waved and smiled. "Uncle Zach and I had ice cream!"

She caught her daughter and hugged her fiercely. "Oh, my darling, I was so worried. Mama couldn't find you!" She ran her fingers through Amanda's hair, held her close, kissed her. "What would I do if I lost you, too? I told you to stay in our room."

"But Mama!" said Amanda with a high-pitched giggle, as she struggled out of Bella's grasp. "Uncle Zach said I could come."

Bella rose and marched to Zach's side, where he was lining up a shot. "How dare you!" She batted the croquet mallet from his hands, catching him off-guard. "How dare you take my daughter without letting me know. Didn't you get my note?"

Zach scowled. "Don't be dramatic. She was safe with me." He bent to retrieve the mallet.

"And I'm supposed to guess that? You might have left me a note, for God's sake. I was frantic. I've spent half my dinner hour searching, working myself into a frenzy, imagining the worst..."

He glared at her. "It was a good thing I found her. No food, dirty clothes. Nice way to care for my niece."

His words were like salt on the fresh wounds of guilt Bella has struggled with all morning. "I brought food."

"Sour milk."

Her throat tightened by waves of shame, and Bella found it hard to say anything for a minute. When they passed, she went on the defensive. "I brought her food as soon as I could. I left you and Mrs. Halley a note. It said to come and find me, for the key, and... Didn't you get it? I left it with the front desk."

"No, I didn't get a note. Neither did Nancy, or we would have..."

"How did you get Amanda out of the room, then, without the key?"

"I jimmied the door."

"You what?" Bella's throat tightened again, but this time with frustration and anger. "You broke into my room? You took Amanda? You didn't leave me a note or have the courtesy to send a message?"

Zach waved his hand. "Calm yourself. I'll take you to tea for the second half of your dinner hour. How about it?"

"No, thank you. You've done quite enough. Come along Amanda." Bella held out her hand.

Amanda looked up from her croquet mallet. "Don't want to."

Her words triggered a flood of panic inside of Bella. She was losing control of her daughter. "You'll come now."

"Don't want to." The child stood glaring at Bella. "Want to stay with Uncle Zach."

"I'll look after..." Zach began.

"No!" Bella's control snapped. She rushed to Amanda and picked her up bodily, wrenching the mallet from her hand. She couldn't stand to think that Amanda preferred someone else over her, not after all her sacrifices for the child's welfare. "You will obey me, or I shall never allow your uncle to treat you again."

Amanda kicked and screamed as Bella marched resolutely away.

Zach watched them go in silence, shaking his head. He recalled the photograph of his brother and Bella, so obviously happy together. He remembered how sweet Bella had been, even on the morning of the funeral. Now she reminded him of a shrew.

He picked up the mallets and shoved each one back into the rack. Then he flopped into a chair and watched the scene around him. Nannies and mothers ran after their young charges, warning them away from the edge of the precipice, chastising them for fighting, exhorting them to stay within sight.

Maybe he should have left a note, he thought. What did he know about children?

Spying Amanda's doll under the tree, he heaved himself out of the chair to retrieve it. Brushing off bits of grass, he tucked the plaything under his arm. He'd bring it back, apologize to Bella, promise to leave a note the next time. That thought surprised him. He really had enjoyed his afternoon with Amanda, teaching her to hit the croquet mallet, sharing bites of ice cream, listening to her childish prattle. He actually wanted there to be a next time.

Humming "Skip to My Lou," Zach strolled over to Bella's room. As he came down the hall, he heard a sweet, strong voice singing a lullaby. The phrasing, the tenderness in the song, caught his imagination. Slowly advancing toward the sound, he stopped in front of Bella's door. Entranced, he leaned against the door to listen.

"In a garden of roses, in a garden of love..." she sang. "We shall be together, together once more."

Zach raised his hand to knock but stopped as he heard her voice break down into a shattering sob. His first instinct was to open the door, to rush inside and comfort her, but Amanda's voice held him back.

"Mama, don't cry. I'll be good. I promise."

Zach knelt down and propped the doll by the door, carefully arranging it in a sitting position before tiptoeing away.

Eleven

The next day started off on a happier note.

After Zach told her what had happened, Nancy Halley had insisted on taking care of Amanda. Bella went off to work in a much calmer state of mind.

Even Katie's haughty demeanor and barbed criticisms didn't bother her. After a while, Katie changed tactics.

"You're really coming along fast, Mrs. Smith," she said, after Bella had made up the tenth room of the morning. Katie plumped the pillows on the bed, then smoothed the coverlet while Bella finished dusting and straightening the tops of the vanity and bureaus.

"Why thank you, Miss Lindstrom. You're a good teacher."

"Call me Katie. By the way, I've been meaning to ask you about your brother-in-law."

Bella was immediately wary of her question. "Oh? What about him?" Katie's tone of voice sounded quite casual, but Bella suspected her intentions.

"He's a very handsome man," Katie said, flicking her feather duster along the tops of the windows and down the draperies. "I heard he's just back from the war."

"Yes."

"I hear he's a very good player."

"Yes, he is."

"Is he married? Or engaged?"

Bella wasn't sure what to say. So this was what Katie had in mind. The truth was probably the safest. "Not that I know of."

"I'd really like to meet him." Katie turned to Bella. "Properly, I mean."

"Well, I'm sure you'll run into him soon enough." Barely able to control her rising annoyance, Bella turned to fetch some clean washcloths from the cart.

"I'd like you to introduce us," Katie said.

Bella froze. "But Miss Lindstrom. Katie. I thought you were..." she searched for the right word. "I thought you were sweet on Mr. Ruckler."

Katie laughed delightedly. "Sweet on him? Oh, I'd hardly call it that. Let's just say *he's* sweet on me. But compared to the leader of the hotel band, well." Her pealing laughter rang out again. "Well, there is no comparison, is there?"

Bella was incensed. These people were so awful. Is this what goes on in the staffs of all hotels? Surely, not. And she was surely not going to help Katie in her little romantic games.

"So, when will you introduce me? We should do it just before I go off duty."

"I'm sorry," Bella said. "I barely know my brother-in-law. I only met him a week ago, after my husband died. He didn't even want to bring me up here. So, I try to stay out of his business, let alone make social introductions."

She glanced up at Katie, who was giving her a look that could whither a newly-bloomed rose. "If I did introduce you, I doubt it would work in your favor," Bella hastily added.

"Humph!" Katie folded her arms firmly. "Fine. If that's the way you want it, that's the way it will be. Let's go. We have six more rooms to finish. And Mr. Ruckler wants the ballroom floor scrubbed down, and the room set up for the afternoon tea dance, too. I think you can do that job."

Bella knew she had ruined her chance to make a friend of

Katie Lindstrom. But somehow, she was glad. At least she knew how things stood.

~

It was late morning when Bella approached the entrance to the ballroom.

She could hear the band rehearsing inside. Opening the door, Bella saw the musicians on the low stage that lined the short end of the room. She picked up her pail and scrub brush to go inside, closing the heavy mahogany double doors behind her as softly as she could. For a few minutes, she listened, swaying to the band's lively waltz. Then she glanced at the large grandfather clock against the opposite wall. It was nearly noon. If she didn't start soon, she'd never finish scrubbing the enormous floor and setting up the gilded chairs and refreshments tables in time for the afternoon's dance.

Zach nodded hello to her. She smiled back and pushed a stray strand of hair back behind her ear. Mentally, she rehearsed an apology for yesterday's confrontation.

"Take a break, boys," Zach said after they finished the number. "I have to talk to someone." Wearing a smug expression, he ambled over to Bella and leaned against the doorway. "So. Still angry about yesterday?"

"Are you?" she replied. "I'm sorry. You rescued my daughter and I chastised you for your pains."

He leaned closer, his eyes sweeping the length of her body. "Chastised? That's putting it mildly."

Conscious of his eyes on her, Bella tucked her hands, red and wrinkled from dirty wash water, behind her back. "I was upset. I guess I didn't realize how many hours the shift was. And didn't think about making arrangements for Amanda. I'm grateful for you taking her to dinner. Nancy came by this morning and insisted on looking after her. But I have to find someone to look after her for my entire shift. Mr. Ruckler told me if Amanda made any trouble..."

She broke off, wondering whether it was wise to complain about her new employer.

"What did he say would happen?" Zach asked, his eyes narrowing.

"That I would be let go."

Zach frowned. "You let me deal with him. Meanwhile, I'll keep Amanda out of trouble while you work. I'll even leave a full itinerary."

"I don't expect you to watch Amanda for my entire shift..."

"Why not? She's a sweet little thing. I enjoy her company," Zach answered.

"But you've got the band and lots to do. And you told me... " She was thinking of what he had said on the walk up to the Mountain House only two days ago; that he wasn't about to take on a bunch of relatives he hardly knew.

"Nancy, John and I have it all planned out," Zach said firmly.

Bella was touched by his insistence. It seemed genuine, and very out of character for her black sheep brother-in-law. "I'd be very grateful to you all. I worry about her. She was never rude or disobedient before. But this place, all that's happened..."

"She'll be all right, now, you'll see." Zach waved off her concern. "By the way, I left the doll by the door. Did she get it?"

"Oh yes, thank you. She did." Bella smiled. "Daniel gave her that doll before he went to war. Amanda takes it everywhere."

"When I brought it back, I heard you singing," he said. "You have a pretty voice. I didn't recognize the song."

"'A Garden of Roses.' It's an old song. It was my mother's favorite. You don't know that one?"

Zach shook his head and leaned closer to Bella. "Maybe you could teach me how it goes?"

Bella couldn't help but smile back. "I'll teach it to you any time you like."

"How about now?"

"Oh, well." Bella glanced at her pail and scrub brush. "I don't think I should." Guiltily, she reached down to pick them up. "I'm supposed to clean this floor and have everything ready in time for the tea dance. I thought I'd start in this corner over here if it wouldn't disturb your rehearsals."

He shrugged. "It won't disturb us. But teach me the song, first. Take ten minutes, no more."

"Well, I really shouldn't." Bella protested.

Zach took her pail and brush from her hands and set them on the floor. Then he caught her hand and led her over to the musicians. "Mrs. Smith is going to teach us a song. It's called 'A Garden of Roses.' Anybody know it?"

The musicians scratched their heads and shrugged their shoulders. All except John.

"Think it goes something like this," John said, tucking his violin under his chin. He began to play a tune. "That it?"

Bella nodded, then looked at Zach.

"Go ahead, sing the words."

She nodded again, cleared her throat, and plunged in, slightly off-key. "When I was just a child of six and you were a lad of seven..."

Bella abruptly stopped. John put down his violin.

"I'm sorry," she apologized. "It seems to be the wrong key for me. Can we try it in F, perhaps?"

John raised his eyebrows, nodding at Bella as if she had said something brilliant. Then he looked over at Zach and grinned knowingly.

"Key of F, eh," remarked Zach. He returned John's grin. "The lady knows her music."

"We'll see," John answered, tucking his violin once more under his chin to play.

Bella listened to the introduction, softly humming to see if the new key matched her range. She nodded, a bit more confident now. "When I was just a child of six, you were a lad of seven. We spent our days at play, at play, in your mother's garden of roses."

Zach picked up his cornet, tapping his foot in time to the music. He gave her a nod of encouragement. Bella was proud to be able to repay him, even in this small way, for all he had done for her daughter. "And you declared your love for me, in your mother's garden of roses."

The band joined in one by one, picking up the thread of the tune, embellishing it with extra notes and trills that lifted Bella's spirits and her voice. Forgetting her aches and sorrows for the moment, she sang all four verses of the sugary old tune. She was glad to see approval in Zach's expression. He applauded enthusiastically when she finished.

"That was wonderful," Zach said, coming over to her. "Could you write down the words for me?"

"Of course." Bella's cheeks burned from excitement as the other musicians added their kudos to Zach's.

"You have a beautiful voice. Good enough to sing with the band!" Zach moved closer to her. "What do you think, boys?"

"Sure enough!"

That's right!"

"Yes, indeed!" came the replies.

John Halley smiled and added, "We sure could use a pretty voice to make us sound better."

Bella laughed and shook her head modestly. "You're so kind. But I'm no singer, although it was fun. You're all wonderful. Plunging right in on a song you don't even know."

The musicians laughed.

"If you will excuse me, however, I have my work to do." She began to walk back to her pail, but Zach dashed up and caught her lightly by her arm.

"I meant it. You sing very well." Zach was not grinning now, nor wheedling her. His dark eyes bore right into Bella's. It unnerved her.

"I sing well enough," she protested. "I'm not a trained singer. I was off-key at first."

"It was the wrong key at first. You knew enough to change it. You know how to read music, don't you?"

"I played piano when I was young. That was a long time ago." Bella turned from him, but he caught her hand this time and whirled her around to face him. His dark eyes glinted with excitement.

"Listen! Come to the dance tonight. I'd like you to sing that number with the band." He squeezed her hand and drew her closer. "As a favor to me."

Flustered, Bella quickly stepped back. "Oh, really, I... No. I'd be too nervous."

She didn't want to disappoint her brother-in-law, especially now that he had taken such an interest in Amanda's welfare. But things were moving too fast. She just wasn't able to think clearly. She saw the disappointment flicker across Zach's face.

"My father always loved to hear me to sing," she quickly tried to explain, "and I never minded when it was just for my parents. Or for a few friends. But the few times I sang or played piano for one of their parties, my palms would get all sweaty. I'd feel faint and sick to my stomach. I just couldn't sing up there," she ended, pointing to the stage that lined the far wall.

"But you didn't feel that way just now?"

"No." The realization surprised her. "No, I didn't. How odd." She smiled. "Well, that was because, well, it was different. It wasn't in front of an audience. Which it would be if I sang at the dance. Besides, Mr. Ruckler, he... I don't think he would approve."

Zach shrugged his shoulders. "Who cares what Ruckler thinks? I just thought you'd enjoy it. And I'm pretty sure the guests here would." Once again, he looked deeply into her eyes.

Bella felt the familiar butterflies in her stomach at the thought of singing in front of all these guests. Some of them might know her from the old days. She backed away. "I don't think so. I'm sorry."

"Never mind," Zach said, returning to his usual brisk manner. "It's not important. We'll be taking Amanda to dinner with us at half past six. What time do you get off work?"

"At seven."

"When you finish, change for dinner and then join us. I'll keep a dish warm for you." He grinned and pointed a finger at her. "And don't say no. I can tell you from experience that any guest of mine will be treated properly, even if she happens to be one of the maids."

∼

It was half-past seven when Bella finally joined Zach's table that evening for supper in the great dining hall.

"I feel strange," Bella told him, as he stood up to hold out her chair for her.

"Why?"

"You're all so well dressed and I..." She glanced down at her brown silk gown. It was ten years behind the fashions, with wide hoop skirts and a boxy peplum jacket. In her old neighborhood, no one noticed. But here, in the company of fashionable guests, some of whom wore the latest Parisian fashions, Bella knew she looked dowdy.

"You could wear a feed sack and you'd outshine the others," Zach told her.

She looked at him in astonishment. "Thank you."

From the corner of her eye, she saw the door to the massive kitchen open. Mr. Ruckler stood there peering out. Since her seat faced the kitchen door, she was a captive audience for his subsequent performance. He scowled in her direction and tossed his head like a bull, his ruddy cheeks flushed with resentment.

"Mr. Ruckler's watching me," Bella whispered to Zach.

"So? Don't worry about him." He patted her arm. "You're safe with me." Then Zach rose and turned deliberately around. He must have stared down the staff manager because Mr. Ruckler immediately disappeared behind the door. Zach sat back down and gave a reassuring wink to Bella.

She couldn't help laughing silently behind her white linen napkin, amused by her brother-in-law's triumphant expression. A quick glance around the room reassured her that no one else had been privy to their little drama.

Bella ate a little, but soon lapsed into a sleepy stupor. She scarcely tasted the codfish cakes and turtle soup. Despite the lively conversation, she drifted off into silence. As she felt her eyes start to close, Bella shook herself awake. It didn't matter. Her daughter kept the conversation going, and Zach obliged Amanda with his undivided attention.

"The band starts in at nine tonight," Zach said, as they rose from the table. "Will you come?"

Bella stifled a yawn and shook her head. "I can barely keep my eyes open now. And there's work early tomorrow."

"I'm not sleepy, Mama." Amanda tugged at her mother's hand. "May I go visit Aunt Nancy?"

"You mean Mrs. Halley."

"She said I could call her Aunt Nancy, Mama. She said she'd tell me a story before bed." Amanda pouted, her stance indicating a readiness to win her point. "Please, please, please?"

Too tired to argue, Bella nodded her consent. Amanda's mood changed instantly. She grinned and threw her arms around her mother's skirts. "Oh, Mama, I love you!"

They climbed the stairs to the Halley's room on the third floor. Bella felt another stab of envy when Nancy opened her door. The room was not much larger than Bella's, yet the furnishings were ten times grander.

A collection of exquisitely dressed bisque dolls adorned the bed. Ornate toiletries were arranged on the small vanity table, including an emerald and gold-trimmed hairbrush and hand mirror. Several leather-bound books were stacked on the table, along with the latest fashion magazines and a copy of Punch, the popular monthly periodical. A chain of handmade paper dolls, cut from marbled paper, lay across the desk.

No wonder Amanda wanted to visit.

Bella stared at the china dolls with a sinking feeling. She'd never be able to provide her own daughter with expensive play-things, or pretty clothes, or a room so fine. She had never cared about frippery or missed the wealth of her youth when Daniel was alive to fill their home with his love.

"Don't worry about Amanda," Nancy said. "I'll bring her

back before long. Unless you'd enjoy hearing a bedtime story, too?"

Bella managed a smile as exhaustion once again took over. "Thank you, but I'd only fall asleep."

"I'll walk you back to your room." Zach offered his arm.

"There's no need..."

"No need?" He laughed and slipped an arm about her shoulder. "If I don't, you might fall asleep on the way down the staircase. Besides, the band is all set up, and I've got a quarter of an hour before we start."

In the soft evening air, they walked back to Bella's room in silence, his arm still firmly around her shoulder.

Zach grabbed a candle from the hall table to shine the way to Bella's door. She fumbled for her key. He took it from her hand, opened the door, and placed the candle in the glass hurricane lamp on the chest of drawers.

"Are you sure you won't come tonight?"

Bella groaned, her muscles aching from the exhausting work of hauling buckets and scrubbing floors on her knees. She was still standing in the doorway, massaging her neck, craning it from side to side. "All I want is to tumble into bed."

Zach moved around her and chuckled softly. "You're not cut out for this kind of work."

"I'm doing fine, thank you. I'm strong."

"That's why your neck is aching, right?" Zach teased. Slipping his hands under her own, he began to rub her neck with a slow, soothing circular motion.

"Ah! That feels lovely."

"I'm good at this." His fingers dug deeper into her shoulder muscles as he kneaded out the painful knots. "You just lean back and relax."

Bella closed her eyes. She thought of Daniel, pretending that it was his warm hands caressing her, his soft laughter that floated out to her. Allowing her body to relax, she began to sway to the rhythm of Zach's movements. Back and forth, his fingers eased her sore muscles and set up a glow inside her that slowly spread down the length of her body.

"Feel better?" Zach finally said. His voice sounded far away.

Bella shook her head and stretched her arms wide, finally shrugging her shoulders. "Much better. Where did you learn to do that?"

"Oh, here and there."

She turned to face him. "Thank you. For everything."

"Everything?"

"For taking care of Amanda, for taking me to dinner, for bringing us here..."

"I owe my brother's wife and child that much."

Bella smiled back. It was the first time he had referred to Daniel as his brother, instead of "half-brother." They were making progress.

"Good night, Mrs. Smith." Zach bowed low and pivoted smartly on his heels.

"Good night, Mr. Smith," she called after him, watching him stride down the hall. Yes indeed, she thought, perhaps her brother-in-law had a human side to him, after all.

Twelve

"**D**amn you!"

Mr. Ruckler, head of the hotel and kitchen staff, cuffed a boy's ear as he passed by with a breakfast tray. "No salt cellar on that tray! And where's the jam pot? Be quick about it!"

It was not even six a.m. and already Mr. Ruckler was on a tear.

In the three weeks she had worked here, Bella felt she was just about able to cope with the workload. But she was wrong. The summer season at the Catskill Mountain House arrived in earnest, bringing a steady stream of guests that first week of June. All the best people—and those who wanted to be—came to Mountain House to see the sights and to be seen. Industrialists and tycoons vied for a table with artists, poets, and old New York families. And they expected stellar service.

"Number seventeen and be quick about it!" Ruckler bellowed at the hapless boy, who slapped the missing items onto the tray. "Next time you forget, you're out on your arse! Well? What are you waiting for?"

Bella lowered her head, hiding her embarrassment as she finished folding linen napkins for the waiting stack of breakfast trays. She felt someone move up behind her.

"Mrs. Smith," Mr. Ruckler whispered into her ear. "How are you this morning?"

"Tired, Mr. Ruckler." She tried to step away from him, but he effectively trapped her between him and the long counter.

"Sleeping poorly?"

She kept her back to him, feeling uncomfortable at his nearness. "You'll excuse me, sir. I have to fetch the chocolate pots." Shrinking from him, she tried to slip away.

He caught hold of her arm. "I might have a remedy for your sleeping problems." His voice was husky with emotion.

Bella froze with disgust, mentally cursing the man for his crudeness. "Shorter work hours?" she managed to quip.

"That could be arranged," Ruckler murmured, his other hand clamping onto her waist.

She broke away from him, baring her teeth in a cold smile. "I wouldn't want you to be accused of favoritism."

"Let me worry about that." He reached after Bella.

She flitted from his grasp. She saw him turn his head, glaring at those who dared to look his way.

"Get on with your work!" he snarled. He took her by the arm. "Come with me, Mrs. Smith. Bring your pail and scrub brush. I've a job for you."

Bella reluctantly obeyed. If only she didn't need this job. She owed three dollars on her room and board, and five more to Zach. She had hoped to put aside fifty dollars by the end of the summer. She couldn't quit just now.

"Certainly, Mr. Ruckler. Just tell me what room."

"I'll have to open it for you. The door is locked." He jingled his heavy ring of keys, then kicked at a bucket with the tip of his toe. "Take your things. Hurry up. I have other things to see to."

Grabbing the empty bucket, she marched to the huge hot water boiler. Steaming water hissed into the bucket. Bella tossed in a slab of coal tar soap and tucked a scrub brush into her apron pocket.

"Let's go." With quick, long strides and a jangling of keys, Mr. Ruckler led her out of the kitchen into the huge dining room, past a sea of empty tables set for three hundred guests and breakfast at seven.

Bella's arms ached with the weight of the full pail as she followed him into the hall.

He stopped abruptly in front of the private dining room and unlocked the door.

"We'll be using this room tonight. First time for the season. So I want it sparkling." He stood waiting in the doorway.

She'd have to slide past him to enter. The cunning wretch, she fumed, wondering if he could hear her pounding heart. "Perhaps you should stand back, sir. I wouldn't want to splash this soapy water on your clean trousers."

"Of course." His eyes narrowed as he stepped back and waved her inside. She moved to the far end of the room. Plunking down her pail, she turned her back to him, removed her scrub brush, and knelt to plunge the brush into the steaming water. She drew a sharp breath as the water scalded her hand. Hearing Ruckler's footsteps, and the sound of the door closing, Bella breathed out a sigh of relief.

"Never mind that," Ruckler said, startling Bella. She heard a soft click and froze. She looked up. He was just putting his keys back in his pocket.

"What are you doing?" she asked, trying to keep her voice as calm as possible.

He leaned back against the door and studied her for a moment. "Such a proud woman you are, Mrs. Smith. Too proud for the likes of me, now?"

"For God's sake," she whispered. "My husband perished less than a month ago. I am still in mourning."

"I'm not asking you to stop mourning him," he said, inching closer. "I'm only asking for a favor."

"What favor?"

Feeling trapped and helpless, Bella began scrubbing the floor with wide strokes, slopping water around her on the polished wood floors as a barrier against Ruckler. He planted himself in front of her, his legs spaced apart. She ignored him, scooting back a bit. He reached down and brushed her chin. She swatted his hand away.

"Don't be coy with me, Mrs. Smith. I know you must be lonely. Even your brother-in-law has no time for you. Wouldn't you rather do less arduous work? Spend more time with that bonny child of yours? I could arrange that, for a favor or two." He reached down again and stroked her cheek.

Again, Bella swatted him away. Choking down her fear, she scrubbed more vigorously.

"I can also arrange to have you take over in the scullery. Scrubbing crusted pots all day. Or in the bakery, where the temperature will bowl you over." His voice held a note of cruelty.

Bella kept her head down. "Find someone else. Katie likes you."

"Katie is a pretty girl. You are a beautiful woman." He stepped nearer, his boot squelching in the soapy water. His finger grazed her cheek. Bella flinched.

"I want you, is what I want," he insisted.

"Please," she pleaded. She scrambled up and stood very tall. "You really don't want to do this."

Her words were cut off, as Ruckler pulled Bella to him and kissed her roughly.

Repulsed, she struggled and squirmed, unable to kick him through layers of petticoats, unable to turn her head from his kiss.

She punched at him.

He pushed her hands away.

She slapped his cheek.

He pushed her, hard.

Bella stumbled against the pail. Then she deliberately kicked it over in his direction, sending a cascade of steaming water splashing over his legs.

"Damn!" He jumped back with a yelp of pain, releasing his hold on her. "You little bitch. You'll pay for that."

He winced and picked frantically at his sodden trousers.

Bella's contempt for him roused her courage. "Don't you dare touch me," she said. "Don't you ever..."

"Really?" He reached out, grabbed Bella by the back of her neck, wrenched her into a crushing kiss, then pushed her back against the wall so quickly that she almost lost her footing on the slippery floor. "So what are you going to do about that, my fine lady!"

Too stunned to move, Bella felt her courage falter at the sound of his scornful laughter. She watched him unlock the door and leave.

"Animal!" she spat after him. She felt the bile rise to her throat, as she shook herself violently.

A cold resolve formed inside her. The next time Ruckler tried to touch her, she would scream, fight back, bring the whole hotel-full of guests down to witness his animal behavior.

No one would ever intimidate her again.

So this was her punishment for resisting Ruckler, Bella thought. Six hours of scrubbing heavy skillets and saucepans. Of breathing in the stench of rotting potato peels and scraps in the refuse bin. Her arms and shoulder blades throbbed. The small of her back burned with pain from bending over the sink.

She picked up the last small cast-iron skillet, grateful for the end. The young, homesick girl beside her twittered endlessly about brothers and sisters and cows and picking strawberries back on the farm until Bella wanted to scream.

Her thoughts were of the murderous variety; reflections on what she'd do if Ruckler touched her again. She tried to think of happier times with Daniel, but those memories no longer held any power to soothe her.

A loud crash and clatter sounded, punctuated by a wail of horror.

Bella and the scullery maid dashed to peer out of their doorway into the main kitchen. A mousey woman in a house-maid's uniform stared down at a mess of broken crockery, her mouth open, her eyes wide with fright as Ruckler ran into the room.

"I, I, I just turned 'round and..."

Bella recognized the woman as her next door neighbor, the one with the wailing infant. They had exchanged a few words now and then. Instinctively, she took a step in her direction, filled with compassion for the woman's predicament.

"You stupid cow!" Ruckler roared. He quickly crossed the room and boxed the woman's ears between his hands. She cowered, raising her arms to protect herself. Ruckler grabbed her by the arm. "Don't you raise your hand to me!" He forced her to the floor, pressing her arm backwards. The woman collapsed, sobbing.

Bella froze, fear flooding her brain. She clutched the skillet tightly.

The staff manager struck the woman, his beefy hands raining blows on her arms as she raised them again in a protective gesture. "Stupid cow! Stupid, clumsy, stupid..."

An overwhelming desire to stop this man swept away Bella's fears.

"Leave her alone!" she commanded. She swung the skillet in a deliberate arc aimed at Ruckler's shoulder. The glancing blow caught Ruckler off guard. He grabbed at his shoulder, opening his mouth in a roar of surprise. Seeing her, he roared louder.

"You!" He pivoted and lunged for the skillet, but Bella hopped out of reach, and he sprawled on his chest.

"You leave her alone!" Bella wielded the skillet like a club, ready to strike if he came near. "I'll tell Mr. Beach!"

"Tell the owner? Tell him what?" Ruckler stumbled to his feet. "That you came after me with a skillet? Intended to kill me because I put you in the scullery?"

She stepped back as he rose but kept the skillet high. "Because you beat this woman. Don't you try to deny what you did. With all these people as witness."

"What witnesses?" Ruckler eyed the staff. "Charlie! What did you witness? Eh?" The old man shook his head and turned away. "And you, Anna? What did you see?"

The sloe-eyed woman smiled slightly and shook her head. "Nothing, sir."

"You want him to beat *you* that way?" Bella cried to the woman. "He will, unless you speak out." One by one, the staff turned away from her plaintive gaze.

"It's your word against mine." Ruckler flexed his arms, circling her like a vulture. "Who do you think he'll believe?"

"I think he'll believe me," Bella said, her voice conveying icy disdain. "He'll believe the daughter of—" Even as she started to say her father's name, she realized that he might not believe her. Her father's name no longer held power. Yet she knew Charles Beach would remember her mother fondly. Yes, he would believe the daughter of Elizabeth Vanderlyn Gale.

"I may have fallen on hard times," she insisted, "but he'll remember me. And he'll take my word."

Something of her certainty must have communicated itself to Ruckler, because his bravado wavered for an instant and his next words lacked conviction. "Get out. You're dismissed. And if I even see you around here after today, I'll have you thrown in jail."

Bella bent down and put an arm around the cowering, weeping maid to steady her shaking body. With as much dignity as she could muster, Bella helped the woman up and they walked past the red-faced manager and out the door.

"You're dismissed!" Ruckler shouted. "Think you're high and mighty, do you? Don't come back here begging for a job. You hear me? No references! None!"

His strangled epithets followed them down the hall.

Thirteen

⁓

"What you need is another singer."

Gabriel Kramer smiled as he made the suggestion.

But Zach wasn't smiling when he looked up. He stopped buttering his warm muffin." What's the matter?" he asked curtly. "Am I off-key?"

"Of course not," Kramer answered. "It's just that you don't sing enough. Since the war, people like to hear the words of the songs. They like Stephen Foster tunes, marching songs, a bit of operetta. Stirring words, sentimental clap-trap. That sort of thing."

Annoyed with this critical assessment of his profession, Zach stabbed at the butter, scraping his knife across the muffin so hard that it crumbled in his hand. "But I sing well, when I sing?"

"Of course you do." Kramer leaned back in his chair. "The ladies adore you, as always. I wouldn't have had you back all these years if they didn't. But you can't sing and play the cornet at the same time, now can you. Things have changed since the war. Got to keep up with the competition. Gilmore's band has a new woman singer every time you turn around. Two, sometimes. So does Dodworth's and Levy's. A regular slew of Swedish Nightingale types."

"If they added an organ grinder and a monkey, you want me to hire them, too?" Zach dumped the muffin into his dish and brushed the crumbs from his hands.

"Just thought the fourth most popular band in the country would want to keep up with the competition. What happened to that woman John hired to sing with the band at the Manchester Hotel last month? She was pretty good. I heard she sang two nights with you and then she was gone."

"She was late for rehearsals. Late for shows. Started acting like some prima donna."

Kramer laughed. "Don't like to share the limelight with anyone, do you, you old dog?"

"I don't tolerate nonsense." Zach gulped his coffee. It was cold.

"Of course not, of course not." Kramer shifted forward in his seat and tapped briskly on the table. "I'm not saying you need a woman, necessarily, but someone else to sing. Think about it."

Zach scowled. "You know, Gabriel, just because you got me my first job, and just because we're friends, doesn't mean you can tell me how to run my band."

"I'm serious, Zach."

"So am I. It'll mean going to New York to find someone. Then working with her. It'll take time."

"Take your time. You've got the whole season ahead of you. Put an ad in the papers. Send a telegram to the agents." Kramer pushed back his seat. "More coffee?" He snapped his fingers, and a waiter scurried over. "Coffee here. Oh, by the way, I meant to ask. How's your niece and brother's wife doing?"

"Fine. Just fine." He recalled the morning Bella sang with his band. If only she hadn't been so shy, Zach would have already solved the problem of a singer.

Kramer nodded, grinning. "Mr. Beach saw you with the little girl and wondered if you'd gotten married, but I set him straight. First time I've seen the domesticated side of Zach Smith, though. It's rather charming."

"Don't think I've gone soft, Kramer." Zach scowled as the

waiter returned with a silver pot and poured a stream of steaming, fragrant coffee into Zach's china cup. Its pungent aroma rekindled his appetite. "Just remember, old man, I can still whip your butt, same as I did ten years ago."

"I remember." Kramer waved the waiter away from his own empty cup. "That reminds me. I heard someone requested the song *Marching Through Georgia* last night. I was told that you ignored him."

Zach gave him a hard look. "What of it?"

"You know the routine, Zach. We like our guests to be happy. If they ask for *Dixie* or *Marching Through Georgia* I expect them to hear it." He leaned forward and lowered his voice. "Myself, I don't give a rat's tail what side of the war you fought on. But there are plenty who do. The kind just itching for their own fights. Don't give them provocation. I'm serious about that, Zach. You know how Mr. Beach feels about anything that tarnishes the Mountain House reputation."

Zach's stomach tightened at Kramer's warning. He recalled the drunken guest who spat his tobacco juice at his feet two nights ago, after his sharp calls for *Marching Through Georgia* were ignored.

"Whad are yooo, a Reb or somethin'?" the man had challenged. "We got us a Johnny Reb, here?"

Good thing someone hauled the man away before Zach jumped down and slugged the idiot. The last thing he wanted to play was a song that romanticized the devastation he witnessed in Georgia after Sherman's march.

"Eh, Smith?" Kramer repeated. "The war's over."

"Tell your guests that."

"Smith!"

Zach looked up and forced a smile. "Sure. No problem. Anything to keep our guests happy."

"That's the ticket!"

When Kramer left, Zach took a gulp of the hot coffee and choked. It burned his lips. As he slammed down the cup, coffee splashed across his sleeve and on his waistcoat.

"Damn!" he cursed softly, although there was nobody else in the dining room at this hour. He dabbed at the coffee with a napkin, but quickly gave it up. He'd have to go and change before he picked up his niece.

Zach took the stairs two at a time, realizing that he'd left Amanda by herself for nearly an hour.

It was too bad Nancy had one of her sick headaches this morning or he could have left Amanda with her. Perhaps he should have taken his niece with him to the meeting.

As he approached his door, he reached into his waistcoat pocket for his key. But there was no need. The door was already open. Someone was humming and moving around inside. For a moment, he thought perhaps it was Bella. But as he stepped over the threshold, he saw the back of a young woman wearing a starched white maid's cap. Her blonde braids hung down to her waist. She was much taller than Bella, reaching up easily to the top of the window as she flicked her feather duster across the draperies.

"Excuse me," Zach said.

The young woman whirled around, flashing a smile at Zach. "Oh, sir. You startled me!"

She didn't look startled, Zach thought. "I didn't mean to."

"Oh, of course not," she answered. "I'm the one who should apologize. I had no idea you would be back so soon." She tucked her feather duster behind her back and gave him a coquettish bat of her long, blonde lashes.

Her voice held a trace of foreign accent. Norwegian or Dutch, perhaps, Zach thought.

"Is there something I can do for you, sir?"

There was no mistaking her tone. She was flirting with him. Zach recognized the signs from long experience, and she was a flirt if ever he knew one. A part of him was flattered. She was pretty: a blonde, buxom young woman with cornflower blue eyes and a teasing smile.

"As a matter of fact, there is something you can do for me," he said. "I spilled some coffee on my waistcoat and shirt."

"Oh, dear!" the maid exclaimed, moving quickly to his side.

"Let me look at that." She took his arm and turned his sleeve toward her. "Oh, that's terrible. Perhaps a little soap and water?"

"Perhaps you might be good enough to take this down to the laundry when you return?" Zach looked into her eyes, which now gazed into his with undisguised ardor.

"Oh, anything for you, sir." She batted her lashes at him again.

He chuckled at her brazen manner. "That's kind of you." He began to unbutton his waistcoat. "I'm in a bit of a hurry. I have someone waiting for me."

"Oh, in that case, I'll just finish up here and take your things when you're done," she said. "Or would you prefer me to wait outside?" She moved over to the door, as if to leave.

Zach smiled. The little minx was really quite charming, in her own way. "What's your name?"

"Katie," she said brightly and softly shut the door. "Let me help you with those buttons, sir."

"Thanks, I can manage," Zach said. It had been a long time since he had flirted with a maid. He'd forgotten just how pleasant it was to have this kind of attention. But it wouldn't lead anywhere today. He had to get Amanda. Funny how his priorities were changing.

Katie helped him off with his vest, then folded it neatly, laying it on the bed.

"Let me help you undo your cuffs," she said, as he fumbled with the gold cuff links that fastened his shirt sleeves. Her fingers were nimble and precise. "Now the other." He held his other arm out.

"I've seen you around the hotel. You're the band leader, isn't that right?"

"Yes," he said. "Zach Smith."

"I'd love to come and hear you play sometime, Mr. Smith," she said, holding out the gold jewelry. "If I could get away early from my duties. Or maybe I could come for the last set?"

Zach took the cuff links from her and held her hand for a moment. "That would be nice. Thank you for your help, Katie."

He turned away in the direction of his drawer, but Katie beat him to it and drew out a perfectly-starched, white shirt. "Here, sir. Let me help you."

Zach chuckled again as he undid the gold stud in his collar. This one was not going to take no for an answer, he could tell. He drew off his soiled shirt and handed it to her. She took it and tossed it next to his vest. "What a handsome man you are, Mr. Smith."

"Are you flirting with me, Katie?" Zach teased.

She held out the new shirt but didn't give it to him. "Flirting, sir? I don't know what you mean?" She giggled, playfully pulling back the shirt.

"My shirt, please," Zach said. He held out his hand. "Come on, now. I'm late."

"Can't they wait?" Katie said, holding the shirt close against her bosom. "A few minutes? A quarter of an hour?" She giggled again.

"I'd like to, but, uh ..." Zach grabbed the shirt. He tugged at it, as Katie held it more firmly. "Another time."

Reluctantly, she let him have the shirt. Her mouth drew into an exaggerated pout. "Is that a promise, sir?"

"Let's call it a distinct possibility," he answered, pulling his shirt on.

"I'll hold you to it." She stepped in front of him now, gazing into his eyes.

Zach ignored her, tucking in his shirttails.

Katie lifted her lips to his. The old Zach would have not hesitated to kiss her. But all he could think of was Amanda, waiting for him in that musty room. He snatched up his pocket watch, checking the time. He had promised to return in one hour, and it was already quarter past.

"Another time," Zach said, holding her hands firmly as she reached to button his shirt. "I have to go."

Fourteen

"Will you come with me to see Mr. Beach and tell him about Mr. Ruckler?" Bella asked the maid, who was still sobbing as they walked down the hall to their rooms.

The other woman stopped walking and gaped at Bella. "Are you a crazy person? If I go to the owner, my husband'll lose his job, too. It's the streets then. With no references, no prospects, it's the streets..."

Bella started to protest. "But we can have him fired, and then..."

"I know you mean well," the woman interrupted, wiping her eyes with a handkerchief. "But I need this job. I'm going to apologize to Mr. Ruckler. To beg, if I must. I need this job. Whatever it takes." The woman grimaced, then disappeared into her room.

Bella shuddered, recalling Ruckler heavy-handed seductions only that morning. She knew all too well what it would take.

Sagging against the wall, her frustration and anger blotted out all hope. *Why?* she silently raged. Why did this terrible luck seem to plague her?

Then she thought of Zach. Of Nancy's story about the boys in the band being stranded. He'd been in tough situations. Perhaps he could advise her.

Bella began to breathe easier. She'd find another position. Maybe she'd talk to Mr. Beach after all.

Fitting her key into the lock, she threw open the door. Amanda sat on the bed, a forlorn expression on her jam-smeared face.

"Darling! Why aren't you with Nancy?" Bella rushed to bed and hugged Amanda. She lifted a corner of her apron. "Let me see that face? Did you stick it directly in the jam pot, my love?" she teased.

"No." Amanda raised her face to Bella and submitted calmly to being washed. "I guess it woozed all over me."

"I guess so. We'll need some water and soap for this job." Bella rose and dipped her apron into the pitcher of water on the washstand. "Come here."

Amanda scampered over and lifted her face obediently again, then grinned.

Bella marveled at the change in her. Under Nancy's care, she was blossoming, turning into quite an outgoing, friendly child. She had made several friends, and Bella often saw her playing and running with the other children, as happy as she had ever been.

She straightened the child's new plaid pinafore, a present from Nancy, and lifted her up. "Have you been here all day?"

"Oh, Mama! Aunt Nancy's head is sick today. She has to stay in her room. I'm so glad you're here."

"So am I, love." She cuddled her daughter tightly. Whatever happened now, she must take care of Amanda. "Where's your uncle? Is he rehearsing with the band?"

"He told me to wait here for one hour until he finished some business." Amanda wriggled out of Bella's arms. Clambering up onto the bed, she pointed to the mantel clock on the dresser. "The big hand was here." Her outstretched finger touched the number ten. The clock now read thirty minutes past eleven. "Is that more than one hour?"

Bella frowned. "Yes. Well, maybe his business took a lot longer than he figured. Let's go find out."

Amanda's face lit up. "Oh, let's!"

They walked over to the main hotel, Bella keeping a watchful eye out for Ruckler. Only the desk clerk shot her a look of annoyance as he coped with an agitated guest.

As they climbed the staircase, Amanda prattled on about all the things she and Aunt Nancy usually did together.

"That's wonderful, darling. Here's Uncle Zach's room." A distinctly feminine giggle came from behind his door. Bella knocked. "Zach?"

The giggle came again, and then a low voice said something. Bella couldn't make out the words. She knocked again. At the third giggle, Bella's impatience got the better of her. Her hand slipped down to the knob and, in one smooth motion, opened the door.

Zach stood there in his shirtsleeves, his buttons undone, holding the hands of a woman dressed in the gray and white uniform of the hotel's maids. The woman stood with her back to Bella, her face tilted up to Zach's, but Bella knew by the long, flaxen braids that it was Katie Lindstrom.

"Zach!"

"Bella?"

Katie whirled around to give Bella an icy stare. "Get back to work," she hissed.

Bella ignored her. Was this why he had left Amanda alone? "How could you?" she cried, her cheeks flush with anger.

"How could I what?" Zach stepped in front of Katie and pushed the maid back behind him.

"Leave Amanda alone for... for her?" Bella stammered.

"I was in a business meeting..."

Bella let out a gasp. "Oh, is that what this is? A business meeting?"

Angrily, Zach took her arm and led her firmly into the hallway. "That's enough. This is none of your business, Bella."

She thought of Ruckler and what he might do to Zach if he found out Katie was throwing her favors at someone else. "Don't you realize if Mr. Ruckler finds out that you tried to seduce..."

"Nobody is seducing anyone." He shut the door firmly behind him, holding Bella at arm's length.

"Uncle Zach?"

Zach noticed his niece for the first time. "It's all right, Amanda. I was just coming to get you."

"Will you listen to me?" Bella snapped, tugging on his arm. "She's Ruckler's mistress..."

"Bella, this not the time for such a conversation, especially in front of Amanda."

"But...but..." Bella sputtered.

"Don't meddle in my private life." Zach's eyes warned her not to say more.

Bella stared at him, her mind a swirl of emotions. "Fine!" she spat. "Let her make a fool of you. Sometimes you make me so angry!"

"The feeling's mutual!"

"And if that's how you look after my daughter, don't bother."

Zach's grasp tightened on Bella's arm. For one moment, she was afraid of him. He abruptly let go of her arm, then shut the door in her face.

"You won't have to worry about us anymore!" she yelled through the door.

For one moment, Bella stood absolutely still, listening, hoping Zach would return. Instead, she heard a low giggle.

That did it! Seething with fury, Bella snatched Amanda's hand, marched down the steps, stormed through the main entrance, through the yard and returned to her own room.

She slammed her door hard, as if that might alleviate some of the pent-up anger inside her. A voice from the next room yelled out something unintelligible. Then someone began banging on the adjoining wall.

Bella pounded back. "Mind your own business!" she yelled. She pounded again for good measure, then rushed past Amanda, who had sunk to the floor in alarm, sucking her thumb for comfort, and clutching her doll.

Bella threw open the lid of her trunk. Tugging open the

drawers of the chest, she flung clothing, toiletries, handkerchiefs, and her hairbrush into the trunk with abandon. She aimed a blue perfume bottle that had been an anniversary present from Daniel. It shattered on the edge of the trunk, spraying toilet water and glass over the floor.

Horrified, Bella stopped and stared at the broken bottle that lay in bits and pieces, like her dreams.

～

"What did she mean about you and Ruckler?" Zach pulled away as Katie tried to embrace him after Bella's intrusion.

"She's just jealous. Maybe she just wants you all to herself."

As she tried to put her arms around him again, Zach took a step back. "Are you Ruckler's mistress?"

"What's it to you if I am?" She planted her arms on her hips and thrust out her chin, swaying seductively. "He doesn't own me. Ruckler." She said it with a dismissive flip of her hand. "He's a swine, but he is in charge. I'm sweet to him. He lets me have the easy jobs. Your friend won't play the game, so she gets what she deserves. Scullery duty."

Her pretty mouth twisted contemptuously, as she leaned into Zach and batted her eyes. "She's just jealous."

Strange, he thought, how the same gesture that had attracted him earlier now repulsed him. "What do you mean, she won't play the game?"

Katie laughed and tossed her head. "Ruckler got her alone this morning. She dumped a pail of water on him. At least, that's what I figured, since his trousers were wet when he came back. Next thing you know, Mrs. Goody-Goody's scrubbing pots in the scullery all afternoon."

She laced her arms around Zach's neck to draw him closer.

Got her alone. The phrase sent a crawling sensation down the back of Zach's neck. So that's why Bella had burst in on him. With both hands, he broke Katie's embrace and stepped back.

"You're talking about my sister-in-law." He glared at her. "And you. You'd have to be pretty low or pretty scared to sleep with the likes of Ruckler. Which is it?"

She tossed her head. "You men. All alike. Can't stand a woman having more than one man, now can you? How many women have you had?"

"That's enough." Over her pouts and protests, Zach firmly guided the maid out the door, then shut it and locked it. Feeling like a fool, he finished buttoning his shirt, then reached for his vest and jacket.

It was time to get the whole story.

~

"Bella?" Zach knocked on the door. "It's Zach. Can I come in?" He heard a patter of footsteps on the bare floor. The door swung open.

His niece stared up at him, anxiety reflected in her eyes. He lifted her into his arms. The child clung to him, laying her head against his shoulder. The stench of sickly-sweet violets assaulted his nose.

"Oh, Uncle Zach," Amanda whispered in his ear. "Mama's upset." She pointed to the corner.

Bella heaved an armful of dresses into the trunk with rigid, jerky motions. Broken glass and untidy piles of books and clothes surrounded her. Her face was streaked with tears. It broke Zach's heart.

"Bella."

She didn't answer.

He tried to make a joke. "What'd you do? Put on a whole bottle of perfume?"

Bella simply turned her head away. Zach's mind raced with scenarios of Ruckler forcing her, defiling her, God knew what else. Quieting his thoughts, he gently let Amanda down.

"Don't worry, sweetheart," he whispered, patting the child on the head. "Wait here."

He walked slowly over to Bella. "Did Ruckler hurt you today?" He touched her shoulder.

She twisted her body away from him. In a voice so low that Zach had to lean forward to hear her, she moaned, "I should have never come here."

"Tell me what happened." As gently as he could, Zach laid his hands on Bella's shoulders. Bella shuddered violently, but this time she didn't jerk away. "I'm listening."

She turned and stared into his eyes with a hateful expression that took Zach by surprise. "Why should you care?" she hissed.

"Of course I care. I…"

"I was fired," she spat back. "By your great friend, Ruckler. Now you won't have to be burdened with us. You can go back to Katie." She turned her back to him.

"Ruckler's not my friend," Zach said. "Neither is Katie. She told me about the games they play. I didn't know. I swear, I didn't know."

Bella didn't answer. She simply went limp. Anger at Ruckler, at Katie, at himself burned in Zach's stomach.

"If he touched you, if he hurt you in any way, I'll make sure he pays."

"I'm the one who paid," Bella said in a dull voice. "So you don't have to trouble yourself about us. We're leaving." She bent down to pick up the pile of books by her feet.

"Leaving?" He glanced over at the child. Amanda was huddled on the floor, sucking her thumb. She watched him with round, sad eyes. "Leaving for where?"

"For anywhere!" Crouching on the floor, Bella heaved books into the trunk one by one. "I'll find something to do. A governess. A companion. I'll work in the hat factory if I have to."

He knelt next to her and laid a hand on her arm. "Tell me what happened. I'll try to fix it."

"We can't fix it." Bella's voice quavered. She sank down to a sitting position, her skirts billowing around her. "Mr. Ruckler evicted me from the hotel."

Fifteen

The story came out in ragged, unconnected phrases, but Zach managed to piece together a picture of what had led to Bella's dismissal. Amanda crept over. Zach drew the child to him, slipping his free arm protectively around her shoulder. He struggled to hold back his mounting anger.

"When I saw him beating her..." Bella choked. "I had the skillet in my hand. I just wanted to make him stop. That's all I could think of. I hit Ruckler with the skillet. It was in my hand. I wasn't afraid. I just swung it at him..."

She drew in a sharp breath and turned to face Zach. "I could have killed him." She began to sob. "I wanted to kill him. Oh, God, oh God! I'm so ashamed!"

Sensing that Bella needed to be held, Zach gave Amanda a reassuring squeeze before slipping his arm from her shoulder. Then he pulled Bella to him, rocking her as he would a sobbing child. "You were trying to protect someone. To stop someone. It's all right."

Zach tightened his grip and rocked her more slowly, humming the lullaby he had written for Daniel, as if the tune could alleviate her pain. He felt Amanda tuck her hand into the crook of his arm.

Slowly, Bella's sobs subsided, and she grew quiet in his arms. Zach silently vowed to prevent anyone from ever hurting them again.

"We can't stay here," Bella said in a small voice.

"You're damned right you're not. It's a rotten room, anyway," Zach said. "We're bringing your things into my room. I'll move in with Billy for a few days until I can get another room."

She lifted her head and pulled away from him. "No, no. I mean we can't stay in the hotel."

"Oh yes you can." He traced a wet trail of tears down her cheeks with his forefinger. "You bet you can." He wanted to wipe away all her pain. But all he could do was smile at her.

"But Mr. Ruckler said if he saw me here, at the hotel, he'd have me thrown out."

"To hell with Ruckler." Zach smiled again. This time it was a grin because he suddenly knew how to fix everything. "He wouldn't dare to evict the new singer in the hotel's most popular band."

Bella blinked, staring at him. She was clearly confused. "The what?"

"The new singer in Smith's Cornet Band." He pointed to her. "You."

She stared at him blankly. "Me?"

"Why not? You need a job. I need a singer."

"No, you don't."

He chuckled. "Oh, yes I do. Got to keep up with the competition. They're all bringing in women singers. That's what the hotel manager wanted to talk to me about at breakfast. So instead of having to go all the way back to the city to look for a singer, I have you." He smiled at her skeptical expression. "You've got a wonderful voice, Bella. I told you that."

"But I've never sung professionally. All those people."

"Every singer has got to start somewhere." He turned to Amanda and pulled her close. "Amanda, don't you think your mother will make a good singer in the band?"

The child nodded eagerly.

"See, Amanda agrees."

Bella stared at him, shaking her head. She was obviously struggling with the idea.

"It's better than working in the hat factory," Zach added. "That's if you could even get your old job back."

Bella took in a deep, ragged breath. "I suppose I could try." She looked over at her daughter. "For Amanda's sake."

"That's the way! You'll be wonderful." Zach heaved himself up from the floor. Amanda scrambled up beside him. He reached out to Bella and was gratified when she took his hand and allowed him to help her rise.

As they faced each other, Zach knew the status of their relationship had subtly shifted. For once, he saw trust reflected in her violet eyes.

≈

"Listen to the mockingbird. Listen to the mockingbird."

Bella sang the song hesitantly, her voice small and barely audible above the band in the cavernous ballroom. The last time she sang here was in jest. This was serious business. Conscious that the musicians would be judging her abilities, Bella could not stop her voice from shaking. Her hands shook, too, and her knees threatened to buckle. She felt as if she could hardly breathe, let alone sing.

"Still singing where the weeping willows wave," she finished lamely.

Zach gestured the band to stop. Sighing, he turned his back to Bella. She longed to run out of the room.

She could have told him that his plan was doomed to fail, but his excitement had bolstered her confidence. Yesterday, he'd moved all their possessions into his room, made her and Amanda comfortable, told Amanda a wonderful bedtime story, and assured them everything would be fine. Now he was probably quite disgusted with her.

"Okay boys. Let's take it again. This time, Bella, you just listen. Feel the pace, the timing of the stops, the trills and the riffs." Zach turned back to her and smiled. "You're just nervous. Tell you what. Close your eyes and just listen to the music."

Bella nodded. Swallowing hard, she squeezed her eyes shut. Her fists were clenched, her jaw tight. She heard Zach whistle the first seven notes of the refrain. The band joined in the cheerful tune.

Unable to stop her thoughts from returning to the past, Bella recalled one of the few times she had sung for her father's guests, standing in front of them in the ornate, gas-lit music room of their New York townhouse. She had been so frightened of making a mistake. When she forgot the words, one of their guests snickered, and everyone began to titter. She had been mortified then, in front of friends. How could she ever sing in front of a roomful of strangers? She began to tremble just thinking about it.

"Ready, Bella?" Zach's voice cut into her thoughts. "Let's try it again."

Miserable, Bella opened her eyes. Zach tapped his foot and beat the time with his free hand. He whistled the refrain and once more the band played the bars of the introduction. Billy hit the bass drum and Peter struck the cymbals together with a resounding crash; her cue to come in with the first stanza.

She swallowed hard and plunged in, her fists still clenched at her side, the notes sticking in the back of her throat. "I'm dreaming now of Hallie, sweet Hallie, sweet Hallie."

Zach cut the band off with a slicing gesture and spun around. Bella screwed up her eyes, expecting to hear him curse her for singing off-key. Instead, she heard him chuckle.

"You look as if you're about to face the guillotine." Zach chuckled again.

Bella opened her eyes. She felt miserable.

"Take a break, boys. Come back in about, oh, fifteen minutes. John and I are going to work with Mrs. Smith for a bit."

The musicians put their instruments down and headed for the doors.

"Bring back some cold lemonade!" Zach called after them.

Deeply embarrassed, Bella hung her head. "I told you, I'm not much of a singer."

Zach picked up his cornet and sat down on the nearest chair.

Absently, he ran a hand down the gleaming silver. "Is that what you think? You can't sing?"

Bella nodded, miserable.

"Well, that's part of your problem, then. We've heard you sing. You've got a grand voice." He looked at John, who nodded in agreement. "John thinks so, too. Come here." He crooked his finger at her. "Come on over here. I won't bite you." He wasn't smiling, but his sober expression was gentle.

Feeling like a child facing an unwanted lecture, Bella plodded reluctantly toward the two men.

"Closer." Impatiently, Zach reached out and took her by the hand, pulling her to him. He turned her so that she faced away from him and placed his hands around her, resting them lightly just under her rib cage.

"What are you doing?" His touch embarrassed Bella.

"Don't move. Now, take a deep breath."

"Why?" She squirmed against the pressure of his hands.

"Take a deep breath," Zach commanded.

"Very well." Bella inhaled.

"Your stays are too tightly laced. You can't breathe." Zach dropped his hands and began to unbutton the back of her dress.

"Just what do you think you're doing?" Bella wrenched herself out of his grasp, thoroughly shocked.

"I just want to loosen your stays." Zach glanced at John, who shook his head with an embarrassed smile.

"To help me sing?"

"Yes." Zach's expression was completely serious. "In order to sing, you need to be relaxed and able to breathe." He pulled her toward him again with a gentle tug to show he meant business.

"Zach, Zach!" John's voice was calm as usual, but he was on his feet and at Zach's side in a heartbeat. "This is a lady. A respectable lady," he lectured gravely. "You don't go unbuttoning a lady's bodice, partner. What are you thinking?"

Zach looked genuinely puzzled and hurt. "John, it's business." He turned back to Bella and shrugged. "It's pure business." He turned to John again. "She can't sing in that contraption. I'll be damned if I know why all these women have to wear the damned things, but she sure can't sing in it."

"I know that," John said patiently. "But you can't go undressing a lady. I'll get Nancy to come and help her undo the stays."

"Oh, for Pete's sake!" Zach groaned. "We haven't got ten years, John. We've got to teach her everything we know in less than a week."

"Gentlemen! Gentlemen!"

The two men turned toward Bella as if they had forgotten she was standing there.

"I can loosen my stays myself in two minutes," she declared. She turned away from Zach and put her hand on the small of her back. "Since you already started, you can help me unbutton down to here." She indicated a spot with her finger. "And no further!" she added sharply. "I can manage from there. I'll just slip into the ladies' powder room at the end of the hall."

John nodded at Zach, who threw up his hands in mute exasperation and quickly undid the last few buttons.

"Thank you," Bella said primly. She clutched the bodice behind her at the nape of her neck to keep the top closed. With her other hand behind her back, she held the bottom, trying to look as dignified as the ridiculous situation would allow as she walked toward the exit.

"Wait a minute, Bella." Zach slipped out of his jacket and brought it over to her. "There." He draped it gently around her shoulders. "Is that better?"

"Sometimes, Mr. Smith, you *can* be quite the gentleman. Thank you."

"Frankly," he called after her, "I'd be happier if you took the damned thing off altogether. You'll sing much better without it."

~

When Bella returned, Zach was pacing the floor, practicing running chords on his cornet. He stopped and put down his instrument. She came and stood in front of him, then turned her back to him, signaling that she was ready to resume her lesson. Her stomach began to flutter, and the sensation moved up into her chest and throat.

"Now, breathe in," Zach commanded. He again placed his hands on her diaphragm, sending a series of shivers through her despite four protective layers of clothing. Suddenly, his fingers began moving gently, as if he were searching for something. He gave a low whistle. "What do you know, you took the..."

"I'm ready when you are," Bella interrupted him firmly, putting her own hands over his to still them. She had removed the offending corset and knew that Zach had felt its absence.

Trembling at her own audacity, Bella concentrated on what she had to do. She took a deep breath.

"Now hold it," Zach told her. "Don't breathe out. But take in more air."

Bella tried, but it felt so strange that she couldn't suppress a giggle. "How can I take in anymore?"

"This is not a joke. It's serious. Breathe in."

Bella forced herself to concentrate, still conscious of his hands against her.

"Hold it. Now take in more air." At Zach's request, she wheezed and gulped in as much air as she could, trying not to laugh at the absurdity of it. She felt her diaphragm expand far more than normal. "Now sing a high note and hold it out as long as you can."

Bella opened her mouth and plunged into a high C, amazed at the volume of sound and her new-found sustaining power. Finally, she gasped and breathed in again, clutching his hands still around her waist. "That was wonderful!"

"Again. Breathe!" he commanded. "More. Give me a D flat, John. Sing the note, Bella."

For the next ten minutes, Bella breathed in and sang out repeatedly, until she confidently sang on her own. Zach still held her firmly, calling out the notes to John. "Now breathe in and do the first line of 'Mockingbird.' Ready John?"

With a deep breath, Bella sang, "I'm dreaming now of Hallie, sweet Hallie, sweet Hallie!" Her voice was on key, loud, and vigorous. "I'm dreaming now of Hallie, for the thought of her is one that never dies."

She heard a smattering of whistles and claps, as the returning band members took their places and picked up their instruments to join in. One of the porters brought in a tray of lemonade behind them.

Flushed with excitement, Bella craned her head to look at Zach. His expression was still serious, but his dark eyes sparkled.

"Keep singing," he called to her. "Enjoy it."

Bella felt as if she had flown off the mountain into the sky. She was dizzy at her new-found powers. Her voice soared to the ceiling and expanded to fill the room. She felt she could sing and sing forever.

When he took his hands away, she felt less sure of herself, faltering once on a high note. His cornet came in on the same high note, and she lifted her voice to join it. With a flourish, they ended the song.

"Oh, I can't believe it!" Bella spun around and grinned at him. "You're a genius!"

He took her hand, gave it a quick squeeze, then twirled her around. "Well, boys, what do you think? Have we got ourselves a singer?"

To the appreciative hoots of the band members, Bella improvised a quick curtsy.

But it was Zach's approval she wanted. "Are you pleased?"

"Quite pleased." Zach's eyes revealed nothing, but his smile flashed approval. "You done good, Mrs. Smith. But we've got a lot of work in front of us."

∿

It had been a good rehearsal, Zach thought. Certainly a surprising rehearsal in more ways than one.

Zach watched Bella pour out a glass of lemonade with sure,

graceful motions. John was right. She was a lady, all right. But she was no prude. Taking off that corset proved she had guts. That she would do whatever was needed to get the job done. That pleased him. She was such an eager pupil on her first lesson, the rest of what he needed to teach her about singing would be easy.

What wouldn't be as easy would be keeping his emotions in check after today.

All the time he was standing next to Bella, her rose-scented perfume was assailing his senses. It had taken real willpower to keep his mind on the task at hand. With the right clothes and the right music, Bella Gale would drive men wild.

He wasn't sure he liked that idea.

"You sure picked a real peach this time," trombonist Paul Bruner said. "I wasn't so sure this morning."

"Yes siree, she's a peach all right, she is," agreed Billy Parisher, the drummer. "Those eyes, boy oh boy, are something to write home about. What color would you call 'em?"

Zach felt the sting of jealousy as the young musicians discussed Bella as if she were fair game. He'd put a stop to that right now. "So you like her, huh, lads?" He draped an arm around their shoulders.

"She's a peach."

"Yes. My peach." Zach caught himself quickly. "I mean, she's my family. I don't want her bothered. Get the picture?"

Paul and Billy looked at one another, then nodded.

"Got it," Paul said.

"What about that Katie?" Billy gave Zach a leering wink. "She keeps asking me about you. You got something going with her? That ain't fair."

Zach chuckled. "No, Billy, I don't have something going with her. Katie's all yours if you want to try."

The drummer's eyes lit up. "Well Hell, yeah!

"Wait a minute, I've got dibs, too," Paul protested.

"One thing you should consider, boys. Either of you know Ruckler?"

"Yeah, that son-of-a-Sam who's in charge of the kitchen help," Billy said.

"What about that piece of slimy soap scum?" Paul asked. "You know what he had the nerve to do yesterday? Cuss me out for having a couple of bottles of whiskey in my room. As if I didn't pay for 'em."

Zach drew them in and lowered his voice confidentially. "Katie's with Ruckler. Apparently finds him irresistible."

The boys groaned.

"Oh, brother, she's all yours," Paul said, digging Billy in the ribs.

"Forget it," Billy said. "I ain't touching' her."

"I know just how you feel, boys." Zach turned serious now. "Ruckler tried putting his paws on Mrs. Smith. Either of you see him coming near her, you let me know. I'm just looking for an excuse to knock his teeth through his eyes."

Zach tightened his grip on Billy's shoulder and feinted an upper cut to the lad's mouth. The drummer flinched, then nodded enthusiastically, his head bobbing up and down.

"Sure thing, Zach."

"Pass it on to the other boys, will you?"

"Yes sir. We will," Paul agreed. "I'd like a shot at that old coot myself."

Zach grinned. By the time word got round the band, Ruckler would be dead meat if any of them caught him looking sideways at Bella. Not only that, but the word would also be out that Bella was off-limits to the rest of the boys in the band.

"Here's your lemonade." Bella was at Zach's side, offering him a cold glass. "And yours, John." As she reached past Zach with a second glass, he inhaled her sweet perfume.

He longed to kiss her. But all he had to do was remind himself that she was Daniel's widow and the urge passed just as quickly. Lifting his glass, he drained it, thinking the tart and sweet liquid a poor substitute for his real thirst.

The men packed up their gear and sauntered out into the hall.

Bella finished her lemonade, then started toward the back door.

"Bella?"

She turned, startled, then laughed as Zach crooked his finger at her. "Come here a minute."

It seemed to Zach that she floated across the room. She held her chin high. Her eyes shone with excitement.

"You did well today." Zach took her hand and squeezed it gently.

"Did I?" She squeezed his back excitedly. "You think I'm ready to sing with the band?"

"Not so fast." He saw a flicker of anxiety in her eyes. "Don't worry. It's just that I want you to be so well rehearsed that your debut at next Saturday's formal ball will cause a sensation." He drew her closer, still holding her hand. "Not only do I want you to come to all the rehearsals, I want you to come and listen to us each time we play. You'll get paid this week, same as the boys."

She nodded eagerly, her head tilted up to him, two bright pink spots coloring her cheeks. "Thank you."

Zach felt the warmth of her small hand in his, felt the world tilt as if he were drunk. Words eluded him for a moment, but he forced his mind to return to business. "I asked the seamstress to measure you for a new gown and a corset that will let you breathe. You'll need a whole wardrobe. She'll be in your room at three o'clock tomorrow."

"Fine."

"You won't forget?"

"I won't forget. But I have to run now and get Amanda."

"And Bella? I just want to know one thing," he said in a low voice. "What did you do with that corset?"

Her face turned red, but she looked quite pleased with herself. "So you noticed."

"You knew I did."

"I left it in one of the stalls," she whispered, still blushing. "I have to run and get it now."

"Too bad," he whispered back. "I was hoping you threw it away!"

She seemed shocked at the suggestion. "I'll have you know I'm a respectable lady."

Zach watched her hurry away. *That's what I was afraid of, Mrs. Smith,* he thought. *That's what I was afraid of.*

Sixteen

Bella had been standing on a low stool in only her chemise, corset, camisole for over two hours. She felt like one of Nancy's china dolls, made to pose this way and that according to other people's whims. Her neck ached, and her legs were stiff from balancing for so long. Yet the dour dressmaker barely noticed her discomfort. She measured her from top to bottom over and over, ordering her to change into a new petticoat and camisole for each new dress. She jammed dozens of straight pins into the undergarments, creating a sort of template from which she would sew each dress.

At regular intervals, Bella was ordered to step down and put on a robe, so Zach could come in for his opinion. After all, he was not only paying for the dresses, he wanted to make sure they were exactly to his specifications.

"You can step down now," the seamstress said. "I need to see which fabric Mr. Smith wants for this dress."

Bella slipped the robe on, wrapping it tightly around her.

The seamstress rose and opened the door. "You can come in now," she said, ushering Zach over to the big armchair. With a sigh, Bella stepped back up on the stool as Mrs. Florsham held up first a white piece of embroidered fabric, and then a pink lawn.

"White. The dress should definitely be white," Zach said. He stretched his long legs out on the rug and folded his arms across his chest. His curly head tilted as he coolly appraised the scene. "With some red trimmings."

"What kind of trimmings, Mr. Smith?" The dressmaker's voice was weary and pinched.

Zach rose. "Two silk ribbons, like so." He reached out and traced a series of scrolls down the fabric, starting from Bella's waist down to her feet.

"Held up by tiny rosettes of red ribbon at the waist?" the dressmaker suggested, making a notation in her pattern book.

"That sounds good. Yes. But we'll need this dress for next Saturday night. Can you make it in time?"

"Of course. I can." The dressmaker sniffed, adjusting her spectacles as she bent forward to stab another pin through the hem.

Zach looked up at Bella and smiled. "What do you think?"

"I didn't know you had so much interest in ladies' apparel." Bella hesitated. "I think the neckline is too low."

Zach shook his head. "In this business, a little provocation never hurts. Within the bounds of good taste, of course." He winked. "You'll be the most striking woman ever to grace the hotel."

Zach turned briskly to the seamstress. He thanked her for coming.

"Of course," the woman said, one eyebrow arching beneath her spectacles as she methodically wound her tape measure and gathered her pins into her sewing box. "When you've taken off the petticoat and corset, Mrs. Smith, just have them brought to my sewing room." She stood up and tucked her sample book under her arm. "Do you still want the blue gingham for the afternoon tea costume, Mr. Smith?"

"Yes, Miss Florsham. Just as we discussed. And a second one in the yellow fabric with the scattered roses that Mrs. Smith seemed to favor." Zach ushered the seamstress to the door, then bent to lightly kiss her hand.

"You are a true artist, Miss Florsham," he told the startled woman. "You will turn Mrs. Smith into a work of art, I'm sure."

The seamstress responded with a curt "thank you" and left. Zach turned back to Bella and helped her down off the stool.

"Thank goodness," Bella said, putting the stool back by the vanity. "I thought she'd never finish. Will we see you for dinner, then?"

"No, I'm dining with the Ben Schoeten party tonight. I promised Gabriel I would dine with two families this week. Part of the job." He smiled at her. "I'd much rather dine with you and Amanda."

"Oh, it won't be so bad," Bella said, settling in front of the vanity. She picked up a hand mirror and a brush. "We'll see you after dinner, at the show tonight."

"Umm huh," he said absent-mindedly. "You know, you'll need to do something a bit more fancy with your hair." He walked over to her, studying her as she removed her hairpins and began to unbraid her hair. "Yes, something, I don't know. Maybe curls or something swept up to one side. Nancy knows. She reads those Peterson magazines. She's very good at doing hair."

"I'll talk to her about it at dinner tonight," Bella said, brushing her hair with vigorous strokes. She put down the brush and stretched her arms wide. "Standing on that stool for so long made me stiff. My neck hurts." She rolled her head from one side to the other.

Zach moved up behind her and placed his hands on her shoulders. He began to knead them slowly, working his way up to her neck. She relaxed, caught up in the languid rhythm of the massage.

"Ummmm, that feels very nice."

Bella leaned her head back and closed her eyes, relaxing completely until she felt his breath on the nape of her neck. Then his warm lips brushed against her cheek. Bella's eyes opened, and she stood up with a start. Had she simply imagined that Zach had kissed her?

He pushed aside the stool that lay between them. For one moment, time seemed suspended as they searched each other's eyes. Then he kissed her.

It was a kiss unlike any she had ever experienced. His lips

nuzzled hers, then took possession of her entire mouth, warming it, softening it, licking it up with unabashed delight. His arms crushed her to him, his fingers kneading her flesh now to inflame, rather than relax her.

Warmth flowed through her, effervescent as champagne, intoxicating her entire body. Her body was responding as ardently as if it were Daniel kissing her. But this wasn't Daniel. How could she feel this way with a man who was not Daniel? *My God, what was happening?*

"Zach!" she cried. He looked up, then bent to kiss her again, but she raised a hand against his mouth. "Please don't."

Zach pulled away, his expression changing in an instant from passion to resentment. He shook his head vehemently once, then twice, and choked out an apology. "I'm sorry. I'm sorry. Just forget it ever happened."

Yanking open the door, Zach disappeared down the hall.

Bella stared after him. Slowly, she closed her door and leaned her head against it.

Forget it ever happened?

She ran her fingers over her lips that were still enflamed by his kisses. She felt an ache of loneliness deep within her. She could feel his fingers against her shoulders, as if they still caressed her skin.

Wrapping her arms around herself, Bella stumbled toward the bed and sank down on it, feeling more confused than ever. She stared up at the ceiling, unable to dispel the feeling of that kiss. It had awakened desires that frightened her. Desires that were completely incompatible with her private vow to never love another man again.

"Let me just tuck in this last little curl." Nancy fussed and pulled at Bella's curls until at last she sighed. "Well, that's the best I can do. Let me get a mirror."

Bella's stomach fluttered as if a flock of butterflies had taken up residence. In just one hour, she would be singing in front of hundreds of people. Some of them would have known her parents. Hopefully, most of them wouldn't remember her or connect Bella Smith with the Silk King's daughter.

"Here." Nancy held up a mirror to the back of Bella's head. "What do you think?"

Bella held up her own mirror, adjusting it until she could see the lovely cascade of curls. She caught her breath. "Nancy, you're a wonder! It's gorgeous. Absolutely perfect. Just like the fashion plate in Peterson's magazine."

"Stand up! Let's see the whole effect," Nancy urged. "Come on!"

Bella drew off the towel Nancy had used to protect the red-trimmed, white satin gown that had been delivered just that morning by Miss Florsham. She stood up and stepped away from the vanity.

"Turn around!" Nancy said. "Turn around."

Bella slowly revolved, getting the feel of the new gown. Her old hoop skirts had been replaced by one with a more tapered front silhouette, which billowed out behind her. The skirt was a slimming front panel of white, trimmed down each side and ruffled across the bottom in red satin. Miss Florsham had gently gathered the fabric at either side and at the back with rows of red silk rosettes and tassels. The underskirt was bright red, with no less than six bands of white silk ribbon trim and two rows of ruffles. The bodice was a flattering princess style, with puffed sleeves edged in red silk. She wore a pair of long, white silk gloves that decorously covered her arms above the elbows.

But the neckline! It was a good six inches lower than any of her day dresses and daring enough to make Bella blush at her own reflection in the mirror. She had remedied it somewhat by folding her old lace fichu around her shoulders and pinning it just above the neckline. Nancy had rearranged the fichu so that it slightly bared her shoulders.

"That dress is divine," Nancy cooed. "Just divine. It shows off your lovely white shoulders, my dear. Oh! I know. Amanda, my love, would you get that box of powder there on your Mama's dresser?"

Amanda rose from her nest of dolls on the bed and scampered to do Nancy's bidding. "Oh Mama, you look so pretty."

"Thank you, my darling," Bella called to Amanda. Then she lowered her voice. "I just don't know if I can go through with this, Nancy. I feel sick inside."

"Nonsense." Nancy gathered the scattered hairpins and paper she had used to crimp Bella's hair. "You know all the songs. You've rehearsed all week. You sing like an angel. What more is there? Besides, Amanda and I shall be watching tonight. Sing to us."

"Yes Mama, sing to us!" said Amanda, returning with the powder. "You always feel better when you sing to me."

"You're right, my darling child. Who made you so smart?" She kissed her daughter, then took the powder and gave it to Nancy.

"God did," Amanda said, as if indignant that her mother didn't know.

Bella patted her daughter's cheek. "Yes, he did, and I'm quite glad of it."

"Hold still, while I dust your shoulders," said Nancy, as she patted the powder over Bella's shoulders and neck. Amanda's eyes grew wide with adoration. "Mama, you look just like one of Aunt Nancy's beautiful dolls. Doesn't she, Aunt Nancy?"

"Much more beautiful than any doll," Nancy answered. She put down the powder. "Come with me, Amanda. We'll scoot downstairs and leave your Mama to rest a minute." She glanced at the mantle clock. "Oh, dear. Nearly seven. And I haven't kissed John for luck yet."

They darted out the door, giving a quick hello to Zach on their way past.

He knocked softly.

Bella turned from the dressing table and looked up. Zach stood in the doorway, exceedingly elegant in a black silk frock coat and a bright sapphire blue silk waistcoat. She hadn't seen this particular outfit before.

"You look quite dashing," she said, taking a step toward him. "New waistcoat?"

"New suit. All the boys and I got measured in New York before we came. These arrived last week, and we thought we'd save them for your debut. Like it?"

Bella smiled. "Very much."

"Is it all right if I come in?"

"Of course."

Zach stepped inside. Even though he left the door open, his nearness made her nervous. This was the first time he had come to her room since the night he had kissed her. All this week, she had contrived to meet with him only when others were around. For his part, Zach seemed to have decided to keep his distance, acting brisk and businesslike whenever he had to address her.

For a long moment, she and Zach merely gazed at each other. His expression suddenly softened, but his dark eyes burned with intensity as he looked her up and down. He gave a long, low whistle.

"I'd say you're going to be the belle of the Mountain House." When she didn't smile, he added, "Pun intended."

She smiled nervously and twisted her handkerchief. "I wish I felt as confident as you."

"What's the matter?" Zach sank into the armchair and frowned. "Backing out on me already?"

"No. But I feel, oh, I don't know." She blushed, embarrassed at her churning emotions. "I'm all fluttery inside."

"Just an attack of stage fright. Everyone gets it. You're ready. Just look at me and everything will be fine."

She drew the handkerchief back and forth through her fingers. "I know. Yet it feels just the same as when I was a child."

"But it isn't. And everyone, including the audience, wants to have a good time."

The knot in her stomach tightened, despite Zach's encouraging words. "What if someone heckles me, like that awful man heckled you on Wednesday?"

"Just heckle him back."

"I couldn't!"

"I'll heckle him for you, then. The boys and I will hop down and twist his arm until he begs for mercy." He grinned at her. When she didn't smile, he added, "I'm only joking, Bella." He stood up. "Shall we go?"

"Couldn't I just wait here?" Bella asked, reluctantly picking up her new white silk reticule. "Just until the second set, when you introduce me?"

Zach chuckled. "Sit up here alone until you're so worked up you decided not to come down at all? Oh, no. You'll come down now and sit with Nancy and Amanda, sip a glass of champagne, and relax to the music."

Bella looked at him doubtfully. "Relax?"

"Chin up. You'll be grand," Zach said, as he gestured for her to walk through the open door. "After you, Mrs. Smith."

～

Bella stood on the side, listening to the last few choruses of the ever-popular Stephen Foster tune, "I Dream of Jeannie with the Light Brown Hair." The song was to lead into Zach's introduction of her. It finally ended to polite applause.

"Thank you, ladies and gentlemen. Thank you, thank you."

The applause died down, as the men ushered their ladies off to the sides to change dancing partners. Zach waited a moment, then blew a fanfare.

"Ladies and gentlemen. I would like to introduce you to a lovely new singer making her debut here at the Catskill Mountain House. She's an American beauty, and like Jenny Lind, can sing like a Nightingale. Please warmly welcome Smith's Cornet Band's new American Nightingale, Miss Bella Gale!"

His introduction caught Bella entirely off guard. Her nervousness vanished, replaced by exasperation. How dare he use her maiden name! As if she had never been married to Daniel at all! As if she didn't have a child by proper wedlock! It was too much! And besides, people would know who she was, after she had been so careful to use her married name. Zach never said a word about using the name Gale. Not to mention that ridiculous title of American Nightingale! The more she thought of it, the more her fury grew.

In a rage, she marched on stage, ignoring the applause and the buzz of speculation that rippled through the room.

She marched right up to Zach, thrusting her chin out. "How dare you use the name Miss Gale, when I was properly married to your brother!" she whispered. "And how dare you call me that ridiculous title!"

For a moment, Zach stared at her, stunned. Quickly recovering his poise, he stepped back, raised his cornet and blew a fanfare in her direction.

Bella jumped back from the deafening blast, outraged at his cheekiness. She turned to the audience. She heard titters from the crowd. Instead of making her cringe, the laughter emboldened her.

"Well!" she cried, putting her hands on her hips. "I'd say the leader of the band needs to learn a few manners."

Turning back to Zach, Bella opened her mouth to demand an apology. He raised his cornet again and blew another shrill fanfare. Then he turned to the audience. "Never let a woman get the last word."

The audience roared with delight at the impromptu exchange. Her anger now white hot, Bella took in a deep breath and turned back to Zach as the laughter died down. Without a moment's thought, she let go with a shattering high C, holding it out of sheer spite, shaking her head at Zach as if he were a naughty child.

Zach let her go, his eyes twinkling, his fingers twitching, eager to blow his horn. When she finally popped the end of the note, her eyes blazing, her entire body preening at her achievement, the audience cheered.

She curtsied to them, acknowledging her due. She felt quite proud of herself for showing up Zach and winning all the applause to herself.

Then Zach blew a high note, holding it out and diving and swooping around it. His face reddened as he wrung the last ounce of breath to sustain it. Billy did a drum roll, and the audience clapped and cheered.

All heads turned to Bella, nodding expectantly as they waited to see what she would do next. Her body still trembling, her eyes still ablaze, she folded her arms and turned to Zach.

"You may have won that round, Mr. Band Leader," she said loudly, shaking her finger at him. "But just you wait until I get you after the dance!"

Zach laughed out loud with the audience, clearly flabbergasted by Bella's impromptu outburst. She knew he thought this was all in fun. But she was not laughing. She meant every word of it. After the dance, she would demand an apology and make him promise to use her proper married name.

"All right, boys," she announced when the laughter had died down. Her anger fueled her confidence, as well as her wish to get this evening over with. "Enough of childish contests. Let's sing a song about Hallie, sweet Hallie, and the mockingbird that's singing where she lies."

John laughed and winked at her, tucking his violin under his chin and immediately picking up the introduction of *Listen to the Mockingbird.* The rest of the band followed his lead, and soon Bella was singing and moving about the stage with ease.

Throughout her five songs, the audience was warmly attentive and filled the dance floor, eagerly bestowing their approving applause after each number.

Bella had forgotten her fears. She searched out the audience to spy Nancy and Amanda. They sat off to the side by the well-stocked refreshment table, nodding happily like a pair of squirrels as they nibbled on dainty cakes and ices. Bella smiled at her daughter, who waved excitedly and clutched at Nancy's arm.

She continued to gaze around the room, catching the eyes of many of the guests, smiling and nodding directly to each. They seemed to like her. How silly to have been afraid, Bella thought.

The end of her set came all too soon. Bella curtsied, overwhelmed by the thunderous applause and shouts of "Bravo!" and "Encore! Encore!"

Zach, of course, had prepared an encore for her to sing, should the audience ask for it. Yet, Bella was amazed that they should want it. Tears of joy blurred her vision. She raised her hands to quiet the audience.

"You are all so very kind," she said, her voice trembling with exhaustion and gratitude. "I am so glad you enjoyed the set, and, of course, the wonderful musicians in Smith's Cornet Band, who will continue to entertain you for the rest of the evening."

Turning to the band, Bella applauded the musicians. She could not have done so well without their help, and at this moment she loved them all. Every one of them had added at least a word of advice on one song or another.

The musicians beamed back at her and took their bows, as the audience joined her in applause. When she looked at Zach, he winked and pointed a finger at her. Although Bella smiled in return, she added a warning look that signaled her continuing ire over the use of the name Gale.

"Thank you all so much," Bella said, turning back to the audience, raising her hands for quiet as she had seen Zach do so many times. "For my last song tonight, I shall sing an old favorite of mine, a lovely ballad. It's not written on your dance cards, but the song is called 'In a Garden of Roses.' I hope you enjoy it."

To the gentle strains of John's violin, Bella began to sing the old melody. She sang it for Amanda. When her gaze connected with her daughter's, she felt totally at peace.

Oh Daniel, she thought, how I wish you were here to share this with me. And yet, if you were, I wouldn't be singing to this audience.

As her eyes roamed the room, she noticed a small movement at the back. There was Mr. Ruckler! Staring at her. Even from this distance, across this enormous expanse of floor, the hatred in his eyes burned bright enough for Bella to see.

She sang the last phrase of the song, her emotions in a swirl. Bella took a deep curtsy and a deeper breath to steady her exit off the stage.

Clutching the nearest chair, she was aware only of the

unceasing pounding in her chest. Panic flooded her senses, blocking out the sounds of the ballroom. Her knuckles whitened as she gripped the chair's gilded back. Ruckler! His eyes had conveyed a potent hatred. She steadied herself and fled the ballroom for the safety of her own room.

Seventeen

s Zach accompanied Bella on the last stanzas of her encore, he experienced a disconcerting mixture of emotions.

The showman in him was ecstatic. Bella was superb as a singer, just as he knew she'd be. Better in fact. She'd had the audience eating out of her hand with that impromptu bit in the beginning.

But the bandleader in him was peeved. Just what the hell did she think she was doing, taking over his job, telling the band when to start in on the next song? He didn't appreciate being totally upstaged.

As she took her final curtsy, Zach strode to the front of the stage, riding the wave of applause and excitement that Bella had generated. "That was Miss Bella Gale, the American Nightingale, who will be appearing with the Smith's Cornet Band from now on. Right now, we shall take a short intermission. So take some refreshment! Catch your breath. We shall return."

Zach looked around for Bella. He spied her nearby, bent over a chair, grasping her sides. Something must be wrong. He saw her run out of the room. His eyes roved over the room to where Nancy had been. Apparently, she had seen Bella's odd behavior, too, and with Amanda in tow, was heading for the far exit.

Concerned, Zach tried to make his way through a growing crowd of well-wishers to see if Bella was all right.

John ran to him and clasped his hand, thumping him on the back. "She was brilliant! Did you two work up that beginning?"

"She did that all by herself."

"Well, it worked. They loved it." He thumped Zach on the back again as the other musicians crowded round to add their congratulations.

Distracted, Zach broke free of them and headed for the far exit.

Before he reached it, the desk clerk was bearing down on him, with the scowling Ruckler close behind. "Mr. Smith. I'm Mr. Farris, assistant hotel manager. Mr. Kramer had business in town tonight. He put me in charge. We have to talk. Come out in the hall with me, sir?"

"Wonderful new singer!" twittered a lady in blue wearing a diamond tiara. "So very witty."

"Absolutely delightful!" said a portly man in a black frock coat. "Good show. Good show."

"This way," the desk clerk said, taking one of Zach's arms. Ruckler took the other. Both men were six foot tall, a few inches taller than Zach.

"Hey, get your hands off me," Zach growled. The two men ignored him, propelling him out the door and down the hall. But out of the corner of his eye, Zach saw John pick up his fiddle case and follow close behind. "What's your problem, Ruckler? Haven't you got enough to do pawing your maids?"

"What kind of joke do you think you're pulling?" Ruckler demanded.

"Mr. Ruckler tells me that this new singer used to work for us in the kitchen." The desk clerk released his hold on Zach's arm.

Zach shook off Ruckler's hold. "A pure waste of talent."

"Mr. Ruckler also tells me she was dismissed for insolence."

Zach narrowed his eyes, hot anger surging down to his hands, which he doubled into fists. "It was the other way around. Ruckler was the insolent one."

"He'll side with her, of course," Ruckler sneered.

"You bastard. You tried to force yourself on her. Locked her in the private dining room." Zach's voice crackled with mounting rage. "Is that standard procedure with all your new maids?"

Farris raised one eyebrow and glanced at Ruckler, who glared back, but said nothing.

"Sure, ask him about the beating he gave a maid for knocking a dish off the counter," Zach continued. "Ask him about the women he lets have the easy jobs for sexual favors."

Ruckler tensed his shoulders and raised his fists. "You're a fine one to talk! His boys have romanced half a dozen of my maids since he's been here."

"Jealous, Ruckler?" Zach raised his own fists. "Because my boys don't have to threaten them to get a kiss?"

"You'll have to fight me, too." John Halley immediately stepped up behind Zach, raising his violin case in a threatening gesture.

Farris snapped his fingers. "No need for fisticuffs."

Ruckler slowly lowered his hands to his side. John lowered his case.

"I'm far more concerned about the kind of signal we'll be sending to the other servants when they see this woman elevated to a higher status," Farris continued in a condescending tone. "We can't have dissension in the ranks."

Zach snorted. "If you're concerned about dissension, get a new head of staff. Your boss knows the whole story. And he's approved Miss Gale's contract. I suggest you wait until he returns to take it up with him. In the meantime, Bella stays." He turned on Ruckler. "And you! Mr. Kramer told me he warned you to stay away from Bella. I'm telling you, it had better be very far away from her!"

A patter of footsteps and excited voices approached the trio. "Ah, there he is!"

Zach turned to see the hotel owner, Charles L. Beach himself, flanked by Mrs. Cornelius Vanderbilt, wife of the millionaire transportation mogul, and another couple Zach didn't readily recognize.

Mr. Beach extended his hand to Zach. "Just came to congratulate you on your new singer, Mr. Smith. Reminds me of Jenny Lind, that dear woman who graced us with a visit before the war. Wonderful. Wonderful!" He pumped Zach's hand enthusiastically. "Where is the charming woman? I believe her mother and father, the Russell Bertram Gales, were frequent guests here. I had the utmost respect for her mother. Dear woman."

"Yes, but her father and all that horrible business!" Mrs. Vanderbilt exclaimed. "We wondered if she really was the daughter of the Silk King. She's weathered the scandal very nicely."

"Glad you enjoyed it, Mr. Beach," Zach answered. "I'm sure I can arrange to have the ladies meet Miss Gale."

"I should like to know if she will appear throughout the season," Mrs. Vanderbilt said.

"Ah, we were just discussing Miss Gale's engagement here at the Mountain House," Zach answered, turning to Farris.

"Yes, yes," Farris said quickly, smiling and bowing stiffly. "I, uh, expect Miss Gale will be here throughout the season."

Zach saw Ruckler's scowl deepen. The man had been overruled by the owner and the patrons. He'd backed down from Zach's fists. He would not dare to interfere again.

"Yes," Zach agreed. "We have a season's contract."

"R.H. Macy here," said the man at Mr. Beach's side. He gestured to the other woman. "My wife would like to meet this Nightingale person, too."

Zach glanced around. "I'm afraid Miss Gale has left the stage. She's probably very tired. But I shall be sure to convey your wishes and introduce you tomorrow."

"Yes!" cried Mrs. Macy. "Tell her to meet us for tea in the arbor."

"Wonderful idea," Mrs. Vanderbilt agreed. "You'll arrange it, Mr. Beach?"

"Of course," the owner replied. "Oh, Mr. Ruckler is here.

Head of servant staff. You'll take care of a special luncheon, won't you?"

"Very good, sir." Ruckler's face had gone quite red. "A special luncheon tomorrow." He bowed and turned to walk away, but not before shooting a murderous glance in Zach's direction.

≈

"And they all lived happily ever after."

Bella closed the book of fairy tales she had been reading to Amanda. She tucked the scalloped-edged sheet over her sleeping daughter, who had lost her struggle to stay awake. It was half past ten, far past Amanda's normal bedtime.

Bella was much calmer now, but whenever she thought of Ruckler's scowling glare, she felt a knot of fear form at her temples. A low knock on the door made her jump.

"Who is it?"

"It's Nancy! I'm back."

Bella unlocked the door and let Nancy in. She was holding a bottle of blackberry brandy and two small glasses.

"I think you need a drink after tonight," Nancy whispered, careful not to disturb Amanda's slumber. "I went back down to the ballroom. Zach said he would stop by with John after the band finishes up. He asked if you were alright."

"You didn't tell him about Ruckler, did you?"

"No. Of course not. But I do think he should know about it." Nancy poured two small measures of the brandy, offering one to Bella. "He saw you run off the stage."

"I don't want him to know." Bella sipped at the brandy. "It was foolish of me to panic just because he looked at me," she added, more to convince herself than to convince Nancy.

"I don't think so at all. That man is a nasty bit of business, I'd say. And the boys should know, in case he makes any further trouble."

"I'll tell him if he asks, but otherwise, he's got enough on his mind." Bella took another sip. The blackberry brandy warmed a little path down her throat.

"Well, Ruckler aside, everyone seemed pleased with your performance. People were buzzing about you down there. Zach said you did yourself proud."

Bella extinguished the bedside lamp. "I wish I could say the same about him."

"Why? I thought he was in fine form tonight," said Nancy, as the two women moved to the front of the room. "The whole band was better than butter." Nancy sat on the small divan, smoothing down her skirts.

"Musically, I'm sure they were." Bella sank into the armchair. "But I was hardly pleased that he introduced me as Miss Bella Gale."

Nancy pursed her lips. "I wondered about that. He didn't discuss it with you?"

"He didn't even mention the possibility. Miss, indeed. American Nightingale, indeed."

Nancy clapped her hands over her mouth to smother a wail of amusement. "So you really were angry at him. That was no play acting?"

"It certainly wasn't."

"You have to admit, though, that the name is a wonderful play on the Nightingale business. I mean, people do associate it with the Swedish Nightingale."

"The point is, I'm a properly married woman with a legitimate daughter. Not to mention the fact that the name Gale will stir up associations with my father's scandal and..." Bella sighed deeply. "I just wish he'd consulted me first."

A knock on the door startled both women. Bella froze for a moment, wondering whether it was Zach or Ruckler outside her door. Quickly, she rose and stood with her ear to the door. "Who is it?"

"It's John!"

Nancy's expression brightened at the sound of her husband's reedy voice. Bella opened the door.

John and Zach were arm-in-arm, wearing wide grins, their eyes crinkling with tipsy delight. Zach held an open bottle of champagne. John held two glasses in each hand.

"Celebration time!" Zach said, leaning toward Bella to give her a kiss.

She stepped nimbly out of his way and opened the door wider to let the pair inside. "Sshhh! Keep your voices down. Amanda's sleeping."

Zach's grin changed to one of dismay. "Sshhh!" he said into John's ear. The two tiptoed exaggeratedly into the room. "Hello, Nancy!"

"Sshhh!" John warned him. He tiptoed over to her and kissed his wife lightly on the cheek. "For a toast!" He held out the glasses. Nancy took two, raising them in front of Zach, who poured a shaky stream of bubbly into each.

Bella was disgusted. They were drunk already. She wasn't about to let him off the hook for tonight's mischief. Zach held out a glass to Bella.

"Here's to the most beautiful Nightingale in the land!" he cooed, his eyes shining, his lopsided grin dissolving into a frankly adoring, open-mouthed stare. "To Bella."

"Here, here!" John tipped back his head and drained his glass, as Nancy took a sip.

"How charming," Bella said. "Allow me to make a little toast of my own. To a man who knows how to take advantage of a woman's assets for his own benefit." She raised her glass high, then took a sip.

The two men exchanged glances, obviously confused.

"How clever of you not to mention that you'd be using my maiden name to your advantage. You just erased six years of marriage to Daniel! And what do I say about Amanda when you insist on calling me Miss Gale? People will think..." She was so angry she couldn't finish.

"Bella!" Zach wrinkled his brow in concentration. "What the blazes are you talking about?"

"American Nightingale. That's what I'm talking about. Miss

Bella Gale. That's what I'm talking about!" She was in his face in three quick strides. Her voice was low, but it crackled with anger. "That was no play acting. I was really angry. From now on, I'm Bella Smith. Or at least Bella Gale-Smith! Do you hear me? Or I'll never appear with your band. Never!"

Zach stared at her, his dark eyes registering bewilderment. But it was John who sprang up from his wife's side, swaying slightly from the effects of the champagne, to defend his friend.

"You say that after all he's done for you?"

Nancy pulled at his jacket with a soft, "John, there now," but her husband would not be silenced.

"You ran away after the performance, no doubt angry, like a peeved child. You left him there to deal with Ruckler and Farris by himself."

Bella's eyes widened at the names.

"Yes, he defended you," John continued. "They were ready to have him toss you out, threatening to get rid of the whole band. They didn't want some former kitchen maid who'd been sacked showing up in such glory."

"John, that's enough." Zach turned away, the bottle of champagne dangling from his hand.

"No, it's not enough." John took a step toward Bella. His voice was soft as ever, but there was an indignant righteousness that made it ring with authority. "He defended your honor, called Ruckler out about what he'd done to you. At the risk of a beating, I might add."

Bella looked at Zach, at his bowed head, his drooping stance as he faced the door. Her stomach tightened at the thought of Ruckler hurting him. She made a small involuntary sound in the back of her throat, her hand flying up to her lips to stop it.

"And that was before Charles Beach came up to him, with Mrs. Vanderbilt and the Macys in tow to congratulate him and you on a wonderful performance. They wanted to meet you, but you had run away."

A confusion of thoughts swirled in Bella's mind: guilt over the encounter between Ruckler and Zach; and alarm over the name of

Vanderbilt, whom her father had always despised. Mrs. Vanderbilt would surely relish the embarrassing story of the daughter of a prominent family come down in the world as a singer in a resort, even one so famous and respectable as the Catskill Mountain House.

"They've arranged for a luncheon in the arbor to meet you tomorrow, and you very well better show up," John finished in a severe tone of voice, "or I for one, shall never be friendly with you again."

Bella raised her head and stared at John. This man, who had always been a kind, sweet-natured gentleman to her and Amanda was obviously convinced that Bella was in the wrong.

"I understand what you are saying, John. I'm sorry, Zach. I'm sorry you had to deal with that horrible man. But you must understand how I felt. I'm a respectable widow with a child. And if these society women think I've never married, well... I don't want Amanda to suffer. And the Gale name..." She hesitated. "It once was well-respected. It's not my father's fault that it is now considered infamous."

Overcome with emotion, Bella took out her handkerchief, dabbed at her eyes, then blew her nose. Looking over at John, she added, "Never fear, John. I'll attend the luncheon tomorrow, swallow my pride, and allow Mrs. Vanderbilt to have her fun. And she will. But I warn you, it will be at our expense."

Eighteen

What should have been a night of celebration disintegrated into a night of strained emotions. John and Nancy headed for the door.

"You coming, partner?" John asked, pulling at Zach's sleeve.

"In a bit," Zach said. "I've got something to discuss with Bella." He watched them go, leaning against the wall by the open door, the bottle of champagne still dangling from his hand. When he turned back to Bella, she could see misery reflected in his dark eyes.

"Are you really that mad at me for using your name?"

"I was."

He frowned, then squatted down, fingering the neck of the bottle, deep in thought. "I'm sorry," he finally said. He was looking down at the floor. "I didn't mean to insult Daniel's memory or ruin your reputation. I just thought it sounded right. Miss Bella Gale, the American Nightingale. If you want, we can use Mrs. Bella Gale-Smith, but it just doesn't have the same ring to it."

"I would prefer it, thank you."

Zach looked up at her and shook his head slowly. "God, Bella, you were superb tonight." He grinned up at her. "You had fire in you! Your quick wit. Everything about you. Your beauty, your voice."

She said nothing.

"Aren't you feeling anything? Aren't you pleased at yourself?"

"No. No, I'm not pleased with myself."

He reached out and caught her hand, pulling her down on the floor with him. "Can't you let yourself be happy, even if it's just for a few hours on stage?" His voice was full of tenderness. "It hurts to see you so sad. So sad underneath."

"You know why I'm sad."

"I know." Zach dropped her hand. "I know."

They sat side by side in silence for a moment, each lost in a maze of thoughts.

"Why did you run away tonight?" Zach finally broke the silence. He looked deeply into her eyes and brushed a stray lock of hair from her forehead. "Why?"

"I saw Mr. Ruckler. He stared at me with such hatred, I just ran away. Like a, like a scared little girl. I'm not proud of myself. I shouldn't have panicked so."

"You don't have to be scared of him ever again. I put him in his place." He reached for her. Bella turned her head away. Zach dropped his hand and said nothing. He played with the half-empty bottle again, rolling it between the palms of his hands. "I'll bet Daniel always protected you."

"Yes. Yes, he did. Not that we ever had any real enemies. But yes, he tried to shelter us from the harsher side of the city. From poverty."

"Did he want to go off to war?"

Bella looked at him, startled at the question. "He thought the Union cause was just. I don't know what you mean."

"Did he burn with desire to sign up?" Zach sighed again, leaning his head back against the wall, letting his legs sprawl in front of him. "Did he think war was filled with glory?"

"He didn't want to leave us. He was drafted." Daniel's face rose before her, his eyes filled with pain of their parting at the train station. Bella had been holding Amanda, not yet two years old, in her arms. "We didn't have the three hundred dollars to pay for a deferment, for someone else to take his place. But even if we had, I know he would have gone anyway. He believed that free men had an obligation to protect their country."

"If I had had a wife like you and a little girl like her, I never would have gone to war!" Zach wiped a sleeve across his eyes.

She turned and saw that his cheeks were wet.

"My uncles burned for the war, for the glory of it. For saving their way of life, the ideals they held dear. I never could see the point."

Bella's heart swelled with sympathy. "Then why did you go?"

"I've asked myself that question a thousand times." Zach drew up his knees and rested his arms on them. "I was visiting Uncle Aaron. New Year's in '61. There was endless speculation about secession. Would Georgia go along with South Carolina, Mississippi, and Florida? Join the new Confederate States?" He took a long swig from the bottle of champagne. "My uncle was a senator. A few weeks later, he rides all night from the capital to tell us the day Georgia voted to join the Confederacy." Zach ran a hand through his hair, lost in memory.

"I can remember the energy in that room when he told us Georgia had seceded." Zach's voice took on a faraway quality. "Volatile as lightning. I remember my uncle said—you may be a Yankee boy from birth, but you're a Georgian in your heart. Said he'd understand if I chose against them, but if I did, I should go before I was arrested or lynched for a Union spy."

Zach took another gulp of champagne, then wiped his mouth across his sleeve. "What else could I do? He gave me my first cornet. Taught me about Mozart and Haydn. Said I should compose my grand symphony when my own father tried to destroy it!"

He choked back a sob and stared at her with anguish in his eyes. "How could I say no? How could I say that war was a waste of time and life? Hang the Confederacy! Hang the Union! I didn't care about either one. I only said yes because I loved him for being a real father to me."

Aghast, Bella tried to take in what he was saying. "You fought on the Confederate side?" Daniel had never mentioned it. Her father-in-law had never mentioned it. Perhaps they had not known. "My God. You're a Rebel?"

Zach looked deep into her eyes, as if he could see the past reflected in them.

"In the space of three years, three uncles and two cousins died. Thad that first year at Bull Run, victorious deaths for old Stonewall's glory! Macomb at the Battle of Shiloh the next spring. Uncle Horace at Port Royal Island against the monster Sherman. Uncle George, dying of dysentery in a Union prison. And Uncle Aaron with a bullet in his leg, fleeing Sherman's devils, watching them set fire to everything south of Atlanta."

He gripped her arm. She instinctively put her arm around his shoulders and drew him closer. He clung to her like a lost child.

"There, there," she murmured. "There, there."

Bella felt a swirl of confusion and compassion. A Rebel, she thought. He might have killed Daniel if they had met on the battlefield. Yet, how could he not help his uncles? His cousins? The people who believed in him. She smoothed his hair and murmured more soothing sounds. She felt his body stiffen, as he struggled to contain his emotions. Suddenly, she didn't care what side he had fought on.

"I've never told anyone," he whispered, pulling away from her. "I've never told how I felt or what I saw. That all the time I fought with them, I knew they would die. I kept expecting to be shot. To be cut down. But there I was, right up until Lee surrendered in April. God, was it only this year? Grant gave the orders to let all Confederates return home without harassment or imprisonment. He gave us food because we were starving. He showed us the kind of mercy my father preached about."

Zach slowly released his grip on Bella's shoulders and slumped back against the wall. Wearily, he took in a deep breath. She took his hand and held it gently in hers.

"What did you do?"

"I went to New York. Back to John and Nancy. I walked, I

hitched rides on wagons going North. I got lucky and found a schooner willing to take me on to New York harbor. Took me two weeks. That's when I found Daniel's letter."

"You never went back to your uncle's home?"

"I was there when it was burned to the ground. There was nothing left. A bunch of rubble and ashes in mounds where the house and the barns and the... Nothing left. Nobody left. It was all for nothing! In the end, my father was on the right and moral side. Slavery was wrong. The Confederacy was doomed from the start," he said bitterly, slamming his fist into his palm. "I see that now. They all died for nothing. And for the life of me, I can't shake this feeling that I should have died there, too!"

Bella gasped and caught his hands in hers. "Don't say that, Zach! President Lincoln said their deaths would unite us into one great nation."

He looked at her angrily. "That's not the point. Why them? Why not me?"

"Because I don't know...because you were meant to write your symphony." The thought popped out of Bella's mouth before she knew she had uttered the words.

He stared at her with a scornful, skeptical expression.

"You said your uncle nurtured your dreams of composing a symphony. Don't you see?" Bella gently stroked his tear-stained cheek. "The symphony wasn't destroyed. You weren't killed. It must be for that reason."

"Stupid reason," he whispered, searching the room as if he expected the answers to be written on the walls. When his gaze came back to rest on her, his eyes held a glimmer of light within their depths. "Who knows? Maybe you're right."

"Of course I'm right." Bella smiled. "Come on, now. It's late. You need to get some sleep." She rose and held out her hand to help him up. "We both do."

Once he was standing, he reached out and tenderly stroked her cheek. Whatever else he was thinking remained locked in his heart.

"Let me help you back to your room."

"No, I'm fine now. Really. I'm all right." Zach took a step toward the door. "Did anyone ever tell you that you are an angel?"

"No."

"Well, I'm telling you. You are an angel." He took her hand and raised it up to his lips. "Goodnight, Mrs. Bella Gale-Smith."

~

Zach stumbled down the steps and out through the back lawn yet managed to find his way back to his room. Billy was already snoring softly in his own bed when Zach unlocked the door. After pulling off his boots, he removed his jacket and vest and tumbled into bed without bothering to take off his shirt and pants. Immediately, he fell into a dream:

He sees himself walking along a country path. In the distance, he sees a footbridge suspended over a swiftly running creek. Amanda is there. She points down.

In the gurgling water, dozens of paper sailboats bob and swirl. A brass button floats by...a blue sleeve ripples in the current...a gray trouser leg...a sword...a body.

Zach reaches for Amanda's hand. She slips past him into the woods, her laughter a distant note that echoes against a turquoise sky. "Amanda!" He crashes through thickets and trees. Has a glimpse of scarlet-striped pinafore. "Amanda!" Her name dies on the wind. Smoke drifts in. Sulfuric fumes sting his eyes. He blinks twice. What place is this?

The low boom of a cannon answers his silent query. He looks down at his gray trousers and muddy boots. He looks up at the backs of Rebel soldiers, crouched behind crude barriers of brush and branches. He knows this place. He is afraid. He starts to shake with fear.

Amanda skips through his vision, slipping in and out of the men as they lay down a pattern of gunfire across the divide. He runs after her, heedless of bullets and smoke and the roar of the cannon.

"Amanda!" She dances across the wide expanse of meadow, headed straight for Union soldiers who train their weapons upon her.

Zach runs, surprised that no bullet can touch him. What is this power, this immunity that protects him? He runs to the beat of his pounding heart, reaches for the hem of the scarlet pinafore.

Amanda points in the distance. "Papa! Papa!" She runs to the figure at the edge of the woods.

Daniel stands by himself, the buttons on his blue Union uniform aglow under a single shaft of light. "Amanda! Amanda!" Daniel scoops the child into his arms. The army band surrounds him, playing "Dixie" and "Marching Through Georgia." That's wrong, Zach thinks. Sherman was later. He walks toward Daniel, offering his hand.

Daniel clasps it and smiles. "Good to see you, brother."

Zach's throat is dry. He stares at Daniel's hand in his. "I'm sorry you had to die."

"Am I dead?" Daniel's smile fades. He puts Amanda down. "And you, too?"

"No," Zach tells him. "Only you."

"Why me?" Daniel cries out, his face contorting with anger and bewilderment. "I have a wife. I have a daughter. Why me?"

Amanda slides down from Daniel's grasp. He turns his back on Zach and walks away. The band plays taps. Amanda puts her arms up to Zach. He kneels down. She pats Zach's cheek. Her voice gurgles like the bubbling brook. "Will you buy me a cottage? With pink flowers and pink sugar cakes?"

Zach blinks back his tears, and the child dissolves. He is still kneeling on the ground, but cradling Uncle Aaron in his arms. "You're a true son of the South," the old man says. "My true son." Zach smooths the old man's brow, damp with fear and streaked with blood. "Why did you die, instead of me?" The old man wheezes and rasps out garbled sounds. "Tell me why?" Uncle Aaron dies in his arms. "Tell me why?" Zach pleads with the darkened sky. "Tell me why! Damn it to hell, someone tell me why!"

Thunder answers his cry. A bolt of lightning strikes the ground, knocking Zach flat on his back. His heart is beating hard. His

breath comes in short, ragged puffs. His father's face peers over the
thundercloud. His words reverberate within its sound, "I saved it for
you all those years."

Zach fought to wake up, rising through the depths of sleep into
growing consciousness. It took a moment to clear the last vestiges
of the disturbing dream from his head.

The soft ticking of the mantle clock helped him fix his senses
in the present. He lay there for a long while, listening to the sound
of Billy's snoring. Then he rose and pulled on his boots before
unlocking the door.

Outside, the night sky was crowded with stars. The moon was
edging toward the horizon. A faint breeze rustled the trees. An
empty swing suspended from the oak tree creaked, swaying
to-and-fro.

Zach looked up at the stars. "Why?" he whispered. An odd
notion came to him. He felt as if he were on a vast stage, waiting
for the footlights to shine. Standing motionless for many minutes,
Zach strained to hear the shifting melodies of the sighing winds.

Suddenly, he heard the refrain of the fourth movement of his
symphony, like a gift from the heavens. The refrain that his father
had interrupted. The refrain that he had never been able to recreate. The music swelled inside his head as he hurried back across the
lawn to the entrance of the servants' quarters.

Once inside his own room, he fumbled to light the oil lamp by
his bed. Its glow spread across the small desk, disturbing the sleep
of Billy Parisher in the far bed. The drummer groaned, then
turned over and resumed his snoring.

Sliding open the drawer, Zach snatched a sheaf of music paper.
He dipped his pen in the inkwell and furiously jotted down the
notes in his head. Consumed by the music, he wrote and wrote
until the section was finished.

Blinking, he looked up. It was dawn. He rubbed his eyes and
glanced down at the paper again, afraid this, too, had been just a
dream.

But it was there, every note, every stanza, just as he had heard it in his head. He clutched the papers in his fist. Was this why he had been spared, as Bella said? How could that atone for so many deaths? For so much carnage?

Whether it did or didn't, what it came down to was this: his life was the one that had been spared. It was up to him to ensure that it wasn't wasted.

Nineteen

The next morning, Bella took Amanda to breakfast. Since she didn't expect that any of the band would be up for hours yet, she asked to be seated at one of the smaller tables that lined the west bank of windows. As they sat waiting for their breakfasts, Amanda suddenly jumped up from the table.

"Amanda!" Bella scraped her chair back and ran after her. "Where are you going?" She caught up with her daughter as Amanda threw her arms around a little girl.

"Oh, Sissy! Mama! Mama! Can Sissy have breakfast at our table? Oh, please, oh please?"

"Well, certainly. That's if they want to, dear. They may have other plans."

"Come to my table. Come on!" Amanda cried, and the two little girls skipped off hand in hand.

Bella looked up into the face of a tall, blond, well-dressed gentleman. His hair was slicked back and parted in the middle. His moustache was close cropped.

"Mrs. Smith, I imagine? Or is it Miss Gale? I'm afraid I'm a bit confused."

"Yes, I'm sorry. It's Mrs. Smith. Gale is just a stage name."

"Charmed, Ma'am. I'm Sissy's Uncle, Robert Kane. At your service." He bowed stiffly, then looked at her again.

"We were just about to have breakfast, Mr. Kane. I think the girls have already decreed that we share a table."

"Yes. I think they have." He gestured for her to lead the way. When they arrived at the table, the two girls were already splitting a stack of buttermilk pancakes with blueberries and syrup. Bella's poached egg was waiting by her place. Mr. Kane pulled out her chair.

"This is rather embarrassing," Bella said. "I'm afraid it may take a while to get your breakfast. But at least, let me pour you some coffee. And there is plenty of toast and jam to start."

"That's very kind of you," Kane said.

Bella motioned to the waiter, who came and took Mr. Kane's order. "Thank you, Charles," Bella said, recognizing the elderly head waiter who had been so nice to her on her first breakfast in the staff kitchen. It seemed ages ago, although it was only a month. "How is Anna? And Mrs. Quinn?"

"Oh, fine, my dear."

"Is Mr. Ruckler in a better mood these days?"

"A touch, madam. A touch." Charles' eyes twinkled. "I'll tell the kitchen to hurry with this order."

"You seem to know everyone here," Mr. Kane said. "Do you come every season?"

"I did when I was young. Amanda's age. But I haven't been here in many years." Bella buttered a slice of toast. "And you, Mr. Kane?"

"This is my first time. I usually have so much business to take care of. But since Sissy's parents died last year, I've tried to take some time off here and there, and take her places. She'll be staying on with her governess, and I'll be coming up every weekend or so."

"She's lucky to have such a devoted uncle." She passed him a plate with slices of buttered toast.

"Thank you. I heard you sing last night. You have quite the voice. And you're quite amusing. Is the band leader your husband?"

"No. My brother-in-law. My husband died..." Bella's voice caught in her throat.

"My condolences. In the war?"

"No. He was in the Union Army. No, it was a streetcar accident. A few months ago. It's hard to believe. And my brother-in-law was good enough to find me a job here."

"Had you sung with him all along?"

"No. Last night was my first night in front of an audience."

"That's hard for me to believe. You seem as if you had been doing that for years."

"I'll take that as a compliment."

He raised his coffee cup to her. "It was meant as one."

Charles returned with Mr. Kane's breakfast and a second stack of pancakes and blueberries for the girls. As he ate, Kane spoke mostly of his various business enterprises, which seemed to take him all over the Eastern seaboard.

"You are not from New York, sir?" His name was not at all familiar to her from any of the old New York families.

"How did you guess, Mrs. Smith? I moved here from Ohio eight years ago, as a pitchman for the railroads."

"Really? What is a pitchman?"

"Someone who is paid by the railroad to get people back East all fired up about moving West."

"I see. Did you have many takers?"

"Thousands."

"Really? Why did you stop?"

"I found far more lucrative opportunities in New York. Especially during the war. Many opportunities to find things that other people found hard to come by."

"Did you serve in the war?"

Mr. Kane's eyes narrowed and his expression became guarded. "Ah, well. I was able to purchase a deferment."

"I see," Bella replied, suddenly feeling less than friendly to this man.

"I can see you disapprove," Kane said.

"To be honest, yes, I do. My husband felt that too many able-bodied men bought their way out of service to their country. He felt that was unfair to the working-class and poor immigrants who could not afford the sum of three hundred dollars. He said he didn't blame the Irish mob who rioted against the draft on that terrible night in New York City. He blamed the rich who passed their responsibility onto others."

Mr. Kane thoughtfully chewed the last morsels of his fried egg and toast. "Not every man should be expected to make the same contribution to the war effort, my dear Mrs. Smith. In my case, I would have made a very poor soldier for General Grant. I have no skill with a gun. However, I feel I did make an important contribution to the war effort. I was able to procure many items for the Union Army and deliver them to where they were needed. Guns, munitions, food, blankets."

Bella considered this. "But you might have done that anyway, as an Army officer in the quartermaster division."

"Talk to any soldier. They'll tell you the quartermasters have been notoriously inept at delivering supplies ever since the days of General Zachary Taylor and the Mexican War." Kane looked at Bella with a cool expression.

"Perhaps that's true," Bella conceded. His argument seemed persuasive enough, but somehow she felt he was too calculating about it all. "Did you make any profit on those transactions with the Union Army?"

"A little." Kane smiled wryly and wiped his mouth on his linen napkin. "That's not a sin in a country that prides itself on free enterprise. It's one of the freedoms your husband fought for, is it not?"

"Yes, I suppose it is," Bella said, feeling as if she had just been checkmated by a rather foxy opponent.

"Then perhaps you have judged me too harshly, Mrs. Smith." Kane peered at her expectantly, as if he was trying to make a rude little girl see the error of her ways.

"If I have, Mr. Kane, I do apologize. The war's end is still so recent."

"Apology accepted, Mrs. Smith." Kane pulled out his pocket watch. "As lovely as our tête-à-tête has been, I'm afraid I must go. I have an appointment."

"Working? Even on holiday?" Bella asked.

"Yes, actually. I do some business here. We supply many of the bedding and linens to the hotel, as I believe your father's firm once did." Kane stood up. "Come along, Sissy. I'm afraid we must leave."

The girls looked up with woeful expressions on their sticky faces.

"Why don't you allow Sissy to stay?" Bella said. "I'm not busy until lunchtime. Would your business be completed by then?"

"It would," Mr. Kane said with a stiff bow. "I'd be pleased to have the opportunity to see you again, Mrs. Smith. Would you have dinner with me tonight?"

"I'm afraid I can't tonight. I have a prior engagement."

"Then next Saturday for lunch."

"I'll have to check my engagements," she insisted.

"Do. I'm determined to dine with you again, Mrs. Smith." He gave Sissy a pat on the head before he left.

Bella watched him go, wondering if he realized how much his words had distressed her. He had a knack for twisting the truth. She wondered what his "contribution" to the Union Army had really been.

Bella looked around and caught Charles' eye. He came over at once. "Is there any more coffee, Charles? I'm afraid Mr. Kane finished the pot."

"Certainly, Mrs. Smith." He quickly returned with a silver coffee server and poured her a cup. "I didn't want to say anything in front of the gentleman there, but I overheard Mr. Ruckler talking with Mr. Farris about making some trouble for the band-leader. I fear they are hatching some nefarious plot. I wish I knew more. But I have my ears to the ground."

Bella was stunned, both at the news and at Charles' kindness in conveying it. "Thank you for the warning. Please, don't get yourself in trouble on my account."

"It would be a pleasure, Mrs. Smith." His broad face beamed. "Ever since we saw how courageous you were that day, we've all banded together whenever he's started in on any one of us. And when Michelmas said he saw you rehearsing with the band, why, it just rallied us right around the flag, so to speak."

He looked around. Then he lowered his voice further. "Of course, there's some here that don't stand with us. But they are in the minority, Mrs. Smith. They are in the minority."

∼

"Where can Zach be?" Bella asked Nancy. It was a quarter of twelve. Nancy had met Bella in the front parlor, armed with magazines, books and paper dolls for Amanda. "I don't want to face those women alone. You don't know how scathing Mrs. Vanderbilt can be, even when she's acting perfectly pleasant."

"John went to fetch him. He can't have forgotten," Nancy said.

"Oh, never mind. I'd best get it over with." She was wearing one of her new tea gowns, the yellow one with scattered roses and a high white lace collar. She straightened her bonnet and pinched her cheeks to give them color.

"Wish me luck." Bella held her head high. She swept through the front doors and across the lawn to the arbor where an elaborate luncheon was being set out on a white linen-covered table under a spreading oak tree.

As she approached, a group of four were already taking their seats. She recognized the owner, Mr. Charles Beach, impeccably dressed as usual in a dapper frock coat and emerald waistcoat. The elderly Mrs. Vanderbilt was slender and elegant, dressed in a rose silk taffeta gown cut in the newest princess style from Paris. She wore a cluster of tiny white roses on her bonnet, and a diamond pendant as large as an egg around her neck.

Bella assumed the portly gentleman and his plump companion had to be the department store mogul and his wife. The woman was dressed in a high-waisted, blue-striped gown with three rows of bows, topped by a perfectly hideous straw bonnet trimmed with blue feathers. With one last glance around the yard for Zach,

Bella squared her shoulders and marched over, smiling as brightly as she could manage.

"Why, here she is, our dear little nightingale!" Mrs. Vanderbilt, voice dripping honey, turned to Mrs. Macy. "Isn't she a beauty?"

The men rose. Bella nodded to them. But she acknowledged the Commodore's wife first. "Mrs. Vanderbilt." Bella nodded politely and extended her hand to the elderly woman. "How nice to see you again." Underneath all the finery and jewelry, the elderly Mrs. Vanderbilt had always struck Bella as a lonely, nervous woman, overshadowed by her powerful husband.

Mrs. Vanderbilt extended her own for a fleeting second, just grazing Bella's fingertips. "So unusual to see the daughter of a prominent businessman venturing onto the, well, musical stage, so to speak. One wonders whether you are following in the footsteps of that unfortunate young woman, Clara Louise Kellogg."

The middle-aged woman beside her tittered and reached over to tap her husband's knee. "Remember her? The little society girl who went and sang that scandalous opera. What was it?"

"Faust, my dear. Dreadfully improper," Mrs. Vanderbilt answered. "Thank goodness my own daughters and granddaughters have more sense. Still, it's a different world than when I was young. One wonders what your dear mother would have thought of it, Miss Gale. Or is it Mrs., now? I was told you have a daughter."

Bella bit her lip to keep her from saying something she'd later regret. Instead, she looked squarely at Mrs. Vanderbilt and mustered every bit of dignity she could before responding.

"It's Mrs. Daniel Joshua Smith. My dear, sweet, late husband was in the Union army. And now I am forced to make my way in the world and support my daughter. I'm only using my maiden name because the band leader likes the pun that it makes of the word Nightingale."

Bella was pleased to see a brief expression of sympathy on Mrs. Vanderbilt's face. She turned toward the other strangers in the group. "I'm sorry, we haven't been introduced."

"So sorry, my fault," Mr. Beach said. "This is Mr. Rowland

Hussy Macy. He owns that fabulous five-story establishment in Manhattan."

Bella gave him a dazzling smile and extended her hand. "Ah, the famous Mr. Macy. What a pleasure to meet the man behind New York's most prestigious store." She didn't add that she had never been in the store and couldn't afford to shop there.

The formidable man took her gloved hand in his and kissed it. "Delighted." He patted her hand. "Enjoyed last night very much. Your voice is quite lovely. So sorry about your late husband. You do him proud."

"Thank you, sir. You are most kind."

"Rowland!"

"Ah," Mr. Macy dropped Bella's hand. "Yes, uhmmm, allow me to introduce my wife, Mrs. Macy. Louisa."

"Charmed." Bella held her hand out to Macy's wife. The woman nodded, and following Mrs. Vanderbilt's lead, barely grazed Bella's fingertips in the barest of formal acknowledgement. So, Bella thought, these women were not in the least bit willing to accept her on their terms. As she had feared, she was to be the butt of their private joke.

"Please, sit down, Miss Gale." Mr. Beach motioned to an empty chair. "Some tea, or would you care for some lemonade?"

"Tea, thank you." Bella sat down. She accepted a cup of steaming tea from a frock-coated waiter who served the party. She recognized him from working in the kitchen; one of Ruckler's favorites. The man raised a disdainful eyebrow at her, completing her discomfort. Where was Zach, anyway? He got her into this mess. She hoped he would come to rescue her soon.

Mr. Beach steered the conversation away from Bella, suggesting sights for the party to see and forthcoming amusements at the Mountain House. Then talk turned to the racing season and the relative merits of the Goshen and Saratoga racing courses.

Out of the corner of her eye, Bella saw Zach hurry toward the party. She breathed a sigh of relief as he bowed to the ladies and apologized for being late.

Mrs. Vanderbilt positively gushed over Zach, especially when he took her gloved hand and kissed it in the European fashion. "So charming. Oh, Mr. Smith, I do adore your little band and your little nightingale."

"Yes, we enjoyed your music so much. Such lovely waltzes." Mrs. Macy said, fluttering her hand out in hopes of a similar treatment. When Zach obliged her, she almost swooned.

"You must come and play at one of my granddaughter's coming out parties," Mrs. Vanderbilt said. "And do bring the dear American Nightingale. Miss Gale, we'll invite a number of families that you'd remember. The Jamisons, The Rowlands, the Berrys— weren't you engaged to the youngest Berry boy? It will be such a lark."

"Oh, I'm sure it will." Bella eyed Zach and gave him a dour smile. "We so look forward to it, don't we, Mr. Smith?"

Twenty

By the afternoon tea dance, Bella's nerves were still on edge over the disastrous luncheon.

Her stomach did their familiar series of flip-flops. She wiped her palms on her handkerchief and watched Zach from the side of the stage. Why wasn't he ever nervous in front of an audience? Happy as a lark, cool as a cucumber, that was Zach before each show. An impromptu audience under the oak trees on the lawn invariably brought a gleam to his eye. He was made for this, Bella thought, fighting against her own nerves. I am not.

She kept adjusting the lace fichu, trying to strike a balance between baring her shoulders and covering her décolletage as much as possible. Reaching in her reticule, she fished for the scrap of paper with the light banter Zach had written out for her. Where was it? She felt around, almost turning the little purse inside out. Oh, no! It had disappeared. She tried to recall the gist of it, but her mind was a blank. She couldn't remember one word of it, although, truth to be told, the witticisms hadn't struck her as particularly humorous to begin with.

From the stage, Zach caught her eye. "Ladies and gentlemen, Smith's Cornet Band presents their one, their only American Nightingale, Miss Bella Gale!"

Swallowing her panic, Bella still felt a little spark of anger. He was still using her maiden name, not Bella Gale-Smith, as he has promised! Whatever happened from here on was all Zach's fault, she thought, coaxing the sparks into a glow of indignation that might carry her across the stage.

Zach looked expectant, waiting for her to deliver her first line as rehearsed.

She stopped several feet from him, unsure of what to do. Then, she turned toward the audience and shrugged her shoulders. Might as well confess.

"I was supposed to say something witty here." She pointed to Zach. "The band leader wrote it down for me so I wouldn't forget." She leaned forward and put her hand up to her mouth, as if she were telling the audience a secret. "Don't tell the bandleader, but I lost the paper he wrote it on."

There were a few titters in the audience, and one man in a blue frock coat guffawed and slapped his knee.

"Look at this man," Bella said, her confidence rising a notch. "He thinks I'm one of those addle-headed females." She hurried across the stage to face the man, who was nodding in agreement. "Isn't that right, sir? Well, don't tell the bandleader, but after reading what he considered witty, I lost the paper on purpose!"

A wave of laughter swelled. Bella laughed, too, at the response. Thank goodness, she had averted disaster. Moreover, they liked her. Or rather, they liked the Nightingale. Somehow, she had left her old shyness behind when she stepped onto the stage. She felt like a different person, confident and slightly daring, with all her nervousness vanished.

She turned to Zach, not surprised to see a grin dancing on the corners of his mouth. At this distance, she couldn't see his eyes, yet she knew they sparkled with mischief, maybe even a hint of anger. As soon as the laughter died down, he lifted his horn to his lips and blew a sharp fanfare. When the audience turned *en masse* to look at him, he lowered his horn and crooked his finger at Bella in a reprise of the gesture he had used at her debut.

"Come here," he said, wagging his finger at her. "Come heeeere!" he sang.

"Oh, nooo-oooh!" she sang back.

He took a step closer. "Then I'll come the-eeere!"

The audience giggled as Zach sidled closer to Bella. Big Harry marked each sidestep with a playful moan of his bassoon. She held her breath, unsure of what Zach's next move would be, praying he wouldn't totally embarrass her for the impudent remarks.

When Zach was but a foot from her, he grinned and wagged his finger at her as if chastising a naughty child. Then he put his hand up to his mouth, pretending she couldn't hear. "Don't tell the singer, but just wait 'til I get her after the show!"

The audience roared with delight to see the tables turned. Before their laughter had died away, Zach signaled the band, and Bella gratefully launched into a comic song "Folks That Put on Airs."

As she sang the words, alternating stanzas with Zach, it occurred to her that for the first time since she had come to the Mountain House, she was actually enjoying her work. Under the dazzling glow of the giant crystal chandelier, the dancers were a swirl of color and movement. Bella was glad to lose herself for an hour in the music.

When her set was over, she hurried to the refreshment table, eager for some cooling lemonade for her parched throat.

"Allow me," said a young gentleman. He reached for the ladle and filled one of the cut-crystal punch glasses for her. "Such a beautiful woman shouldn't have to pour herself."

"Thank you so much, sir." Bella took the glass and quickly sidestepped out of reach before the young man could trap her at the table. She nodded politely at a few women who nodded in her direction.

"Miss Gale!" cried a young man that Bella recognized as a painter she had been introduced to recently. He stopped her. "Do you have a dance card? May I please have a waltz with you?"

"So sorry! I can't today." She gave him an apologetic smile. "Next time!" And she deftly slipped away.

"Excuse me, Miss Gale, I'd like to talk to you."

Bella turned around, recognizing the older man in the blue suit who had laughed and slapped his knee at her opening joke. "Hello." She extended her hand. "I hope you enjoyed the songs as much as you did the jokes."

He smiled with a wide, toothy grin. "I did indeed. Which is why I'd like to talk to you for a moment." He ushered her into a corner apart from the crowd, shielding her from well-wishers with the bulk of his body. "Now then, Miss American Nightingale. Allow me to introduce myself. Frederick J. Feniwinkle, impresario extraordinaire. I book acts for a touring company of theatrical and musical events, traveling from here to St. Louis and touring in Europe. Only the best places book our talent. And I am here to offer you a contract."

Bella stared at the man, aware that her mouth was hanging open and no words were coming forth.

"Ah, I have that effect on most young artists," Feniwinkle continued, smoothing his bushy whiskers with pride. "Do you have a contract with the Smith Cornet Band?"

"I... "She stopped, realizing that she didn't know one thing about the business side of the band. "I might. I mean... Yes."

"Ah, not to worry. Such talented singers should scarcely worry their pretty heads about business."

"Perhaps you could speak to Zach Smith, the band leader. You'd want to book the whole band, wouldn't you?"

"Not necessarily. Oh, they're good, but I have a much bigger band lined up, a 25-piece orchestra looking for just the right singer. Now, I've found her. Never heard better."

"Well, thank you," Bella said. "I'm sorry, but I hardly know what to say. I'm really very new to this."

He drew a little closer to her, smiling wider now, lowering his voice as if they were conspiring together. "To tell the truth, I think you're better than this band gives you credit. I know Zach Smith from way back. He likes the spotlight for himself. He's not a bad character, mind you. And quite a generous one, with the ladies and his musicians," he added hastily, as Bella opened her mouth to protest. "Still, he does only give you a few songs to shine in. But shine you do! And your comic wit, it's wonderful. I could make you a star, just like Jenny Lind. Take you to the continent. You could sing for the crowned heads of Europe."

Bella stared at the pompous Feniwinkle, overcome by an urge to laugh. Surely, he was full of himself and a flatterer as well. His offer seemed fantastical to her; especially the bit about singing in front of the crowned heads of Europe. "Well, that's very kind of you, Mr. Feniwinkle. I'm perfectly happy right here."

"Don't dismiss me out of hand, Miss Gale."

"I promise, I shall give your offer the proper amount of thought it deserves."

"Do! Do! Delighted to have talked with you. My card." He produced a gold-edged card with the flick of his wrist. "Room number two-thirty-five. I shall be staying on for a bit. My pleasure, Miss Gale." He bowed and then backed away from her. A surge of young men moved in quickly to surround her, as if Feniwinkle had been a dam keeping the tide of male admirers at bay.

What a perfectly awful notion, Bella thought to herself as she tucked Feniwinkle's card into her reticule. As if she would want to traipse around the country with a bunch of strange musicians! Hardly the life she had in mind for Amanda. She laughed at the absurdity and began to work her way through the crowd.

Zach scowled as he eyed the small knot of young dandies who hovered around Bella like a swarm of pesky bees, buzzing with small talk and flattery. She seemed to be enjoying the attention, bestowing her bright smile and charming laughter on the men. Reluctantly, he turned back to the society matron who was crowing in his ear.

"You must have Miss Gale come to dinner with us tonight, Mr. Smith. I simply must have her in our party. She is divine!" The elderly woman dressed in a forest green gown clasped his hand to her sagging bosom. With delicacy, Zach wriggled out of her grasp.

"I'm so sorry, Mrs. Dorchester. We'll be at the Van

Houghton's table tonight." Out of the corner of his eye, he saw Bella blush and accept a flower from the noted painter, David Chevalier.

"Then tomorrow night, Mr. Smith," the older woman insisted, reaching once again for Zach's hand. "I insist."

"Yes, yes, tomorrow." Zach looked down into the over-eager face of the wealthy Philadelphia dowager and smiled. "I'll just go now and tell Miss Gale." He bowed and edged his way out. "Till then."

He was waylaid by John. "Well, Zach. How does it feel to have a popular new singer with the band?"

Zach scowled. "She's popular, all right. Too popular. And getting a little too unpredictable to boot."

John laughed and clapped him on the shoulder. "Can't ever be too popular. Or so you've always told me!"

"I might have been wrong." Zach watched one of the hovering admirers lean close to Bella and whisper something in her ear. Something that caused her to blush again. "Think we ought to rescue Bella from the hordes?"

John tilted his head to one side, giving his friend a long, appraising stare. "If I didn't know you better, I'd say you were jealous."

"That would be breaking my cardinal rule," Zach replied dryly. "Just protecting the band's assets from the wolves is all."

Bella looked up and caught Zach's eye with a smile of relief. Zach saw her lips move and heard the collective groan from the admirers' circle as she made her way through the throng, accepting another rose to add to her burgeoning bouquet.

Zach held out his hand and plucked her from the circle, tucking her hand protectively under his arm. The scent of her perfume and the warmth of the afternoon stirred up his amorous feelings, which were stronger than ever after the tender sympathy she had shown him last night. But he knew that on her part it had been nothing more than her generous and sympathetic nature in responding to a friend's grief.

"Thank goodness you came," Bella said as they walked toward

the ballroom's exit. "I thought I'd never get away. They were sweet to give me flowers, though. I think the audience really likes me."

Zach laughed at her innocence and resisted the urge to pull her closer. "Do you doubt it?" Then in a sterner tone of voice, he asked, "Did you really forget the paper with the notations we wrote down?"

"I really did. I'm sorry. It's as if I turn into someone totally different when I step out onto that stage."

"Can't say I like being overshadowed by you. But you've got good instincts. Just don't start acting like a prima donna. Or telling me how to run the band."

"That's the last thing I would do." She hugged his arm to her as they squeezed through the doorway and out into the hall. "I felt totally at ease today. I have you to thank for that. You're a wonderful teacher."

Zach changed the subject, secretly pleased by her compliment. "What was Amanda up to today?"

"Out with Nancy, her new friend Sissy and her governess. She adores that child. The child's uncle, however, is a strange sort of man. He rather unnerved me. He asked me to dinner next week. In fact, I've had a dozen invitations to dinner tonight."

"I hope you turned them all down."

"I certainly did."

"Good. We're dining at the Van Houghton's table. And tomorrow night with Mrs. Dorchester's party."

Bella's smile faded, and she dropped his arm.

"What's wrong?" Zach asked.

"I hope it won't be another session like today's luncheon. Are they going to invite us to their table just to snub us? Because honestly, Zach!"

"I'm sorry about that, Bella," Zach said. "They're not all like Mrs. Vanderbilt. I didn't realize she invited you solely to humiliate you. That won't happen again, I promise."

Bella said nothing, but she didn't believe him.

"Look, you spent your childhood here," Zach continued. "You

know that it's a very peculiar little community. Old money rubs shoulders with new money, even when they would never do that back home."

"That's true," Bella conceded.

"Most of the women are up here by themselves, waiting until their husbands get around to joining them on the weekends. They're bored. They're looking for any novelty that comes their way. When Jenny Lind came here, lady singers became respectable. The old Mrs. Dorchester of Philadelphia isn't going to invite us to dinner at her mansion, any more than the young Mrs. Van Houghton and her set would have us back to her townhouse in Manhattan. But they're both desperate to have us at their tables, just to spice things up."

Bella sighed. "And just what are they going to expect me to do? Serenade them?"

"I suspect," Zach said with a chuckle, "they're hoping you'll regale them with tales of your wild life on the stage."

"Well!" She laughed. "Aren't they going to be disappointed!"

"Oh, if you reminisce with Mrs. Dorchester about the old days at the Mountain House, I think she'll be happy. As for Mrs. Van Houghton, she'll do all the talking anyway."

Bella sighed again. "I was hoping for a quiet evening."

"You're the most exciting thing here at the moment. Have to take advantage of it while it lasts."

They strolled outside, heading toward the front lawn and the rock ledge.

"I had a rival offer today," Bella said, inhaling the aroma of her flowers.

Zach stopped short. "What do you mean?"

"Don't look like that. It wasn't a serious one, I'm sure." Bella reached into her reticule for the little card. "Here, do you know this man? He claimed to know you."

Zach looked at the card. "Ah, Feniwinkle. I saw him today ogling you. I figured he'd try and steal you away."

"I thought he wanted to book the entire band," Bella said, taking the card back from him.

"Let me guess. He wants to book you on one of his tours and make you a star. Have you sing for the crowned heads of Europe."

"I guess he tells that to all the new singers."

"Not all. Just the good ones." Zach sat down in one of the wooden chairs that faced the view. "So, do you?"

Bella settled in a chair next to him. "Do I what?"

"Want to go on tour with him? After you finish out my contract, of course."

"Why would I want to do that?"

"Because he could make you a star." He tipped his hat over his eyes to shade them from the sun. "There are bands that are bigger and better known than mine."

Bella laughed. "I'm surprised to hear you admit it."

"I'm not a fool, Bella. Especially when it comes to business. You're good. You're special. And you certainly deserve to take your singing as far as it will take you. Make some money for you and Amanda. Even sing before the crowned heads."

"Have you?"

"Have I what?"

"Sung before the crowned heads?"

"Once or twice," he said, his mouth slowly spreading into a bemused smile. "They're not all that exciting. For one thing, they don't applaud very loudly. They clap like this." He patted his fingers lightly against his palm.

"Do you ever stop joking?"

"I'm not joking." Zach sat up and looked at her. His expression was serious. "I'm telling you; you're going to get many offers. I'm sure of it. I wouldn't have put you in the band if you didn't have something special about you. And I won't blame you for taking other offers. It's a big world out there. There are rich opportunities, and who am I to hold you back?"

Bella sat back, unsure of what to say. Unsure of what she was feeling. Did he want her to go? To sing with other bands? "Is that what you think I should do?"

"I wouldn't blame you if you did." He settled back into the chair and pulled his hat down over his eyes.

Bella sat very still, not sure of why she felt as if she were going to cry. "I don't think it would be a very good life for Amanda," she said at last. "I don't think I'd like to leave her with strangers."

Zach said nothing.

"What will you and John and the others do after this?"

"End of September and October, we're in Boston and Philadelphia. In November and December, we have the holiday season in New York City. Then in the spring, we're in Washington and Maryland. Then, back here. In the winter, everyone heads for home, wherever home happens to be."

"Oh."

"I'd be more than happy to keep you on with the band, Bella. As long as you'd like. But we're moving around, too. And as you say, it's not a very good life for Amanda."

Bella swallowed. Tears sprang to her eyes. "But with you, I'd always have..." Her voice quavered. She wiped away a tear. "I mean, Amanda would be with people she loves."

Zach lifted his hat. "Bella, are you crying?"

"Yes!" Bella said, her voice breaking. She fumbled for a handkerchief. "And I don't know why."

He reached for her hand. "What's wrong?"

"Because I hadn't thought about what would happen after all this ends." She sniffed back the tears. "Oh, everything is happening too fast! I don't want to be with strangers. I don't want Amanda to be with strangers." The words caught at the back of her throat. "I don't want to be alone again."

"No one is saying you have to." Zach gripped her hand even tighter. "No one is saying you have to go with Feniwinkle. Or anybody."

She wiped her eyes with her handkerchief. "Wouldn't you miss Amanda?"

Zach nodded. "I would. Very much. I'd miss you, Bella."

She looked up at Zach, a smile brightening her tear-streaked face. "I'd miss you, too. You and John and Nancy. Even the boys. I'd miss you all."

Zach's expression seemed to falter for a moment. "We'd all

miss you." He stood up. "But nobody's missing anybody for at least two more months, so let's not worry about that. And right now, I have an appointment I completely forgot about. I'll see you later, Bella. Don't forget, dinner with the Van Houghtons tonight. You can bring Amanda if you like. They have a little boy."

Zach walked away from Bella as quickly as he could. He didn't have an appointment at all. He just didn't trust himself alone with her anymore.

He thought she was going to say that she would miss him. Him alone. He hoped she would say that she had some feelings for him. But she didn't. She said she would miss all of them. Him and John and Nancy and the boys. Not him alone.

Why the hell did he have to fall in love with his brother's wife? If he was going to break his cardinal rule and fall in love with anybody, why with her, of all women? The knowledge burned a searing path down his throat as potent as any whiskey.

He knew Bella would not lightly turn to another man. It might be months, hell, years before she would allow herself to fall in love again.

And even if she did, she certainly wasn't the kind of woman who would be satisfied with a casual relationship. Bella possessed the soul of a romantic. She was strong-willed and could take care of herself. He had seen that. But from any man she did decide to give her heart to, she'd expect fidelity, trust, love, and respectability for her child in return. Everything Daniel had given her.

Everything, Zach suspected, he was incapable of giving any woman.

Twenty-One

I t was Sunday, blessed Sunday. Bella had felt a strong need to attend church that morning. She and Amanda caught a ride in one of the stagecoaches down to the town. Inside that quiet chapel, she felt soothed by the preacher's sonorous tones. She raised her voice to join the congregation on the sweet, old-fashioned Protestant hymns she had sung as a girl. Their forthright tunes and heartening lyrics lulled her into a feeling of deep peace.

Afterwards, they wandered through the streets, poking into the few stores.

Amanda chose several pretty sticks of candy and a book of colored paper dolls with the most intricate costumes Bella had ever seen. The book cost thirty-five cents, far beyond her budget only a few months ago. But now, having received her first week of pay; the amazing sum of twelve dollars, Bella felt rich enough to splurge on luxuries for her daughter. She even bought a sketchbook, colored pencils, and a small watercolor set, thinking it might be pleasant to emulate her mother and try and capture the beauty of the place. They topped off their excursion with a stop for cakes and tea at Mrs. Gully's Tea Room.

By the time they returned to the Catskill Mountain House, it was early afternoon. Amanda was invited to play croquet with a group of little girls on the lawn. Bella lounged nearby in one of the lawn chairs, oblivious to the chatter and the clank of croquet mallets around her.

Idly, she flipped through the box of stereoptic cards that one of the waiters had offered to bring her. She had chosen a set showing the canals of Venice. Inserting the first card into the stereoscope, she stared through the lenses at the three-dimensional image. Two happy people sat in a gondola, as the gondolier in the striped shirt leaned on a long pole thrust into the water to steer the boat.

Venice. It was where she had been born, during an extended stay in Italy on one of her parents' business trips. The Italian midwife had called her "Bella bambino," and her father had insisted they put the name Bella on the birth certificate. Her parents had taken her back to Venice for her tenth birthday. They had had such a good time there.

Sighing, Bella put down the stereoscope.

"Dreaming of something?" Nancy sank into the seat next to Bella with a companionable sigh of relief. "Feast your eyes on this." She crinkled the newspaper in her hands, folding it in half again before thrusting it in front of Bella.

"What's this? Gossip columns?"

"Stock market. I think you should put your money in the two companies circled there. They're going to make a mint in the next three or four weeks, I hear."

Bella squinted at the small rows of type. "Consolidated Mercury, Limited, and… "she glanced at the second circled figure, "Lackawaxen Steel." Shaking her head, she glanced at Nancy, noticing her smug expression. "What about them?"

"I put five hundred dollars on each of them six months ago. They've taken off. Got a hundred and fifty percent return." Nancy grinned. "And I have it on good authority that the owner is poised to make a killing."

Bella sat up straight and stared at the two names again. "Five hundred dollars? That's a fortune! On whose good authority?"

"Now, now. I never give my sources away. But I have my ways of getting information. I'm telling you to put whatever money you can risk on these two. You'll get double back by the end of the year."

"Nancy, I have no knowledge of investments."

"You don't need any." John's voice came out of the shadow that passed over Bella's head. "Nancy knows enough for all of us."

Intrigued, Bella asked him to explain.

"She's been investing my money and Zach's for years," John explained with quiet pride. He sat down on the grass next to Nancy's chair and stretched his legs. "Made enough to keep us all comfortable, even during the war."

"So that's what you read every day! And I thought it was just the gossip columns."

"You'd be surprised what you can find out from the gossip columns," Nancy said. "I once read that this couple was ruined by some scandal and had to raise money fast. They had some property in a little farming town on Oyster Bay, on the north shore of Long Island. I made them an offer and bought two cottages for a lot less than building them new."

"Cottages? You've more than one?" Bella gazed at Nancy with new respect. "I can't believe you could be such a wizard of the stock market."

"That's her secret," John said with a laugh. "None of the pompous stockbrokers and investors take her seriously. She's sly, my wife, she is."

"We're not the Vanderbilts," Nancy added. "We've only the one cottage. Zach has a cottage, too. It's our winter home. It only takes a few hours to get to the city by steamboat."

Bella's heart skipped a beat. An image of a tidy little cottage with a garden came into her mind. "Zach never said a word."

"Oh, he isn't there as much as we are," John said. "Sometimes he gets bored and goes into the city to play. And he used to spend a lot of time down South with his family."

"It's a snug little town," Nancy added. "Not fancy. But we built a bandstand so the boys could play whenever the urge strikes. It's where they rehearse new numbers for the next season. All the townspeople come to hear them."

Bella gazed at John and Nancy with envy, not for their money, but for what they had built together. "Do you own a great deal of stock?"

"A few thousand dollars' worth, with Zach's. Some gold, too, of course, as a hedge. Nothing we can't afford to lose. I buy and sell according to the market and my inside information." Nancy said it as casually as if she were talking about buying a new hat.

Bella's mind reeled. "You're wealthy, yet you still travel with the band."

John and Nancy looked at each other and burst into laughter.

"The stocks are our nest egg," Nancy explained. "The band is our business. And with the extra income, we can afford to travel first class and stay in much nicer rooms on the road."

"What else would we do?" John added. "When we retire, we'll settle down in Oyster Bay. It's beautiful there."

Settle down in Oyster Bay, Bella thought. What a lovely notion. "What does it look like, that cottage of yours?"

"Oh, it's very nice." Nancy took John's hand. "Ours looks right out on the bay, with a grand front porch and lots of windows to let in the light. And we have three fireplaces. John loves a fire in the hearth."

"And roses everywhere, climbing over the house," John added.

"Zach's, too?"

"Oh, yes," Nancy said. "Zach's favorite spot is the willow tree in the little meadow. That's where he sits and plays."

She saw him in her mind, under the willow, surrounded by the water and roses. Tears sprang to her eyes. What was wrong with her today? Clutching the stereoscope, she brought it up to her eyes to hide her tears. "It sounds lovely."

"Yes," Nancy said. "We hope you'll come and stay with us during our two-week hiatus in September. Oh, I'd love to show you and Amanda the bay! And there's some very nice children who live there."

"We'd love to come." Bella lowered the stereoscope. "Well, I'll have to invest my few dollars, as you advised, Nancy. Perhaps one day, I can build a cottage there, too. Amanda would love it."

"Speaking of Amanda, I heard something I thought you might want to know," said Nancy. "I was talking with Mrs. Pendergast's niece, Miss Sidlow, and she told me that Sissy's uncle is no gentleman."

"Whatever are you talking about, Nancy?"

"The little girl that Amanda is with today," Nancy said patiently, "is the ward of this Mr. Kane. And Mr. Kane is the financier that ran guns around the blockade and made a bundle of ill-gotten money from selling weapons to the Rebels during the war."

Bella put down the stereoscope. "How do you know all this?"

"Miss Sidlow's second cousin is related to Mr. Kane's mother. And her cousin said Mr. Kane approached him about investing in the gun-running business. Said he could guarantee two hundred percent profits. That was two years ago. And Miss Sidlow's cousin said no, even threatened to turn him in. But when he told the authorities, someone must have been bribed, because nothing ever came of it."

Bella was speechless.

"Well, I figured that you should know who Amanda is spending time with." Nancy reached over and patted Bella's shoulder. "You let me know how many shares to buy for you. Don't wait too long. Have to catch your opportunities while you can."

With her debut behind her now, Bella had settled nicely into a pleasant routine of rehearsals, concerts, teas and dinners with Mountain House guests. She spent mornings and many afternoons playing croquet and other games with Amanda or taking her daughter for walks along the wooded paths that Bella remembered from her own childhood summers. On restless nights and quiet afternoons, she sketched in her book.

She was doing that now, sitting in one of the slatted chairs, trying to capture the ever-shifting shades of blue sky and green across the valley as the clouds drifted across the face of the sun.

"Bella!" From the hotel veranda, Nancy was madly waving a handkerchief to get Bella's attention. "Bella!"

"Mama! Aunt Nancy wants us," Amanda said, looking up from her drawing of a cat. Or maybe it was a dog. Bella couldn't quite tell.

"Gather up your things," Bella said. "Let's find out what she wants."

The two ran up the wide, white steps of the hotel and into the shade of the deep veranda.

"Aunt Nancy! Look at my goat. I drew it all by myself!" Amanda waved her piece of paper in front of Nancy's nose.

Nancy took it, "oohed" and "aahed" in appropriately appreciative tones, then pronounced it the most perfect goat she'd ever seen. Only then did she turn to Bella.

"Zach and John are looking for you," Nancy said. "They've called a rehearsal. Zach just finished a new waltz. He wants to try it out."

"Oh, well! So much for a quiet afternoon," Bella said, tucking her sketchbook firmly under her arm. "Would you like to come and watch rehearsal, Amanda?"

"Oh yes, Mama! Can I sing, too?"

Bella laughed and shook her head. "I think you are much too young to make your debut. But you can sing along with us."

As they approached the ballroom, they could hear snatches of music, stopping and starting and stopping again.

"Good, Bella's here," announced John, as the women came through the doorway. "Amanda, too."

Zach spun around. "Hello there, Little Missy! Come on up here. It's about time you paid your Uncle Zach a visit!" He held out his arms and caught Amanda as she hopped up onto the stage into his arms.

Bella's heart swelled with pride. Amanda was so sweet. And Zach had been so good to her. He had his own special way with her; simple, direct, and openly affectionate. He was very much like Daniel in that he treated the four-year-old with great respect, never talking to her as if she were stupid or in the way.

But while Daniel had always been extremely gentle with Amanda, Zach tossed her around and teased her as if she were a little boy.

Amanda seemed to love it. She squealed with delight even now, as Zach lifted her high into the air. "Do a bird, Uncle Zach! Do a bird!" And he flew her around in a circle, while she arched her back and flapped her arms as if they were wings. When he stopped, she begged for more.

Zach deposited her on the ground and wiped his brow. "That's enough for one day, Little Missy."

"Uncle Zach? Will you come to my birthday picnic?" Amanda was tugging on Zach's vest.

Zach squatted down next to her. "When's your birthday?"

"On Tuesday next. Mama promised we could go on a picnic." She smiled and held up five fingers, then furrowed her brow in concentration as she counted each finger again to be sure. "Five! That's how old I'll be."

"Five!"

She nodded emphatically and held up her hand again. "This many. Count it."

"One, two, three..." He counted her fingers. "It's five alright. Well, that calls for a celebration."

"Will you come?"

"I'll talk about it with your Mama. We'll see."

Amanda's smile turned into a pout. "But Mama said I could invite you. Didn't you Mama?"

Bella nodded. "Uncle Zach may have business to take care of, dear."

"But if you don't come," Amanda cried, "then it's only Mama and me. Aunt Nancy's brother is coming on Tuesday, and Sissy went home and won't be back until weeks and weeks." Her little voice cracked with emotion. Her lower lip began to quiver.

Zach scooped her up in his arms and tossed her in the air. "In that case, Little Missy, I can't let you down. I'll be there!"

Amanda squealed with joy. When Zach set her down, she scampered off to join Nancy on the settee at the far end of the oak paneled room. There they settled in happily to read and cut out paper dolls.

"Let me explain why I called a rehearsal, Bella," Zach said, reverting to his usual businesslike demeanor. "I wrote a new waltz. The Fifth Avenue Waltz, I call it. We've just started in learning the introduction. Now, there are no words. But I had an idea for some new dance steps to go with it. And I was thinking that you and Paul Bruner could demonstrate the dance to the audience on the first two stanzas. It would be a novelty, something fun for one of the afternoon tea dances."

Bella looked amused.

"You do know how to waltz, don't you?" Zach asked.

"Oh, I think I can remember how," she teased. "Let's see, one, two, three, one, two, three." She twirled and bowed.

"Good. Paul, come over here. Now, you start with a regular waltz step, but on the fourth turn, the music pauses on the second and third beat. That's when you twirl Bella under your arm."

Paul's eyebrows rose so high, he looked quite comical. "Twirl her? Under my arm?" he croaked. "I don't know, Zach."

"Come on, it's not hard." Zach coaxed Paul as if he were a child. "Try it."

John took up his fiddle and played the first six bars of the tune, demonstrating the pause and where the music came back in. Paul gamely held Bella and waltzed her awkwardly around the room but couldn't quite get the hang of the twirling business.

Zach grimaced and strode toward them. "Paul, you have to twirl Bella like this." He took her hand and raised it high, twirling her with a firm hand. "And Bella, when the music comes in again, you take one step, a little hop and then kick up your right heel behind you. It's a kind of a flippant, flirtatious kick. At the same time, you look away from your partner. As if you're being superior."

Bella thought about it, then quickly twirled and did the little kick, with an insouciant toss of her head.

"That's just what I wanted," Zach said, nodding in appreciation. "Perfect."

"Uhm, Zach? I don't have to kick, too? Do I?" Paul asked.

"No. The man doesn't kick. But he looks away in the other direction from his partner at the same moment. Think you can do that?"

Paul rolled his eyes and took a deep sigh. "I guess so. Here's goes nothing."

John started to play the beginning of the waltz. Paul wore a painful expression as he whirled Bella through the motions. He forgot to stop on the pause, then came back in a step too late, throwing off Bella's kick.

The other musicians were snickering among themselves, trying hard not to laugh out loud.

"Try it again, John!" Zach called patiently.

Bella felt sorry for Paul. He gripped her hand awkwardly, and she could feel him stiffen as the boys' laughter reached their ears.

"Just relax," she whispered to him. But her words were in vain. He shuffled and stiffly ushered her through the steps.

"You look like a wooden soldier up there," Zach called out. "It's supposed to look like you're enjoying the dance, Paul."

The others laughed out loud as the miserable young musician tried yet again. Finally, Paul had had enough.

"Gosh darn it, Zach. I'm willing to try anything once. But I can't do this with them all laughing at me. Make 'em stop, will ya?"

Zach looked like he might call for quiet, but instead, he burst out laughing himself. "You're a great French horn player, Paul, but you're no dancer. Come on back up here." He turned to the other musicians, who were still laughing. "All right. Who's next up to try? Can't spare Billy, but Billy can't dance. What about you, Harry?"

Big Harry blanched. "Me? Oh, no, not me, Zach. I can't dance. Not me."

"Jeremy? How about you?"

The skinny flute and piccolo player just shook his head. "Just call me Two Left Feet."

"Don't look at me," cried Peter, ducking down behind the piano.

"What about you, Zach?" Billy Parisher cried. "You been dancin' all over our room for the last week, figuring out them steps. How 'bout you dance with her?"

"And I can play the cornet part on the French horn," Paul chimed in.

Zach looked at John.

"Guess you're the only one left, partner," John said, tucking his violin under his chin. "Ready when you are."

Zach nodded and stepped down to join Bella. They joined hands. Zach pulled her closer to him, holding her firmly around her waist. "Just follow my lead. Four bars, twirl, hop and kick, then repeat, then four bars of whirling to the left, then to the right. OK?"

"Ready when you are," Bella replied.

"Give me the first sixteen bars at half tempo, John."

The music started. Bella gave her full attention to Zach. They began to move slowly through the various sections of the dance. It was not a particularly difficult dance and Bella soon had it down perfectly.

In the last few weeks of singing with the band, she had come to appreciate Zach's absolute command of everything musical. Nothing escaped his ear. When he played, he was one with his cornet. One with the music. So it was not surprising that he would be the same way as a dancer. He didn't just move around the floor to the music, as Paul had done. He was attuned to the music, as if it flowed out from inside him.

What surprised her was how she could follow him so effortlessly. She hadn't danced in years. But somehow her feet seemed to know what he wanted her to do, without more than a word and a movement of his hand. They were a good match, she thought. She was only a few inches shorter than him. When they whirled, Bella's feet scarcely touched the dance floor. She felt as if they were dancing on a cloud of music. It was magical. As the music speeded up to full tempo, Bella forgot everything else and entered the spirit of the dance. She ended with the little backward kick and a toss of her head.

Everyone applauded. Zach whirled her away from him, and she curtsied deeply. Bella felt almost giddy.

"You are full of surprises!" she told Zach. "Where did you learn to dance like that?"

"Here and there," Zach answered dryly. "Mostly in Georgia. Every gentleman must know how to dance. What about you? Did Daniel take you dancing?"

Bella laughed softly. "No. I haven't danced in years. I did take dancing lessons when I was a girl. I tried to teach Daniel a few steps, but he didn't care to dance."

"That's not surprising. I'm sure my puritanical father saw to that. He thought dancing was one of the seven deadly sins." He turned to the musicians. "All right, now. Everybody got their music? Let's work on this for an hour, then call it a day. We can finish up at tomorrow's regular rehearsal."

Bella felt suddenly awkward and somehow deflated. He hadn't said a word about her own dancing or whether she had performed it the way he had wanted. She started to walk away, but Zach called her back.

"Where are you going?"

Bella turned. "I thought you were finished with me."

"You'd deny me the pleasure of another dance?" He stepped toward her. He took her hand and drew her to him, once again placing his arm firmly around her waist. "You dance like an angel, Mrs. Smith. You sing like a nightingale. I'm a very lucky bandleader."

Before she could reply, the music started, and she was whirling in Zach's strong arms, adrift on the music of the Fifth Avenue Waltz.

Twenty-Two

T he morning of Amanda's birthday was sultry and hot, so Zach decided to take them to the coolest place he could think of; the caves at Kaaterskill Falls.

At the front desk, Zach collected the picnic hamper he had ordered. It was filled with smoked salmon, roasted chicken, potato salad, fresh raspberries, beaten biscuits, plum jam, and a half-dozen pink sugar cakes; one was inscribed with Amanda's name in white icing. The child was clearly excited. She hopped along beside Zach, begging to peek inside.

"No, it's a secret," Zach teased her, as they made their way to the front porch. "You'll just have to wait until we get there. Ah, there's our pony cart."

A white horse and a canary-yellow governess cart with red spoked wheels were waiting for them at the hitching post.

"Oh, Uncle Zach, it's the prettiest cart!" Amanda cried, flying down the steps ahead of the adults.

"Zach, this is so nice of you," Bella said quietly. "You went to a lot of trouble."

"No trouble at all." Zach hoisted the hamper behind the seat. "There! Now Amanda goes in." Lifting the giggling child high into the air, he swung her into the cart.

Then he turned to Bella, offering his hand. She looked lovely in a yellow sprigged muslin dress and a lemon-colored bonnet that set off her violet eyes and rosy complexion. Hiking her skirts, she climbed up onto the cement stepping block to step into the cart. The pony shifted and took a step.

"Whoa!" Zach exclaimed, hopping quickly up beside Bella. He fell against her as the tiny cart lurched forward. The peal of her laughter and the warmth of her body resting lightly against him made him feel both elated and miserable with desire.

"We're off," Zach said, and clucked his tongue. "Hold on!"

The horse trotted along the wooded path past the Laurel House. Just past this small inn was a rustic cafe. From its porch, a long wooden staircase led down to the bottom of the falls, where a curtain of water churned and bubbled into a wide, rocky pool.

Zach stopped the cart, hopped out, and lifted Amanda down first. He pointed to the bottom of the falls. "That's where we'll picnic," he told Amanda. "There's a shady grove down there."

"But Uncle Zach," Amanda said, clutching her uncle's arm, "how will we ever carry our picnic basket way down there?"

"Don't you worry. They'll drop it down to us. It's rather ingenious. Wait and see." He winked. "Think you can walk down all those stairs?"

"Oh, yes! I shall run right down!"

"No running!" Bella warned from her seat on the cart. "Or you shall fall headlong down."

Zach caught Bella lightly as she hopped down off the high step to reach the ground. "Thank you very much, sir."

He bowed low and kissed her wrist. "You're very welcomed, milady."

"Such elegant manners for the black sheep of the family," she teased him.

"Something about you brings out the Southern gentleman in me." Zach gazed into her eyes. He was thinking how much he wished he could tell her that he cared for her. But Amanda's insistent cry that they "come and see" distracted him.

"Coming, darling!" Bella caught up her skirts with one hand

and grasped her parasol with the other, turning with a dazzling smile to follow the child into the gazebo.

Zach clapped his straw hat firmly on his head and hoisted the hamper. He was enjoying this outing. But a niggling thought kept creeping into his mind. Had he done all this for the child? As much as he loved the little miss, he had to admit that he was trying to woo Bella. Ridiculous! Even if she did someday decide to love again, why would she fall in love with an old rogue like him?

Yet he wanted her. He could have turned to other women; the Mountain House was full of lonely females eager for romance. The boys asked him often to come with them on this or that outing, and even hinted about this maid or that one who could be invited for him. He hadn't been interested. He wanted Bella. No one else. That much was achingly clear to him.

Even if she did come to care for him, she wouldn't want the kind of relationship he felt most comfortable with. She'd want marriage, with all its inherent responsibilities. And that was another matter entirely.

He could almost hear his father's ghost sneering at him: *"What? You be faithful? A whoring, drinking, carousing devil such as you?"*

Shaking off the unpleasant thought, Zach quickened his pace. He followed them into the cafe, where he arranged with the proprietor for the hamper and a bottle of his finest champagne to be lowered down, then delivered by one of the young guides to the picnic grove.

Clattering down the wooden mountainside stairway, Zach, Amanda, and Bella sang "Skip to My Lou" in the clear morning air. As they descended, the steady hiss of the falls grew louder.

"Oooh!" breathed Amanda, captivated by the sparkling wall of water beyond the stairs. Bella and Zach each instinctively reached for Amanda's hand when they reached the first landing, where the cave was.

It was cool and dark here. Bella folded up her parasol.

"This way," Zach said, motioning them to follow him. It seemed as if he were taking them into the waterfall itself.

Amanda pulled back. Bella also hesitated.

"You've never been this close before?" Zach yelled over the roar of the falls.

Bella shook her head. "No. My mother didn't think it safe."

Zach grinned. "It's quite safe, I swear to you. I've been through here many times. Came back without a scratch."

Bella looked up, uncertainty still showing in her expression.

"Will we drown, Uncle Zach?" Amanda's voice wavered.

"Nothing to fear," Zach said. "This goes behind the falls into a wonderful cave. Come along. I'll show you."

He gently shepherded them onto a rock ledge that hugged a sheer rock wall, and suddenly they were in a vast, dome-like cave.

"Look," Zach cried, squatting next to Amanda. He pointed up at the huge roof that bowed out in a perfect semi-circle hundreds of feet above their heads. "It's like the great amphitheater at P.T. Barnum's, only bigger!"

Zach hoisted Amanda on his shoulders. "Reach up!" he cried. "You'd have to be a giant to touch the ceiling!"

He felt Bella's hand on his arm, clutching him in excitement. "It's marvelous!" she cried. "I never imagined it, even from what I've heard! So enormous!"

Zach smiled, feeling a bit smug that his birthday surprise was turning out to be quite a success. "We'll walk along this rock shelf. Perfectly safe, see? It runs around the entire back wall of the cave."

About twenty other visitors were meandering along the rock shelf. Several of the more intrepid guests had stepped down onto the vast concave floor of the cave, leaning on tall staffs, working their way toward a pile of boulders that stood in front of the curtain of falling water.

"It's amazing, isn't it?" Zach said. "The water falls from one-hundred and sixty feet above us. Some of it splashes on the ledge of this cave, but most of it continues to fall another hundred feet to the pool at the very bottom."

One of the guides stationed inside the cave handed Zach and Bella tall walking sticks.

"Feeling daring?" Zach asked Bella.

"In what way?"

"Let's walk down there," he said, pointing to the cave's floor, "and get close enough to feel the spray of the waterfall."

Bella took in a sharp breath. "Is it safe?"

"Safe enough," cried Zach. "Come on! Hold on Amanda!" Using the walking pole, Zach picked his way down off the walkway, with Amanda still sitting on his shoulders.

"Oh!" Bella stood there for a moment, staring at the falls. She held out her hand to stop Zach, but he turned back and was laughing at her, as was her daughter.

"Oh, Mama! It's fun!"

"You little dare-devil, you!" Bella shifted her parasol, hiked up her skirts and jabbed the walking stick down onto the sandy floor to steady herself. One of the guides sprang to her aid.

Zach watched her approach, holding Amanda's feet firmly against him. "That's it," he encouraged her.

Bella clutched onto the guide's arm as if for dear life. Her expression was strained with fear. When she reached Zach, she thanked the guide gravely. Then she surprised Zach by slipping her arm around his waist, her shoulder snuggling just under his.

Zach felt as if they belonged that way, one family. The thought caught him by surprise.

From here, the floor of the cave was relatively smooth and sandy. He led them down within a few feet of the pounding waters. There Bella stopped, refusing to take another step. Her face was pale, her eyes round with fear.

"There's nothing to be afraid of, Bella." Zach eased Amanda to the ground in front of her mother. He gently slipped his arm around Bella's shoulder once more, and felt her body lean into his.

"Do you like it, Amanda?" Zach asked.

The child had both her hands pressed to her ears but looked up at Zach and Bella with a wide-eyed grin on her face.

"Want to go closer?" Zach took a step. Mother and daughter both squealed and hung back again. "No? Well then, wait here for me!" Away he spurted, over the last few feet of dark sand to touch the nearest boulder under the falls. He heard their squeals of terror.

"Come back!" Amanda yelled, her eyes round with excitement. "Come back!"

"My goodness, Zach! You'll be killed!" cried Bella, holding her hand over her heart.

Zach turned and waved. "Come on over! Feel the spray!"

Mother and daughter shook their heads adamantly. "No! Come back!" they yelled in unison.

Zach raced back to them, scooped up Amanda and dashed away with her toward the boulder. The child kicked her feet, squealing and shouting and laughing.

Suddenly, Bella was at Zach's side, tugging at his arm, a note of terror in her cries to let Amanda go.

Immediately, Zach put Amanda down on the sand. He turned to Bella, who was now pounding his arm. Catching her to him, he shouted her name over the sound of falling water. "I wouldn't put Amanda in danger! My God, Bella. The edge is another twenty feet away. It's perfectly safe. I'd never hurt either of you."

Bella became still. They stared at each other for a long moment. Just as he was afraid he had ruined the whole outing, she pulled away from him and gave a playful swipe at his chin. "Oh, I should know better. You will have your fun."

"You don't trust me?" The hurt feelings welled up in his voice.

"It's just that I suddenly pictured the two of you dashed against the rocks and I... "Bella swallowed hard. "I couldn't stand it if anything happened to Amanda, or to you!"

Zach felt jubilant. She did care about him. He took her hand. "Bella. Do you trust me?"

She looked up into his eyes. "Yes."

"Then come here with me. You, too, Amanda. Give me your hands. We'll go slowly."

He led them to the nearest boulder. They leaned forward slightly, stretching out their hands until they could just feel the spray of water on their fingertips. They stood there for a long time, their bodies absorbed the pounding rhythms that reverberated around them and under their very feet.

Zach broke the spell, leading them back to the safety of the rock ledge.

"Sometimes, you have to face life head on." Zach looked into Bella's eyes. He could see the fear had been replaced with calm trust. He smiled at her, his heart joyous with the knowledge that she did care for him. "Now, then. Ready for that picnic?"

Twenty-Three

As the Fourth of July approached, a steady procession of stagecoaches brought more guests to the biggest weekend celebration of the season. Many of the newly arrived guests were younger than the society matrons who had filled the Mountain House with their children in June. The air was rife with gossip and flirtatious laughter, as well as the swaggering energy of young Wall Street men in high spirits and business suits.

The day itself dawned bright and hot. Every balcony and balustrade at The Mountain House had been decked in red, white, and blue bunting. A huge American flag had been hoisted high over the hotel's wide front lawn, and now rippled proudly in the wind. A bandstand was arranged facing the hotel, and the smell of spit-roasted pork and fresh blackberry pie permeated the air.

"When's the parade, Mama?" Amanda asked, as Bella brushed the tangles from her hair. "Ouch! I want to march, march, march!"

"Yes, dear. Everyone will march past the Stars and Stripes as the band plays."

"And I want to see the pie-eating contest," Amanda continued. "Ouch!"

"Sorry. Yes, we'll see the pie eating contest."

"Billy says Big Harry's going to win. He can eat a whole pie in five minutes, he says."

Bella laughed, picturing the bassoon player, hands tied behind his back, chomping his way through a whole blackberry pie. "No doubt he can."

"And Aunt Nancy says there's to be a singing contest. I want to sing, Mama."

"And what will you sing?"

"When Johnny Comes Marching Home Again, Hurrah, Hurrah!" she said. "Ouch! And will you sing, Mama?"

"No, dear. I'll be singing at tonight's dance. That's all the singing I want to do." She finished tying a red, white, and blue bow in Amanda's hair. "There now. We're all ready to go."

Amanda whooped and ran out the door.

"No racing down the stairs, young lady!" Bella called after her. "You wait right there, while I get my bonnet."

Bella and Amanda descended into a hotel lobby crowded with people. They had to elbow their way through, squeezing past the spectators who lingered on the veranda and lined the steps leading to the lawn. Children raced back and forth in impromptu games of tag. Couples walked arm in arm. Three officers in Union uniforms were passing around a silver flask, as a young woman in a pale pink gown simpered and swayed before them.

"Mama, what are they drinking?" Amanda asked.

Bella raised an eyebrow. "Lemonade, dear. Come along."

Bella craned her neck, looking for Nancy or John, or one of the other boys. She didn't see Zach anywhere.

"Mrs. Smith! How delightful to run into you again."

Bella turned and saw Robert Kane, Sissy's uncle. He was balancing two tall glasses, and a wrapped bundle.

"Ah, Mr. Kane." Bella smiled politely. "Back up for the holiday?"

"Yes. Sissy and I got in yesterday. Excuse me, my hands are full or I would tip my hat. You look well. And how is little Annie?" he asked, smiling down at Amanda.

"Amanda."

"I'm sorry, Amanda, of course. Sissy is over past the arbor with her governess, waiting for the archery exhibition to start. Would you care to join us?"

Amanda tugged at her mother's hand. "Mama, please! Mama, please! I want to see Sissy!"

"Well, I suppose. But the pie-eating contest starts at nine o'clock, darling, and we wouldn't want to miss seeing Harry, would we?"

Truthfully, Bella didn't feel at all like joining the man, but Amanda continued to tug at her sleeve. She finally fell into step with Mr. Kane. When they reached Sissy, the two youngsters hugged each other joyfully, jumped up and down, and fell into a heap on the blanket where the governess was busy brushing ants from her skirts.

"Well, this is lucky, running into you like this," Kane said smoothly. He passed the drinks and food to the governess. "So, tell me. How have things been at the Mountain House?"

"Fine," Bella said, lifting her fan to wave in front of her face.

"Would you care to sit, Mrs. Smith?"

"Thank you, but I think I'll stand. I'll have a better view."

"Is your engagement calendar completely filled, or is there a chance of having dinner with me this week?" Kane said.

"I'm sorry. It is. Business before pleasure, I'm afraid." Bella hoped her words didn't sound as sour as she felt. The man was a war-profiteer and if it hadn't been for Amanda's friendship with his ward, she would have told him in no uncertain terms that she was not interested in his company.

"And your dance card for the ball tonight? That can't be full already?"

Bella was trapped there. "No," she admitted.

"Then I would like to claim the first waltz," Kane said, taking a sidestep closer to her.

"The first waltz is always taken, Mr. Kane. I dance it with my brother-in-law as part of the act."

Kane's eyes and mouth betrayed a flicker of irritation. "Then I insist on a Schottische and a polka."

"As you wish." She turned her eyes toward the field where the archery targets were set up. "I believe the event is starting."

Kane moved even closer, his shoulder touching hers. He was tall, a good six inches taller than her. She shifted her weight, casually moving back a step.

The crowd applauded as the contestants, four men and two ladies, stepped up to the marks and took up their bows. All the contestants wore white suits and straw hats, with a quiver of arrows strapped to their backs.

"I get the feeling, Mrs. Smith, that you don't care for me."

Bella turned to him with what she hoped was an innocent look on her face. "Why do you say that?"

"You're rather cool toward me. I gather you would prefer I not bother you with my attentions."

Bella measured her response carefully. "My husband died only a few months ago. I'm sorry, but I'm afraid I'm rather cool toward every gentleman, no matter how nice."

"Not so cool toward your brother-in-law, however."

Bella looked at him sharply. "He is family, sir," she said acidly.

"Of course," Kane said. "I understand. I wondered ..." he paused. "I wondered if you could set something straight for me, Mrs. Smith. I heard some of the gentlemen talking and they mentioned that Mr. Smith refused to play *Marching Through Georgia* a while back."

Bella felt a cold shiver trail up her spine. The crowd burst into applause as two of the contestants hit the bull's eye. She applauded with them, testing an answer out in her head. "Yes, it's unfortunate, isn't it, that men keep asking for war songs now that the war is over."

"Why wouldn't he want to play that song?"

"Perhaps he is tired of war songs, sir. After all, he just returned from the fighting."

"Ah, but fighting where? Several men speculated that he, perhaps, fought on the wrong side."

Bella was furious. How dare he stir up trouble? "You, sir,

fought on neither side." As soon as she had said it, she knew it had been the worst thing she could have said.

"So it's true. He's a Confederate."

"Mr. Kane..." Bella was trembling with so much rage, she had to breathe deeply just to get the words out. "The war is over. If the great General Ulysses S. Grant, whom *my* husband fought under, could be magnanimous enough to allow all the Southern soldiers to go home unmolested, we should be equally as willing to let them get on with their lives."

For a moment, Kane was silent. The crowd cheered again as one of the ladies shot her arrow cleanly through the bull's eye. Bella applauded. She stopped when she felt Kane take her arm. She turned to see his cold hazel eyes boring through hers.

"Not all of us are so magnanimous, Mrs. Smith." Kane turned and stalked away through the crowd.

That night at the Patriotic Gala, the crowd was boisterous and demanding. A younger set had crowded the ballroom, calling out names of songs they wanted the band to play.

Bella felt skittish all through her set. Mr. Kane had appeared for his two dances. Bella obliged him, then quickly excused herself, much to Kane's obvious displeasure. She headed for the back door, hoping to slip out without notice. She wanted to check on Amanda and Nancy.

"Thank you, ladies and gentlemen." Zach lifted his cornet. "This next song..."

"Where's the Nightingale?" cried someone from the dance floor.

"Bring back the Nightingale!" another took up the cry.

Zach once again held up his hands to quiet the growing murmur over Bella's whereabouts. "Miss Gale is just taking a break..."

"When will she be back?"

"Yes, bring her back!"

"We'll bring her back in just a bit," Zach called out calmly. The crowd buzzed louder. The band members shifted uncomfortably, eyeing each other nervously. Zach looked unperturbed. He raised his hands again. "Let's do the Doggy, boys," he called out.

But before the band could strike the opening notes of the playful ditty, someone shouted, "Play *Marching through Georgia,* Rebel boy!"

The audience gasped, horrified, yet titillated at the same time.

All eyes turned to the stage. Zach scanned the crowd and noticed the man Bella had pointed out as Sissy's uncle, grinning in a smug, self-satisfied way. A cold wave of conviction swept through Zach: This was a declaration of war from a jealous rival.

"Go on! Play *Marching through Georgia,* you gray bird!" someone else shouted. He looked over and saw Farris staring at him.

"He's a Confederate!" a third voice cried. Zach turned sharply to see Ruckler in the back of the room, waving his fist in the air.

The crowd began to shriek and whistle, ladies hurrying from the dance floor as three Union officers in full uniform thrust themselves angrily into its center to openly challenge Zach's loyalty.

Several young Wall Street men eagerly removed their frock coats, rolling up their sleeves in anticipation of a fight.

For once, no ready response came to Zach's lips. He felt his stomach tighten in revulsion. He would not play the hated song.

"'Marching through Georgia' be damned!" he cried.

The band members looked at each other in confusion. Zach gave them no signal or indeed even seemed to notice their presence. He had balled up his fists and was staring down a particularly vociferous old man who called him, "Rebel scum!"

Older men, staying well back around the perimeter of the room, began to call out shouts of encouragement to the Union officers. But they made no effort to join the fight.

"Come on down here and fight, you Confederate coward!" one of the soldiers cried.

Zach jumped down from the stage and was immediately surrounded.

Billy Parisher quickly sized up the situation.

"Charge boys!" he yelled. And in an instant, Billy, Peter, Paul, and John, had jumped down to Zach's side. The young Wall Street dandies joined the small knot of flailing arms. And the rest of the distinguished male guests, standing well out of harm's way added their sharp curses to the air.

∼

Bella had been exchanging a few words with Charles and Anna at the rear exit when she heard the terrible challenge. Turning back, she saw Zach frozen on the stage, and heard him condemn the song.

For a moment, Bella stood rooted to the spot, gasping as Zach jumped down and the band members took after him.

"My God, Charles!" Bella screamed. "They'll kill him!"

"I'll go fetch help," Charles said, and slipped out the exit.

Bella ran up on stage. She saw Billy jump on the back of one of the Union officers. John and Paul were struggling against two of the Wall Street dandies. And in the middle of the fray, she saw Zach being held by two men, his arms pinned behind him, as a soldier took a swing directly at his face.

"Stop them!" Bella screamed. "Stop them!"

But not a guest in the room lifted a finger to help.

Wildly, she ran to the piano and began to pound out 'Marching Through Georgia' in harsh chords, shouting the words of the chorus over and over again in an attempt to gain the crowd's attention.

Slowly, the crowd began to hush until only the grunts and groans and guttural cries from the small band of brawlers could be heard. Eventually, the exhausted brawlers began to look up, too.

"That's what you wanted to hear, wasn't it?" Bella berated the crowd. "Well now it's been sung, for all the good it does. You men ought to be ashamed of yourself, crying for war songs when the war has taken so many brave men."

She glared at the men closest to her. Their faces wore a look of shock and shame. The room was silent.

"Look what you've done!" she cried. "This is a respectable hotel! You ought to be ashamed. You're frightening the ladies. This is no saloon for you to brawl in! Shame on you!"

As she continued to talk, the young brawlers began to sheepishly pick themselves up and dust off their evening clothes, stem their bloody noses, and straighten their vests and cravats.

"Answer me this!" came a self-assured voice from the far corner of the room. "Is your bandleader a Johnny Reb, or not?"

Bella felt her cheeks flush hot with anger. "The war is over, sir. No matter which side you were on, we are all united now."

"No, madam," the voice replied, and she finally saw its fair-haired owner. Robert Kane. "It's not that simple. Traitors are traitors. And they're not welcome in New York."

Bella said the first thing that came to her mind. "Mr. Kane, if I were you, a man who is said to have run guns into the South to make a quick profit, I would not broach the subject of loyalty or traitor. How many of these good people's fathers and sons died needlessly because of your efforts to prolong the war?"

Both Kane and Zach looked up at her in shock. Before either of them could speak, Gabriel Kramer leaped up on stage and held up his hands. Behind him, their sleeves rolled up, came six burly men; porters used to hauling trunks and heavy boxes, who would have no trouble subduing an unruly crowd.

"Ladies and gentlemen." Kramer's voice was confident and cool. "Coffee is served on the veranda. This evening's entertainment is over. Please clear the room. Thank you very much."

He and his men began to shepherd the crowd through the wide doors and down the stairs, taking care to separate the disheveled brawlers from each other.

Bella ran to Zach's side, gently touching his bleeding lip. "Are you hurt?"

He wiped his mouth on his sleeve. "I'm fine." He brushed her hand away.

"Are you angry at me?" Bella asked in surprise.

"At myself."

Zach turned to go, but suddenly Kramer was there, blocking his path. He stared at Zach for a long moment, shaking his head.

"You'd better come with me, Zach. We need to talk," Kramer said. "You, too, Miss Gale."

~

"Damn it, Zach!" Kramer said again, as he paced back and forth in front of his office window. "Why the hell couldn't you have just played the damnable song and have done with it?"

Zach did not answer. He leaned against the wall, arms folded, licking his bloody lip.

Kramer looked helplessly at Bella, who only sighed from her seat on the backless settee. John Halley gave no indication of his emotions either, standing quietly beside Bella.

"Zach, Zach, Zach," Kramer continued. "I warned you, didn't I? Your reputation survived a four-year absence. Now it's ruined. And for what? For a song?" He stopped in front of Zach and threw up his hands.

"I wouldn't play that song then," Zach said quietly, looking directly into Kramer's eyes. "I won't play it ever."

Kramer shook his head and growled in disgust. He walked back to his desk and collapsed heavily in the big leather chair. "You're not allowing me to help you, friend. You're stubborn as the day is long."

"Nothing new," Zach said.

"Mr. Beach has very few choices now. He can let the band go for breach of contract." Kramer's chin sank onto his chest for a moment. "He probably won't want to do that, but he doesn't want to lose patrons either. Or he can let Zach go and keep the band on under a different name."

"He couldn't!" Bella cried. "It's so unfair! It wasn't Zach's fault."

"Yes, it's damned unfair," Kramer agreed. "But Mr. Beach has one ironclad rule. There are no disturbances at the Catskill Mountain House. No unpleasantness. Ever. It's immediate grounds for dismissal or breach of contract. I'm powerless to do anything about it. It's his hotel and his reputation."

"You're right, as usual, Gabriel," said Zach quietly. He heaved himself away from the wall. "It was my choice not to play that song. And I'll take the consequences. But Mr. Beach still needs a band."

He walked behind Bella and placed his hands firmly on her shoulders. "Ask him if Bella and the band can stay on for the rest of the season. John leads the band. If you want to change the name, fine. Call it the Halley Band and the Nightingale."

"Zach! You can't!" Bella cried. The band was everything to him. She craned her neck to look up at John. "John?"

John's normally calm face was tense and red, but he said nothing.

Zach's strong hands massaged Bella's shoulders. "Sshhh, sshhh, Bella. This is necessary. We can't lose everything because of my mistakes."

"But—" Bella began.

"Don't worry," John cut in. "As soon as we leave here, the band will resume Zach's name."

"That's hardly fair to you," Bella protested.

John shook his head angrily. "Oh, it's fair. I've no wish to lead the band, except when it's necessary. We've always been equal partners in the band, but Zach's the front man with my blessing. I took over while he played soldier. I'll take over now, although I've a mind to say the hell with it and just walk away."

"Gabriel?" Zach said quickly. "Will you deliver our offer to Mr. Beach in the morning?"

"Of course. I think he'll agree." He clapped Zach on the back. "I'm really sorry about this, Zach."

"I know you are."

"But I can't sing without you there!" Bella blurted out.

"Of course you can." Zach squeezed her shoulders. "If John can do it, you can do it. I have complete faith in you. It's for all of us. For the Halleys. The boys. Amanda. For all of us."

"But what will you do?"

He shrugged. "I'll work on my symphony."

Bella nodded up at him, recognizing what was at stake. If he could give up his place, she could carry on for him. For all of them.

Twenty-Four

It was late the next morning when Kramer came to let Zach and John know the verdict: Mr. Beach would keep the band on if the name of the band changed. He also wanted Zach to leave by the end of the week.

"I'm sorry," Kramer said, his shoulders sagging. "I tried."

"The hell with this," John snapped. "Let's all leave. We've got bookings elsewhere."

Zach looked at John in alarm. His partner had never been this emotional. "No John. I can afford to go without pay for a while but…"

"So can I."

"Yes, but the boys and Bella can't," Zach said firmly. "And it's far too late for them to find anything to fill in now." He looked at Kramer. "Gabriel? What's the chances that if the band finishes out the contract, Mr. Beach would book us again next season?"

Kramer hesitated. "Better than if you all left him without a band. But I couldn't promise."

Zach turned to John. "Let's do it this way. We'll cut our losses. We'll pick up the pieces."

"Damn it, Zach," John said. He stuffed his hands in his pockets. "We just started to get everything back together and now this."

"I know. But it's not like we're starting from square one. The band is good, you've done a fine job. And Bella's the most exciting singer we've ever had. I know it's a lot to ask of you..."

John studied his shoes for a long moment, lost in silence. Then he looked up and gave a resolute nod. "We'll do it your way, Zach."

"Mr. Beach wants the card changed tonight." Kramer said. "What shall I call the band?"

"Ask John. He's the leader now." Zach sat back in the chair. He stretched his legs and took a long sip of coffee. Strangely, he felt as if a load of bricks had been lifted from his shoulders. The decision had been made. Now it was out of his hands.

"Nightingale's Orchestral Band," John replied grimly.

Kramer wasn't smiling. "Are you sure that's wise? Can she handle a full season of eight shows a week, three to four sets a show?"

"Absolutely wise," John said. "She is the draw now that Zach is out of it."

John's words had sent a twinge of jealousy through Zach. *Out of it,* he thought. *I am out of it.* Shaking himself, he stood up. "Settle things between you. I'll be back."

Zach strode out of the office and headed for the back door. He had no wish to run into anyone at this moment, only to get as far away from the main hotel as possible. He made his way around the side of the building, skirting wide to avoid the burly porters who were lashing trunks to the back of the stagecoach.

Then he saw Robert Kane, the one who had instigated last night's uproar. Kane was handing up two large satchels to the porter standing on the coach's rooftop. "Have a care with these," Kane shouted.

Nearby, Kane's young niece and her governess waited patiently with a small group of departing guests.

Zach's emotions smoldered into murderous thoughts. *He's leaving,* he thought. *Good! That's one less rat around to bother Bella.*

Zach continued in the direction of his room, mulling over what to do without his band. He couldn't stay on here for more than a few days, just enough to see that Bella was all right. Maybe he'd go home, back to the cottage at Oyster Bay to work on his symphony.

He pictured the house standing against the sandy Long Island harbor, a glint of morning sun illuminating the wide porch. Gulls crying and wheeling overhead. He'd finally have time to trim back that tangle of climbing roses. To repaint the carriage house that held his black carriage with the gold striping. To sit under that graceful weeping willow and dream of Bella, and wonder what the band was doing, and worry about the future.

He laughed aloud. That was a new one for him. He had taken so much for granted in the years before the war.

He'd been so arrogant to think that he could simply go on living a bachelor's life for the rest of his life. So certain that he'd always have the band. That he'd always be its leader. That people would always want to hear his music.

Arrogant enough to think that whenever he felt lonely, he'd only have to look the right way at any woman he chose to have all the warmth and companionship he needed, without any of the responsibilities.

Now, those responsibilities seemed desirable.

He pictured Amanda skipping through the garden. He imagined Bella sitting on his porch, her shining face upturned to welcome him home. Imagined what it would feel like to wake up to her in the sun-drenched bedroom in the fine mahogany, four-poster bed. He pictured himself sitting with her on the porch at night, gazing at the stars and listening to the gentle lap of the tide along the beach.

Coming out of his reverie, Zach saw he had wandered to the cliff that looked out over the valley below. He remembered that night when he had heard the chords of the final movement of his symphony here. Staring across the vista, Zach immersed himself in the sweep of grays, greens and blues of the sky and the land and the winding ribbon of river.

Idly, he jiggled the change in his vest pocket and felt the hilt of his pocketknife. Removing it, he flipped it into the air, then caught it, flipped it again, then missed. It clattered on the rock under his feet. He bent down to retrieve it, and then stood up, dizzy from the panoramic view that shifted suddenly as he readjusted his gaze.

Suddenly, he heard the chords of the final movement of his symphony again, swelling in his brain. Only now, they held a skewed, melancholy note, soaring out of the full chord.

Zach broke into a run to reach his room. Vibrating with pent up anticipation, he sat at his desk and carefully laid out the score of his symphony in front of him.

His eyes roved over the notations, mentally translating them into music: the procession of drums, the boom of cannon fire, the sweet refrain of "Dixie" in counterpoint to the driving strains of "John Brown's Body." This last section had inevitably focused on war; on the innocence of the newly-inducted soldier to the realities of death and killing. He had been working on it all week, had reached the tricky climax where he had thought of re-introducing the themes of "Daniel's Lullaby" and "Taps" once more, as brother faced brother on the battlefield.

The idea had excited him: the realization that the mosaic of his life, as well as the threads of this unfinished symphony, finally had a tale to tell; one of brother against brother in a war where glory and infamy, kindness and viciousness, valor and cowardice existed side-by-side.

Now, the idea ignited him. It was the last musical asset he had. The only work left for him to do. He took out another sheet of music, dipped his pen into the inkwell and wrote the first decisive chord of the last movement.

Bella hesitated outside the door to Zach's and Billy's room. Then she knocked softly. The door was slightly ajar. She pushed it open a few inches and listened for a sound.

"Zach? May I come in?" She pushed open the door another few inches and looked in.

Zach was at the desk, in his shirtsleeves, hunched over a sheaf of papers. He was writing furiously.

"If I'm disturbing you, I'll come back."

"Not at all." He put his pen down and stretched his arms high over his head.

Bella smiled. She came in, holding a basket covered with a linen napkin. "I brought you some sandwiches and a bottle of lemonade. Nancy said she hadn't seen you for hours. I thought you might be hungry."

Zach stood up and took the basket from her hands. "That was a very sweet thing to do. But then, you are an angel." He smiled at her and put the basket on the corner of his bed.

Bella blushed and took a step backwards. "It's just a few sandwiches. I was worried about you."

"Worried? About me?" Zach felt a surge of emotion at her words, but he stopped himself from reaching for her.

"Yes. I thought you might be distraught. The whole situation is terrible. It wasn't even your fault."

Zach shook his head. "Don't think about it anymore. What's done is done."

She looked at the desk covered with sheets of music. "Were you writing your symphony?"

"Yes. It's going well." He rubbed his eyes, then looked up and smiled at her again. "At least I think it's good."

"Of course it's good," she said, brushing one of the pages with her fingertips.

"It will be, since I'll have plenty of time to work on it now."

She looked up, startled. "Does that mean...?"

"Yes. Gabriel Kramer gave us the news early this morning while you were out with Amanda."

"And...?"

"Beach insists I leave the band, but he's keeping you and the others on under a new name."

"Oh no! Oh, Zach!" Her eyes reflected sorrow and pity as she reached a hand to him in sympathy.

Zach took her hand briefly, then abruptly turned back to his music. He didn't want to see the pity reflected in her eyes. He wouldn't stand for pity, especially from her.

"If only there were a way to convince Mr. Beach that he was wrong! Maybe if I talked to him?"

Zach caught her hand again, but this time to stop her. "No! There's nothing to be done. You have nothing to bargain with."

"I do have something to bargain with. I'm going to tell him the truth, that I can't sing with the band unless you're there."

He took both her warm hands in his, rubbing the soft tips of her fingers.

"That won't solve the Rebel problem," he said quietly. "And it won't help the boys keep their jobs, not to mention your own."

Bella began to protest, but he shushed her.

"Now that I'm out of it, John says you are the draw for the band. Whatever happens, we have to preserve the band." He looked deeply into her violet eyes, drowning in their reflected sorrow. "That's our future."

She said nothing, but averted her face from his gaze. "We've burdened you so, Zach. If I hadn't insisted on coming with you."

"Don't say that Bella. This had nothing to do with your coming." He turned her face gently to his. "I'm going to finish this symphony, Bella. I was thinking it would be better if I went back home for a month, then met you all in Boston."

"Oh, Lord! Must you?" She pulled away from him, her eyes brimming with tears.

He didn't know if the tears were a sign that she would miss him, or simply panic at the thought of performing alone. A great tide of misery washed over him. "It'll be all right, Bella. I'll stay until the end of this week. But I need to keep out of sight."

"Won't you even come to watch me?" Her voice was low and tentative. "To rehearse with me? I don't know enough songs to carry the band. And who will I banter with?"

Zach looked at her for a long moment, trying to figure out how to put into words the agony of her request. How could he explain that it would be misery for him to stay on and watch them on stage? To hear them play his songs. To watch John lead his band. How could she even begin to understand?

"Of course I'll rehearse with you," he finally said.

"Oh, thank you!" She threw her arms around him, embracing him fiercely. Then she abruptly pulled away. "I'm sorry I'm not more confident. But I need your help, at least for the first few times. I wouldn't know what to do up there alone. I depend on you so when I'm on stage."

"Don't apologize," Zach said, longing to take her in his arms. "I'm asking you to do a great deal."

"I'll make you proud of me, Zach." She gave him a peck on the cheek. "I'll leave to your work, now. And your sandwiches." And in a moment, she was gone.

He put his hand to the spot she had so casually kissed and held it there for a long time as he stared at the pages of music in front of him.

Twenty-Five

As she waited at the far end of the hallway to go on stage that night, panic burned through Bella's stomach. This was nothing like the familiar flutter of stage fright Bella had always felt before a performance. Her heart pounded so hard, she could barely breath. How would she ever sing?

Zach massaged her shoulders, whispering something in her ears.

Bella thought back on her short month with Zach's band. Always, no matter how nervous she was before going on, Zach's smile and his banter instilled courage, and the band's lively music buoyed her spirits. But tonight, there would be no one to tease, despite John's steady presence. Indeed, the music would sound different without Zach's soaring cornet solos.

Her feet tapped nervously, as the urge to flee rippled through her body.

"Breath in." Zach put his hands on her diaphragm as they began the familiar routine of warming up her voice.

Bella obliged him, but in her mind, she flew through the door, down the main stairs, out the hotel door, down, down, down the winding mountain pass, running until she reached the safety of her old rooms in Mrs. Oster's building, where she and Amanda and Daniel had lived together.

Amanda's face rose in front of her, with her sweet dimples and cornflower blue eyes, and that stubborn look she had cultivated as of late. And dear Daniel's image hovered in her vision.

That image broke her spell. Daniel was gone. That was the cold, hard reality.

Bella took in a deep breath and hit her note, reassured by the familiar feel of Zach's strong hands on her waist. She had to do her best. She couldn't run away. She was the breadwinner now and had better behave like one.

"That's your cue," Zach said, giving her shoulders one last squeeze.

Bella could hear John's voice announcing The American Nightingale. The crowd's chatter continued and then subsided into an expectant hush.

"Oh Lord," she breathed. "Get me through this." Squeezing Zach's hand for luck, Bella swept through the door and onto the stage and plunged into *Listen to the Mockingbird*, which had by now become her trademark.

The burning sensation in her stomach soon subsided with the lilt of the music, giving way to mere butterflies. As the band swung into the refrain of Stephen Foster's popular ballad, "Old Folks at Home," she caught John's eye. He winked at her, and she felt a bit better.

Putting aside her emotions, she sang the song with as much enthusiasm as she could muster. Her concentration was broken when a young man in the front yelled out something unintelligible. She tried to ignore him, but as she finished the Stephen Foster tune, he came closer to the stage and yelled again.

"Where's your gray bird, Nightingale!" This time, his comment was quite audible. Sticking his thumbs in his waistcoat, the boy puffed out his chest with evident pride.

Bella felt her face redden as a burst of laughter greeted his jeer. She realized "gray bird" was a euphemism for Zach's Confederate background.

Anger propelled her toward the young man. She glared at him, ruffling her skirts, and began to sing without accompaniment.

"Shoo fly, don't bother me. Shoo fly, don't bother me." She leaned over the stage and waved her hand at him in a dismissive gesture, her anger flashing in her narrowed eyes. "Shoo fly, don't bother me, for I belong to Company C."

John and the boys came right in on the song, and Bella made another dismissive gesture.

As the brazen young man shook his fist at the band, several couples swept onto the dance floor. The crowd tittered and laughed at her put down.

She glanced over in triumph to where Zach was standing just inside the far door and caught him in a rare, unguarded moment. She saw his sad, faraway expression suddenly harden into a mask of bitterness. Her buoyant feelings turned to lead.

Then, as he caught sight of her, he flashed a grin. Raising a clenched fist above his head, he shook it in a gesture of triumph.

Bella turned away, shaken. She had been so caught up in her own fears, she hadn't thought about how tightly Zach's very soul was bound up in this band. How much it hurt him to stand out in the hallway and listen tonight.

The final irony was that the band could never mean that much to her. She would gladly trade places with him. She would do anything to restore him to his rightful place as band leader. If only she could find some way.

Zach's fingers twitched as the band swung into the next song, aching to work the valves of the coronet. He jammed his hands into his pockets, but his brain mentally played each note, throat constricting as if he were actually blowing into his horn. He winced as Billy came in a fraction too soon on the drums.

"No, no, Billy boy," he muttered. He couldn't stand this a minute more. He stalked down the hall, down a flight of stairs, and out of the hotel into the night air.

Drawing a cigar from his inner coat pocket, Zach lingered on the porch steps to light up. But his pent-up energy would not let him smoke there in peace. He jogged down the porch steps and kept walking until the grass ended and the ground turned into an exposed floor of bare, smooth stone, bathed in moonlight.

The band music drifted out from the second floor of the hotel, Bella's sweet voice floating above the melody line. It sounded unreal to Zach, as if it were a dream somewhere far off and unconnected to him. The night air was cool. He wished Bella were here with him, or he on stage with her and the band.

Squatting down, Zach studied the various names and dates carved into the bare rock. Lovers' names. Artist's names. Children's names. He ran a finger over the nearest ones. Some had rough edges that caught at his fingertips, as if they had been chiseled only yesterday. Others were smoother to the touch, worn by footsteps, rain, and wind.

He stood up thoughtfully, studying the names until he saw a large smooth space. In his mind, he pictured the words "Smith's Cornet Band" carved there in big flowing letters. And a date: 1866. Next year, he vowed silently, his band would be back here, with himself at the helm and Bella at his side.

Reaching into his vest pocket, he removed his mother-of-pearl handled pen knife. He would carve the words deep into the rock floor. But as he opened the ornate knife, he looked at its small blade and chuckled. It would take him a year and a day with this bitty knife. He snapped the blade shut and returned it to his pocket.

First thing tomorrow, he'd purchase one of those chisel and hammer sets the rockhounds were always using. Then he'd carve his promise and his legacy deeply into the rock where it could never be erased.

"I thought that was you, Smith. What's the matter, don't enjoy the music anymore?"

The harsh voice put Zach on his guard. Slowly, he turned around and came face to face with Ruckler.

"I would have thought you would be on your way by now," the manager said with a smirk. He scratched his long, bushy beard. "Back to wherever it is you Rebels come from."

Zach removed his cigar between his teeth and calmly blew a series of smoke rings, which floated up into the night air. "I come from New York."

"That makes it doubly traitorous, then." In the moonlight, Ruckler's face was in half shadow, but his piercing eyes glimmered with hatred. "Traitor."

Zach said nothing. Inside, he began to gather his restless energies into his center, coiled tense and ready to spring. His senses were fully alert, as if he were back in the army, waiting for the rush of enemy and the sudden bursts of gunfire to break the boredom of camp life.

"I ought to run you off," Ruckler continued, taking another step closer, raising his fists into a boxing stance. "I ought to throw you right off this cliff."

Zach grinned silently, dropped his cigar, and with deliberate menace ground it slowly under his heel. His fingers were itching for a chance to pay Ruckler back for once and for all. But he knew how to bide his time.

"Well?" Zach stared into Ruckler's eyes and inclined his head. "What are you waiting for?"

Ruckler hesitated a moment. He raised one fist but shifted his weight back as if ready to retreat. "I've got my job to think about. But don't think I wouldn't be able to do it, Smith. Besides, you're as good as gone from here. And your high and mighty mistress will be left wide open."

Zach became as still as a tiger before it leaps for its prey.

"You're right, Ruckler. I'm as good as gone. You've seen to that." Zach noticed that his words had caused Ruckler to relax into a less wary position. "As good as gone," he added softly.

Ruckler threw back his head and laughed. "We'll see who she turns to when you're not here to watch over her."

"Dangerous position, though," Zach continued thoughtfully, as if he had not heard Ruckler's remark. "Yes, indeed. Unlike you, I have nothing more to lose."

For one moment, Ruckler's eyes widened as Zach pulled back his arm and landed a blow that smashed his nose. His second blow hit Ruckler squarely in the stomach, knocking the wind out of him. Ruckler doubled over. A third blow on his neck sent him sprawling in the dirt.

Ruckler lay there, gasping for breath. Zach nudged his shoulder with the tip of his boot. "Stick your nose in my business again and I'll make sure you won't be able to breathe through it."

Ruckler groaned.

"And if you so much as look the wrong way at Bella, I'll make sure your eyes are permanently shut." Zach bent over Ruckler, his foot resting firmly on the man's rump. "Even if I'm not here, my boys will protect her. They'll let me know if anyone tries to bother her. I'm not a forgiving man, Ruckler. No one threatens what's mine —my career, my band, my sister-in-law—and gets away with it."

Ruckler clutched his nose and groaned again.

Zach looked up. A small knot of people had gathered on the porch, whispering, and pointing.

"Is there a doctor in the house?" Zach called to them casually, strolling toward the hotel. "The man over there met with a little accident.

~

Exhausted, Bella took her last bow and gratefully sailed offstage. She had never realized how much effort it took to sing all night. Zach had made everything so easy for her.

She looked around for him in vain, but he was not there. She saw John making his way toward her, fiddle in hand.

"You did well, tonight," he said. "A real trooper. It's a lot to carry off a full night. I'm proud of you."

Bella smiled wearily. "Thank you, John. From the first, you've been a kind and encouraging friend. I can't thank you enough." She took his hand. "But it was you who made everything go smoothly tonight. I have a lot to learn."

John squeezed her hand affectionately. "It's late. We'd best be catching some winks."

"Zach isn't here. I wonder...."

"It's tough for him to stay and watch," John said. "He's probably back in his room, working on his symphony."

Bella nodded. "I guess so."" She felt a movement behind her and turned around.

Zach was there, framed in the doorway, grinning broadly. "You two did me proud, tonight. The band's in good hands."

"Zach!" Bella ran to him. His strong arms caught her and held her, as she looked up at him. "Oh, Zach, you did watch us after all!"

"Of course I watched you. I was prowling around all night."

Bella stood back a moment and gazed at him. Something about him was different. "You look decidedly pleased with yourself," she said. "What have you been up to?"

"Not much." Zach winked at her. "A totally uneventful night for me. Come on, let's all go for a walk before bed. It's a glorious night!"

≈

It was nearly eleven o'clock when Zach finally put his pen down and pushed back his chair.

The glow of his oil lamp flickered against the dark windowpane. Billy and the rest of the band had probably finished for the night and would be packing up.

Even with his aching back and bleary eyes, Zach felt a ripple of deep satisfaction. The last stanza of his symphony was finally finished.

The entire final section had come in a rush of furious work over the last two days. True, it was only the first draft; more tedious work lay ahead to score each stanza for a full symphonic orchestra. He could finish that in Oyster Bay. But the composition was complete.

The act of stepping down from his responsibilities as bandleader had uncorked some sort of spigot that allowed the music that had been stored all these years in his head to gush forth. The result was like fine, aged wine.

At the thought, Zach smiled and reached for a glass to pour himself a brandy, feeling the need to mark the occasion with a bit more formality than a pull from the bottle itself.

One task remained. Turning back to his desk, he drew out a sheet of stationary to write a letter to an old friend who now played bass violin in the New York Music Society orchestra.

He would send Abraham Bronson a first draft of the symphony, in hopes that the society would commission it for their autumn or spring season. He drew out a second sheet of stationary and wrote a short note to a sheet music publisher offering three new tunes for sale, including "Daniel's Lullaby."

He tucked the letter into his coat pocket. He would post it in the morning, traveling into Catskill himself. He certainly wasn't going to let this letter fall into the hands of Ruckler or Farris, who handled the daily mail.

A bit of brandy remained in the snifter. Holding the glass up to Bella's photograph on the wall, he whispered her name. He wanted to share this with her. After all, it had been Bella who had urged him to finish the symphony. Bella, through Daniel, who had pushed him to open the package from his father in the first place.

Grabbing his candle and his manuscript, Zach set out for the main house to wake Bella.

At her door, he softly knocked. She would be just going to bed. Perhaps she was already asleep. He knocked again, listened, then thought better of it. He'd wake Amanda. How stupid of him.

"Who's there?" Bella's voice on the other side of the door was tentative and wary.

"It's Zach! Are you awake?"

"Zach!"

He heard the key in the lock turn. The door flew open.

"What's wrong?" Her face was filled with anxiety, as she looked up at him. She was dressed in a robe, and her hair was down around her shoulders, loose and long and lustrous in the candlelight. The sight of her took his breath away.

"Nothing's wrong. Everything's right." He smiled at her. "I finished my symphony. I just wanted someone to tell."

Even as he said the words, he felt foolish. But in the next moment, Bella's face was radiant with excitement. She opened the door wider and waved him inside.

"Oh, Zach, that's wonderful!" she whispered. "Of course, you wanted to celebrate! Come in, come in."

He stepped inside. In the flickering candlelight, he could see Amanda, asleep in the big bed, her thumb in her mouth, her arm locked around her doll.

"I'm sorry, this was foolish. I'll show you in the morning. I don't want to wake Amanda."

"You won't," she whispered. "Come out on the balcony. Nancy and I often talk out there after I come back. Amanda won't hear us. She's fast asleep."

"Here it is." Waving the sheaf of papers in his hand, he followed her. "The last movement."

"I knew you'd finish it. Hum it to me. What does it sound like?"

Zach chuckled. "It's hard to hum a symphony."

"Well, try!" She sat down in one of the little wooden chairs and motioned him to pull the other chair next to her.

He began to explain the harmonies and competing sounds, whispering snatches of the melody as Bella nodded and smiled, or closed her eyes and listened.

"I'm sorry. You're sleepy and I'm..."

"No," she whispered. "I want to hear. Keep talking. I like to hear you talk about your music."

So Zach talked for a while longer, until she drifted off to sleep completely. He sat there for a long moment, content to gaze at her.

"Bella," he whispered. She didn't seem to hear. "I have to go away from you soon, and it's the hardest thing I've ever had to do. To go away and not tell you how much I love you. How much I want you. How scared I am to tell you because you might not share my..."

Bella moved her head. "What? What?"

He stood up. "Bella?" He shook her arm gently. "Bella, wake up. You should go to bed."

Her eyelashes fluttered, and she opened her eyes. "What? Oh, Zach. Oh no, I fell asleep. I'm sorry."

"I put you to sleep talking about my symphony. I just hope that's not a reflection on its appeal."

She smiled sleepily. "You're always joking." She patted his cheek. "I'm just so tired."

"Come on," he said, helping her rise and walking her to the bedroom. "You need to go to bed." As she drew back the covers, Zach locked the balcony doors. When he turned back around, she was taking off her robe, oblivious, it seemed to him, of his presence. Watching her silhouette in the semi-darkened room, he wanted to take her in his arms and tell her he loved her.

"Bella?" he whispered.

"What?"

He shook his head. "Nothing. Goodnight. Don't forget to lock the door behind me."

Twenty-Six

It was nearly noon when Zach awoke the next morning from a deep sleep.

He'd been dreaming of holding Bella. As he stretched, he almost expected to feel Bella beside him, warm and drowsy. But, of course, it had only been a dream. He was alone in his narrow bed.

Zach sat up and saw that Billy had also gone out. He rose and headed for the washbasin to splash his face with water and shave. After he dried himself, he turned around and noticed a note on the floor near the door. He picked it up and unfolded it.

Dear Zach,

Billy said you were still asleep. We didn't want to wake you. Amanda and I went to breakfast at nine. Nancy and I are taking Amanda on a children's outing at ten. I'm so happy you've finished your symphony! Join us if you wake. After rehearsals, we'll celebrate tonight at dinner! I'll ask Mr. Kramer for the private dining room at 6 o'clock. Don't be late! We have a show tonight."

Affectionately,
Bella

The note filled Zach with conflicting emotions: a measure of gladness that Bella had gone to the trouble of arranging a celebration dinner. A touch of melancholy at being left out of things. Bella and the boys had their day filled with rehearsals and shows. Nancy and Amanda had their amusements. Well, he had his work, too. The first task was to mail a copy of a first draft of his symphony to his friend at the Music Society in New York City.

Driving to the postal clerk in town would take up much of the afternoon, he thought. But when Zach got to the desk, there were no carriages to be had.

"Surely, there must be one, even a horse that I can ride into town," Zach said.

The desk clerk didn't even bother to look up. "Sorry. Nothing."

"It's vital I post this package today," Zach said, trying to keep his voice neutral.

The desk clerk raised his head and gave Zach a long, cold stare. "I'm sorry. I have *nothing* for you. You may leave the package at the desk, if you wish. It will go out with the next stagecoach."

"I'll bet," Zach retorted. Jamming his package under his arm, Zach stalked away. If he had to, he vowed, he'd walk all the way down the mountain road to post it.

"Mr. Smith!" A feminine voice reached him from across the room. "Mr. Zach Smith!"

Zach turned. The voice was familiar. Yet it took him a moment to recognize the tall, willowy woman descending the main staircase. She wore a stylish blue walking suit, and a cascade of blonde curls tumbled out from one side of her blue bonnet. Then he saw her face as she drew closer. It was Charlotte Courtland.

"Mrs. Courtland." Zach hurried over to her. "It's been so long."

"It's Countess *Vallenchin du Lac*, now." Charlotte grabbed both his hands. "I thought that was you!" Her blue eyes twinkled with warm affection. "The old Mountain House has been a dull place without you these past years. I'm glad to see you've survived that wretched war, *chéri*."

"Survived it, yes." He sighed, as her words stirred up sad feelings about the war. But he tamped them down, and smiled, truly pleased to see her after so many years.

"And survived it well from the look of you." Charlotte gave him a once-over glance, her hands fluttering over his vest and up to his neck. "Still the handsome rogue."

"You look positively ravishing, Charlotte. Nancy told me you had married a Parisian count. Paris seems to agree with you."

Charlotte gave a throaty, low chuckle and tucked her arm possessively through his. "Walk me outside. I've rented a carriage. One day here and I'm bored silly already. Of course, now that I've seen you...."

"I'm surprised you'd want to be seen with me."

"Why wouldn't I?"

"Johnny Reb and all that nonsense with the riot..."

"Hold on, mon *chéri*," she stopped short and patted his arm. "You'll have to start from the beginning. It's obvious I've missed something vital here. I've only just arrived yesterday." Her eyes glittered, as she shot him a saucy look. "You mean to say that I've missed a full-fledged riot at the respectable old Mountain House? I have the worst luck!"

Zach guffawed. "Nothing ever ruffles your feathers, does it, Charlotte?"

"No. That's what tons of money and widowhood at an early age'll do for you." She winked and hooked her arm through his once more. "So tell me what trouble you've gotten yourself into, my dear, handsome fellow. I'm all ears."

Zach stopped her. "Listen, did you say you've rented a carriage?"

"And a driver. I'm bored already with the respectable company in my party. I only come here for the fresh air, you know."

"I need to get to town to post this parcel as soon as possible and there isn't a carriage to be had." Zach indicated his manuscript. "Would you mind a detour and some company?"

"I can think of several detours I'd like to take with you!" They approached a line of three carriages in the driveway. "Find out which one is mine, *chéri*, will you? This is turning out to be a much better day than I expected."

"Now, Charlotte," Zach cautioned. "At the risk of losing both my transportation and your company, I have to be honest with you. I'm afraid I'm hopelessly in love with someone."

"Oh my," Charlotte said, and stuck out her lower lip in a pretty pout. "Who is she? A rich young thing?"

"Afraid not."

"Anyone I know?"

"No one you know," Zach said.

Charlotte stared at him with a look of surprise. "Are you serious about her?"

"Yes, Charlotte, I am very serious about her."

"Are you going to marry her?"

He hesitated, mulling that question over in his mind. "I think I might like to," he said, almost surprised to hear himself say it. "The thing is, I haven't declared my feelings to her yet."

Charlotte frowned but didn't say a word.

"Still want me along?" Zach said gently.

"Well, I am disappointed," she said, reverting to her old, familiar teasing ways. She winked at him. "War does such funny things to people. I'd never take you for a one-woman man. I promise, however, not to try and tempt you, or kiss you wildly, or sully your new-found virtue. Even though I'd like to."

"I thought you were a married woman again?"

"I am. But he's stayed behind in Paris," she said lightly. Zach noticed a forlorn look cloud Charlotte's expression for an instant. He wondered if her new marriage was an unhappy one.

Zach helped her into the carriage, then climbed in next to her, tucking his parcel at his feet. "Thanks for allowing me to tag along despite ruining your expectations."

"No matter," she said, flashing him a brilliant smile. Tucking her hand into the crook of his arm, she snuggled close. "Even otherwise spoken for, you're still one of the more fascinating men I could choose to spend an afternoon with. Now, I want to hear about this riot. And, more so, about this lady love who has managed to inspire your honorable intentions." She rapped on the side of the carriage. "Drive on, driver!"

~

That evening, John and Nancy waited with Bella on the porch. John perched on the railing, puffing a cigar and scanning the horizon for a sign of Zach.

"It's past six," Bella said, pacing the wide front porch of the mountain house. "I left him a note about dinner."

"Mama?" Amanda tugged at her mother's skirts. "I'm hungry."

"Yes, I know, dear. We'll just have to eat without Uncle Zach." Bella's mouth was tight with disappointment. She had ordered an extravagant dinner in the private dining room to celebrate the completion of the symphony. Now the band members and Gabriel Kramer were devouring it on their own. "John, maybe you should take Amanda in and eat. I'll wait."

"Why don't you come, too?" John said. He stubbed out his cigar and rose with a resigned sigh. "Waiting isn't going to bring him any sooner. He probably hitched a ride down to the post office and can't find a way back, is all."

Bella nodded. "You're right. Might as well eat something so the dinner isn't a complete waste. Come on, Amanda."

The boys in the band were noisily eating their way through roast leg of lamb, stuffed and rolled veal birds in wine sauce, and roasted potatoes. Bella tried to choke down some of the food but had little appetite. She was exhausted. If it hadn't been for Zach, she might have skipped supper altogether in favor of a nap.

The band's heavy schedule was beginning to wear her down, especially without Zach there to trade off singing duties. Now it was all up to her, and, truth be told, she felt somewhat resentful. Zach hadn't come to rehearsals or backstage these last few days to help bolster her spirits. She could understand it, she told herself, as long as she knew he was working on the symphony. She knew he was keeping out of trouble by staying in his room. And yet... Where was he now?

Billy Parisher tapped her arm. "Say, Bella? Ain't that true?"

Bella glanced up. "I don't know, Billy. I'm sorry." She hadn't been paying any attention. She felt dizzy and anxious and out of sorts. "Will you excuse me, please? Nancy, I'll be right back. If you could just keep an eye on Amanda."

Bella pushed back her chair and fled the room before anyone could question her.

Hurrying through the lobby and the main door, Bella veered off for the furthest corner of the nearly deserted hotel veranda. Throwing herself into one of the rocking chairs, she fell into a stupor of disappointment and exhaustion. She felt tears sting her eyes and brushed them angrily away. She had gone to so much trouble to make this a nice celebration for Zach, to give him something special, and he hadn't even bothered to show up.

The sound of squeaking carriage wheels coming up the path caught her attention. Bella sank back into her chair and closed her eyes, so that whoever it was would think she was sleeping. Voices caught her attention.

"Well, I hope I haven't caused you to miss your dinner, *mon chéri*."

"I'm not too late. Charlotte, I can't thank you enough for the ride into town and for a charming afternoon. It was just like old times."

Bella's eyes flew open. It was Zach. Craning her neck a bit, she could see him helping a tall, blonde woman from the carriage. As she stepped down, Zach lifted her hand and kissed it. Bella's throat tightened. Her eyes raked the woman's profile, taking in the expensive clothes, jewels, hat and hairdo, the rouged cheeks and lips. So that was why he had been late. He had gone off somewhere with this woman. A woman she didn't recognize from any of the guests at the Mountain House.

"I'm in your debt, Charlotte."

"You're always in my debt." Drawing him close, she kissed him on the cheek. "I'll go in first, so people won't talk. Good luck with your *affaire de coeur*. When you do marry your lady love, you will invite me to the wedding, won't you? I promise to behave myself. And if things don't turn out the way you hope, well. Look me up again."

The woman disappeared into the hotel. Zach stood there a moment, unaware that Bella was watching him. He pulled out his pocket watch and shook his head. "Lord, I'm late."

Bella was confused. Lady love? A wedding? What could the woman have meant? Zach wasn't engaged. Or was he? Suddenly, she felt embarrassed to think that Zach might learn she had eavesdropped on his conversation. She pressed herself further into the chair as Zach bounded up the steps, but he never even glanced in her direction.

She waited until Zach had disappeared inside the front door. Then she quietly slipped out of the rocker and followed a short distance behind him. When she reached the private dining room, Zach was already seated at the head of the table, smiling as the boys joked about him being late.

"Glad you could make it for your own howdy-do," Billy teased him.

"Hey, did anybody save a veal bird for the guest of honor?" joked Big Harry.

"Bet you ate his share," Pete joked.

"Time for a toast," Gabriel Kramer said, raising his glass.

"Now, Gabriel, wait until Bella gets here," Nancy gently reprimanded him. "She's the one who put this dinner together."

"I'm here," said Bella, slipping into her seat next to Amanda. She quickly raised her glass and smiled. "Here's to Zach's new symphony."

"Here, here!" came the cries around the table as they all lifted their glasses to Zach.

Zach grinned. "Let's hope the New York Music Society likes it. I just got back from posting it off to them."

As Zach and the others exchanged their customary banter, Bella quietly sipped her wine. She felt quite detached from the gaiety around her, as she tried to puzzle out the little scene she had witnessed between Zach and that woman. If Zach was getting married, he hadn't said a word about it to her. There was no reason he should, she reasoned. And he certainly deserved some happiness, after all he had been through in the war.

Yet, somehow, the thought of Zach marrying made Bella feel even more lonely than ever.

~

That evening, while the band played without him, Zach wandered out in front of the hotel, past rows of old people nodding off in their rocking chairs on the hotel's wide veranda.

He'd had an enjoyable afternoon with Charlotte, tagging along as she shopped. She had talked of her new life as the Countess Vallenchin du Lac; of her fondness for the witty old count, who had no wish to join her in the "wilderness of America," as he called it; of his dozens of boring relatives; and of her homesickness for the New York scene of her youth.

"We're getting older, *mon chere*," she had complained to Zach, in a voice filled with such longing he couldn't help but kiss her. And that had been the funny thing. There had been no passion in that kiss between old lovers. Only the warmth of an old, old friendship.

Zach slipped into in an empty Adirondack chair, tipping his hat over his eyes to induce a nap. For what seemed like an hour, he sat there, trying to relax. But on checking his pocket watch, no more than ten minutes had passed.

He jumped up from the chair and surveyed the scene in front of him. A few children ran in circles, teasing each other as they played a lively game of blind man's bluff in the waning light.

He watched them for a while, amused by their antics. Lighting a cigar, Zach felt at loose ends. He longed to play with the band. Longed to talk about his symphony with Bella, as he had done last night. He would have to leave soon, maybe even tomorrow, and he didn't want to leave her. He had told that to Charlotte.

"Tell her you're in love with her," Charlotte had advised.

"Maybe she's not ready, but how else will you know whether it's worth the wait?"

She was right. Yet, the only time he had dared to say the words was the night on Bella's balcony, when she had fallen asleep. He didn't think he could bear it if she told him she couldn't love him. That would destroy everything. How could they ever work together on stage again? It would be too painful.

He had surprised himself when he told Charlotte he was considering marriage. But now, a voice very like his father's kept running through his mind: *What? You, the whoring devil? What makes you suddenly think you can become a faithful husband?*

He'd never been faithful to any woman in his life. That was the unvarnished truth of it. He'd quickly grown tired of them all—all except Charlotte, who had made it clear from the start that he was not rich enough or old enough to be her husband.

With Bella, it was different. His feelings for her went beyond physical attraction.

Lost in thought, Zach wandered out to the edge of the grassy lawn to where it joined the rock ledge. Two boys were sprawled on the ground, busily chipping away at the stone. A lump of coal lay near one of the boy's feet. He saw they had used it to write out the words they were now busily carving.

"What are you doing, gentlemen?" Zach asked.

One stopped his tapping and looked up, eying him suspiciously. The other boy kept tapping his hammer against the chisel, totally absorbed in the process.

"We're carving our names, Mister," the boy said with a scowl. "What of it?"

"Nothing much," Zach said lightly. He peered over the boy's shoulder, taking a long puff as the boy resumed chipping the stone.

After some time, the tow-headed boy who had scowled at Zach jumped up. "I'm done with mine," he announced. "Jamie, you almost finished? We've got to go in soon."

"Would you be willing to sell me your chisel and hammer set?" Zach said. The boy looked up at him in surprise. Zach took a long puff on his cigar, then blew a smoke ring to impress the boy. "I'd like to carve my own name here, tonight. But all I have is this pen knife." Zach reached in his pocket and pulled out the pearl-handled knife. "Either of you gentlemen willing to trade me?"

"Let's see!" The towheaded boy snatched the knife and pulled it open, examining it closely. "It's a real good one." He tapped the pearl handle with the point of his chisel. "This real?"

"Genuine mother-of-pearl," Zach said.

"All right, it's a deal." The boy handed over his rock hammer and chisel.

Zach held the tools up to the light for inspection. "Fine specimens," Zach pronounced. "Pleasure doing business with you."

The two boys suddenly looked over toward the hotel.

"Mama's calling," said the dark-haired boy, scrambling up from the ground and gathering his tools. "Let's go, Randolph."

Zach watched the boys run off. He knelt down to pick up the lump of coal they had left behind. Scanning the rock floor, he found the bare spot where he had envisioned carving the band's name the other night.

Zach calmly wrote the name "Smith's Cornet Band" in flowing script on the soft rock. Then, he added the year 1866, when he hoped to return next season. He nodded, pleased with the look of it.

He removed his jacket and rolled up his sleeves. Taking up the chisel and hammer, he sat down, and began to tap out the first letter with sure, steady strokes. He intended to carve his promise to return next year so deeply into the rock that it would stay there until the end of time.

Twenty-Seven

"Hello, Billy," said Bella at breakfast the next morning. "Hello, Billy!" echoed Amanda. "Want some of my pancakes?"

Billy patted Amanda's head. "Naw, you eat 'em. I ain't got much of an appetite this mornin'."

"You're up early," Bella said. "Care for some coffee, at least?"

"Much obliged." The lanky drummer pulled out a chair and sat down next to Bella. He accepted the cup of coffee she handed him, then stared gloomily into its depths.

"Sugar?"

"Sure." Billy accepted the sugar bowl. He dropped three lumps into his cup, then listlessly stirred the coffee.

"Something the matter?" Bella asked. He seemed unusually moody this morning.

"Zach's gone."

Bella put her own coffee cup down. "When?"

"He packed up and caught the early morning coach. He's taking the afternoon steamer back to the city." Billy stopped stirring and simply stared into the depths of his cup. "Said he said all his goodbyes last night at the dinner, and couldn't bear to say 'em all over again."

"Oh, Billy!" Bella instinctively reached for his hand.

The drummer looked up at her with an expression of woe. "Won't be the same. And him just back from the war and all." He shook his head back and forth. "Won't be the same."

"Mama?" Amanda asked, her expression grave. "Is Uncle Zach going away?"

"Yes, darling," Bella said. "Just for a little while. He's hoping to get his symphony played in New York City."

"What's a symphony?"

"Oh, a grand musical composition played by fifty musicians all playing different instruments," Bella explained.

Amanda's face lit up with pleasure. "Can we go?"

"Sure can, Little Missy," Billy answered, affectionately mussing up her hair. "Zach said we'd have front row seats." He turned back to Bella, his mood brightening a little. "Zach says he's got a good chance at getting it played, because he heard the Society was look-ing' for somethin' new. Something' for a benefit concert for war orphans and widows and such."

"Mama?" Amanda was waving avidly at another table, where a young red-haired child was beckoning to her. "There's Caroline. Can I go over to her table? I'm finished."

Bella turned around. Another one of Amanda's new friends. She seemed to make a new one every day. The youngster's mother was nodding and smiling, gesturing that Amanda was invited to come over. "Of course, dear. But nowhere else."

"Yes, Mama." Amanda kissed her mother on the cheek, then skipped over to the other table.

"Maybe I will have a piece of toast." Billy reached for the silver salver. He slathered butter and jam onto a slice, then proceeded to devour the toast in big bites.

"Billy, how long have you known Zach?"

"Well, now, let me think," Billy said, his mouth full of toast. He wiped his lips on his sleeve, then remembered and used the napkin for the last few crumbs. "Nigh onto ten years since I been with the band."

"You can't be more than twenty, twenty-two," Bella said in surprise.

"Twenty-four last February," Billy said, taking a gulp of his coffee. "Met Zach when I was fourteen. Been on my own since I was twelve. My ma had ten of us all crammed in one cabin. She kicked us all out of the house one by one when we was old enough."

"At twelve?" Bella was shocked.

"Sure. There weren't much food nor nothing else." Billy slathered more butter and jam on a second piece of toast. "Anyways, I was always drumming on anything I could find. Got me a job with a traveling tent show."

"What's a tent show?"

"Revival. Gospel stuff. Preaching' and making the lame walk and all." He studied Bella as if she were a strange specimen. "You never been to one?"

"I don't think they have them in New York City," Bella said.

"Humm." Billy considered this a moment. "Maybe not. Anyways, we was in St. Louis, set up down by the muddy old Mississippi. And Zach's band was playing at a fancy hotel in town. So one night, I says to Gordy—he played fiddle, but nowhere near as good as John—I says, Hey, Gordy, let's go down to the hotel and hear us a real band. And don't you know, even though it was a public dance, they took one look at us and kicked us right out.

"Well, Gordy was all for going back to the tent show," Billy continued. "But I says to him, let's go around the back of the hotel by the stage door. You could hear everything from there. I never heard such fine music. When Zach and John came outside in-between sets to have a smoke, I just starting talking' to them and drumming on boxes. Zach says, stick around, we can play together after the show. I decided then and there to just follow his band. Been with him ever since."

Bella was touched. Zach liked to pretend he was unsentimental. But here, he had taken in this young, untutored boy and helped him become a professional drummer.

"Another slice, Billy?" She held out the salver with the last piece of toast.

"Thanks."

"I wondered, Billy, if you knew if Zach was engaged to some-one," Bella asked.

Billy stopped buttering his toast. He looked at her keenly. "Why you askin'?"

"Because, well..." Bella hesitated, then blushed. "When I was on the porch waiting for Zach yesterday, I saw him get out of a carriage with a very beautiful woman. And I overheard her ask Zach if he would invite her to his wedding."

Billy looked embarrassed. "Oh. Right. Zach mentioned that Charlotte, I mean, uh, Countess Du Loc or something like that, gave him a lift into town yesterday. She married some Frenchie last year. Zach and her are old friends."

"But has Zach mentioned that he's getting married?" Bella gently persisted.

Billy choked in mid-chew, sputtering out a few crumbs. "I ain't heard nothing about a wedding." He cleared his throat loudly. "But I can tell you Zach is in love with only one person I know of. I ain't never seen him so miserable love-sick over a woman the way he is over you, Bella."

For a long moment, Bella couldn't seem to find her voice. "Me?"

"Hell, yes. He's been littering' up the room with paper trying to write a song about you. Bella this. Bella that. Crumples up the paper and throws it on the floor. If that ain't lovesick, I don't know what is!"

Bella was stunned. It was not the answer she had expected.

"Billy, you must be mistaken. Zach is not in love with me just because he's writing a song." She thought about this for a moment. "Is he?"

Billy looked at her and shook his head slowly. "See, that's what I can't make out. He ain't even told you. Usually, he sees a woman he wants, he goes right up to her, sweeps her off her feet, and that's that. But with you, he ain't said a word. But I saw the way he looked at you whenever you two dance that waltz. Hoooo, boy! He's got it bad, all right. I guess he ain't said nothing on account of your husband being dead and all. And your husband being his brother and all."

Bella sat back in her chair, her hands clasped over her mouth. Zach in love with her? Her head reeled with the thought.

"It can't be," she said at last.

Billy looked at her and grinned. "Sure is. As sure as I'm sitting here talking to you."

∼

For the last two days, Bella had sat down every morning, intending to write to Zach. She wasn't sure what to say, or even how to say it. She yearned to find out if Billy was right. And who better to ask than Zach himself? Yet, her own feelings for Zach were such a jumble, she simply couldn't figure out how to broach such a delicate subject.

"I was talking to Billy..."

No, that wouldn't do.

"Billy mentioned that you were in love with me."

She crumpled up the paper and threw it into the wastebasket. No matter how she phrased it, it always sounded ridiculous.

This morning, she had tried to write Zach again with the same result. In need of strong coffee, she dressed Amanda and herself, and went downstairs to breakfast. Gabriel Kramer was just coming up the steps.

"Mrs. Smith! I was just on my way to your floor. I have a letter from Zach for you." The hotel manager, dapper as usual in his charcoal gray silk frock coat and his close cropped beard, held out a creamy vellum envelope. "Had one from him myself. Sounds like he's making good progress on the symphony."

Bella took the envelope he offered and felt her cheeks grow hot with excitement. "Thank you. I was just on my way down to breakfast. Will you join us?"

"Another time, I'm afraid," Kramer said. "I have several matters to attend to. Guest problems that need to be smoothed over."

"Then I won't keep you."

"I just wanted to say that Mr. Beach is very pleased with the band. You've done an admirable job. I know you don't have much experience, but you handle yourself well on stage and off."

"Thank you, Mr. Kramer. I appreciate that."

"Good day, Mrs. Smith. Good day, Amanda." Kramer straightened his silk cravat and hurried past them.

Bella ordered breakfast and buttered slices of toast for Amanda. Coffee arrived. After exchanging pleasantries with the servers and cutting Amanda's waffles into bite size pieces, Bella finally had a moment to slit open the thick envelope that bore her name. Inside were two folded sheets of stationary filled with Zach's distinctive, bold script.

"What does it say, Mama?" Is Uncle Zach coming back?"

Bella scanned the pages to find something appropriate to read to Amanda. "Ah, he says, 'How is Little Missy?'"

"That's what he likes to call me," Amanda interrupted. "What else, Mama?"

"He says, 'I hope she has become the world champion at croquet by now. I miss her very much. When you get back to New York City, I plan to take her out to the best bakery in town and buy up all the pink sugar cakes they have!' How about that?"

Amanda nodded eagerly. "When? When can we go?"

Bella laughed. "Not until September."

"How many days is that?" Amanda looked thoughtful. "This many?" She held up six fingers.

"Oh, many more than that, I'm afraid," Bella answered with a sigh. "The rest of July, all of August, and then it's September."

Amanda pouted. "That's ages and ages." She turned back to her breakfast of waffles heaped with raspberries and cream.

"Yes, ages and ages," Bella agreed.

"Bella!" Big Harry was making his way through the dining room toward Bella's table. "Any coffee left?"

Bella sighed. She folded the letter and tucked it back into her reticule. "Of course, Harry. Sit down and I'll pour you a cup."

~

Between the demands of Amanda, rehearsals, social obligations, and the evening show, Bella's busy schedule left her no chance to finish Zach's letter until nearly midnight. When she finally returned to her room, Amanda was sleeping soundly, and Nancy was yawning over a book.

"How is she?" Bella whispered.

"Fine, as usual," Nancy whispered back. She closed her book, stretched, and yawned again.

"Oh, Nancy. I'm so sorry about these late nights."

"Nonsense. I'd just be sitting up reading anyway, waiting for John to come home. I'm used to the hours." Nancy scrutinized Bella. "But they don't seem to agree with you."

"You're so right." Bella unlocked the doors to the small balcony and sank into one of the twig chairs. Nancy joined her. "Amanda's up with the birds every morning. And I can't seem to drop off to sleep right away."

"I know. You're all wound up. John gets the same way. What you need is some nice chamomile tea. I had a pot brought up for you. You can sit out here and relax for a few minutes. There's a lovely moon out tonight." Nancy stood up and patted Bella's shoulder. "I'll see you tomorrow."

Bella grasped Nancy's hand and looked up at her. "I don't know what I'd do without you. I truly appreciate your friendship, dear Nancy."

"And I yours," Nancy said, giving Bella's shoulder a final pat. "You've become family."

"You don't know how happy that makes me feel."

"Goodnight."

Bella rose and locked the door after Nancy left. She walked softly to the bed and kissed her sleeping daughter, gently tucking Amanda's out flung leg back under the covers. Her daughter sighed in her sleep.

"I love you so," Bella murmured, stroking her curls, thinking of Daniel and their life together back in the old apartment. It seemed a lifetime ago, yet it had only been a few short months.

She poured herself a steaming cup of chamomile tea and took it outside on the balcony. With the bright moon giving enough light to read by, she opened Zach's letter.

Dear Bella,

I am sitting under a weeping willow tree, reading a volume of poetry by Yeats. I should be working on the timpani section of the symphonic score, but the day is too fine, the sky too blue, and the waves too inviting to stay indoors. I hope you will come to stay at Oyster Bay with us for the winter, when the landscape has a different kind of beauty. There are plenty of cottages here for rent. I want to take Amanda ice skating on the lake, and take you out on the ice boat with me. I think you would enjoy the feel of the wind in your hair as you skim along the frozen bay.

The New York Music Society has selected my symphony for a special concert to be held in aid of war widows and orphans. A worthy cause. September 16. I have a lot of work to do to get ready. I will be conducting the orchestra, something new for me. In fact, I will be spending the next week at the Music Society, holding auditions in Castle Garden to put together an orchestra. I will reserve a row of seats for all of you. I hope you will allow Amanda to come, too.

How is Little Missy? I hope she has become the world champion at croquet by now. I miss her very much. When you get back to New York City, I plan to take her out to the best bakery in town and buy up all the pink sugar cakes they have!

If you were here now, I would play the sections of the symphony for you on the piano and the cornet, instead of trying to hum them to you like I did that night.

I hope you are well. Don't wear yourself out. The band can be a hard taskmaster, as I well know. I am writing another waltz— where all this music is coming from, I haven't any notion, but it just seems to be pouring out of my pen. When we get to Boston, I

will teach you the steps. Tell the boys hello for me. Don't let them run you ragged. Kiss Amanda for me. Take care of yourself.
　Zach

Bella stared at the pages, reading certain phrases over and over, imagining Zach's voice as she did: *If you were here now...I hope you will come to stay at Oyster Bay... I think you would enjoy the feel of the wind in your hair... Take care of yourself.*

A slight breeze sent a shiver down her back. She stood up, folded the letter and slipped it back into the envelope. Outside below her, she could see two people walking hand in hand along the path to the arbor. Their backs were to her. They stopped, kissed, then embraced. As Bella watched them entwined in each other's arms, she shivered again, not from the wind but from loneliness.

How could she have been so blind? How could she have not realized that he cared for her from the way he had held her when they waltzed? From the night he opened his heart to her about the war and his childhood? From the afternoon he had kissed her? Had he been in love with her even then?

She missed him terribly. Was that love? She pressed the letter to her heart. Was it love in the same way she had loved Daniel? Yes, she thought. Of course, she thought. That's why she kept expecting to see him on stage with the band; to hear his knock at her door; to have him sit down to dinner at her table.

Turning from the window, Bella decided she was ready to take a chance. She would write to Zach and tell him what Billy said. She would make it clear that she still needed time, but that she had feelings for him, too. If Billy had somehow gotten it wrong – if Zach wasn't in love with her after all, he would quickly set her straight. And if he did love her... Oh!

Her heartbeat quickened with the thought of that possibility. Before she lost her nerve, she sat at her desk and lit a candle to write by.

Twenty-Eight

"July's half gone," Ruckler said to Farris as they sorted through the bags of morning mail in the back office. "I'll be glad when the season is over. A bit of quiet and a sojourn in the big city."

"I know what you mean," Farris replied, tossing several letters his way. "Here's one for someone on your staff. And a bill from the greenhouse."

"This one's addressed to the tea house in town," Ruckler said, holding up an envelope. "Wonder how it got in with ours?"

"Put it in the basket for the late-afternoon pickup," Farris said.

"Right-o," Ruckler replied. He stepped into the hall and tossed the letter into the outgoing basket at the front desk. That's when he noticed the name "Zach Smith" written across the only other envelope in the basket. It was addressed in care of the New York Music Society. There was a return address for the Mountain House, but no name indicating the sender.

Ruckler glanced around the lobby to make sure no one was looking his way. Then he took the letter and stuffed it into his pocket. He walked back to the office whistling a tune and resumed sorting the mail. "Yes, the big city with all its nightlife," he said. "I'm looking forward to a turn in some of those fancy houses I told you about. Eh, Farris?"

When the mail was sorted, Ruckler returned to the kitchen and set the envelope over a boiling kettle to steam it open. "Mind your own business!" he growled at one of the maids who attempted to peer over his shoulder.

Charles, the headwaiter, also came over and was duly rebuffed. "See to your polishing," Ruckler scolded. "Look sharp!"

Retiring to the privacy of his tiny office next to the pantry, Ruckler unfolded the pages of the letter, carefully smoothing them out. Threading the ends of his spectacles over his ears, he peered at the elegant script. Bella's name caught his eye at the bottom of the last page.

Gleefully, he began to read the letter. He skimmed over the first page of niceties about the woman's brat, rehearsals with the band and a reference to a concert.

On the second page, Ruckler's eyes widened, and he let out a low whistle. "What do you know about that?" he muttered as he read:

Billy said he was sure you were in love with me. His statement took me quite by surprise. I had no idea. I assumed you felt affection for Amanda and me but had never thought of anything further.

I admit that I haven't wanted to think of any other possibility. The afternoon you kissed me left me bewildered as to my own needs and emotions. After Daniel died, I vowed to never love again. First, because I couldn't imagine falling in love with anyone else. And secondly, I felt I never wanted to risk my heart again. All the people I dearly loved are gone.

When your letter came, it was clear from your fond tone that Billy might be right. So, despite the awkwardness I feel in broaching this subject in a letter, I felt that I should give you some clear indication of my own feelings. I find that I have feelings for you beyond that of a sister-in-law. And in pondering those feelings, I realized that I could fall in love again—especially with you. I say this so you will not have to wonder anymore. The rest I leave in your hands.

Bella

Ruckler sucked his teeth as his mind began to work through a plan. Perhaps he could get a bit of revenge by not sending the letter on. Then Smith would never know that his sister-in-law was on the brink of returning his affections. He could nip that little romance in the bud.

But eventually, they would see each other, and it would come out. All he would have done was delay the inevitable. As he reread the last paragraph, a more interesting prospect occurred to him.

I find that I have feelings for you beyond that of a sister-in-law. And in pondering those feelings, I realized that I could fall in love again – especially with you.

Ruckler's eye scrutinized the lines. *I find that I have...*fell at the end of a line, with a bit of space after it. As did the words, *I realized that I could...*

With two small alterations, he could change the entire meaning of the paragraph. He took up his pen and a blank sheet of paper. He scanned the letter again, looking for the words "no" and "never," then practiced writing those words until he could match Bella's handwriting.

He was good at this. He had learned over the years how to make discrete bookkeeping changes under the petty cash column to cover his "bonuses," as he thought of them. In his new job, he had cleverly added items to an order already signed by Gabriel Kramer, so that an extra box of fine soap or a bottle of wine could be "borrowed" without being missed.

When he was satisfied with his forgery, Ruckler took the letter and neatly wrote in the words in the blank spaces.

With a deep sigh of satisfaction at his own artistry, Ruckler folded the letter and slipped it back into the envelope. He lit a stick of sealing wax and dribbled it along the edges of the envelope to seal it back up.

"There now, Miss Nightingale." He gave the envelope an affectionate pat. "See how you like being turned down by the one you fancy." He snickered and removed his glasses. "And you'll never even know why!"

Choosing the musicians who would perform his symphony and discussing arrangements with the management of Castle Garden had been a tiring four-day affair for Zach. He was glad he had decided to book rooms at the Dumont Hotel, instead of taking the ferry back and forth each night from Oyster Bay.

But now he had the best orchestra in New York City. The only chair not filled was the first violin. That would be held open for John Halley.

He had booked three days of rehearsal time to fill out the rest of the week. Then he would go back to Oyster Bay and fine tune the symphony until it was time to rehearse it twice more before its debut.

Charlotte had surprised Zach by sending a note to say she was in the city to satisfy some family obligations. Great Aunt Amelia's seventieth birthday was to be celebrated on Saturday, Cousin Geraldine's wedding was in August, and Cousin Benjamin's engagement party was planned for the third week of September, after which she planned to return to Paris.

"I received a note from Jemmie at Castle Garden, asking for my patronage for various events. He knows I can never refuse his requests where music or art or a children's charity is concerned. He mentioned you would be in town for auditions. May I attend? I'd love to hear some of your symphony, mon chéri."

In fact, Charlotte was so taken with Zach's symphony, she immediately offered to underwrite the cost of a second matinee performance.

"I know it will be a magnificent concert," said Charlotte.

"And raise quite a bit of money for the War fund," Zach said. "Thank you for being so generous."

"It's for a good cause," Charlotte replied, unfurling a large, lacquered fan. She waved it once or twice to stir up the air. "Gives me something to do." She waved the fan again. "It's awfully stuffy in here. How about lunch? And then I think I'll go back to my townhouse for a nap. This weather is too stifling for anything else."

They walked up the red-carpeted aisles, past row after row of gilded chairs and emerged into the ornate, marbled lobby. As they approached the heavy wooden outer doors, a young man waved Zach over to the box office.

"A letter addressed to you, Mr. Smith."

"Thanks." Zach took the cream-colored envelope, closed with green sealing wax. He turned it over. "No name." But he recognized the handwriting. Bella's.

"From your lady love?" Charlotte teased.

"Maybe."

"Oooh. Mysterious, aren't we? Never mind," Charlotte said, taking his arm. "Let's go to Delmonico's. I'm in the mood for steak and oysters."

Zach smiled. "No champagne?" he teased.

"Of course. Champagne is the only beverage I drink since I've become a countess, *chéri*."

"It was the only thing you ever drank," Zach replied, and laughed as Charlotte swatted at him with her fan.

It was two o'clock by the time Zach returned to his hotel. In the gilded lobby, he chose an armchair in a secluded corner. Flagging down a passing waiter, Zach ordered a whiskey and soda. Then he settled back to read the letter.

Dear Zach,

It was such a nice surprise to receive your letter today. We are all so glad to hear that your symphony will be performed in September. The boys can talk of nothing else, and John seems to spend all his spare time practicing his part. Amanda and I will come, of course. Nothing could keep us away.

I read Amanda the part in your letter about how you plan to buy her pink sugar cakes and she is most excited. She had been rather sad after finding out that Mr. Kane and his ward Sissy have left the hotel, so your plan cheered her. She is well and happy and misses you very much.

Oyster Bay sounds lovely, and I am sure Amanda and I would enjoy a visit there very much. Nancy and John have offered to have us stay with them. Or we could, as you suggest, rent a cottage for the winter.

Zach smiled at the thought of Bella coming to Oyster Bay. He turned the page, then caught his breath. *Billy had told her...oh, my God...* And then he read the words that broke his heart:

...I find that I have no feelings for you beyond that of a sister-in-law. And in pondering those feelings, I realized that I could never fall in love again—especially with you.

Zach's eyes stung. He blinked back tears, reading the words over, once, twice, then a third time. There was no mistake. He slammed his fist on the little marble table and felt the sting from the impact. He crumpled up the letter, balled it into his fist, then gulped down the remainder of his whiskey and soda.

Bolting from the lobby, Zach took the stairs two at a time. He reached his door, unlocked it and once inside, slammed it shut.

"How could she!" he cried out to the empty room. He threw the balled up letter in the wastebasket. It was all so cool, so proper in language, so friendly. But her words were cruel. *Especially with you.*

He felt as if his father were sitting there, mocking him. *Who could ever fall in love with such a whoring devil such as you?*

Damn her! he thought, his mind plunging into despair. *That's what you get for breaking your cardinal rule!*

Twenty-Nine

"Oh, the places we wander, the places we roam, be it ever so humble, there's no place like home!"

Bella concluded the afternoon concert with the wistful song. The small audience began to disperse even before she had sung the last notes. The heat of August was oppressive, even on this mountain top hotel. Few people had been in the mood to dance; those who had tried soon collapsed into seats to cool themselves by furiously fanning the air with their dance cards.

Sharing their torpor, Bella had switched to singing softer, nostalgic tunes, the sweet old songs that had been popular before the war. She had no energy for anything more exciting.

"What we all need is a good cold glass of lemonade to revive us," John Halley said, as the boys began to pack up their instruments. "Peter, would you mind getting us some?"

"Just lemonade?" Peter said with a smirk.

"Unless you can find something to spark it," John replied. "Bella? Lemonade for you?"

Bella nodded and let out a long sigh. "My throat is parched." She threw her head back, feeling the sweat trickle down the back of her neck.

"Got a letter from Zach," John said, snapping the locks shut on his violin case.

Bella froze for a moment. She hadn't received any letters from Zach since she wrote to him. "How is he?"

"He's fine. Says hello to everyone. He sent me my part for the symphony."

Bella managed a smile. "That's wonderful, John." Then a terrible thought struck her. "Does that mean...will you have to go to New York to rehearse?"

John laughed softly and shook his head. "It's all right, Bella. You should see your face. No, I won't leave you here on your own. I'll rehearse here, then have one day with the full orchestra the day before the concert."

"Oh, I'm relieved," she said. "I know it will be harder for you that way, but..."

"Ah, here's the lemonade." John nodded toward the double doors, where Peter and a maid had appeared with a pitcher of lemonade and a tray of glasses. "Shall I get you a glass?"

"I think I'll go with you. I want to say hello to someone," Bella replied.

When she reached the buffet table, the maid, whom Bella had recognized as Carrie Quinn, was filling tall glasses with the icy refreshment. She held one out to Bella, then proceeded to pour another for John.

"Hello, Mrs. Quinn. How's your little boy?"

The young woman smiled. "He's grand, Miss. Just grand! That was so kind of you to offer to take him to the barbecue last Saturday. So kind, indeed. And Mrs. Halley and Amanda took him out yesterday for a bit of running around."

"He's a sweet boy," Bella said. She noticed the sparkle in Carrie Quinn's eyes. "You look quite cheerful today."

"We all are, Miss." The young woman blushed, then shrugged her shoulders with a grin. "We all have good reason, Miss."

"What's happened?"

"Haven't you heard?" She looked around, then in a low voice said, "Mr. Ruckler was sacked last night, Miss."

Bella stared at her in wonder. "Sacked?"

"Yes." She giggled. "Caught stealing from the hotel, he was

now. Charlie was suspicious for some time. And he finally had an opportunity to tell Mr. Kramer. And Mr. Kramer caught Ruckler red-handed. There was a case of wine and champagne, and boxes of fine soaps and silver bud vases, even, all crammed in a big trunk in his room."

Bella looked at John. "Did you know about this?" she said.

"No." John shook his head. "Tell us more."

Carrie Quinn glanced around the room again, as if worried that someone would stop her. Then she grinned. "He tried to deny knowing how they got there. But Mr. Beach came himself, he did. Oooh, he was fit to be tied when he saw that trunk. And the next thing you know, there was Mr. Ruckler hurrying down the hallway, carpetbags in hand. Two of Mr. Kramer's big porters escorted him right off the premises. My husband, Michelmas, saw it all."

"Well!" Bella was speechless. Then she nodded her head. "Well done! Good for Charlie."

"Good indeed, Miss," Mrs. Quinn agreed. "Charlie, I mean, Mr. Douglas, has been promoted to head of servant staff!"

At that news, Bella impulsively leaned over and hugged Carrie. "Oh, I couldn't be happier for you all. He was so awful."

Carrie Quinn stepped back, a bit startled at Bella's effusive response. But her smile was broad. "Charlie, I mean, Mr. Douglas, says it's all because of you. He says after you defended me against Mr. Ruckler that morning, he found the gumption to bring Mr. Ruckler to justice. So we owe it all to you, Miss."

Bella laughed. "Well, you tell Mr. Douglas that I'll be around to congratulate him myself tonight at dinner. And perhaps he'll take a glass of champagne with us at dessert."

Carrie Quinn nodded and winked. "I'll tell him, Miss. I'll tell him, sure."

～

"Now be careful with that trunk!"

Nancy was in full command, as the staff helped packed up the band's belongings on their last morning at the Mountain House.

"No, no! Just leave that. That one there, you can take that. But leave the big one yet, until I've changed into my traveling dress."

Bella stood in the doorway, trying to catch Nancy's attention. Finally, Nancy came over to her.

"Packing up is the worst chore," she said to Bella. "But I'll be glad to see the city again. And John is so excited. And nervous. By the time we get to New York, he'll only have a day to rehearse with the orchestra before the symphony. But he knows the part by heart."

"Nancy." Bella held a finger to her own mouth to make Nancy listen. "Where is John? He said he wanted me to go along with him to talk about next year's contract with Mr. Beach."

"I think he thought you were meeting him at Mr. Beach's office." Nancy's attention was once more diverted. "No, not that one!" she cried.

Bella grabbed her arm. "Can Amanda wait here?"

"Of course, dear. Bring her over and then run along to John. Don't want to keep the owner waiting."

"Ah, Miss Gale." Charles Beach stood up at Bella's entrance into his office. So did John Halley and Gabriel Kramer, the hotel manager.

"Good afternoon, gentlemen." Bella smiled at John, who beamed back. She nodded at Kramer.

"Have a seat. Have a seat." Mr. Beach motioned her to the empty chair. Then he settled into his own. "Well, now. You've been very well received here, Miss Gale."

"Thank you, Mr. Beach. You're very kind."

"Nonsense. I'm looking forward to you returning next year."

"As we all are," Kramer added.

Bella took a deep breath. This was the moment she had been dreading. "I'm not sure if I will return, Mr. Beach."

There was a moment of confusion that hung in the air.

"What?" John said quietly.

She avoided his eyes. "I'm sorry..." she began, but Mr. Beach cut her off.

"You are simply joking, aren't you, Miss Gale?"

"Not really. I don't enjoy performing, sir. And my daughter is very young. I'm not sure this is the kind of life..."

"See here," Kramer said, standing up suddenly. "Why, Mr. Halley specifically said you would return."

"The band certainly will," Bella said quickly. "And Zach, of course, but..."

"Mr. Halley, did you know about this?" Beach turned his stare to John, who wore a stunned expression.

"No, sir. I did not." John spoke quietly, fixing his gaze on Bella.

"I'm sorry, John," Bella said. Then she turned back to Mr. Beach. "I didn't tell Mr. Halley, because I didn't decide until just this morning. But you don't need me..."

"On the contrary. You are the draw." Mr. Beach's voice was firm.

"That's right," Kramer echoed.

"But Zach is really who people come to see," Bella protested. "People will forget all about the war by next summer. And then..."

Mr. Beach cleared his throat. "Now see here. I have done a number of unusual business arrangements because I wanted to keep you in the band. Smith's Cornet Band is finished. People have long memories. They might—and I stress the word 'might'— tolerate him as long as you are with the band. But, by God, without you, they'll stay away. I know my guests."

She turned to John. "That can't be true. It's Zach they come to see. They will..."

"Not without you." John's long fingers played with the brim of his hat. "Mr. Beach is right."

Bella felt crushed. "You can't tell Zach that. It'll kill him, John."

"I know." John sighed.

She stared from one man to the other. Suddenly, the room was stifling. She felt as if she were gasping for air.

"You'll excuse me. I need to think." She stood up, then motioned the men back down as they began to rise. "No, sit. I'll be back. Give me just a few minutes. I need air."

She left the room. The outside door was nearby. Bella flung herself against it and bolted into the bright sunshine. The drive was lined with carriages, as the last of the guests and their mountains of luggage prepared to depart.

She hurried past them, paying little heed to the din and confusion. Drawn by the cool vista, she wandered toward the stone bluff. Her eyes scanned the sweep of green valley and river, and the purple-shadowed mountains beyond.

She felt lost. She hadn't heard from Zach since she wrote him that first letter more than a month ago. She had sent him three more letters since then, but still had no response. Something had happened. She was sure of it. Perhaps Billy had been wrong. He had not been in love with her and resented her assumption. Or he had, but...here, she had no answer.

For some reason, she looked down at her feet. Chiseled into the rock were the words "Smith's Cornet Band, 1866."

She knelt down, running her fingers over the numbers. She knew that Zach had carved it. That it was his promise to return next year and restore the band.

How could she stand in his way? Mr. Beach had made it clear that Zach might be invited back if she returned.

Besides, she reasoned with herself, what other way did she have to take care of Amanda? Some vague notion of becoming a governess or ladies' companion for one of her mother's wealthy friends? Slowly, Bella ran her hand once more over the rough stone, tracing the carved letters. Then she rose, dusted off her skirt, and turned with calm resolve toward the hotel.

The three men rose once more as she entered the office.

"Mr. Beach." Bella took a deep breath. "I simply can't return next year unless Zach Smith is in charge of his band."

Mr. Beach sat down heavily in his chair and scratched his head thoughtfully. "You've been fine without him for the last two months. And John Halley has run this band without him for four years. Why do you need him?"

"Mr. Beach, I've never had any ambition to sing," Bella said. "The only reason I'm here with the band is that my dear brother-in-law saw some talent in me I had not even guessed was there. He was the one who taught me how to sing in front of an audience. I was terrified. He taught me how to project my voice. How to talk to the crowd. How to listen to the band. How to give a performance. Designed the very costumes I wear. The only reason I continued with the band was to keep it going until he could come back. It's been very hard for me to work without his support."

She looked deliberately from Kramer to Beach as she made her final point. "With all due deference to the fine job that Mr. Halley has done in his absence, everything you said about the band being so much better this year *is* due to Zach Smith."

"Such as?" queried Mr. Beach.

"Such as the back and forth banter that you find so amusing. All Zach's idea," Bella said.

"And?" Mr. Beach persisted, raising his eyebrows.

"The *Fifth Avenue Waltz*. Written and scored by Zach Smith. And he devised the dance steps, which *you* said, if you recall, were immensely clever."

Mr. Beach conceded with a slight nod of his head. "Go on."

Bella glanced at John. He was leaning back in his chair, a faint smile hovering on his lips as he watched her.

"The funny songs, like *The Wind Blew Mr. Murphy Away*. And, your favorite, *The Little Gal from the Big Hotel*."

"Let me guess," Mr. Beach said. "Zach wrote them?"

"Yes," Bella said. "It was his idea to invite the guests to participate in singing contests. You remember how excited Mrs. Barron and her daughters were when they won? And the weekday children's concerts under the gazebo?"

"Let me guess," Mr. Beach said. "Zach's idea, too."

"Correct," Bella said.

"And don't forget," John added quietly, "the Sunday afternoon classical music programs. They were very popular. We haven't been able to do those since Zach left. He did all the arrangements."

Mr. Beach let out a long sigh.

Bella took a step closer to the owner's desk. "Don't you see, Mr. Beach? Except for that one incident, which I admit was terrible, Zach Smith has added so much to your hotel since he returned. As I told you once before, I believe that Mr. Ruckler was the instigator of that terrible incident. It was not Zach's fault."

"And what if someone else next season asks to hear *Marching Through Georgia*? What then?" Mr. Beach asked quietly.

"I believe that no one will ask, Mr. Beach," Bella said. "This has been a terrible year...the war's end...President Lincoln shot...a terrible year. But by next season, I think the hottest of tempers will be cooled. Don't you think most of your guests will have put the war behind them by then?"

Mr. Beach mopped his brow and tucked his thumbs into his waistcoat pockets. "I admire your loyalty, Miss Gale. You remind me very much of your dear mother. All right, I concede your points. Zach Smith is responsible for all of the things that make the band special. If you agree to come back, I'll invite Zach Smith to return as well. On a trial basis."

He held out a pen to Bella.

Elated, Bella seized the pen and bent to sign her name "Mrs. Bella Gale Smith" next to John's signature on the contract. Deftly, she added a codicil; she would not appear at any time that Zach Smith was not in charge of Smith's Cornet Band. This way, Mr. Beach had to keep his promise to invite Zach back. She wrote it onto all three copies of the contract, then signed her name to each.

She turned the document around and offered it back for Mr. Beach's perusal. He read it and began to shake with laughter.

"You also remind me of your father," he said. "You're a very deft businesswoman, Miss Gale. Quite persuasive."

Bella smiled, pleased at the comparison. "Please initial it, sir, next to the codicil, Mr. Beach. I want it to be legal. And Mr. Kramer, will you witness that change and sign next to it also?"

Kramer's eyebrows lifted. "Certainly, Miss Gale. Certainly."

When they were done, Bella took one copy for herself.

"Miss Gale." Mr. Beach stood up. "I will enjoy having you back next summer."

"Mr. Beach," Bella said with a broad smile, extending her hand to him. "I will expect you to reserve me a slightly larger room next summer. One with a balcony, of course."

As she left the office with John, Bella gripped the contract tightly in her hand. Her heart was pounding. No matter what happened between her and Zach, they would be working together next summer.

Thirty

"**B**ella! Nancy! Over here!"

Billy Parisher waved to Bella and Amanda as they made their way with Nancy to the first row of gilded seats at the ornate Castle Garden concert hall in New York City.

Bella grinned and clasped Billy's hand, as the other boys in the band nodded, waved, and greeted them in a noisy tide of welcome.

"Zach will knock 'em off their feet!" Paul Bruner crowed.

"Be the best thing this old place has ever heard, it will," Big Harry said, punching Billy playfully in the shoulder.

"Hey, Bella!" cried Peter. "Maybe he'll want you to come up and sing something to warm up the audience."

"Amanda, honey, watch out," cried the bassoon player Harry. "They'll be sending you out soon enough to sing a couple of solos, if I know Zach Smith."

"This'll put the band back on top," Billy said.

Bella blushed at the young men's high spirits. She noticed glances of annoyance from some of the other patrons. But she didn't really mind. The boys were as excited about Zach's symphony as if it were their own.

Soon, the crowd settled down into their seats. Nancy gripped Bella's hand. "I'm so excited. John's always wanted to play in a real symphonic orchestra. Oh, Bella, it's so wonderful."

Bella patted Nancy's hand. "I know." But inside, her excitement was reserved for thoughts of Zach. How would he greet her? Why hadn't he ever answered any of her letters, when she knew he had written to others at the Mountain House? What had happened?

She shook her head to clear her thoughts. Whatever it took, she would try to make things right between them; right enough so that they would at least be able to work together.

The lights dimmed, and the curtain rose on the vast stage. The musicians were assembled in a semi-circle. Nancy pointed to the left. "There! There's John. Oh, I'm so excited! Look Amanda!"

The crowd hushed, and a familiar figure strode across the stage to the center podium, accompanied by a wave of applause. It was Zach, resplendent in white cravat, black frock coat, and his signature sapphire blue waistcoat. Bella caught her breath, taking in his tangle of curls, the cut of his strong jaw, and his muscular, lithe body. Everything, from the tilt of his head to the jaunt of his step, set her heart racing. She had almost forgotten how dazzling a figure he cut.

The boys in the band, of course, went wild, applauding and whistling loudly. Several people sitting immediately behind Bella hissed and loudly denounced the boys' rudeness.

At one time, those remarks of censure would have deeply embarrassed Bella. Now, she realized, they no longer had the power to bother her. She merely laughed and added her own applause to that of the boys in the band.

Zach bowed, then turned to face the orchestra. He lifted his baton. The applause died. The hall fell silent. The overture began with the clear, delicate strains of John's violin, coaxing the sweet refrain of "Daniel's Lullaby."

Bella felt her entire body melt at the familiar tune. She began to cry, so overcome by the memories of Daniel and Zach. The memories mixed together and flooded her mind, filling her at once with a confusion of love and sadness, regret, and joy.

A low murmur of strings rose to join John and subtly shifted the lullaby into a lament. A choir of voices joined in next. The melody shifted into a religious oratorio and then into the Southern spirituals as the choir sang, "Swing Low, Sweet Chariot, coming for to carry me home."

A canon boomed, and a startling military drum beat intruded. The brass section breathed life into two military airs, one Confederate and the other Union, a fugue of disparate melodies played in counterpoint to each other. The music built into a swelling crescendo, as Zach laid out the musical themes of home and rivalry between brothers, frivolity and religion, the intrusion of war, love and hatred, honor and death.

Bella caught her breath, understanding Zach's work in more personal terms than the audience would. This was his life, made into something higher, brighter, more universal, encompassing his own experience with the larger one of the nation at war.

Throughout the concert, Bella let herself be swept along with the music. She was amazed at Zach's command of this vast orchestra. Of how he had woven so many popular songs into the fabric of his symphony. Her eyes never left Zach. They followed his every movement with longing. She yearned to touch him, to tell him how much she cared for him, and how sorry she was that he had lost his band all these months.

Yet as she listened to his music, she realized that no one could ever destroy Zach's gifts and talents.

His band and his music were more than a mere livelihood. They were his life and soul. And whatever sacrifice it meant on her part, she had to give his band back to him, if nothing else.

The last notes of the symphony ended to shattering applause. She saw Zach gesture to the orchestra. Only after the musicians had taken their bows, did he turn to take his due. Humbly, Zach bowed low and then turned once more to the band, gesturing for them to rise.

Bella's chest swelled with pride and love. When Zach turned once more to the audience, she saw his eyes scan the first row. They settled on Nancy first, and he grinned. Then on Amanda, and he smiled. When his eyes met Bella's, they narrowed. His mouth tightened for a moment. Then he quickly looked away.

The boys in the band roared with approval. Bella's heart plunged into despair. She blinked back the sting of tears. Something was very wrong. She must find out what it was and make it right again.

~

"Brilliant!"

"A masterpiece!"

Zach pushed through the crowd of people waiting to shake his hand and offer congratulations.

He smiled and thanked his admirers who sang the praises of his symphony. Yet his eyes were fixed on the raven-haired beauty at the far end of the room. Noisy accolades and exuberant wishes for success receded into a dull hum. Shining faces and effusive smiles merged into a colorful blur as Zach steeled himself to greet Bella.

He couldn't ignore her. But anger welled up inside him. Why did she have to be here tonight to dampen his evening?

"Hello," he said evenly, as his sister-in-law and niece reached him. He picked up Amanda and threw her high in the air.

"We came!" Amanda cried. "It was so much fun, Uncle Zach!"

He laughed, although he felt it was a hollow laugh. His love for this child had now been tainted by those words that haunted him every night. He gave her a quick kiss and put her down. "I'm glad you came, Amanda."

Bella said nothing as she took Amanda's hand. She only looked at him with a calm dignity. "Bella. You're looking well," he told her, keeping his tone of voice formal and his emotions detached as possible.

"Thank you. You are looking well, too." She glanced down at the floor, and her cheeks turned scarlet. Then she gazed up at him with wide, violet eyes. "The symphony was magnificent, Zach. Your uncle would be so proud."

Zach looked at her, unable to say a word. He wanted to hold her, shake her, demand an explanation of that letter. Demand how she could stand there and say those words of praise when she had written that hateful letter. But now was not the time or place, he reminded himself. Instead, he forced himself to smile. "Thank you."

Then, as more people crowded up to him, he heard his name being called. "You'll excuse me, I have other people to greet," he told Bella, not daring to look into her eyes. "I'll see you later, eh, Amanda?" He patted her hair and winked at the child.

"Yes, we'll see Uncle Zach back at the hotel tomorrow. Come along, Amanda." Bella gently tugged Amanda's arm and, to Zach's relief, turned to go.

≈

"Coming to the party, Bella?" asked Billy Parisher. He had bumped up against her as Bella made her way toward the massive outer doors that led to the street.

"No, back to the hotel," she answered, careful to keep her voice neutral.

"Aw, you're gonna miss all the fun," Billy said. He lifted Amanda up and swung her on his shoulders. "Come on. Say you'll come."

"Say yes, Mama!" Amanda cried, catching Billy's enthusiasm.

"It's far too late for little girls," Bella chided her daughter gently. "I must get Amanda to bed, Billy."

"Then, let me flag down a cab for you, Bella," Billy said, suddenly turning serious. He swung Amanda down gently. "You and Amanda wait in here. It was raining out there when the boys and I were having a smoke."

"No need, Billy," Bella began. But the musician only gestured for them to remain behind.

"Won't take me but a minute, and I'll come back to get you." Then he quickly disappeared.

True to his word, Billy returned within ten minutes, holding a dripping black umbrella. "Here, get underneath. I've got a hackney waiting."

Bella and Amanda huddled under the umbrella, as Billy

ushered them through the door and out into a cold and steady drizzle.

"Lettin' up some, but it's still a foul night," Billy exclaimed, as he lifted Amanda into the waiting cab, and then helped Bella up inside.

To Bella's surprise, Billy hopped inside the hackney too, giving the dripping umbrella a shake or two before closing the door.

"Honestly, Billy. There's no need for you to miss out on the party. Amanda and I…"

"Nope." Billy cut off her protest with a sharp rap on the roof and fell back against his seat as the cab lurched away from the curb. "Told the driver where to take us. Can't let you go back by yourself. Ain't safe in this big city."

Bella was touched. "Thank you, Billy. You're very kind."

He grinned at her, as the carriage swayed and rocked along the cobbled and rutted avenues. "Some concert, huh?"

Bella nodded.

"It was magniferecent!" said Amanda, enthusiastically mispronouncing the word. "The most magniferecent music I ever heard."

Bella smiled but said nothing.

"Bella?" Billy asked in a low voice. "Do you want me to ask Zach what's the matter with him? It don't seem right that he…"

"No!" Bella looked up at him with a sharp expression.

"But I can see you're miserable. And I can see that he's miserable. Now, maybe…"

"No!"

"But I feel bad about tellin' you, and then him not writing you in all that time…" he continued, a pained expression on his face.

"Not a word, Billy," Bella said firmly. She wanted to cry, she wanted to shout at him: *Why did you tell me that he loved me? If I had never known…* But, in her heart, she knew it wasn't Billy's fault. "When the time comes, I will approach Zach in my own way and find out why he is so angry with me." She gazed sternly at Billy, and her heart melted a bit at the anguish she saw reflected in his pale blue eyes. "It's not your fault."

~

After an hour more of receiving congratulations, the crowd thinned until Zach was left with a small circle of friends that included several musicians from the orchestra, John and Nancy, Charlotte, and the boys in the band. Plans were made for a late supper in a private dining room at the Fifth Avenue Hotel and the happy group piled into waiting carriages.

"You're awfully quiet, chéri," Charlotte observed, as she cuddled next to Zach. "She's unnerved you."

"Hardly," he said sourly.

Charlotte laughed in that low, throaty chuckle of hers. "Oh, Zach. You'd better have it out with her. I still say my women's intuition tells me there's something strange about that letter."

Zach said nothing. There really was nothing to say. It was Bella's handwriting. "Charlotte, if you want to last the evening, don't mention it again," Zach warned her.

"Mention what, chéri?" she answered coolly.

~

It was nearly noon by the time Zach rose and dressed the next day.

He carefully knotted his cravat, adjusted his waistcoat and frock coat, then looked himself over in the full-length gilded mirror. The charity matinee would begin at three o'clock. There was plenty of time for a leisurely late breakfast before heading over to Castle Garden.

He locked his door, pocketed the key, and headed toward the staircase. Then he saw Bella on the landing, hurrying toward him.

"Hello, Zach." Bella's voice was warm but guarded.

Zach froze. He managed a polite nod. "Hello, Mrs. Smith. Where's your daughter?"

"Downstairs with Nancy and John. We were going into lunch, but Amanda forgot her doll."

Zach nodded and started to walk past her.

"Zach. Can you wait a moment? I would very much like to talk to you."

He froze again, then shook off the feeling. "There's nothing to talk about."

"There's everything to talk about." Bella stepped toward him and tentatively touched his arm. "About whether I'm singing with the band when you go to Boston. About next summer's contract." She hesitated. "About why you never answered my letters."

His guarded expression said nothing, but his voice was cold. "You made everything perfectly clear in your letter. There wasn't anything for me to answer."

"There was everything to answer. I told you how I felt..." she began.

"You certainly did," he said, turning toward the stairs.

"Zach, please." Bella ran to him, catching him by the arm. "Can you please just wait until I get Amanda's doll? Then we can talk somewhere quietly."

Zach stopped, taking in a deep breath. But he said nothing.

"I'll only be minute," Bella said. She ran off down the hall toward her room. She fumbled with the lock, finally pushed open the door, swept the doll off the bed, and hurried back out.

Zach was gone.

"Zach!" Bella cried angrily. She hastily locked the door, grabbed the key, and raced to the landing. She could see Zach below her on the wide, carpeted staircase, just rounding the next landing. "Please wait!" she cried and gathered her skirts to fly down the stairs.

Zach tipped his head back and shook his head wearily, but he stopped on the landing.

She arrived breathless and angry.

"You could at least..." she said, taking a deep breath, "give me the courtesy of...of an explanation as to why you didn't answer my letters!"

"What was there to say? I was sorry you felt that way?" he said.

"Felt what way?"

"Ah, don't." Zach shook his head. "You're not good at playing games, Bella."

"Felt what way?" she persisted.

"I'm not going to talk about this in the hallway." Zach started down the second set of stairs.

Bella started after him. "Just tell me this: Are you engaged to someone else? Is that why you wouldn't answer my letters?"

Zach stopped on the staircase and turned to her with an expression of outrage. "Engaged? Engaged? To someone else? God damn it, Bella!"

"Well, I can't think of any other reason why…"

"Oh, I see," Zach interrupted. "It would make you feel better about the whole thing!" Abruptly, he turned and started down the stairs. "I don't have time for this nonsense."

"Will you please hear me out?" Bella cried, hurrying after him again. She was almost to the third landing, when the doll slipped out of her hands. Reaching out, she stumbled on the steps, unable to stop herself from going down.

A small cry escaped her lips as she hit the landing hard.

Thirty-One

Zach glanced back to see Bella sprawled on the landing. Sprinting up the stairs, he knelt next to her.

"Are you all right?

Bella sat there a moment, too stunned to answer. The wind had been knocked out of her. She put a hand to her heart to calm herself.

"Can you rise?" Zach asked in a concerned tone. "Or shall I call the doctor?"

"I'm fine. I just..." Bella took a deep breath. "I just have to catch my breath."

"Let me help you up." Zach held out his hand.

Bella clasped his hand and rose shakily with his help. "I'm fine. Really, I am. Oh, dear! No, I'm not." She drew her hand over her forehead, then began to weep. "I don't understand what's happening. I really don't."

Zach put his arm around Bella and led her to a small sofa in a small alcove just off the landing. He had no idea what to say to her.

"Sit down," he finally told her.

She collapsed on the sofa, wiping her eyes with the heel of her hands. "All I want to know is why did you never answer my letters?" Bella looked up at him with such misery in her expression that Zach reached out to smooth her hair.

"There was nothing left to say. You made it very clear."

"That I loved you?" Bella asked.

Zach froze. He dropped his hand. "That you couldn't love me."

"What are you talking about?" Bella said angrily.

"What are you talking about?" Zach snapped back. "This conversation is at an end." He rose, spun on his heel, and turned toward the staircase. Two couples were coming up the stairs.

Bella rose off the couch. "Don't you dare walk away from me, Zach Smith. You owe me the courtesy of an explanation!"

"I don't owe you anything."

She ran to him and pulled his coattail. The first couple on the staircase hesitated, shrinking back against the wall.

Zach spun around. "You're making a scene," he whispered angrily.

"Then sit down and talk to me, or I shall make a bigger scene," Bella retorted.

The first couple looked embarrassed, but the second gentlemen, a large man with a black cape and tall stovepipe hat, waved his hand dismissively in Zach's direction. "Take your lover's quarrel somewhere else, my good man, or I shall have the management up here in jig time."

"I'll give you jig time," Zach muttered. But he turned back in Bella's direction. "All right. We'll talk. Over there." He stalked over to the sofa and sat stiffly at the farthest end.

Bella followed, perching on the other end, spreading her skirts to create a barrier between them.

They both breathed hard, then turned to each other at the same moment.

"I don't..."

"There isn't..."

They both stopped. Zach looked away. When there was no word from Bella, he said testily, "Well? You had something to say to me. Say it."

"I do have something to say to you," she began quietly, drawing her hands together in her lap. "What I wanted to say to you was...well, what I wanted to ask you was, first, if Billy was right when he said you had been in love with me. That's the first question. And the second is, if that's true, well then, why, when I wrote you back that I cared for you, why..." She shook her head crossly, her voice cracking with emotion, "why are you angry with me?"

Zach was silent for a moment, mulling over her words. "When did you write me that you cared for me?"

"In my first letter, of course," Bella said.

He shook his head in exasperation. "Well, I must have gotten some other letter," he said caustically. "Because the one you wrote me said you could never fall in love again, *especially* with me!"

Bella's expression changed to one of alarm and confusion. "No!" She reached out and gently touched the sleeve of his jacket. "I never wrote such a thing to you."

"Don't do this," Zach began.

"I said that I never thought I could give my heart again, that's true. I didn't think I ever could." Bella stopped and folded her hands again, bringing them to her lips.

"If that's what you feel, then..." Zach began.

"It's not what I feel now!" she cried, turning toward him. Zach looked away. Bella touched his hand. This time, he did not pull away. "I missed you. All the little things we shared. Being on stage together. Dinner. Playing with Amanda. Walks. Talking about music. I realized that I did have feelings for you, feelings beyond that of a sister-in-law. And that I was surprised, because I realized that I could fall in love again, *especially* with you," she said.

"What?" he whispered, half in anger, half in disbelief.

"So I don't understand why you're so angry with me." Bella's eyes searched him, then welled with tears.

Zach's throat was so tight he could hardly speak. "You wrote 'never.' That's what you wrote." He grabbed her by the shoulders. "'*I* find that I could *never* fall in love again. *Especially* with you.' Those were your exact words."

"No." Bella shook her head, her face a study in outrage. "No. I swear. I wrote to tell you that I wanted to *return* your love."

"Then..." Zach stopped. He let her go, feeling new anger at

what he was beginning to suspect. "Where did you post those letters?"

"At the hotel desk, of course." Bella's face suddenly registered comprehension. She gasped. "Oh, God! Oh that monster! Do you think Ruckler...?"

"Or Farris."

"They sort the mail together in the mornings," Bella said, clapping her hand to her mouth. "I should have remembered. Zach, I didn't write 'never.'"

Zach took her by the shoulders again, but this time his hands were much gentler. "Swear to me!"

"I swear to you! I swear it on everything I hold dear to me!" Tears coursed down Bella's cheeks, as she gazed into Zach's questioning eyes. "Oh, Zach. I don't blame you! You must have felt so betrayed. But when you never wrote back, after that sweet, lovely letter about Oyster Bay, after you wrote how much you missed us, I knew. I knew something was wrong."

"My God, Bella. Can you ever forgive me?" Zach drew her into his arms and held her for a long moment without saying a word. "Ruckler must have picked up your letter and twisted the words around somehow," Zach finally said. "It's his style. The man's a bully and a coward. That letter was his retaliation for..."

"Hush!" Bella didn't let him finish. She embraced him again, pressing her cheek against his.

Zach held her tighter, pressing her to him as if they could merge into one person and never have to part. When they finally did pull apart, Zach saw that Bella's eyes were still filled with tears. Yet her face was radiant with happiness.

"Bella, I've been miserable all these months without you. And to think I almost let Ruckler ruin everything between us." He embraced her again. "I've loved you for a long time."

"You never said a word," she murmured.

"I did once," he added. "The night I hummed my symphony for you. I told you how much I loved you. But you were nodding off to sleep and didn't hear a word."

She kissed him gently as he tightened his arms around her.

"Maybe I did hear you say that," she whispered in his ear. "Maybe my heart heard it. Maybe that's why I knew that whatever was wrong, it could be fixed."

He kissed her again, long and slow. A door slammed down the hall and a voice exclaimed, "Well, I never!"

Zach and Bella both laughed and pulled apart.

"I should get back to Amanda. She's waiting for her doll."

"I'll come with you." He put his arm around her shoulder. "Say you'll come with me to the matinee performance."

"Yes, I'd like that," Bella said.

The matinee concert was every bit as successful as the previous night.

But this time, Zach basked in the glow of his love for Bella. After the concert, he introduced Bella to all the musicians, to the trustees of the concert hall, and even to Charlotte, who was on her best behavior.

"So I finally get to meet Zach's lady love!" Charlotte said, taking Bella's hands in hers.

Bella's eyes widened. Now she knew who Charlotte had been referring to that evening she overheard their conversation. "It's lovely to meet you, too."

"You're a lucky woman," Charlotte said. "He's one of a kind. Take my advice. Don't let him go."

"I won't," Bella said.

Zach and Bella said little on the drive back to the hotel. They were content to cuddle close together, their hands clasped tightly, as John and Nancy and Amanda prattled on about how wonderful the concert had gone. During dinner, they held hands under the table and gazed at each other like a pair of school sweethearts. After dinner, they excused themselves and went for a short walk down the avenue, strolling hand-in-hand.

"I have to go back now. It's Amanda's bedtime."

Zach put his arm around her shoulder and drew her close. "I hate to let you go."

"It's a long trip to Boston tomorrow," Bella said, snuggling closer to him. "I want to make sure everything is packed and ready."

"I know." Zach stopped and pulled her to him. They kissed, then began walking back to the hotel parlor, where they found Amanda, John and Nancy engaged in a game of cards. Amanda hummed contentedly as she tossed out a three of hearts on the little marble table.

"That finishes me off," John said, throwing his cards down.

"Ah, but I can match that," Nancy said, drawing a card from the center pile.

"Mama!" Amanda looked up to see her mother with pleasure. "I'm almost winning at Hearts!"

John nodded mournfully. "She is at that," he said.

Nancy just laughed. "She's a natural."

"It's time for bed," Bella said.

"Can't we just finish the game, please Mama? Please?"

"Ten minutes, no more!" Bella replied.

When the last card had been discarded, Amanda joyfully raced to John and Nancy to give each a goodnight kiss.

"I expect a rematch, young lady," said John as he hugged the child. "What do you say?" Amanda just giggled and nodded.

"Come along," Bella said, her hand outstretched. "It's way past your bedtime."

Zach walked Bella and Amanda upstairs to their rooms.

"This is your room?" Zach said in surprise, as Bella fitted the key into the lock.

"Yes."

He looked at the number, 417, then followed her inside. As she followed Amanda to the washstand, she noticed Zach examining the little door in the center of the room.

"What's the matter?"

"Did you realize that this is a connecting door to the room next door?" Zach asked her.

"Yes. The bellboy said just to keep it locked on my side and the other person would do the same."

Zach gave a wry smile. "I think I'm going to have a hard time keeping my side locked tonight."

Bella's eyes widened. "You?"

"I'm in 415," he said.

He leaned in and kissed Bella hungrily. "I'll be up packing, if you need anything."

Bella smiled. "I might need help with the locks on the trunk," she said. "Amanda has so many new dresses and playthings from the boys that I don't see how I shall fit everything in."

"You can always put the extras in my trunk," he said. "Just knock on my door."

"I'll keep that in mind." Bella kissed him once more before reluctantly pulling away. "I'll see you in the morning."

"Or even before." His eyes twinkled.

Two hours later, Amanda was bathed and in bed, and Bella had packed all but the next day's necessities. She had managed to get the lid down on most of their belongings in the trunk—all except for the stuffed puppy from Harry and Billy's present of a wind-up canary in a gilt bird cage.

She wondered if it was too late to see if Zach had room for the two toys. She eyed the little brass key to the connecting door, which sat on the bureau. She picked it up, feeling the weight of it against her palm. Glancing over at Amanda, she listened for a moment to the soft, even rhythm of her daughter's breathing. Then she stared at the door, picturing Zach on the other side of it.

She closed her eyes and thought back to that night when Zach had first kissed her. That kiss had stirred up such primal and powerful urges that it had frightened her at the time. His hungry kissed had summoned those same passions tonight. This time, she did not want to suppress them.

She leaned back against the connecting door and sighed softly as her imagination recreated his kisses, invaded her senses, and coaxed an exquisite pressure deep inside her; a pressure that coiled tighter and tighter.

Why was she torturing herself like this? He had told her he loved her. She had only to open the door and enter his room, and he would...what?

She knew what. He would take her to his bed, kiss her, hold her, love her, release her from this all-encompassing physical need for him.

She breathed in deeply, willing her senses to calm down as she turned the key over and over in her palm.

When she felt in control again, she picked up the puppy and the cage in one hand. Gently, she inserted the key into the lock. A soft click told her the lock had opened. She knocked softly on the door.

"Zach? Are you awake?"

"It's unlocked!" came the reply. "Come in."

With a trembling hand, Bella turned the knob, pushed open the door, and stepped quickly inside.

Zach was sitting in a blue damask armchair at the far end of the room. His long legs were stretched out in front of him, his stocking-clad feet resting on an upholstered footrest. He was looking in her direction, his face illuminated by the flickering flames from the fireplace. A small leather-bound volume rested on the arm of the chair.

"Hello. I hope I'm not intruding," Bella said.

"Not in the least," he said, putting the book on the table. He stood up.

Bella saw that he was dressed only in his shirtsleeves and trousers. His cravat and vest had been tossed on the empty chair. The top buttons of his shirt were open, revealing his bare neck. His hair was mussed and wild, dark locks fell forward over his forehead. The sight of his smile made her knees weaken and her heart melt.

"Amanda is sleeping. I finished packing. And I...I came to see if these would fit in your trunk."

In a few strides, Zach was at her side. He reached out and closed the door softly behind her. "I'm glad you're here."

He took the cage from her and set it on top of his bureau. "Where'd she get this?"

"Billy. And Harry bought her this last night," Bella said, taking the stuffed puppy from under her arm. "If this keeps up, I'll need to buy a new trunk just for Amanda."

Zach chuckled as he placed the puppy next to the cage. "I'll speak to them about it," he said.

"No. Don't spoil their pleasure," Bella said.

Zach turned to Bella. They looked at each other for a long moment without a word. In the flickering firelight, Bella felt as if she were drifting into a dream, floating disembodied in an ethereal world. To shake the feeling, she walked over to the far side of the room where his book lay open. She picked it up and held it up to the gas lamp in order to read the embossed cover.

"Shakespeare's Sonnets!" she said. "I didn't know you read Shakespeare."

"It was my mother's," Zach said in a soft voice as he walked up behind her. "She loved poetry. I always carry it with me. It was her favorite."

"It's one of mine too," Bella said, running her hands along the gold letters. She turned the book over and turned to the page that listed the poems. "Which one were you reading just now?"

"One I've been reading a lot lately." Zach put his arms around Bella, reaching one hand out to flip the pages to the nineteenth sonnet. "*When, in disgrace with fortune and men's eyes, I all alone beweep my outcast state...*"

"*And trouble deaf heaven with my bootless cries,*" Bella read, "*and look upon myself, and curse my fate.*" She drew in a breath at the sad words.

"*Wishing me like to one more rich in hope,*" Zach continued from memory, hugging Bella tighter. "*Featured like him, like him with friends possess'd, Desiring this man's art and that man's scope, With what I most enjoy contented least.*"

"Oh Zach," Bella said, understanding that the words echoed what he had been experiencing these last few months—exiled from his band, on his own, so miserable that even music could not assuage his despair. She turned to him, her eyes glistening with tears. "It's been so hard for you!"

He took the book from her and laid it on the side table. Drawing Bella into his arms, he kissed her tenderly. Then Zach continued to recite the sonnet by heart.

"*Yet in these thoughts myself almost despising, Haply I think on thee.*" Zach smiled and kissed Bella once again. When he pulled away, he gazed into her eyes and stroked her hair. With each stroke, Bella felt as if she were melting; conscious of nothing but the sound of his voice and the touch of his hands.

"*And then my state, Like to the lark at break of day arising from sullen earth, sings hymns at heaven's gate,*" he recited, cupping her face in his hands. "*For thy sweet love remember'd such wealth brings, that then I scorn to change my state with kings.*"

He kissed her again with growing passion. "I have never stopped thinking of that first afternoon when I kissed you," he said. He scattered delicate kisses down her neck. "The only thing that's sustained me is the hope of winning your love, Bella."

Any remaining vestige of Bella's practical nature had disappeared. She was borne away on an intense wave of emotion and physical longing.

"Hold me." She raised her arms and tightened them around his neck. "Hold me the way you did when we waltzed."

"I love you," he whispered into her ear. His lips nuzzled against her bare neck, scattering soft kisses along her skin. Each one sent a tingling arc down through her body.

She thought she might swoon. Her body was beyond her control now. "Kiss me the way you did that night..."

Then there were no more words. Just the exquisite feeling of floating in the air as Zach carried her off to his bed.

Thirty-Two

Zach laid Bella gently on his bed.

She sighed, stretching one arm out to him.

He leaned over and kissed her, tasting the sweetness of her lips. He kissed her again, this time deeply, and was pleased at the growing intensity of her response.

As he stretched out beside her, she threw her arms around him. Her fingers stroked the nape of his neck. He gazed deeply into her eyes for a long moment, then cupped her face in both his hands and claimed her lips more greedily.

Her lips parted, and their kisses deepened and slowed into a dreamy progression of languorous sensations. They had all the time in the world to explore each other now.

He kissed her cheeks, her eyes, the tip of her nose. She ran her fingers through his hair. He nuzzled the delicate skin just below her earlobe, inhaling her sweet scent. She arched her head back. He scattered warm kisses all the way down her neck to the top of her collar. Undoing the top two buttons, he kissed the hollow of her throat.

Her sighs rose and fell, echoing in Zach's mind like a haunting musical refrain. He felt as if the world had been reduced to one exhilarating chord that vibrated to the tune in his heart.

Zach looked up at her and caught his breath.

She stroked his cheek with warm and gentle hands. "I love you," she whispered.

For a long moment, they were content to gaze deeply into each other's eyes.

Then Zach reached out to undo the remaining buttons on her bodice. Bella's eyes widened for a moment. Zach hesitated, then pulled away from her, fearing that she was having second thoughts.

"What's wrong?" Bella whispered.

"I just... Are you sure you want me to...?"

Bella nodded. "I'm sure," she answered, drawing him closer for another kiss.

Elated, Zach kissed her again and again. "My God, Bella! I'm so in love with you! I can't believe you're really here."

"I'm here," she whispered. Then she reached down and fumbled with the tiny buttons at her throat.

"Let me." Zach gently drew her hands away and undid the remaining buttons.

Bella watched him, a smile on her lips and a dreamy, faraway look in her eyes. Zach drew back the bodice, revealing a camisole underneath that bared an inch more of her creamy skin. He leaned forward and brushed his lips against its silken texture, savoring the feel of her eager response. Then he drew back and helped her sit up to remove the bodice. Bella lifted her arms high, and Zach pulled the camisole up over her head to reveal her corset.

"Ahh, you women. Layers and layers," he teased her.

Bella giggled softly, then swiftly unhooked the six fastenings of her corset. She smiled at Zach more broadly now, but she blushed, too, as she slipped off the stiff garment and dropped it on the floor. Underneath, she wore a second camisole.

"That's better," Zach whispered. "You're so beautiful." And she was: not just her delicate features, and creamy, flawless skin, but her expression, so filled with love and tenderness, was one of the most beautiful things he had ever seen.

"Let me loosen your hair, too," he said, sitting up. She turned slightly to allow him to undo the hairpins that held her coiled braids in place. He unplaited the braids, running his fingers through the long tresses that reached down to her waist.

With a sigh, Bella turned to him and enfolded him in a tight embrace.

Zach eased her down on the bed. He bent over her and nuzzled her breasts through the filmy camisole, eliciting a series of shivers and tiny gasps of pleasure wherever he kissed her. His own ardor was building now as he slipped his hands underneath her camisole.

"Is this the last layer?" Zach asked, easing the fabric higher.

"Yes," she whispered. "It buttons down the front. Here."

Zach undid the six pearl buttons hidden in the soft folds of lace and drew back the fabric. "You're so very beautiful," he whispered again. He stroked her breasts, lightly grazing her nipples, hoping to infuse every inch of her skin with desire.

His hands roamed lower. Inch by inch, he teased the hem of her skirts up along her legs, stroking her calves, her knees, her thighs. Then he untied her garters, slowly rolling down her stockings until her legs were bare and he could stroke the tender flesh.

Bella gave herself over totally to each sensation that awakened wherever his hands touched her. Her entire body vibrated with desire: desire for his kisses, for his touch, for the sound of his voice, for the feel of his body against hers.

When his hands encountered the lacy edge of her underdrawers, Bella's body seemed to catch fire. The intensity of the feeling was almost too much.

"Oh, Zach!" she cried.

"Do you want me to stop?" Zach gazed at her with such a stricken look, that she laughed softly.

"No," she whispered. That exquisite pressure deep inside her coiled tighter and tighter. Stretching out on the bed, she arched her back, yearning for release.

He reached for the side buttons on her under drawers. He undid them and gently caressed the flesh beneath.

Zach watched her body begin to sway and writhe. He fondled

her, determined to stroke her into an ecstatic release. He wondered if she had ever experienced such pleasure before.

Bella cried out as an orgasm broke over her body in wave after wave of relief. Finally, sated and spent, she rolled onto her side, snuggling close to him. He embraced her and she arranged his arms more firmly around her.

Zach was charmed by the gesture and the way she arched her back against his chest. With his free hand, he stroked her hair, losing himself in its silken texture. He scattered kisses on the slope of her shoulder, reveling in her now-familiar scent. A scent of rose-buds. Then he massaged her neck, eliciting soft moans of pleasure.

Every move she made sharpened his own desire, as she slowly stretched her body against his. He reached around and fondled her breasts again.

She moaned softly.

He reached forward to nibble at the lobe of her ear. "We've not finished yet," he whispered.

She turned over to face him, her violet eyes misty and wide. "You're still dressed." She sat up and whispered, "Now it's my turn."

Excited by this new, emboldened aspect of Bella's nature, Zach grinned and stretched his arms back behind his head, inviting her to undress him.

Bella smoothed his rumpled, blue-striped shirt. Coaxing the last four tiny onyx studs from their fastenings, she pushed the shirt open. Lightly, she ran her hands over his bare chest, tracing his sharply defined muscles.

Zach shivered at her touch. He had imagined this many times, but the warmth of her hands, the sensations they conjured up deep inside him were much stronger than his daydreams. He rose up just enough to tug the shirt off and fling it on the floor.

She kissed him and ran her hands over his arms, feeling his muscles flex at her touch. Her hands roamed over his chest again, hesitating at the waistband of his trousers.

Throughout it all, Zach drank in the sight of this voluptuous beauty who explored his body with the most delicate touch he had ever felt.

Suddenly aware of his eyes on her naked body, Bella blushed and shivered.

"Are you cold?"

"No. But maybe we should be under the covers?"

"I want to see you. All of you." He reached up and enfolded her in his arms, enjoying the sensation of her skin against his. He kissed her, and this time she devoured his lips, her passion growing stronger and more reckless with every kiss.

Her hands tugged at his waistband. She fumbled with the buttons.

He swiftly undid them and pulled off his trousers. His body was inflamed with one desire: to be inside of her. Everywhere she touched him produced new sensations. He was amazed at how sharp his senses had become. Amazed at how much he wanted her. His normal detachment from other women, even when making love to them, had been replaced by a feeling of wanting to merge with her so deeply that he would know everything she thought and felt.

"Bella, Bella," he murmured.

She opened her arms to him. He slid on top of her. She parted her legs. He entered her, feeling the snugness of their fit, reveling in the start of that steady rhythm that would bind them together. Their pace quickened, and he felt the world tumble and turn as he clung to Bella and then collapsed on top of her.

A deep sigh of pleasure escaped Bella's lips. Her arms tightened around Zach's shoulders.

When Zach opened his eyes, he saw Bella's face, reflecting such peace and radiance that he felt as though the sun had filled him with its source of light. And then he realized that the source was Bella. No other woman had touched him in this way. No other woman ever could.

≈

The dim glow of dawn was just visible in the window when Zach felt Bella stir in his arms. He tightened his embrace, unwilling to let her go.

"Zach?"

"Uhmmm?"

"I have to go back. Amanda will wake soon."

"Do you have to?" he said sleepily, snuggling closer to her.

"I have to," she said. She kissed him, then tried to pull away.

He started to let her go, then changed his mind. "One more kiss."

She laughed and obliged him. "I don't want to go either."

"Then stay." He embraced her more tightly, luxuriating in the feel of her skin, running her hands over her naked back.

"I can't," she protested gently. "Please. I can't let Amanda see us like this. It would be so confusing."

With a sigh, Zach released her. "You're right. I know."

She slid out of bed, shivering in the morning chill. As she stooped over to retrieve her undergarments, her waist-length hair fell loosely around her.

"You're the most beautiful creature I've ever known," Zach murmured. "And the sweetest. And the bravest. And the nicest and..."

Bella stood up, her arms filled with clothing. She took a step toward the bed. Zach slid over and caught her, pulling her down toward him. "I want to make love to you again," he whispered.

She kissed him, but he sensed her reluctance. "I can't," she said. "I have to get dressed. I'm sorry."

"It's all right," he said, trying to conceal his disappointment.

Bella sat on the edge of the bed and began to pull on her clothes. He watched her in silence, struggling with a mixture of feelings and desires.

"I'm sorry," she said again. She stood up and began to button her bodice. "I'm not sure how to... I've never had intimacies with a man I wasn't..."

"Married to?" The words hung in the air between them.

"Yes." She hesitated, then tugged on her petticoat. "But you have, haven't you? I don't mean it as an accusation."

"Yes." Zach sat up and rubbed his eyes. As Bella pulled her skirt over the petticoat, he reached for his trousers and pulled them on. Then he walked around the bed to her side.

She turned to face him. He drew her into his arms. "You make me feel things, Bella. Things I've never felt for another woman." He stared at her, trying to read her thoughts behind those violet eyes. Was she thinking of him or of Daniel?

Bella clung to him. "Do you...Do you think any less of me for being so... so wicked?" she finally whispered.

"No, no. Not at all," he said in a soothing voice. "You're not wicked. You could never be wicked, my darling Bella."

"But I would be if..." she hesitated. "If we did this again, and we weren't... If someone found us together. If Amanda... I couldn't bear it. But then, oh! How can I bear not to be with you?"

Zach wanted to get down on one knee and ask her to marry him. But a small voice in the back of his head muttered a warning: *A whoring devil like you could never be faithful to any woman.* His throat constricted as the emotions swelled inside him.

"I've never been faithful to any woman. Never had a desire to marry. Not until I met you," Zach finally admitted, struggling to voice his deepest fear.

Bella's face glowed with happiness and anticipation as she searched his eyes.

Zach knew what she expected to hear—an ardent proposal of marriage. But the words stuck in the back of his throat, crowded out by all the old doubts and fears. Then a sudden image of Bella and Daniel's wedding portrait came into his mind.

"I just don't know," he finally said, "if I can be as good a husband as Daniel was."

Thirty-Three

The trip to Boston took most of the next day. It was late by the time Zach and the boys in the band had settled into the Grand Fairmount Hotel for a two-week engagement. Zach was in high spirits, since he was once again the bandleader of Smith's Cornet Band.

At dinner time, Amanda had little appetite. But Bella insisted she come down to the restaurant for something to eat with her and Zach.

"Mama?" Amanda tugged at her mother's arm. "I don't feel good. My tummy feels bad."

Bella peered closely into her daughter's eyes. They looked dull. She instinctively put her hand to Amanda's forehead. It was hot.

"Come on, darling. Let's go find the powder room."

She picked Amanda up and grabbed a napkin, worried that she might be sick before they could reach a toilet or basin.

Zach followed Bella. He was unfamiliar with childhood diseases, but Bella seemed uncharacteristically alarmed. He saw her rush into the lady's privy, holding the napkin up to Amanda's lips; heard the little moans and choking sounds the child made. His heart felt heavy as he waited helplessly outside the door. There was nothing he could do, he knew, but he resigned himself to waiting.

He wanted to be there to comfort them, or to carry Amanda upstairs if need be.

When Bella finally emerged, she was cradling Amanda in her arms. Her expression was grim.

"What's wrong with Amanda?" Zach asked.

"She's burning up," Bella said. Her expression began to break down. Tears welled in her eyes. "She was sick. And now, she's almost unresponsive. I'm frightened, Zach."

"Let me take her upstairs. We'll get the hotel doctor to take a look."

For a moment, Bella hugged Amanda tighter in her arms, as if she refused to let her go. Then, reluctantly, she allowed Zach to take her.

"Go over to the desk," Zach said, "and ask them to send up the doctor. I'll wait right here."

He watched her walk over to the front desk, cradling the child in his arms. "Amanda," he crooned, humming a few bars of Daniel's lullaby. He could feel her warm body. He lowered his head to her, putting his cheek next to her flushed one. He had hoped that Bella had exaggerated.

Bella ran back to Zach. "They're going to find him and send him up." She lay her hand against Amanda's fevered brow. "Oh, Zach!"

"Come on," he said, trying to keep his voice calm.

They stepped into the caged elevator. It seemed to take hours to reach their floor. The attendant threw open the door, and Zach and Bella hurried to their adjoining suite. Bella bit her lip to quell her rising anxiety, as scenes of her daughter lying dead flitted through her mind.

"I don't understand, Bella. How could this happen so suddenly?" Zach asked.

"She's been sick before, of course," Bella replied. "But never this bad. I don't know what's wrong with her."

Her hand trembled as she turned the knob and the door swung inward. She ran to the big bed and turned down the covers on one side.

Zach laid Amanda gently on the bed. Then he glanced over at Bella, who was pouring water into a basin. She dipped a hand towel into the basin, wrung it out, then laid it across Amanda's forehead.

"I need to bring the fever down," she told him. "Could you bring that table over to the bed so I can put the basin on it? And could you bring more cool water?"

Zach hurried to fetch one of the side tables. Then he brought the basin over. "There's water in my room. I'll fetch some more and bring extra towels. What about ice? I'll see if the kitchen has some."

"Yes, that might help," Bella answered. She dipped a second cloth in the water, wrung it out, and laid it across Amanda's forehead. Then she began to undress the child, pulling her clothing off. She laid a second cool towel across her daughter's bare chest, holding back the tears as she saw the spots that had erupted on Amanda's skin. The feverish child cried out and tried to push the cloth away, but Bella held it firmly, her mouth tightening in determination. "Anything to bring the fever down."

The doctor's verdict was scarlet fever.

Children die from scarlet fever, Bella thought. The doctor prescribed belladonna and ice baths to fight the fever.

"It could be two or three days," he warned, "before you see a change."

For the next three days, Bella refused to leave Amanda's side, except for a few minutes to perform the most necessary of functions. She didn't sleep and ate very little. And she refused to go anywhere, even onstage with the band. Instead, she sat in the lavishly furnished room, oblivious to the silk drapes, ornate moldings, the burled walnut armoire, the fluted side tables, and overstuffed chairs.

Nancy sat by Bella's side while Zach and John were rehearsing or performing. Then Zach would come to relieve Nancy and take over running little errands. Mostly, Zach simply kept Bella company.

Watching Amanda lying inert day after day made Zach feel as if his heart was being wrenched out of his chest. The worst was last night, when he had helped Bella change Amanda's sweat-soaked nightgown and saw the rash of tiny red spots that marred the child's delicate skin.

"It's not smallpox, is it?" he had asked Bella. He had had terrible dreams that night: dreams in which he was a small boy again, standing helpless and furious outside the door of his mother's sickroom as she lay dying of malaria, while his father knelt by the side of her bed chanting prayers and supplications to God.

Zach felt just as helpless now, watching his niece. Sometimes he sat for hours, stroking the child's damp blond hair, remembering random moments of happiness he had spent with her in play at the Mountain House. There had not been many of those sweet moments, but he desperately wanted there to be more. He had discovered a whole new world of pleasure and pride in Amanda's childish imagination and accomplishments. And he did not want that to end.

If I could, I'd trade my life for hers, he thought.

But all he could do was offer some small modicum of comfort. He moved over to Bella's chair. She looked so weary. He massaged her shoulders.

"You need to get some sleep, Bella," he pleaded.

Bella dipped another cloth into the basin of cool water, then wrung it out. "When the fever breaks." She carefully folded the fabric, then laid it gently across Amanda's fevered brow.

"I can do this, and you can catch a few winks," Zach said. He was afraid for Amanda, but he also feared that Bella might ruin her own health if she went on this way. "Just sleep for a bit."

She turned to him, her beautiful face etched with sorrow. "Do you honestly think I can sleep when my daughter is in danger of dying?"

"No. Of course not." Zach drew her into his arms. "Oh, Bella. She just has to get well."

Bella sagged against him. He held her even tighter as her muffled sobs shook her body. "She will get well, Bella. She will. She must."

～

Over the course of the fourth day, the band's day off, Zach seldom left Bella's side.

He read her poetry, hummed lullabies, and told her about his boyhood summers at his uncle's plantation in Georgia. He brought her plates of food, pots of tea, and even chocolates, strawberries, and fancy iced cakes to tempt her appetite. She barely touched a bite. He brought endless pitchers of cool water for the wet cloths Bella used to fight the high fever. He filled the bathing tub with ice water, lowering Amanda's feverish body into it, cringing at the spasms it brought on.

"Are you sure this is working?" he would ask. Bella would never reply, only kneel by his side to bathe her daughter with such tenderness that he had to blink back tears.

He massaged Bella's neck and shoulders when he saw the tension strain her muscles. He held her in his arms when she looked as if she was about to collapse from weariness and hopelessness. And privately, he did something he hadn't done since before his mother died; he prayed.

You can't let this sweet, innocent child die. You can't take everyone away from us, Zach prayed. *You couldn't be that cruel.*

But in his heart, he knew that death was as impartial to the sufferings of its victims as the wind was to the leaves it blew off the trees.

It was ten o'clock at night when Zach stood up and yawned.

"You should go to bed," Bella told him.

"Bella, how long can this last?" Zach felt hopeless. He leaned over Amanda's bed and kissed her brow. It was still hot, and yet it felt damp. Beads of sweat broke across the child's skin, alarming Zach further. "How long can she stay burning up like that? Isn't there anything else we can do?"

"No. There isn't. That's the awful truth of it." She began to cry.

Zach caught her in his arms and held her close to him as she sobbed. There was nothing to say. He knew she was right. He had seen plenty of death and there had been nothing to stop it.

"I wish I could make her well," he murmured. "I love you both so much."

"I know you do," Bella said, her sobs subsiding. She clung to him. "I used to think that love was something happy," she said. "But now I know that love is when you stay with someone through the worst that life can hand you, even through death, even when you can't do a blessed thing to help them. That's love." She looked up at him. "I know you love us."

Zach held her tighter, rocking her, stroking her hair. "I do. I do."

"You told me you've never been faithful to any woman. But you stayed with your uncles. You've been there for John and Nancy and the boys. You stayed with us when Daniel died, and you didn't even know us."

"I think I loved you even then, Bella."

He lifted her into his arms and settled her gently into the wingchair next to Amanda. "I'll get us some tea."

He saw her lean forward and kiss Amanda's forehead. Then she gasped.

"Zach! I think the fever broke." She laid her cheek against Amanda's forehead. "Thank God, thank God! The fever's broke!"

He ran to her side, knelt over Amanda and placed his lips on her brow. Her skin was clammy, but it was cooler. He grinned at Bella. "She's going to be all right?" he asked, feeling hopeful for the first time.

Bella nodded, and Zach felt his heart soar. "She's going to be all right!" he cried.

Rising, he pulled Bella up into his arms and laughed in relief as he waltzed her around the room.

∿

The hotel doctor was in his shirtsleeves, having just retired for the evening. But he hurried into the room and began to examine Amanda.

There was a knock on the door. "It's Nancy! What's happening? Zach? Bella?"

Zach unlocked the door to find Nancy and John at the door, their faces full of concern. He grinned at them and put his arms around them both in an exuberant embrace. "Her fever broke. She's going to make it!"

"Thank God!" Nancy cried and began to bawl. "Oh, Lord! Lord! I'm so happy!"

John patted his wife's shoulder and grinned back at Zach. "That's good news," he said quietly, his grip tightening on Zach's shoulder. "Good news!"

Nancy recovered her composure, and moved to Bella's side, hugging her tightly. "Oh Bella! I've prayed so for her to be well. Oh, Lord, I'm so happy for you! How is she, doctor? Out of danger, please God?"

The doctor stood up. "The worst is over," he pronounced. "She's dehydrated. When she wakes, be sure to give her barley water or ginger water, and lots of mashed fruit, applesauce, to replace her lost fluids. I'll want to examine her when she wakes, so I can determine if there's been any brain damage."

Zach felt his stomach tighten. "Brain damage?"

"Yes. When a child has had a high fever for that long, you sometimes get brain damage. But that doesn't happen in all cases." He packed up his case. "Let me know when she wakes up tomorrow." He looked over at Bella. "She needs sleep, or she'll be ill next.

Then he left, leaving them more worried than ever.

"You heard the doctor," Nancy admonished Bella. "You need to get some sleep. Look at you. You're practically sleeping standing up! I'm taking over."

Nancy slipped into the chair by the Amanda's side of the bed.

"Now you go in the other room," she ordered Bella, "and get some rest so when Amanda wakes up, you won't scare her with those dark circles under your eyes."

Bella nodded, too tired to protest anymore. She did need to sleep, so she would be rested to deal with whatever happened once Amanda woke up. "Promise you'll wake me as soon as she opens her eyes!"

"Of course I will," Nancy promised.

Zach guided Bella into the adjoining room He pulled back the covers on his master bed.

Bella fumbled with the buttons on her shirtwaist.

"Let me," Zach said, stepping in front of her. Smiling, he gently undid the buttons, helped her off with her dress, then loosened the stays of her corset.

Bella slipped underneath the covers, grateful for the cocoon-like warmth of the down pillow mattress. Zach pulled the sheets up to her chin, then knelt down next to her and stroked her hair.

"You get some sleep now," he told her.

She smiled sleepily at him and reached out her hand. "Don't go. Stay with me. I... I don't want to be alone. I don't want to think about how close she came to..."

"Of course I'll stay with you."

Zach stood up and gently closed the connecting door. Then he removed his boots and waistcoat. He laid down on top of the covers next to Bella and gently stroked her hair. "It's all right. She's going to be fine. It's all over. We're all together and everything will be fine."

Silver shafts of moonlight spilled through the window. In the pale light, Zach's features were bleached of their color. Bella pulled him to her, her mouth seeking his.

"Zach, oh Zach," she cried out softly, needing to hear the sound of his name.

Her hands tugged at the covers, then his shirt, and soon Zach was undressed and kissing her ardently. She explored his smooth, hard-muscled body, committing its contours and texture to memory through her fingertips.

Zach knelt over her, his smile illuminated in the moonlight. Wordlessly, he parted her legs, running his hands over her thighs. She wrapped her legs around him, pulling him inside of her. He whispered her name. They clung to each other and rocked each other into a joyous release of all the grief and tension of the last four days.

When it was over, Zach kissed Bella gently, awed at depths of emotion he felt for her and Amanda. If the child had died, something in him would have died, too.

"Marry me, Bella. I want to spend the rest of my life with you and Amanda. I'll always be there for you. Always."

Thirty-Four

Z ach stood on the porch of John's cottage.

He gazed at the final autumn blaze of color that flanked the sparkling blue waters of Oyster Bay on the northern shore of Long Island. He breathed in the cool, crisp air.

"I'll miss this place when we start the next season."

John chuckled. "Miss it, huh? You used to get bored." He came up behind Zach and patted him on the shoulder. "Never could stay past Christmas, if that."

Zach smiled, his breath a faint white puff against the chill morning air. "That was before."

"Before the war?"

"Before Bella." Zach turned and grinned at the violinist. "Now I know your secret."

John arched one eyebrow.

"Marriage." Zach turned again and rested his foot on the gingerbread railing of the wide porch. "I used to think that would be boring, too."

"You'll find out in a few hours, won't you?" John clapped Zach on the shoulder again. "I'd say, since I've known you, you haven't been wrong about too many things, old man. But marriage —well, I think you'll find it to your liking. Has a lot to recommend."

John raised his foot up on the bottom rail and folded his arms contemplatively along the top of the railing. "Mind you, you have to find the right woman. A woman you can trust. Someone who never minds listening to your worst ideas. One who loves you enough to stand up to you when you're half-cocked and stand by you when you're in a mean fix."

"That's the most eloquent I've ever heard you wax about marriage. Taking this best man routine a bit seriously, are we?"

"Damn right, I am."

Inside the house, someone was tuning up their instruments. A crash was followed by a shriek, then giggles.

John stepped off the porch and pattered down the steps into the yard.

Curious, Zach jumped over the railing to head his friend off. "Hey! The wedding's in an hour. Where are you going?"

"Your house. Too many guests in mine. A man needs a bit of peace."

John continued across the lawn to the cottage next door and up the porch steps. He eased himself into the porch swing, plunked his feet on the railing, and stretched his arms out behind his head. "Remember all those times we sat here and planned a new season? Wrote new songs? Rehearsed out under that band shell?"

"Yes, I remember." Zach sat next to John. "A lot of years in this old place."

The two men rocked in companionable silence for a moment, their breath puffing faintly in the air.

"A little brandy?" John reached in his hip pocket for a thin silver flask. "Filled it with the good stuff. Have a nip." He unscrewed the silver top and handed it to Zach. "Groom first."

"Thanks." Zach tipped his head back and felt the brandy warm him. He handed it back to John, who took a quick draught. "I been thinking, maybe I'd try for a position at one of the orchestra houses. Bella agreed to perform next season at the Mountain House, but..."

John was silent.

"I'm not sure her heart is in it," Zach continued. "I was thinking we could stop touring so much. There'll be a full railroad service from here to the city in a year or two. We could find a regular job at a hotel in New York City for the season."

"Nancy and I were just talking about that." John grinned. "Seems she's tired of living out of a trunk, too."

"Now, that's a surprise," Zach said.

John looked thoughtful. "We were talking about maybe adopting a tyke or two. See what you've started?"

"Blaming me?" Zach pulled John into a bear hug and tousled his hair affectionately.

"Hey!" John cried. "Watch the hair. Nancy'll give me hell for mussing it up. Sure I'm blaming you. She's crazy about Amanda. Just being around her so much has put her in the nesting frame of mind, so to speak." He leaned back in the swing again. "Truth is, I'm getting too old for this business. Mind you, I don't want to give it up completely. Just make it a bit easier."

"No matter what we end up doing, John, we'll still always work together. The war's over and I swear this country is just revving up. There's a whole new world of music being imagined out there. And we'll be part of it."

"That's a promise," John agreed.

The sound of a carriage arriving made the two men sit up. A shout came from the house. Amanda, dressed in a white organdy dress, flew across the lawn to Zach's cottage, her white ribbons flying in the wind.

"Papa Zach! Uncle John!" she cried.

Amanda reached John first and tugged at his hand. "Uncle John! Come quick. The guests are arriving. Aunt Nancy says you have to open the champagne for the punch!"

"We're on our way." Zach rose and hoisted a squealing, giggling Amanda onto his shoulders. *My niece,* he thought. *No,* he corrected himself. *My daughter.*

❦

Bella waited at the top of the stairs.

She was dressed in the same white satin gown she had made her singing debut in. Nancy had replaced the red roses and trim with pale violet satin and had sculpted Bella's hair into a cascading waterfall of curls.

Nervously, Bella fingered the small bouquet of white and yellow winter roses cut from the vine that trailed up Nancy's front porch. From here, she could see out a small, octagonal window to the cottage next door. It was exactly the cottage she had dreamed of with Amanda. And after today, it would be their new home. The strains of John's violin announced the wedding march. Bella started down the steps slowly, gazing fondly at the scene below, where all the people she loved had assembled.

Her dear daughter was growing into a boisterous and quick-witted child. The boys in the band, whom she had thought so rude on that first stagecoach journey to the Mountain House, were now like family to her. Dear John and Nancy had become her staunchest allies and friends.

Then she saw Zach, resplendent in black evening dress, his signature sapphire waistcoat striking against his dark good looks. Her heart leapt at the sight of him, so debonair and handsome, gazing at her in a way that kindled her desire.

Zach strode to her side and laced his fingers gently in hers. To her surprise, his hand was trembling. She gripped it tightly, and he winked at her, his mouth turning up slightly at the corners.

The music stopped. The minister stepped into place.

"Dearly beloved," he began.

The words took Bella back to the day of her wedding to Daniel. She saw him, blond and blue-eyed, shy and gentle. She recalled how he had taken his vows and heard her own voice in return.

I'll always love you, Daniel, she told him in her mind. *I'll always look at Amanda and see you. But when I look at Zach, I'll see only him.*

"Do you, Bella, take this man, Zach, for your wedded

husband? To love and obey, for richer or poorer, for better or for worse, in sickness and in health, until death do you part?"

She turned to Zach and saw him clearly, with no trace of Daniel at all in her mind. Zach was her trusted confidant, stalwart protector, ardent lover, and her dearest friend.

"I do," she declared.

~

The wedding party was a blur to Zach. The guests ate. They drank. Music played and everyone danced on the porch. The boys took their turns dancing with Bella for luck.

As he watched her graceful turns in the arms of Billy Parisher, Zach was sharply conscious of the good will around him and of Bella's radiance. It felt as if everything in his life had led to the moment he had publicly pledged his love for Bella. With crystalline vision, he also saw how the joy of this day would color the rest of his future as brightly.

For the first time in his life, he felt sorry for his parents. They had been a mismatched pair from the start, he thought. He was luckier. For the first time, he felt a deep kinship and gratitude toward his brother Daniel for leading him to Bella.

As he watched Bella whirl, he craved her touch, her voice. It was time to have her to himself. When the waltz finished, Zach reclaimed his bride.

"Come steal away with me for a moment," he whispered, taking her hand. "I want to show you something I bought for Amanda."

She beamed at him, and together they swept down the porch steps across the grass to the cottage next door. At the porch steps, Zach suddenly scooped her up in his arms and swept her over the threshold. Bella giggled, and pressed her arms tightly around Zach's neck, nuzzling her lips against his cheek.

Setting her gently down, Zach led his bride through the house on the way to see Amanda's surprise.

Bella loved every room: The dining room with its fine Georgian table and chairs, and a sideboard of inlaid burled walnut. Zach's study, with its piano, a huge collection of leather-bound books, and a picture window that offered a superb view of the bay. The bedroom with its mahogany four poster bed and dressers. And the small room that would be Amanda's, with pale, pink-flowered wallpaper and a carved pine sleigh bed.

"What do you think?" Zach said, opening the door to Amanda's room. He pointed to an ornate three-story doll house that stood in one corner. "I saw it when we were in Boston. Do you think she'll like it?"

Bella nodded at the lovely playhouse. "She'll adore it." Then she kissed Zach. "You'll spoil her."

Zach grinned. "I intend to spoil both my girls." He kissed her again and was almost tempted to carry her off to the bedroom. But there would be all the time in the world for that now.

Coming out of his reverie, Zach put his arm around Bella's shoulder. "Let's go out to the garden before we head back to our guests."

Arm in arm, they strolled outside, wandering among the trailing rose bushes. Zach stopped and picked a single blushing bud that lingered on the trellis. "Here's a promise," he said, laying the delicate, pale pink rose in her open palm. "You'll have your garden of roses, with as many as you want."

She brought the flower to her lips and looked up at him. "I love you." She embraced him and they kissed.

They walked out into a wide meadow and sat on the bench under the gracefully arched branches of two willows.

"This is my favorite spot," Zach said, sitting down and pulling her close to him. "I sit here and watch the sun set over the water. I play the cornet and hear a whole symphony in the rustle of the leaves."

The strains of John's violin filled the air with sweet melody.

"May I have the pleasure of this waltz, Mrs. Smith?"

"With all my heart, Mr. Smith."

Zach whirled her around. In his mind, John's violin had

swelled to an orchestra. He could hear the final movement of his symphony.

"I never understood until now," he murmured, "what my uncle once said to me. That love was the greatest symphony of all. I thought that was just romantic nonsense. But he was right!"

He kissed Bella tenderly. Then he whirled her once more, his jubilant laughter ringing out across the lapping waves of the bay.

The End

~

Don't miss out on your next favorite book!

Join the Satin Romance mailing list
www.satinromance.com/mail.html

THANK YOU FOR READING

≈

Did you enjoy this book?

We invite you to leave a review at your favorite book site, such as Goodreads, Amazon, Barnes & Noble, etc.

DID YOU KNOW THAT LEAVING A REVIEW...

- Helps other readers find books they may enjoy.
- Gives you a chance to let your voice be heard.
- Gives authors recognition for their hard work.
- Doesn't have to be long. A sentence or two about why you liked the book will do.

About the Author

Debra Scacciaferro is a former newspaper reporter and arts critic, who lives in the Hudson Valley of New York, where *American Nightingale* and *State of Innocence* are set. After leaving the newspaper business, she worked as a researcher and assistant to her husband, best-selling author Jim DeFelice, and raised her son, Robert. In between, she joined several writers groups, finished three unpublished novels, and began helping other writers polish their books and novels through her business DebraS Novel Services. She is grateful to her dear friend and colleague, Lorraine Ash, author of "Life Touches Life," for introducing her to S.K. Mason, who was looking for a writing partner.

www.debrascacciaferro.com
www.facebook.com/debrascacciaferro
www.facebook.com/debrasnovelservices

Also by Debra Scacciaferro

WITH MELANGE BOOKS

Novels

State of Innocence with S. K. Mason